Books by Bart Spicer

ACT OF ANGER   *1962*

THE DAY BEFORE THUNDER   *1960*

BROTHER TO THE ENEMY   *1958*

THE TALL CAPTAINS   *1957*

THE WILD OHIO   *1953*

New York
Atheneum 1962

Bart Spicer:

Act of Anger

To Betty, as the first

Act of Anger

The roads come into Rincon

out of raw purple mountains that always have a little snow
streaked high in jagged folds.

From the north the road is six concrete lanes, with a black
tar dividing strip that is all you can make out when the sun is
low in the west. You drive in a long tight curve around the
Cobre range and then the road drops away in front of you,
and even if you can't read the sign against the dazzle, something tells you to ease up. Then from the thin shadow of Cobre Peak you can see Rincon far out in the desert valley, just
about hidden under a low-hanging boil of pale dust.

Beyond rough sterile foothills the road narrows to get
through town. It twists along the cramped, Spanish-planned
streets, dips under the Santa Fé tracks and picks up again south
of town, wide and fast, just before you get to the new city airport. It seems to meander from there to the southern moun-

tains because it is running along the old Mexican pack-horse trail beside the San Marcos River. The pass through the Castaño range is not high. The road rises slowly until it disappears into a vague sky.

The road west into Rincon is four lanes of crushed rock bound with asphalt that is beginning to crumble at the edges. It is drifted with sand most of the time and the white-painted divider is barely visible. The Gritón range has high horse pastures, hidden springs, defiles made for ambush. The Apache liked these mountains, and the road follows the Apache trail down from Cochise Springs. Once on the valley floor, the road is an arrow toward Rincon, because the town was a Pima village once and the Apaches seldom bothered to sneak up on a soft target like that. They just waited until the horses were fat, the corn and maidens ripe. Then they rode down to take their share. Apache is a Pima word. It means enemy. The Pima knew what he was talking about.

This is the long line of the desert valley. Behind thin straggling cottonwoods the dry bed of the Rincon River runs straight beside the road, past the fenced cattle range, past the irrigated cotton land, past the bright thickets of new houses that spread north and south into the mountain canyons.

It takes a long time to get through town this way. The road is heavily traveled and not wide enough. But once you are past the pruned palm trees and the little dabs of green lawn shining like victories against the desert, past the downtown business section, the county courthouse, over the stone bridge and past the Rincon hospital and the adobe-and-tin shacks that line the Agroño Wash, the road lifts again into bare broken foothills. This is the beautiful part of Rincon, the land of prehistory, bleak as the moon, dominated by giant saguaro cactuses thrusting high over the pale, harsh talus slopes.

The two highways meet in the center of Rincon. They circle an open area that was once called La Plaza de las Armas in the days when the town was a presidio named San Marcos del Pueblito de Rincón. Now it's just Rincon, and the plaza is Courthouse Square. The low white-plastered adobe building, edged with robusta fan palms, is not high enough to block your view of the other road.

The roads meet here. Briefly, they seem to be one.

But they are not.

THE FOUR-MILE STRETCH of the north road from Cobre Peak through the foothills to the city limits was still county territory. The way Rincon was growing these days, it would probably be lapping over the edges of the county before you knew it. But until the city took over, it remained the sheriff's job to police the road.

The two deputies in the black county car sat low and lazy, each staring out his own window at the pale, hard-packed desert that was beginning to brighten with the false dawn. The man behind the wheel held a stop watch in his hand. In the rear-view mirror he could see the road as it rounded the mountain. From there it was a measured mile to a white-painted telephone pole. If a car covered that distance in less than a minute, it was a speeder, and the county racked up another twenty-dollar fine. An average Saturday night brought out at least fifty freewheeling rooty-toots.

But not this Saturday night. Must probably be a big dance down somewheres in South Rincon, the deputy told himself. He stretched wide, cramping his neck and jaw to choke back a yawn. He was a scrawny man, juiceless and stringy as old jerky. He held the stop watch out to the man beside him.

"Here, Mex, you take it a spell. I got a sore finger."

"Don't call me Mex." The man turned from the window and took the watch. "My people been living in Rincon for two hundred years, so don't call me Mex." He juggled the watch in his hand. "I don't mind, you call me Mex in a friendly way, but you don't say it friendly. I am Deputy Sheriff Juan Alonzo Montero. There's five names. Pick one you like. Don't call me Mex."

The deputy made a sound low in his throat. He pushed the

doorlatch with his elbow and slid from the car. He walked very stiffly, his narrow shoulders high, moving in little finicky steps toward a clump of mesquite. He opened his fly and stood with a strained, reddened face until he was able to urinate.

Montero watched him, his heavy young face blank and brooding. After a moment he turned away. He caught a flash of light from the mirror and clicked his thumb down on the stem of the stop watch. "This one is moving some." He leaned forward, eyes on the mirror.

The deputy came inside and shut the door. He switched on the ignition. The cold motor coughed twice, then settled to a steady rumble. The deputy pulled down the gearshift lever and released the brake. He was ready when Montero stopped the watch.

"Forty-eight seconds, and he's all over the road. Must be a drunk. Watch yourself."

The county car lurched forward, spraying sandy earth in a twenty-foot streamer. It bucked up onto the concrete slab. The deputy slammed the lever into second and pushed the accelerator to the floor. Montero held down the siren button. Behind them they could hear the shrill, agonized whine of a car braking at high speed.

"He's taking the whole road," Montero said. "Better try to stay ahead of him."

Headlights from behind flared inside the patrol car. The driver hunched low over the wheel to shut out the glare.

"I don't believe he'll make it," Montero said. "I bet he can't hold the road."

The whining squeal behind them stopped abruptly. There was a flat spat of sound as if a giant had clapped his hands together just once.

"He's over," Montero said. "Slow down. Let's go back and scrape him off the road."

The speeding car had dropped one wheel over the high edge of the concrete, reeled as it tried to recover, then rocked over on its side. It slid, shrieking and scattering sparks back along the road, then rolled lazily onto its top for a few yards and finally completed its turn to the other side. By then it was a mess.

The deputy braked carefully, turned the county car and headed back. "Jesus, look at that," he said. "Bastard drives that way, he's got no right to own a good car."

"Better pull off the road," Montero said. "I'll set out a flare. You see if the guy's still breathing."

Montero walked north a hundred yards, ripped the fuse on a white flare and balanced it between the southbound lanes. He walked back slowly, taking off his low-crowned Stetson to let the air get to his head. One thin-soled boot kicked against a silver figure in the road, and he picked it up without breaking stride.

The deputy stood braced awkwardly on top of the wreck, holding a twisted door open with his knee and hauling at a thin dark-haired boy with both hands. Montero hustled up to help him. They laid the boy down in the sand beside the road.

"Mex kid," the deputy said sourly. "Where in hell did he get a car like that?"

Montero straightened the boy's legs. He brought his arms down to his sides, feeling a big lump under the sleeve where the bone was broken in the right arm. The boy's shirt was torn, and a thin gold chain with three medals hung against his neck. Two were holy medals, the other a thin silver disk of the kind the nuns give to good students. Montero lifted it and read "Arturo Campeón" engraved on the reverse.

"Tough luck, Arturo," he muttered softly. "Tough luck, you lousy Mex."

The boy was breathing with the quick shallow gulps of shock, but he was breathing and that was the main thing. His face was covered with blood from a scalp wound. His color was bad and his eyes had rolled back somewhere inside his head.

Montero looked up to tell the deputy and saw the old man stroking his hand along the underpinning of the wrecked car.

"Get a blanket out of the trunk," Montero said. "And you better radio for an ambulance. This kid needs a doctor."

"You ought to see this car," the deputy said. "Just look at

it, will you. Chrome-plated underneath. You ever heard of a car chrome-plated underneath?"

"Call the ambulance," Montero said.

"I never even heard of a car like that."

Montero got to his feet and took one fast step toward the deputy.

"What the hell's the matter with you tonight?" the deputy complained, backtracking hastily. "That kid ain't going nowhere. He can wait a minute, can't he? I just want to see what kind of a car he stole."

Montero looked down at the silver figure he still had in his hand: a lady lifting her head to a strong breeze and her clothes sailing out behind her like she was about to fly.

"I guess he stole it all right," he said. "It's a Rolls-Royce. Call the ambulance."

THE NORTHERN PASS of the Gritón range was two thousand feet above the high desert and the first sunlight lay like a sheet of new ice along the graveled road, leaving the mountain valley behind it still dark with purple shadow. A fine-headed heavy white stallion came breasting up the slope in a high-legged rush, eager to reach the light. His rider leaned forward, holding him on the snaffle but letting him make his own pace.

Within the pass the road ran fairly level for a hundred yards, and once the horse had settled into a smooth rack along the flat, the rider pulled him in, neck-reining him in a tight circle and swinging down with a loose-jointed ease. He hooked the bights of the reins with his left elbow and took a cigarette from the pocket of his faded red flannel shirt. He moved back to the limit of the reins and turned his back, shielding the flame when he worked the lighter. The stud watched him quietly, breathing in slow deep draughts.

The rider stood facing into the sun, his sand-colored rancher's hat low across his forehead and throwing a thin streak of shadow that barely reached his eyes and seemed to emphasize his bony nose, his long narrow chin. His cigarette angled up toward his hat brim, and the slightly outthrust jaw gave him an arrogant and vaguely menacing air.

He liked to stop here when he had time, right here where you got your first sight of the long high-sloped valley of La Cañada locked inside the harsh spalled ridges of the Gritón range. The valley floor rolled and bulged for five miles to the east, ending in a narrow pocket that tailed out of sight to the south. There the mountain stream broke through to a small pool, protected from wind and sun, almost hidden except that water can never be hidden in that part of the world. All the buffalo-grass meadows, the lupine and violets, the cedars and pines, the cattle and horses and orchards and gardens and people were able to live in that valley because of the spring and what other water came from the winter rains and the runoff from snow melting in the high Gritones.

Back there on that setback, straddling the spring and shielded by the granite overhang, was the stout adobe-and-stone fort that old B. Kellogg had built for himself in the summer of 1868 when the Apache raiders were still larruping around the Territory like the Golden Horde and lifting every scalp that wasn't nailed down and well protected.

B. Kellogg had money and land scrip enough to file on the entire valley, and with him he had a couple of dirt-mean, long-haired Tejanos and a squad of tough vaqueros from Sonora that liked nothing better than forting up with plenty of water and ammunition and knocking off Apache bucks. There wasn't much profitable ranching in the valley for the best part of twenty years, not until the cavalry finally ran down Geronimo and made the Territory safe for garrison soldiers and merchants and politicians. By that time B. Kellogg was a politician himself. He was also a lawyer, probably because an old Blackstone that he had found in a burned-out cabin was the only book he had to read for some years, and he didn't want the reading to go for nothing. When he had the feel of the new country, he spoke the right words to the right people and laid out the right sum in gold double eagles, and he was appointed

Territorial Governor.

He wasn't the worst governor the Territory had ever had; he was never caught with jam on his mustache, and you couldn't say that about every governor. He did make a pile of money, but in those days a man with good card sense and guts enough to buck the tiger usually made his pile if he lived long enough. Old B. Kellogg was eighty-one when he died, hot-tempered, bull-throated, pig-headed as when he had first looked down into the valley and asked his Pima guide what in hell its name was.

The valley was called La Cañada, the Pima told B. Kellogg. That was before old B. had learned much Spanish. "Cañada" just means vale or small valley in Spanish. Neither the Mexicans nor the Pimas cared much for exploring in Apachería, so they had never gotten around to naming the valley. La Cañada is what it was then, what it still was. A deep and fertile mountain valley, an Englishman might call it a dell, or maybe a dingle if he was that kind of Englishman. A homesick Scot would say it was a glen. Hereabouts it was La Cañada, now and forevermore, amen.

The rider pinched out his cigarette, ripped it open with his thumbnail and let the tobacco drift away on the wind. He drew the stallion to him by the reins and swung up into the light hunting saddle. He let the horse go freehand on the snaffle with plenty of rein.

Once beyond the pass, the stallion edged off the road to a parallel trail and picked his way carefully down the long slope toward the desert. The sun was higher behind them now, but mountain shadows still reached out for ten miles across the desert floor. In the shadow it was cool and dry, a rare combination for that country.

Within the long terraces of foothills the graveled road bore left toward the paved highway and the dingy village of Kellogg Junction at the intersection. The rider glanced only briefly at the cluster of false-fronted buildings, artificially aged and made picturesquely shabby by dirt-colored paint and corrosive acids applied by the movie-set people who had reconstructed the town for a Class B western thriller some ten years before. He spurred his horse across the road.

When he had been a skinny, shock-headed boy, Kellogg Junction had seemed glittering and exciting and refreshingly sinful. Then he had felt a stir of pride in knowing that his name was Benson Kellogg, the same as old B. for whom the town had been named. He had more than once strutted down the splintered boardwalks of the littered streets, pretending with a boy's high drama that he was old B. himself, he-coon of the Territory.

All that was a long time ago, before the movie people had come. Now Benson Kellogg went quickly through town whenever he went at all. It was a cheerless place these days, its Hollywood improvements rotting back into the desert. Once it had been a good enough town. It had had its purpose. Now it was nothing, a ghost town with people walking around in meaningless patterns.

Benson Kellogg put the stud to a narrow irrigation ditch and urged him lightly with the spurs. The horse took the jump in a quick thrust and landed well gathered, tucking himself together like a big cat. He almost pranced as Benson Kellogg reined him along a wagon road running between two irrigated fields.

Beyond the line of foothills the desert valley was nearly flat, broken by wide shallow washes, made lumpy by low unpredictable knolls. Here, where runoff water from the high Gritones first touched the desert, the vegetation was fairly thick. The sagebrush and cactus and mesquite were showing unmistakable traces of new green. Spring was setting in, Benson Kellogg thought. Any day now you'd be seeing the desert flowers.

In the tall grass country you always know when spring comes. The people there call it greenup, and they can see the high water in the creeks, the juicy hot buds about to bust open, smell the warm yeasty dampness of a new season. They don't even have to look at the ground. But in the desert you have to look sharp. Spring can come and go some years and you're still wondering if it isn't about due and you with the sweated shirt steaming on your back and thinking maybe about getting a new hat that doesn't weigh so heavy on your head.

But spring was coming with plenty of warning this year. It had been a fine damp winter and the cactuses were bulging with stored water. It should be a good spring.

Closer to Rincon, Benson Kellogg kneed the stud along a twisting desert path toward a high stand of poplars that circled a wide low knoll. Between the trees he could see flickering glints of sunlight reflected by the windows of his brother's house. He bore sharply left behind the knoll and walked the horse past an irrigated kitchen garden, beyond a low line of adobe stables, and pulled him up at a small stake-and-pole corral. He dismounted, opened the gate and led the stud through.

"Okay, horse," he said softly. "Now let's see how good you really are. Let's see if you can still move with all that winter fat on you."

He lengthened each stirrup leather one notch and snapped the stirrups down. By then the stud was shifting restlessly, curvetting with a lot of roguish neck action and rolling his eyes.

"No band, no audience today, horse. I'll whistle a jig for you, just to start you off. But give us a show anyway. Give us a good show, horse."

He went up into the saddle quickly and smoothly. He settled himself carefully in that well-back, almost straight-legged seat designed to show off a gaited horse in the ring. The stud was tight and nervous between his knees. He brought the horse's head up with the snaffle slowly and called for flexion with the curb. The stud came willingly into the bit. He tossed his head once and then flexed tightly at the poll until his nose was pointed directly at the ground and his small shapely head made a vertical line with it. Gradually he relaxed as he brought his legs under him in answer to hard knee pressure. He was ready then and he stood like a cast figure, perfectly in control.

"All right, horse," Benson Kellogg said, keeping his voice easy and level. "You're the champion. Let's see why." Softly, with heavily accentuated beats, he began to whistle a quick-step. The stud's ears slanted back inquisitively, then cocked eagerly forward again, waiting.

Benson Kellogg eased the snaffle, holding the stud on the curb, and touched him with the spurs. As the big horse reached out, he shook the reins lightly and urged him forward from the walk. The white stud struck out across the dusty corral in a slow, dramatic strutting pace, just short of a four-beat gait, lifting and reaching with fluid precision in a stepping pace, the showiest, most enjoyable to watch of all a horse's gaits. The strong pure line of motion delighted Benson Kellogg.

"That's it, horse," he said quietly. "That's exactly it. Lots of action now. Kick your chin, horse. Lift high. High and reach. That's it."

He took the stud in a quick, cadenced circle. The muted thud of his hoofs was in soft harmony with Benson Kellogg's whistling. Puffs of pale dust rose like smoke around his fetlocks.

"Very smooth, horse. Fifteen miles an hour at the rack and going like silk all the way. Now we know why you're a champion, don't we? Once more around and then two-track up to the judge's box and I'll give you a breather."

The stud turned from the barrier still in his collected rack, came to a balanced pause, passaged briefly, and then strutted diagonally across the corral in a controlled, high-action gait in which front and rear quarters seemed to function independently in a spirited, light-hearted passage.

Benson Kellogg swung down from the saddle and touched the stud's nostrils with the heel of his hand, very lightly. The horse blew out a long breath and nudged against him.

"That was perfect, horse," he said. "Thanks for taking me along."

PAULA KELLOGG lay sprawled and relaxed, naked, on the big rumpled bed. Her eyes were half closed against the glare of morning sun that fell in a direct and warm path across her waist, below the icy glass of orange juice she was balancing between her breasts. She was listening to the noisy splashing of her husband's shower, listening also to another sound that she thought might be the pounding pulse in her head.

She shut her eyes tightly. The sound seemed to come from somewhere else as well, she decided, but it was in her head too, and why shouldn't she have a pounding pulse after all the nonsensical champagne she had drunk last night? It was Burr's fault entirely, she assured herself with smug conviction. He should not have gone dashing off on a mysterious errand of mercy and left her stranded at the Callisons' party until blue o'clock in the morning. She had never realized that lawyers had to answer emergency night calls for clients in trouble. Depends on the client, I suppose, and I wonder who it was. Burr was so funny, being discreet and embarrassed and close-mouthed about it. He is often a dear and darling man, though being married to him takes more effort than he is ever likely to know, and he needs to be reminded that he has a wife who likes sleep more than drunken champagne parties. Well, sometimes she does. What made it even harder to take was the brisk and cheerfully energetic manner of the man this morning. With just two hours' sleep, he should be fumbling around, bleary-eyed and moaning, and instead he's in there wallowing and snorting in his shower and just about to break into song. And that after a vigorous and merry romp in the hay with his eager and delightful and charming wife. Paula giggled softly to herself and stretched lazily. She finished her orange juice in quick sips.

The soft thudding sound stopped briefly. Not the one in her head, the other one. Paula nodded. Now she knew what it was. She opened her eyes to the brilliance of the sunlight. She winced and turned away from the glare. It seemed amazingly foolish to put huge, east-facing windows in a bedroom in that country. It was supposed to give you an admirable view of the mountains. Even if she was a Vermont farmer's daughter and didn't yet understand about living in the desert, she knew it was witless to bring that glaring sunlight into a bedroom. Especially a bedroom where poor Paula Kellogg was trying to recover from an exhausting night.

She drew in a quick, decisive breath and swung her bare

feet down to the floor. She rose and, pulling a light robe around her shoulders, moved toward the windows, reaching for the cords that controlled the Venetian blinds. She was a tall, streakily blonde girl with a normally pale skin that had accepted the desert sun very nicely and was now a light peachy tone that made her seem exceptionally healthy even when she didn't feel at all well.

She paused with the cord in her hand. On a long angle she could see part of the corral where Benson Kellogg was exercising his white stallion. Unconsciously, when horse and rider swept briefly into view, Paula drew her robe closer together in front.

She adjusted the metal slats to bar the strong light and then let her robe drop to the floor. She wriggled into a pair of snug knee-length black pants, put on a loosely woven Mexican cotton shirt and knotted the tails below her ribs. She stepped into a pair of soft huaraches and went across the bedroom to tap on the open door of the bathroom.

"Burr," she called, pitching her voice to make it carry over the roar of the shower. "Burr, Ben's here. Burr, can you hear me?"

"Yo!" he said in a spurious basso. "I hear you. I hear you well. Steak for breakfast, that means." He tested the resonance of his voice again and held a long echoing note. "My God, did you hear that? Alfred Drake never did better."

"Not even George London," Paula said. "But please don't start singing until I get out of here."

A plume of water sprayed at her from the shower and a melodic bellow followed her out the door and down the tiled staircase.

The ground floor was cool and dark, except for the glassed-in terrace off the kitchen that was used as a dining room. Paula went through into the kitchen, scuffling her shoes on the tiles to give warning of her approach.

Two young dark-haired girls looked up from the big center table with startled doe's eyes. Each was nursing a tall, earthenware coffee cup in both hands, hunching protectively forward. From the stove a solid, serene woman nodded and smiled sweetly.

"Good morning, señora," she said slowly, enunciating carefully.

"Good morning, Petra. Hello, Pepita, Aurelia. How are you girls getting on?"

"Good morning, Mrs. Kellogg," the girls said in small shy voices, with that studied, learning-to-speak-good-English precision that they always tried for except when they were too excited or too busy or just forgot.

All three had come from La Cañada, the family ranch that Benson now owned and operated. The two girls were here for training and to go to high school, but Petra was here for keeps. She had been with Burr since his childhood and was as permanent a fixture in his mind as his wife, Paula suspected.

"Mr. Benson has just come," she announced briskly. "I suppose he'll be staying to breakfast."

Petra drew in a sharp breath. "El patrón!" she whispered.

Always the same routine, Paula said to herself. Sometime I'll have to find out about this "patrón" business. It just means landlord, according to my Spanish dictionary, and I'll be mildly damned if I ever before saw anyone take on like that over a landlord.

Petra scuttled to the high refrigerator, pulled out a meat storage drawer and flipped a long beef fillet onto the center table.

Tenderloin, for God's sake! Paula thought. I guess it's all right; the meat all comes from La Cañada anyway, but it seems like an awfully luxurious breakfast, even for a man who won't eat anything but beef, any time, anywhere.

She nodded approval at Pepita, who was chopping mushrooms with a knifeblade that was a flare of light in her quick fingers. She smiled at Aurelia, who was inspecting a basket of tomatoes with a suspicious frown, as if she doubted that any of them would do for the patrón's breakfast. No one noticed when Paula left by the back door.

Benson Kellogg was walking toward her along the flagstone walk bordering the swimming pool. Beside him came Juanito, carrying the hunting saddle on his shoulder, almost running along the rough, nonskid granite border of the pool, talking eagerly, earnestly, to Benson.

When he saw her, Benson smiled and lifted his rancher's hat in awkward courtesy. He's always so *polite,* Paula thought. All that shy, old-world courtesy might seem fakey in anyone else, but it suited Benson. Even so, he never seemed to see *her.* He was always looking at a label that said, "This is my brother's wife." Correction—"my half-brother's wife." Maybe that explained it. Half-brothers were supposed to make an abrasive combination, if you could believe what you read in books. But it didn't seem to work that way with Benson and Burr. They were close and very relaxed with each other. And Benson's constant courtesy was nice, actually. Sometimes it was nice. And sometimes it was warm and comforting. And sometimes it was downright infuriating.

"Paula," Benson said gravely. He touched Juanito's shoulder. "Plenty of oil for that saddle, my friend. It's getting old."

"Sí, patrón," Juanito said. "Like me. Like all of us." He swept his battered straw hat low, bowed to Paula and turned away, moving stiffly on his old-man's painful feet that were cramped into narrow-toed horseman's boots.

"I need a shave," Benson said, fingering the dusty stubble on his chin. "Come in and talk to me. What's been going on? Did you and Burr go up to El Monte this weekend?"

He opened the door of the small annex room he always used when he changed at Burr's house. He held the door for Paula, followed her inside and tossed his hat on a chair. He stripped the rope lashing from his flat package, unwound a length of canvas and wadded it, using it to polish the sides of a legal-size briefcase. It was black leather, smooth and waxy, with a small silver emblem fixed in a top corner.

He dropped it on the bed beside Paula and moved around the room collecting clothes from a closet, from a lowboy dresser; he pulled a pair of shoes from a compartmented bag on the back of the closet door.

Paula rubbed a finger along the edges of the briefcase. "No, we didn't go up. Monte is nice, but I get a little tired of that political mob. I'd like it better if it weren't the state capital. We just stayed home and went to a stupid party last night. What does this thing mean?" She poked her finger at the silver emblem on the black briefcase.

Benson looked back from the bathroom door. "Cattle brand," he said. "BK-Connected, is how you say it. Just means the B is turned around so it can butt against the K. Haven't you ever noticed it at La Cañada? It's on all the stock. Hip for cattle and shoulder for horses."

"Do you realize I've only been up there four times since I came here? Why don't you invite us more often?"

Benson turned on the shower, and the sound of the water muffled his voice. But Paula knew the answer even if she couldn't hear. They did not go up to La Cañada very often because Burr didn't want to, and that was that. She didn't try to talk while Benson was in the bathroom. He wasn't like Burr, splashing and singing for an hour or more. Benson would be showered, shaved and dressed within fifteen minutes at the outside.

He was, except for his shirt. He came stamping back into the small bedroom in a heavy pair of Bedford-cord slacks, muttering under his breath.

"What's the trouble?" Paula asked lazily.

"Shirt," Benson said. "No buttons, or very damn few."

Paula giggled softly. "Burr would have blown the roof off if he'd found a button missing. You're not much like him, are you?" She rolled over and looked at him appraisingly. "You don't look much like him either. You're a little taller, I guess, but Burr is a lot thicker and heavier. Why is that?"

Benson frowned without turning around. "Same sire, different dams," he said shortly. He took another shirt from the drawer, flipped it open for inspection and then put it on.

"It sounds slightly brutal, the way you put it," Paula said mildly. "What's that puckery scar on your back? Somebody take after you with a knife?"

"I don't know," Benson said. He was turned with his head inside the closet and his voice sounded hollow and full of echoes.

"You don't know!" Paula lifted herself from the bed. "You're not serious? A scar like that, and you don't know how you got it?"

"I didn't mean that." Benson hung a matching whipcord jacket on the bedpost and turned away to knot his tie. "I don't know exactly what did it. Somebody was shooting at us from twenty thousand feet down, and he didn't tell us what he was using. Anyway, I've always suspected it was a popped rivet or some other piece of detached hardware from the plane."

"That was in England?"

"While we were stationed in England. It happened over Germany. Got me a nice long leave, so I didn't really care what caused it."

"Got you a wife, too, didn't it?" Paula said with a secret sort of smile.

"It helped," Benson said. He picked up his jacket and loaded its pockets with handkerchief, keycase, coins, wallet and a silver pencil before putting it on. He strapped on his wristwatch and checked its setting by the electric clock on the lowboy.

When dressed he seemed excessively thin because his clothes were cut to fit his body, not some idea of fashion that might or might not be currently accepted. There was no bulge of shirt, no pleats or flaps on his trousers or jacket. His clothes fit him, decently and comfortably. They suited him and he was unaware of them, without interest or vanity in their appearance or his own.

"Ready?" He picked up his briefcase from the bed. "I'm hungry."

"I know," Paula sighed. "You always are." She got up slowly and went outside, holding one hand up as a shield against the strong sunlight. "Ben?"

"Yes, Paula?"

"Ben, talk to Burr, will you? Those political people are

after him again. And this time he's beginning to listen."

Benson half smiled. "For a politician's daughter, you're awfully hard on them."

"Daddy wasn't a politician," Paula said insistently. "He was just a farmer who got elected to the state senate. He liked it because there really isn't much to do in Vermont during the winter. It was sort of a hobby with him, but Burr is talking about the big leagues, Ben, the kind of politics that aims at Washington. Can't you . . ."

Benson shook his head soberly. "It's his business, Paula. I can't interfere."

"But it isn't Burr they want," Paula said sharply. "They don't even pretend it is. Some horrid little fat man told me they just want to list B. Kellogg on the ticket again. Money in the bank, he said. Just the name."

"It's Burr's name," Benson said in a suddenly cold voice. "He can write it that way if he wants to."

"And he wants to," Paula said wearily. "Why? Why does he sign himself B. Kellogg, and not you? You're the oldest. Why don't you use the famous name, instead of Burr?"

"His business, Paula," Benson said bluntly. "Let him handle it."

Then, as if regretting the shortness of his answer, he touched her arm gently. "It's not important, Paula. Don't let it bother you. Why don't you and Burr come up to La Cañada next weekend? I'll show you the new colts and we'll get some mariachis to serenade you. It's pretty up there right now."

Paula smiled, thinly and only briefly, but a good smile. "Thanks, Ben. I'd like to." She tucked her hand under his elbow and walked comfortably in step with him toward the house.

BURR KELLOGG stood in front of the bank of open windows. He could see Paula and Benson walking slowly up the path from the swimming pool, but he did not hurry with his stretching exercises.

The exercises finished, he took a black silk suit out of his wardrobe and tossed it over the back of a chair. He dressed slowly and carefully, as he always did, enjoying it. He chose a black knitted tie with a double gold stripe and went to the mirrored wall to fix the knot just right.

He rubbed an excess of powder from his chin and checked himself again at the mirror to make sure his dark hair was lying smoothly against the back of his neck. His was a broad, square face, full of heavy, vigorous lines, with a wide jaw, a big blunt nose and ears larger than any man needed. It was, he felt, a face that needed the softening effect of thick hair. He ran a finger around inside his lightly starched collar, twisting his head from side to side.

It's too damn tight, he admitted to himself. I'd like to blame the laundry, but I don't suppose I'd fool anybody. I'll have to start watching the calories, maybe cut down some on the grog. He grinned at his reflection, thinking, you'll be thirty-five next month, friend, and that's the dividing line. After thirty-five, the pounds begin to pile up if you're not careful.

Thirty-five.

Burr Kellogg shook his head. I sure as hell don't feel like thirty-five, but that's what the book says. When I was a kid, I used to figure a guy thirty-five was worn out and just about useless. There's an estimate that could stand some latter-day revision. Look at Ben. Seven years older, minus seven days. Close to forty-two. Now there is a good husky number of years. And Ben still looks the same as he did twenty years ago.

Well, friend, maybe we'll give you a couple more good years. But it's about time you started thinking about the future. Maybe you'd better find a plush-lined cubbyhole somewhere and stake out a claim, just in case you ever feel like retiring. Everything is rosy now, so that plush-lined cave would be easy to find, if you want it. All you have to do is reach out and——

Burr Kellogg grinned at himself. He nodded approvingly and went out and down the stairs, humming softly again.

At the table Paula and Benson sat quietly at breakfast, closely together, unconsciously intimate, their backs to the sundazzled glass. To Burr they were visible only as shadows. Benson lifted a loaded fork, saw Burr, and stared with exaggerated interest.

"Court clothes?" he asked. "I thought you finished Friday. Didn't you get a verdict?"

"They weren't out half an hour. 'Not guilty, Your Honor.' They just took time for a smoke and gave it to me on the first ballot." Burr stroked a finger along his wife's cheek as he passed on the way to his chair. "But I have to see Judge Groat this morning. He released my bum, but he didn't release the ten grand my bum had in his wallet, and that money is my fee. I have to show up with my petition and the judge will sign my petition. Maybe he'll sign it. But you know what he wants from me first, don't you?"

"I can guess." Benson reached out to lift another strip of thinly sliced steak onto his plate.

"But you will get it, won't you, Burr? All that lovely money!"

"Don't fret, baby, I'll get it. That's my fee. I'll collect every cent. I earned it. But Judge Groat is going to make me earn it again." Burr sprinkled brown sugar over a bowl of cornflakes, added cream and stirred vigorously. He spoke through a mouthful of noisy cereal. "You're married to a genius, sweetie. Ten thousand bucks for two weeks' work."

"But what about the judge? Why doesn't he let you have the money?"

"He likes to get some free work out of these overpaid trial boys like Burr," Benson explained. "Groat makes a habit of it, I hear."

"Of what?" Paula demanded.

"It's not as bad as that," Burr said. "There are always a certain number of defendants up for trial who can't afford to hire lawyers. The court appoints attorneys for them, but no lawyer who makes a decent living wants his name on the judge's free list. I think you get about fifty bucks from the county, maybe a little more. So whenever Judge Groat awards a verdict to a good lawyer, he usually tries to con him into taking one of the free cases. Or makes him wish he had. A gentle form of blackmail. No trial lawyer can afford to have a judge mad at him."

"So you'll have to try another case for nothing? Just to get paid for this one? I think that's outrageous!"

"You're right," Burr said, trying not to laugh. "But you come and tell Judge Groat. Don't waste it here. And don't expect anyone to feel sorry for me. Look at old Ben sitting there with a big fat grin on his face. You think it serves me right, don't you, boy? Old Ben the Beefeater. Are you ever, ever, ever, going to get finished with that land-grant litigation?"

"Eat your cornflakes, sonny," Benson said easily. "You hotshot trial lawyers don't understand the subtleties of the civil side."

"A true statement, Counselor," Burr mumbled through a mouthful. "Any time a case drags on for sixteen weeks, I don't want to hear anything about it. I'll wait for a digest in the *Law Review*. And anyway, I like cornflakes. What's wrong with cornflakes?" He looked up with a bland, wondering smile. "You know, I'll bet I'm the only guy my age around here who really does like this stuff? I even like peanut butter. I have a lot of depraved tastes."

Benson grinned and Paula laughed outright. "What a shocking confession," she said, touching Burr's hand with a quick surge of affection. "You have just admitted to a happy childhood."

Benson put down his knife and fork and pushed his plate slightly away. He poured a cup of coffee, his face turned away from his brother. Burr frowned quickly, secretly, at Paula and tipped his head warningly toward Benson.

He could guess what had sobered Ben so sharply and completely. It had taken him a long time to realize what a bad life

Ben had lived through after his father had remarried. They didn't talk about it, because Ben was incapable of it, and Burr could still be intimidated by Ben's sudden, cold withdrawal. It would be a lot easier for Ben if he could blow his top once in a while, Burr felt.

He didn't understand Ben and he didn't pretend that he did, but he was probably closer to him than anyone else. It might have been different, and probably a damn sight better, for Ben, if his wife had not been killed during the war. Maybe it would have been better. But better or worse, a woman can get close, and that's what Ben needed—someone whose emotions and desires were as important to him as his own. Ben had a tendency to freeze sometimes. He would clamp himself into a chill, impersonal remoteness, and when he did that he was a totally different, somehow alien person.

I wonder what she was like, Burr thought, Liza FitzAllen Kellogg. Ben always had a nice eye for female flesh and he never had any patience with crap and flutter, so Liza was probably okay. Beautiful too, if that picture in Ben's bedroom was an honest job. She had been English, a soldier's daughter, and she had married Ben in London during his second tour in bombers. That was a good period for Ben. Burr could clearly remember the light-hearted tone of his infrequent letters. And then Liza got killed during an air raid and Ben went cold inside himself. It was still deviling him, Burr suspected. He had watched Ben operating with some of the tasty tourist babes and he had always stayed on top of the game. There was never a time when Ben hadn't had a regular girl somewhere in town. But none of them, Burr felt sure, ever managed to get under that protective layer he had brought home with him. Probably he was scared of another blitz bomb wiping out his future, Burr guessed.

The only good thing left to Ben from his brief marriage was Liza's father, who had shown up at La Cañada some three years back, retired now and sick of life in England, but still an eager, exuberant old guy, noisy with wild stories and hearty, young-goat appetites. What a swath he had cut through the stands of dude-ranch dolls! And he'd been good for Ben, and

he was still there at the ranch, using it as his American head-quarters, and still good. He had a quick, light English voice that must have reminded Ben of Liza and the good times they'd had together before she got herself killed. Her father, old Fitz, was good, but he wasn't good enough, Burr suspected; he would make Ben remember too many things that were better forgotten now.

"Could I ride your pretty trick horse this afternoon?" Paula asked, offering a pretty smile to Ben. "I wouldn't take him far, just up toward the foothills."

Benson turned blankly to look at her. Then he blinked and forced a smile. "Better not, Paula," he said mildly. "The old fellow gets bad-tempered when he's by himself. I tired him this morning and he still has to get home over the pass. Jorge will walk him back when he's had a rest."

"And don't call him a trick horse," Burr said. "It's a wonder Ben doesn't chew your head off."

"Is it bad?" Paula asked innocently.

"He's not a trick horse," Benson explained. "He can do it all, but it isn't a trick when he does it. He doesn't learn routines like a dancer. He does it all under control, on signal. It's an entirely different thing. But don't let Burr trouble you. It's not a fighting matter."

"Well, I think you're being mean," Paula insisted. "Why can't I ride him? I saw Fitz riding him, and he didn't have any trouble."

"Oh my," Burr said softly. "Fitz has been riding rock-skulled horses since the Light Brigade went on a stampede. He's a salty old hard-butted cavalryman. I wouldn't be surprised if he knows more about riding than Ben does."

"At least," Benson agreed.

Paula made a ladylike snort. "I'm not convinced," she said. "I'm going out and pet him anyway. I don't think he's so fierce."

"Only when he's away from the mares," Benson said. "He likes company and he gets fidgety when he's by himself."

"Now there is a sensible type horse," Burr said. "I never

saw one yet I'd give a damn for, except to bet on, but any horse that thinks like that is worth some consideration."

Benson smiled thinly. "I'll tell him."

Just then the outside temperature reached the critical point and the thermostat turned on the air conditioning system with a sudden, audible snap. The soft roar of the compressor was very loud in the still room. Paula groaned at the sound of it.

"Going to be hot today," Burr said with a look at his watch.

"I hate it when that thing comes on so early in the day," Paula said. "It makes the house feel like a cave."

"Then turn it off," Burr said casually. "You about ready, Ben? I'd like to get in early this morning."

Benson nodded. He folded his napkin and pinched it under the flange of his saucer. "I'll just have a word with Petra," he said. "Won't be a minute."

Burr and Paula walked slowly to the front door in companionable silence. Outside, they stopped to inspect the day and then moved around the front of the house toward a wide, enclosed carport. Burr went ahead to put his key in the ignition of his car and switch on the air conditioner.

"What an effete life we live," Paula said mockingly. "Air conditioning at home, air conditioning at the office, air conditioning in the car. All you need is an air conditioned hat."

"Appurtenances of civilization," Burr said absently. "When you live in the desert, air conditioning is just good sense."

"Decadence," Paula offered, tongue in cheek. "Materialism. Loss of spiritual values."

"God, I hate that kind of yatter." Burr leaned against the fender, crossed his arms and glared pleasantly at his wife. "Man has been trying to get comfortable ever since he first ducked into a cave to get out of the rain. The first fire brought indoors wasn't any effete self-indulgence, it was the dawn of civilization! To hell with that crap. I'll take air conditioning, and what goes with it."

"Goodness, what did I say?" Paula asked, dismayed.

"Forget it," Burr muttered. "I get annoyed sometimes. I guess I'm still wound up from the trial. Every time I open my mouth I start to address the jury. I think I'll play a little golf this afternoon if I can get away. Want to come along?"

"No," Paula said sharply. "And you won't play either. You come straight home and get some sleep. That's what you need."

"We'll see how it works out," Burr said evasively. He opened the car door as Benson came around the corner of the house. "I'll call if I can get away."

"Don't call, come home," Paula said. "You aren't getting enough sleep these days. Make him come home early, Ben."

"I can't do a thing with him," Benson said. "He won't even eat his cornflakes when I'm around."

Burr put his arms around Paula's shoulders and bent to whisper in a low, private voice. "I'll make it if I can, sweetie."

"Well, be nice and lazy, anyway. We'll have an early dinner and get to bed by nine."

Burr waved from the front seat of the car. He drove slowly down the curving avenue of poplars, rattled over the iron-pipe cattleguard at the entrance and stopped briefly at the highway. He turned west toward Rincon.

INSIDE THE CAR, with the windows closed, it was very quiet. A hot wind was whipping dusty streamers along the road, but the low persistent drone of the air conditioner blocked out the sound. Burr moved back squarely in his seat. He looked quickly at Benson, then back to the road.

"What's the matter?" Benson asked.

"Did Paula say anything about last night?"

"Not to me." Benson tossed his briefcase into the back and slumped down.

"I had to leave her at the Callisons' party. The sheriff called me. I didn't get home till five this morning."

Benson nodded. "Trouble?"

"Yes. Bad trouble, Ben."

There was something strained about his voice and manner that made Benson frown. He turned to look at Burr, saw the big square hands on the wheel clenched so hard that the tendons stood out in relief, white against the tanned skin.

"Remember Judge Turnbull? Old Famous Amos?"

"Of course I remember him. I used to stay with him and his family when Dad sent me to school in Rincon. It was a long time ago. I was twelve, I think. But I remember him all right. What about him?"

"County patrol picked him up last night. Sheriff had sense enough to call me instead of booking him right away."

"Judge Turnbull?"

"Yes. They answered a call out in that new development south of town. What's it called? Sunnyvale? Sunny Acres? Something like that."

"Get to it, Burr."

"I am fiddling, I guess. I don't like to think about it. This new development was built on the old Turnbull ranch. The judge used to be pretty fond of the place. Logical place for him to go when he ducked out the window, I suppose."

"Alone?"

"Alone. He must have walked ten miles. Then he parked himself outside a house where a truck driver's wife was undressing. Shades up, lights on. Wife looked out the window and damn near fainted. She started screaming and I'll bet she hasn't stopped yet."

Burr was speaking in a slow bleak voice. His normal tone was brisk and sharp, full of animal vitality. Hearing him now gave Benson a feeling of cold apprehension.

"Why?" he asked.

"Truck driver's wife saw the judge out there, standing in the full light from the window. He was watching her and drooling, she said. And milking himself into the oleanders."

"My God," Benson said heavily.

"Yeah. Me too. Judge didn't even stop when the truck driver came running out. He got a hell of a clout on the jaw."

"Judge Turnbull?"

"Famous Amos himself."

"I can't believe we're talking about the same man. Judge

Turnbull was on the State Supreme Court for twenty years. He drafted most of the state statutes. He could have been governor if he'd ever wanted the job. He was——"

"Goddam it, Ben! I know what he was," Burr said angrily. "You don't have to tell me."

"What happened to him?"

"What do you think happened? I drew up the commitment papers and typed them myself. I drove him up to El Monte and got the presiding judge out of bed and had Judge Turnbull in the nuthouse an hour later. For keeps. That was the deal."

"The family agreed to that?"

"Hell, yes, they agreed. Ben, they've been going out of their minds the past few years. There's a granddaughter seventeen years old, and she doesn't dare bring friends to the house. They've done everything they could for him. This was just too much."

"He's one of our great men, Burr. Couldn't you . . ."

"No, I couldn't," Burr said roughly. "Maybe the family might have agreed to keep him, but what was the use of trying to persuade them? That truck driver was wild. He didn't give a damn who Judge Turnbull was. He's only been in Rincon a couple of years, and the judge's name means nothing to him. He wanted the old boy jailed, and don't think it didn't take plenty of work to talk him out of that. The only reason he finally agreed to withdraw the charge was because I promised the judge would be put away. There wasn't any other choice."

"I see," Benson said heavily. "I wish you'd called me, Burr."

"I thought of it. There just wasn't time. You need more than an hour to drive in from the ranch, and this couldn't wait. Anyway, what could you have done? I tell you, there wasn't any choice."

"Maybe not. But Judge Turnbull . . ." Benson shook his head. "We could have tried, Burr."

"Tried what? The old boy's better off where people can watch him and take care of him. Anyway, it's decided now. Reason I mentioned it is the family all asked about you. They weren't any too happy about what happened. They'll be thinking it over and I suspect they'll be wishing they could change their minds. I was wondering if you could go out and talk to them, Ben."

Burr's slow voice dwindled to silence. He was driving in heavier traffic now and he gave it all his attention. He kept his eyes carefully ahead, waiting.

"I'll go see them, Burr. How was the judge?"

"He looked terrible. I didn't recognize him. He was just some dirty old bum in run-down carpet slippers and a torn sweatshirt, with his pants unbuttoned. It wasn't Judge Turnbull, Ben. I don't know what happened to him, but that grimy old bastard wasn't Judge Turnbull."

"Take it easy, Burr."

"I'll take it easy. Don't worry about me. But you didn't have to look at him. He didn't even know me, Ben. Hell, he didn't even know his own name. That wasn't Judge Turnbull."

"But it was, Burr."

"No. That wasn't Judge Turnbull."

After a long moment, Benson said, "I'm sorry, Burr."

"Don't be sorry for me, damn it."

"I'm sorry for all of us."

Burr swerved abruptly into the right-hand lane and flipped the signal for a turn. "I'm going straight over to the courthouse. You want to go there, or——"

"No, I'll stop at the office. I'm not due till ten."

"Okay." Burr drove with close concentration, fighting for every small advantage. After a few blocks he glanced at Benson and grinned. "Boy, she's a rough life sometimes. I wonder how we stand it."

"That's about all anybody can do. Some of us can't do that."

"The hell with it. I'm thinking of some golf this afternoon. Want to get up a foursome?"

"Not today. I'll be busy. We finish up today, and then I have to rough out a brief."

"What's that land-grant case about, anyway? What takes

you so damned long with it?"

"You know. History." Benson reached back for his brief-case. "The dispute goes back to an early Spanish land grant. The problem is tricky and confused because the original language of the lease is vague and all the decisions based on it are not very good law. My client has a good case, I'd say. We have a chance."

"But what do you guys do for four months? What can you talk about that long?"

"I told you. History. We sit in the judge's chambers and argue about the current meaning of a ruling that was handed down to deal with a situation that hasn't existed for a hundred years. It gets involved and pedantic, but I like it."

Burr shrugged. "I suppose this is another one that will have to go all the way to the Supreme Court?"

"Probably. If I get the verdict, it will be a departure from precedent, so it will have to be tested. We should know the answer pretty soon."

"What makes you think you'll get it?"

"Doesn't matter much whether we do or not."

Burr looked at him sharply, his eyes narrowed suspiciously. "Why, you old swindler. You sandbagged the judge? You've really got him?"

"He did it himself. On a point that has been called reversible error once before. I'd rather not use it, but I have it if I need it."

Burr laughed softly. "What a tricky bastard you are. Is there much of a fee involved?"

"Might be. If we win all the way. Otherwise, just the standard rate."

"What's the amount?"

"Five million maybe."

"And you stand to rake in ten per cent?" Burr whistled softly. "God! And here I was feeling great because I'm going to collect a measly ten grand." He eased the car against the curb and leaned across Benson to open the door. "Kindly get the hell out of here before you ruin my day."

"It's just pie in the sky, Burr. It'll be a long time before anything is settled." Benson tapped Burr's shoulder with the edge of his hand. "You take it easy, boy. I'll go see the Turnbulls."

"Okay. Thanks, Ben."

The car pulled away and merged into the morning traffic. Benson went into the building that housed his office and waited for the elevator. The sliding glass doors were painted exactly as the entry doors on the twenty-first floor, with an old-fashioned black-and-gilt lettering that said B. KELLOGG AND SAMPSON in a curlicued arc across the top. Sampson had been a vigorous young attorney old B. had imported to run his office. He had died before Benson had been born. He and Benson's father, who had signed himself B. Kellogg, Jr., had been the senior partners for a long time. When they died, the firm's assets, which included the name, had been sold to energetic juniors. A square-printed block listed the names of the five current senior partners, none of them Kelloggs or Sampsons.

SHORTLY BEFORE NOON a two-motored plane cleared the shadows of Cobre Peak and headed in a long ellipse for the Rincon airport. This was Flight 721 of the Westair Airline. It made three stops in the two hundred and fifty miles between El Monte and Rincon. The pilot was never able to gain much altitude between stops, so he had to thread the mountain passes. Every passenger got a clear and frightening look at the wild jagged country below.

Most of the passengers had seen it all too often before to show much interest, but it was new to Tim Cook. He was a little scared, not enough to show it, but too much to be able to look away. This was not the land you saw from the highway, smoothed and softened by perspective. From above, it was naked, exposed and downright savage. You could see how a man could get lost in those brutal twisting mountain canyons and never find his way home. The colors were pale and mysterious in the clear morning light, unlike anything you ever saw in humid atmospheres. The strange colors were a little frightening too.

The plane leveled off above the airport. Tim sat back and checked his seat belt. He was a small, neatly made man, composed of angles and apparently no flesh. He was too big for a jockey, but he gave much the same impression of alert, nervously quick competence.

He was the first passenger at the door. He almost ran down the stairs. He went straight across the hardstand toward a row of public telephone booths near the main entrance. He held his dime pinched between his lips as he looked up the number of B. Kellogg and Sampson. He muttered it to himself as he dialed.

"Mr. Blumberg, please," he said to the switchboard girl. "Timothy Cook calling. He's expecting me."

He waited impatiently, tapping a finger in broken rhythm against the coinbox.

Blumberg's voice was slow and heavy, almost solemn. "Mr. Cook," he said. "You were lucky to catch me. I was on my way to lunch."

"Maybe it could wait," Tim said quickly. "Nathan Barstow sent me down from El Monte. I've got a lot to do and not much time to do it in."

"Yes, I talked to Nate last night. All right, Mr. Cook. If it's urgent, suppose we lunch here. I often have a bite at my desk."

"Okay, I'll grab a cab." Tim hung up without waiting for an answer. When the state chairman sends a man to see a county chairman, the county chairman makes time to see him. It was that simple.

The trip into Rincon from the south was a dusty, wind-blown ride. Tim sat nervously forward on the edge of the seat, two dollar bills ready in his hand. He paid the driver, went quickly across the sidewalk, got directions from the starter and shifted restlessly until the private cage came down to take him up to the offices of B. Kellogg and Sampson. On the door the name of Jason Blumberg led the list of senior partners. Tim nodded approvingly; it was always easiest to deal with the head man.

In the reception room, a bright-eyed girl looked up from her desk and smiled.

"Timothy Cook. To see Mr. Blumberg."

"Yes, he's expecting you, Mr. Cook. I'll ring his secretary. Won't you have a chair?"

The girl pulled down the key of an intercom box and spoke briefly into a handset. Tim Cook put his suitcase down beside the girl's desk and then moved aside to let a tall man ring for the elevator.

"Oh, Mr. Kellogg," the girl called. "Will you be in at all this afternoon?"

"Five o'clock, for a while, Norma. Not before then."

Not bad, Tim thought, looking closely at the tall man. Not bad at all. From what they told me, I was expecting one of those chesty loudmouths with a lot of hair and a faceful of big teeth. But this one looks human and his voice is all right, judging by that little sample. He's kind of skinny, but the way television makes everybody look like a tub of guts, it's better for a candidate to be skinny. I think he might do okay. Tim Cook nodded to himself. For the first time that day he allowed himself to feel mildly confident about his job.

He said, "Mr. Kellogg!" in a brusque, almost peremptory tone, and thrust out a narrow, nervous hand, forcing the man to take it.

"Yes? You wanted to see me?"

"Mr. Kellogg, I'm Tim Cook from the state central committee. I came down from Monte to see you."

"Not me." Benson shook his head decisively. "You want my brother."

Tim rocked back on his heels and scowled. "How do you know?" he demanded.

"That's easy, Mr. Cook. I'm probably the only lawyer in Rincon who doesn't want to run for public office."

Tim Cook grunted. "You might be good at it," he said, letting his voice rise with a questioning inflection.

Benson shook his head. "We'll never know. I don't intend to try." He stepped around Tim and into the waiting elevator. "My brother's still in his office, Mr. Cook," he said.

Tim turned away from the elevator to find a slim, severe woman in a sober gray suit waiting for him at the reception desk. "I am Mr. Blumberg's secretary," she said in a sober gray voice. "Will you come this way, Mr. Cook?"

Jason Blumberg's office was large and sunlit, a corner room with two walls of glass tinted blue to cut down the glare From a big carved desk a matching conference table stretched down the center of the room. The far end of the table had been cleared to make room for two napkin-covered serving trays.

In his short term of employment with the state committee, Tim Cook had met only a few of the seventeen county chairmen, but Nathan Barstow had briefed him on Blumberg with pungent, brutally direct clarity.

"You'll be seeing Jake Blumberg in his own office. He likes to put on the dog, and he likes people to act impressed. Jake was a poor boy back East, and now he's got a little extra money, he likes to have it out where it shows. But don't let that stuff fool you; he's a shrewd old bird, so whatever you do, don't try to feed him a line of bull."

"Tough, is he?" Tim had wondered.

"He likes to act tough. Speak right out to him. He likes people with bad manners. Damned if I know why. He figures a guy with bad manners can't be a phony. Which shows you just how smart Jake is."

Jason Blumberg rose, smiling easily, his small soft hand ready. He seemed slightly familiar to Tim. He was about middle height, with a fringe of feathery white hair, a bright pink face and small eyes that were almost hidden in deep tired pouches. As he clutched Blumberg's hand in a quick, hard, meaningless politician's grip, Tim looked at the way his shoulders sloped powerfully inside the loose, beautifully cut suit, at his heavy pendulous ears and the large shapely nose that gave distinction to a broad, otherwise undistinguished face.

"Tim Cook," Blumberg said. "Tim Cook. I remember meeting a man named Tim Cook at the national convention in Chicago four years ago. Thought for a minute you might be the same man."

Tim nodded. "I am."

Blumberg eyed him dubiously. "This was a bigger man. Sort of—heavier, you might say. Ran the publicity office."

Tim flicked a thumb back toward his chest. "Me," he said briefly, hiding the quick anger that made his throat feel hot. "I had to quit. I can't live in Chicago any more. I've got about eighteen kinds of allergy that add up to asthma. I had to come out here so I could breathe."

Blumberg smiled a little uncertainly. "Well, your misfortune is our good fortune. We can certainly use a man with your experience. Now let's sit down at the table, Mr. Cook. We can be having a bite of lunch while we talk."

Tim sat in a chair at the end of the conference table. Blumberg settled himself heavily beside him and drew a covered tray closer. He removed both napkins, wadded them and tossed them down the table.

"That's real corned beef, Mr. Cook. I have it brought in special." He lifted a sandwich in both hands, bit an enormous semicircle out of it, chewed and swallowed it down quickly. "Got some news for me, haven't you, Mr. Cook? Good news, maybe?"

"I guess it's good news," Tim said. "Good for somebody. I suppose you heard about Charles MacKelland falling down with a stroke Saturday?"

"Heard about it?" Blumberg lifted both hands. "Why, Nate Barstow was on the phone to me five minutes after it happened. Poor old Charlie. How is he?"

"Not good. His whole left side is paralyzed. There's no chance he'll be able to campaign again this fall."

"A terrible thing," Blumberg said softly, his eyes shining. "Poor Charlie was Attorney General for two terms. Fine terms. He might have become Governor one day, who knows."

"Yeah." Tim bit into his sandwich and chewed slowly,

not looking at Blumberg.

"So I get it?" Blumberg went on, softly insistent. "That's definite? I get to name the Attorney General?"

Tim shrugged. "You get to name the candidate. Nate said your man is named Kellogg. That right?"

Blumberg nodded, his mouth full.

"Had some experience, has he?"

Blumberg swallowed noisily. "Not much, no. He makes a good speech, though, nice and easy. He's never been on a ticket before."

Tim stared morosely down at the tabletop. He scratched his chin with his thumbnail. "Attorney General is a pretty important spot," he said. "Kind of fast company for a beginner."

"It certainly is. And I'll bet you know why it's going to work out fine, don't you?" Blumberg said slyly. "A man like you who used to be with the national committee? Don't tell me Nate Barstow didn't explain it all to you?"

"The name is really worth all that, is it? Who the hell was this B. Kellogg anyway?"

"One of the old names, one of the good old names. What do you think it would be worth in Kentucky if you could put Daniel Boone on the ticket? Or Robert E. Lee in Virginia? Or Sam Houston in Texas?"

"Something, I guess. Not much."

"Mr. Cook, listen to me. You come from Chicago. You know about big cities. You see a couple of good-size cities in this state, and maybe you think that's the state. It isn't. Nah!" Blumberg shook his head forcefully. "Don't you believe it. Ninety per cent of the state is just like it was when settlers first came here, and the people living out there are pretty much the same kind of people. They add up to more than half the voters. They're not ignorant and they're not poor, except for some of the Indians and Mexicans. A lot of things have changed around here lately and, by and large, those people don't much like the changes. What they like is the tough old days. And the tough old names."

"Maybe so," Tim said skeptically. "If I was picking out a

name that was political magic, I'd say Roosevelt. But I can remember a couple of Roosevelts who got walloped."

"Kellogg is different," Blumberg said, hoarsely confident. "Let me tell you. This is the old Kellogg law firm, I guess you know. A lot of my colleagues at the bar would like me to change the name. You just bet they would! I came to work here as a young man, fresh out of Temple Law School, some forty years ago. A long time. Lots of changes since then, let me tell you. But one thing never changed. The solid business came to this office—the land litigation, the title problems, the fights over water and mineral rights, railroad and highway rights-of-way. That's where the money is and up until the time Mr. Kellogg —that's B. Kellogg, Jr.—died, we got most of it. After he died, we were just another law firm. Then, about five years later, after the war, I brought one of the sons in here. And I'll just ask you to guess, Mr. Cook. Just take a wild stab at it. How much do you think our business picked up after that?"

Tim shook his head. "No idea. Lots, eh?"

"Well, maybe I shouldn't be talking about it. Wouldn't want my young men hitting me for a raise. Let's just say that our business improved by some fifty per cent, Mr. Cook. That's what the name means. When some old rancher comes in from his hundred-section spread and wants to sue the railroad, or a mining company, or a neighbor, he starts looking around for a lawyer. The only lawyer he ever heard of is B. Kellogg. He comes in here, right off the street and asks to see somebody named Kellogg. That's all there is to it."

Tim drained his glass and set it down with a soft crash. "Okay. I don't think any name is worth that much, but it's your baby. You get to name the candidate. You pick Kellogg, so Kellogg it is. Nate Barstow wants him up at Monte in time for dinner tonight. He's getting some of the county chairmen in to look him over and start the ball rolling. There's not much time left before the state caucus, so we'll have to get your boy moving around the state. Better tell him not to plan on coming home for a week or two."

Blumberg got up and went to his desk. He spoke softly

into the telephone. He hung up, took a cigar from a box in his desk drawer and came back to his chair, rolling the cigar gently between his hands.

"He'll be here in a few minutes. Going to be exciting news, I can tell you."

"I guess so," Tim said sourly. "While I'm here, I want to talk to his family, take some pictures, rough out some publicity. I'll need a campaign biography. I figured on staying around a couple of days maybe, if I don't run into any trouble." He looked at Blumberg silently until the lawyer had his cigar lighted and drawing well. He waved the heavy smoke away from his face. "What's wrong with him?"

"Wrong? With Burr Kellogg?"

"Let's not kid around," Tim said. "You know what I mean. What is the opposition going to throw at us during the campaign?"

"Why, there isn't anything about him that——"

"There's always something," Tim said wearily. "Take it from me, Mr. Blumberg. The pitiful part is that the poor slob always hides it from his friends, so when his enemies dig it up, it has a real impact on the public. None of that for Tim Cook. I want to know everything about this boy of yours. Every goddam thing that is likely to snap back in our faces. I can handle it if I know. But nobody is going to give me the lily-white routine, so don't try."

Blumberg chuckled. He rolled his cigar moistly in a corner of his mouth. "I like the way you talk, Tim. I like it fine. Straight shooting, that's my kind of talk. All right. I say you won't find anything bad about Burr Kellogg. Local boy, fine old family, went to school here, went to college at Amherst, then Yale Law. Played a little football, served in the Navy, married a nice girl from Vermont last year, no children yet, belongs to all the right things, none of the wrong ones. He inherited some money and he's a soft touch for all the charities. You won't find anything, but go ahead and look. Satisfy yourself."

"I will."

"That doesn't bother me," Blumberg said. "I know Burr

Kellogg like I know myself. What I'm wondering about is Nate Barstow." He closed one eye and squinted at Tim with a shrewd, speculative intensity. Just then he looked a little like old Nate himself, Tim thought. That's probably where he got that stony, one-eyed glare.

"What about Nate?" he asked.

"What does he want my man up there for? We've got the state caucus scheduled for Monte next week. Why can't he wait till then?"

"Your boy may be B. Kellogg," Tim said in a bored voice, "but personally he isn't well known, that's all. He has to start meeting people. Not everybody is awfully damn happy about some unknown kid running for Attorney General."

"He's no kid," Blumberg objected. "What's Nate worried about? Can't he handle the caucus?"

"Caucus? Caucus, hell. The caucus isn't going to decide anything. You know who makes the decisions, don't you? Nathan W. Barstow. He owns three banks and six newspapers and thirteen county chairmen, and he'll hold a caucus inside his dirty old cowboy hat and that's all the caucus you'll ever need to worry about."

"Then why——"

"Figure it out for yourself. Your boy still has to sell himself to Nate Barstow. You've got him in, most likely, but if Nate says he won't do, then it's all off. I don't think Nate is going to be hard-nosed; he just wants to see the guy. The biggest job comes when we try to sell him to the county chairmen. We don't want them getting pissed off and decide to go fishing during the campaign. We'll trot your boy out and let them all get a good look at him. Then they can talk it over a little and try to make themselves believe they're deciding something."

"You don't think much of county chairmen, do you?" Blumberg's unctious voice hardened with the beginning of anger.

"Not much," Tim agreed. "About what you think of them. You've got to have them, but you don't have to listen to them. Where's your boy? I've got to get him started for Monte."

"Well, by God, you are a cool one, I'll say that," Blumberg muttered. "I wonder if you're as tough as you talk?"

"I'm not tough," Tim said heavily. "I'm not anything. Don't bother trying to figure me out, Blumberg. I'm just a hired hand minding the store. I don't have opinions. If I say something, it's Nate Barstow talking, not me."

Blumberg removed his cigar with slow deliberation, reversed it and inspected the brand, blew on it gently and then screwed the cigar back in his tight mouth again.

"You want to go easy when you talk to Burr Kellogg," he said, trying for a casual tone. "Burr is a nice friendly fellow, but he's got a temper. You might find out if you start giving him trouble."

"Yeah, sure. I can see he's going to get along just fine with Nate Barstow."

"I'll handle Nate myself. You just stick to your job, Mr. Cook."

"I will," Tim said easily. "Don't think I won't."

He pulled back the sleeve of his shirt to see his watch. Then he slid down in his chair and folded his arms, pretending a patience that would always be alien to him.

THE RECEPTION ROOM of B. Kellogg and Sampson was deserted when Benson Kellogg got off the elevator shortly before seven o'clock. The lights had been turned down and the air conditioning system was off. The corridors were dim and quiet, musty with a feeling of dampness, like an abandoned ship.

Benson went into his office, sat on a corner of his desk and leafed through a pile of mail left by his secretary. Nothing there that couldn't wait till morning. At the bottom of the stack was a hurriedly scrawled note from Burr: "Ben—Have to take off for Monte in a cloud of dust. I want to talk to you as soon as you come in. Call me at home if you're late. Burr."

Benson rolled his chair back from his desk. He sat and

swung one leg up. He took out his cigarettes, lit one and blew a long plume of smoke at the telephone. He didn't feel like talking to anyone, not even Burr. He just wanted to sit there quietly for a few minutes, not even thinking, just sitting and waiting for enough time to pass so that he would get over being tired and depressed. He had put in a long day; up at five and occupied completely ever since then. But only the last hour had been really bad. Even the strain of finishing his final summation before a querulous, demanding judge had not been half as exhausting as sitting in the gloomy shadowed living room of the Turnbull house, listening to the three Turnbull women trying to convince themselves that they had behaved decently and honorably as good citizens should, that they had done the right, the responsible thing. But the fever of guilt was in them and its heat was not endurable. Benson sighed heavily, surprising himself. He sat up quickly and drew the phone toward him.

He dialed and waited while the mechanism searched down the relays and rang a bell. "Desert Sportswear," a dispirited voice said after a moment.

"Miss Gilbert, please. This is Benson Kellogg."

He listened to the quiet murmur of the open line for a while, staring blankly across the room. He smiled unconsciously when Jocelyn Gilbert lifted the phone and said, "Hello, Ben. It's high time you called me."

"Evening, Joss. I've had a busy day. A lousy day, as a matter of fact. How was yours?"

"Terrible. I'm ready to drop."

"Like to have dinner with me? We could go up to the Skylight Room and eat with the eagles."

"I'd love to, Ben, but I'm awfully tired," she said in a tone of honest regret. "I wouldn't be very good company."

"Just come along and smile once in a while. I'm in no mood for chatter, either. I've had too much of it today."

"We-ell, all right, Ben," she said on a dubious note. "If you're sure?"

"Reasonably sure. I might get talky after a couple of drinks. Pick you up in half an hour?"

"At the apartment, yes. I'm leaving now."

Benson held down the crossbar briefly, let it up and dialed a familiar number.

"Yes, hello?"

"Evening, Paula."

"Oh, Ben, we've been trying to reach you. Where——"

"I've been out of touch. What's up? Burr left me a note."

"I know. You'll find messages all over town. He was calling everywhere right up to the moment his plane left."

"Plane? Where's he gone?"

"I hate to tell you, Ben, but he's gone up to Monte to have dinner with the great Nathan Barstow. Haven't you heard what's been happening?"

"Not a word," Benson said patiently. "But if Nate Barstow is involved, I guess it's political."

"Political? I should say it is. They want Burr to run for Attorney General."

"Burr?"

"I know. It's maddening. I wish you could have talked him out of it."

"It's up to Burr, Paula," Benson said mildly. "Is he going to run?"

"He's wild at the chance. He was charging around like a kid with a new wagon."

"My God," he said softly.

"And he's had to dump his work load on the people at the office. He wanted you to take on something for him."

"I suppose I could. I finished up today. I might find a little spare time. What was it?"

"I don't know, Ben. He didn't say. His plane gets to Monte about seven o'clock. He'll call me from the airport. Can I give him a number where he can find you?"

"I guess so. I'm taking Joss to dinner at the Skylight. Tell Burr to try her apartment first."

"All right, I'll tell him. Oh, Ben, isn't it infuriating? He won't be home for a week. And he left a wheezing little mean-eyed man here when he left. I'm supposed to tell him everything about Burr. I don't even want to talk to him. Could you do it, Ben? Would you mind?"

"Who are you talking about, Paula? What man?"

"Oh, somebody named Cook. He's something political. He wants to talk about Burr's background. He wants to know all about your horrible old grandfather, the one who started this political nonsense. He's asking about Burr's childhood and his parents and schools and——"

"Take it easy, Paula. That shouldn't be much trouble. What's bothering you?"

"Oh, I don't know, Ben. I'm being unreasonable, I suppose. I hate Burr going off like this. I can manage this Cook person, I suppose, but I just don't want to. Could you see him, Ben?"

"About Burr? All right, I'll talk to him. Tell him to phone me tomorrow. I'm staying in town tonight."

"You are?" Paula's voice went soft and strange. "With Joss Gilbert?"

"At the Rincon House. With myself. Where do you get these romantic notions?"

"You know perfectly well where I get them. This is really an awfully small town in some ways, Ben."

"It's growing every day, I hear. Good-bye, Paula."

"Ben?"

"Yes?"

"Don't be angry." ·

"I'm not angry, Paula. I'll phone tomorrow. Good-bye."

Benson dropped the phone back on its standard and left the office. He went down in the elevator and out into the street. He walked slowly among the evening crowd to Navajo Drive, crossed with the light and turned left toward the original Spanish section of Rincon. Here a street was called a calle and sometimes an avenida and most of the houses had names instead of numbers.

Benson rattled the latch of Jocelyn Gilbert's door, found it unlocked and walked through to an open tiled areaway. Straight ahead was a tiny walled patio completely in shadow. Four doors opened onto the areaway, each painted a different pastel, each lettered.

Benson pushed the bell beside the door marked with a dull bronze A. It opened immediately.

"You must have been right behind me," Jocelyn Gilbert said. "I just got out the ice." She was a tall girl, and to kiss Benson she had to raise herself only a little on her toes.

"Joss," Benson said. "You are looking very well for a collapsing shopgirl. You're looking very well for any kind of a girl. I thought you were drooping on the stem?"

"Oh, what a day it has been! I can't bear to think about it. Make us a drink, there's a dear Ben. I want a martini and shower, both ice cold. I'll be just a minute."

Benson shifted to cut her off from the bedroom. He put both hands on her shoulders and smiled. "You really are looking very well," he said softly.

"Oh, Ben. You look lovely too, dear. But wait, please. I'm so gritty." She kissed him again with expert swiftness, moving in his arms so that when she pushed herself away she was in the doorway. She smiled up mockingly and closed the door behind her.

Benson licked the lipstick from his mouth and then lit a cigarette, looking intently at the door as if his mental image of Joss were clear enough to study in detail. She was a startlingly beautiful girl in a subtle but strongly dramatic fashion. She was an almost white blonde whose coloring was not vivid. It wasn't vivid, but it was perfect. She was tall and her body was long, rich and exciting, with high heavy breasts and a swell of hip and thigh that made some kinds of clothes difficult for her to wear. She always dressed with a knowing, expensive elegance that was not common in Rincon except among the winter visitors. But that magnificent body was best suited by no clothes at all. Benson grinned at the thought.

It was hard for him to remember that she was decidedly a young girl, barely twenty-three. She approached and solved, or cleverly evaded, all problems with a clear-eyed, well-considered sureness that normally comes only with maturity when it comes at all. It was remarkable, even admirable, but Benson suspected that it was also an attitude that might at times be chilling and repellent, though he had never seen it so.

Joss was sometimes a little stagey and larger than life. That was one of the few things about her that reminded Benson of her youth. Like all girls who are a little stagey, she sometimes tried a little too hard, and so you had a feeling that you were watching a performance—not a public performance, but a private showing staged for an audience of one: you. A stagey girl is not used to simplicity and doesn't much like it, so everything around her is given a higher gloss, a different aspect, an unusual importance. With such a girl you begin to see things in another fashion, and that is always interesting, though it isn't often restful.

For a while, after they had first met, she had been in love with Benson. That was two years ago and it had lasted for a month until she decided to open her dress shop. After that she was too busy. There had been a time, about a year ago, when Benson had been in love with her. Joss had still been too busy. By now they were used to the idea that sooner or later they would feel the same way at the same time. Then they would do something official about it. There was no hurry.

But maybe there should be, Benson thought suddenly. He went to the high Spanish chest in the far corner and began to assemble the gear for drinks. Maybe it is about time we hurried ourselves a little. After a day like this, I begin to realize I'm not getting any younger. Just thinking about Judge Turnbull is enough to give any man intimations of mortality.

He measured gin and vermouth at eight-to-one, enough for two drinks, and let it stand in the bar glass without ice. Then he poured himself a long four fingers of bourbon, added water and ice and took the glass with him to a chair across the room.

There were too many chairs and couches set around the room because Joss liked to give big parties, but except for that it was a pleasant place.

Benson leaned back and closed his eyes. He drank from

his glass slowly, feeling and liking the first sense of ease that a good quiet drink can give.

When the telephone rang, he did not move. He had for the moment forgotten about Burr and he opened his eyes in mild surprise when Joss came in from the bedroom wrapped in a toweling robe, her hair piled loosely high for protection against the shower spray.

"It's long distance. Somebody in Monte, for you. Were you expecting——"

"It's Burr." Benson came to his feet with a lunge. He put down his glass and threw his cigarette into the fireplace.

The telephone stand was at the far side of the large square bed, in a narrow space that did not allow passage. Benson sat on the bed, lay back quickly, lifted the receiver and sat up again in one swift movement.

"This is Benson Kellogg," he said.

"One moment, please," the operator said. "Here is your party, sir."

"Ben? That you, Ben? Boy, you're hard to find. What are you doing in that beautiful doll's apartment?"

"Guess," Benson said sourly.

"Not me, I'm a married man. Heard the news, Ben? I'm moving up to the big leagues."

"I heard. Are you going to take it, Burr?"

"Damn right. I'll see Nate Barstow at dinner. It's all set. Attorney General. How about that?"

"Yeah, how about it?"

"Not sore, are you, Ben? I didn't mean to interrupt you—"

"I'm not sore. Paula said you were pleased about it. So am I, Burr. Good luck, best wishes. All that. You know. Count on me for a campaign contribution."

"Thanks, Ben. I know you don't give a damn for politics, but I've always wanted to take a flier. I'm glad you're with me. There's one thing I wanted to ask you. Remember what we were talking about at breakfast?"

"Judge Turnbull?"

"No, at breakfast. About me getting assigned to one of the free cases?"

"Oh. Yes, I remember. Is that what you——"

"I want you to take it on for me, Ben. I've laid off everything else on my schedule, but this is something special. Judge Groat really socked it to me before I agreed. I don't want him browned off at me now. B. Kellogg is attorney of record, but you're B. Kellogg too. Old Groat can't get around that."

"Yes, he can," Benson said. "But I don't suppose he'll care if we swap. All right, Burr, if it's that important. What's the case?"

"Thanks, Ben. I appreciate it. I forget the number. It's that pachuco kid named Arturo Campeón they scraped off the road Saturday night. He killed some guy from California up on Lookout Point, then stole his car, a Rolls no less, and cracked it up just outside town. It's not a——"

"A murder case?" Benson broke in sharply. "For God's sake, Burr! What's wrong with you? I haven't been inside a criminal court in nearly ten years. I don't even remember the procedure. I couldn't handle a murder case."

"Wait a minute, Ben. Will you wait a minute? This case wouldn't bother a beginning law student. Campeón is guilty as hell. He admits it. He's already signed a confession. I appeared for him at Justice Court this morning and we waived a preliminary hearing. We just didn't have anything to say. The kid told me he's guilty. He doesn't even argue it. So there's nothing to worry about. You know Frank Sayer, don't you?"

"The County Attorney? I know him, of course. I wouldn't say we were friends. What does that matter? I can't take on a murder case."

"Will you listen?" Burr demanded impatiently. "I've already talked this out with Frank. He wants this conviction on his record. He's up for re-election this year and he has to make a good showing because he wants to go for Mayor next year. Frank wants this conviction and he's willing to stand still for just about anything to get it."

"What does that mean in plain English?"

"He'll go over the case with you, outline his trial plan, show you what evidence he has, let you interview all his witnesses and help you prepare your case. And he won't be sharpshooting you with objections if you push him a little. After all, he wants the trial to go off smoothly, too. So it's all set. How about it, sound okay?"

"Just slow down a minute, Burr. Even if your client is guilty, he ought to get a fair shake. I just don't have enough experience in criminal court. And anyway, what makes you trust Frank Sayer? From what I've heard, he's a man who just might leave you holding an empty sack."

"He's up for re-election, I told you. He can't afford to pull anything. But you're right; he isn't anybody's rose. You have to watch him. But he won't lie to you. You know what I mean? He won't actually say the lie. So watch him. He lies, all right, but he never does it straight out. Just listen to every word he says. Don't take anything by implication, or he'll be leading you by the nose."

"You're not reassuring me, Burr. I don't think I'm the man to help your client."

"Don't worry about helping him. Nobody could help that greaseball. If he had Clarence Darrow and Earl Rogers in his corner, he'd still hang. You don't understand yet. No jury would ever let him off. Frank Sayer could get a conviction on half the evidence he has. Nobody expects you to save the bastard." Then Burr laughed and his voice altered subtly. "What you're worried about is you might walk into that courtroom and make a jerk out of yourself. Don't worry about that. I've already covered it with Frank Sayer. And Jake Blumberg will assign some clerks if you need help with the details. You can use my secretary; she's sharp with trial stuff. And you'll be doing me a hell of a favor, Ben. The truth is, I don't want to handle a losing case now that I'm slated to run for Attorney General. Every lawyer would know it was just a free case and doesn't mean a thing, but it looks bad to the public. It's different for you. This isn't your field and nobody is going to be second-guessing you. Another point: Judge Groat would accept a lawyer with your reputation as a substitute, but he'd never agree to anyone else. I'm sure of that. And I need him on my side, for a while anyway. He cracks a big whip with those downstate politicians. Well, there it is, Ben. Will you help me? Please."

"Burr, it's a hell of a thing to ask me. I'm no trial lawyer."

"I know, Ben, but this case won't give you any trouble. You could walk through it with your eyes shut. It's on ice. Take it from me. Will you do it for me, Ben?"

"I . . ." Benson hesitated, knowing he should refuse flatly, knowing also why he couldn't. "All right, Burr. Where's your file?"

"My secretary's got it. You know Harkie. Thanks, Ben. I knew you wouldn't leave me dangling. By God, it's great to know there's someone you can depend on. You don't know what this means to me. Judge Groat would have burned my butt otherwise."

"Okay, Burr. I'll do what I can. You'd better call me some time tomorrow. I may need some help."

"Will do, boy. Will do. Thanks again, Ben. I'd better get going now. So long, Ben."

"Good night, Burr." Benson lay back to hang up the phone, and when he sat up again he was looking directly at Joss, who stood stiffly before him, knees almost touching his, her clenched hands propped on her hips, glaring at him with an expression of almost comical exasperation.

"He sold you another gold brick, didn't he?"

Benson shook his head. "Nothing like that, Joss."

"It is something like that. It always is. Any time he gets into a jam he yells for help and you always come running."

Benson moved his shoulders impatiently. "He's my brother, Joss."

"He's not. He's your half-brother."

Benson pushed up from the bed. "That makes it harder, not easier." He drew her close and held her warmly to him. "Let's not talk about it right now, please. How about that drink you wanted?"

Joss held herself stiffly for a moment longer, then softened slowly. The long line of her body pressed against him softly.

"Oh, damn you, Ben Kellogg. I wish you were as big a sucker for me as you are for Burr."

A DENSE BUDDING HUISACHE outside the bedroom window moved a little in the light breeze that reached the enclosed patio, and thin moonlit shadows broke and formed new patterns across the floor and walls. Lying still and lax, breathing long, interminable breaths of the warm acacia-scented breeze, Benson felt a detached, swimming sensation inside his brain, as if he were drifting, unresisting, along the bed of the sea, looking up and watching the light move against the surface of the water. Joss shifted beside him, lifted one arm to brush back a wing of nearly white hair that had fallen across her face. She opened her eyes very slowly, then almost closed them again and smiled lazily.

"You were asleep," she said softly. "I saw you. Like a boy. You don't snore. That's quite an asset. I thought all men snored." She put her arm lightly across his chest.

"Clear conscience," Benson said in a quiet murmur. Clear sinuses is more likely, he thought.

"How do you keep so thin?" Joss said in a sleepy voice. "You haven't any blubber at all, and you ate a two-pound steak and a big baked potato and you must have had six of those garlic buns."

"Seven."

"So why aren't you fat, if you eat like that? It's not fair. I have girls working for me who don't eat that much in a week and they still put on weight."

"I don't know. Something to do with metabolism, I suppose. And stop poking my belly." He drew her down close, fitting her head snugly in the pocket of his shoulder. Her breath was warm and slow against his bare chest.

"Love me?" he said.

"No."

"I think you do love me."

"No. That's just physical. Chemistry."

"The hell you say," Benson objected mildly. "That's love."

"Well, maybe. Sometimes."

"Marry me?"

"No, not now. Not ever, probably."

"You sound damn sure, and serious. Why not?"

"I don't know, Ben." Joss rolled onto her back and held a hand across her eyes as if to shield them from a strong light. "I was talking to Burr at a party last week. About you, and the ranch. You've finally gotten over what he did to you, haven't you?"

"He didn't do anything to me, Joss."

"Oh, Ben, don't be so protective. Everybody in Rincon thinks it was a dirty trick, even if you don't. He had no right to split the estate the way he did."

"Of course he had the right. Half of it was his."

"So he took the cash and left you with a ranch that you didn't have money enough to operate. How much did he take, actually? I heard it was a quarter-million."

"About that. But——"

"He didn't want it for anything, did he? He just invested it somewhere else. Why didn't he leave it invested in La Cañada?"

"Burr never liked living at the ranch, Joss. After Dad died, he had a chance to get away completely and he took it. You can't blame him for that."

"But he left you in a bind, didn't he? How long did it take you to pull out of it? Working like a dog, borrowing money at ten per cent from every loan shark in the state? How long, Ben?"

"Don't be so fierce about it, Joss. It's never been that bad. La Cañada has always been a good producing ranch. I switched over to breeding parade horses and I had to raise some capital. But since then we've been doing pretty well. And we'll do better. We're over the hump now. I had to scratch for a while, but it was worth it, don't forget that. La Cañada is worth some effort. But what has all that got to do with us? I don't follow."

"You don't want to. You just don't realize that you have put so much of yourself into La Cañada that you will never be able to leave it. That place is becoming an obsession."

"That's nonsense, Joss," Benson said gently. "La Cañada is my home. I was born there and I'm fond of it. Also, it's a damn valuable piece of property. There's nothing obsessive about that."

"Maybe not," Joss said tiredly, as if she didn't want to talk about it any more.

Benson waited for a long quiet moment, then turned so that Joss could feel him close. "Why don't you come up to the ranch for a while? Maybe you've been away from it too long. Take a week off and poke around with me. It's a good life, Joss. It's the best life I know. I can't believe you wouldn't——" He broke off and looked down at her curiously, aware that she was not listening. "But it isn't just the ranch, is it? There's something more to it."

"Yes, maybe. Oh, I don't know, Ben. I just don't see any place in your life for me. You don't need me. You're all full up. You've got the ranch and your job and you're so busy all the time that you don't even realize you're not very happy." Joss lay with her face to the ceiling, speaking so softly that Benson had to strain to hear. "What's your wife's name, Ben?"

"Liza. But what——" Benson stiffened. He was frowning in the darkness and his voice sharpened. "For God's sake, Joss! What are you trying to do? I thought you were using the past tense, you know that. Liza is dead. She was killed during the war. It was a long time ago. I know she's dead. I loved her and we had a happy time while it lasted and now it's over and I know it's over."

"I'm sorry, Ben. That wasn't fair, was it? But I'm not sure Liza is dead and gone, as you say. Why do you keep her father around, if it's all over?"

"I don't keep him around," Benson said tightly. "Fitz is his own master. We got to be friends while I was in England. When he retired he wanted to visit the States, and naturally I invited him to stay at La Cañada. He makes his headquarters there, but he doesn't spend three months of the year with me. What's got into you, Joss? Fitz is good company, you know that. If my old C.O. retired and wanted to come to La Cañada for a while, I'd be just as glad to have him. Fitz isn't any damn symbol; he's a man, a good one, and he goes his own way. He doesn't look after me and I don't look after him."

"I know, Ben," Joss said, sighing. "I know you're right, but still . . ." She turned to him and stroked a finger gently along his mouth. "I don't know what's the matter with me, Ben. Let's not talk about it any more. We were having such a fine time before I spoiled it. Were you having a fine time, darling?"

Benson drew in a long breath and laughed shakily. "It was pretty fair," he said, heavily judicious. "Not enough food, not enough drinks and a damn sight too little loving. Except for that . . ."

"Oh, dear." She giggled unexpectedly and buried her head against him quickly. "Poor Ben. Could I get you a sandwich, poor Ben?"

"No, thank you."

"A drink then? A nice long———"

"No, thank you."

"You don't mean you want———"

"Yes, thank you. Now you've got the idea."

A NOISY, three-unit parade came out of the low morning sun and rolled along the street toward Navajo Drive, slowing so the patrolman at the corner could flag down the traffic. Benson stopped on the curb outside his office building, hemmed in by the press of early shoppers halted for the free entertainment.

A sound truck with three speakers like morning glories sprouting from the roof went by very slowly, silent for the moment. Close behind them was a stake-body truck loaded with a ten-man cowboy band seated on rickety camp chairs, except for the bass fiddler, who propped himself dangerously against the back of the cab and kept his bow moving even while he rocked from side to side. A red-faced bellower in a white Hopalong hat formed fake chords on his guitar and pretended to strum the strings, always a half-beat off. He fascinated Benson because he was singing in time, and it did not seem possible that a man could have such peculiar co-ordination.

> As I was walkin' down the street,
> Down the street,
> Down the street,
> As I was walkin' . . .

A flapping canvas sign in blue and orange along the side of the truck read RODEO! RODEO! RODEO! JAYCEES ANNUAL ROUNDUP! COME EARLY, COME ALL! SPONSORED BY THE JUNIOR CHAMBER OF COMMERCE, RINCON COUNTY. It was a lot to get on one sign, and much of it was illegible from dragging in the dust. The message was repeated on a banner pinned to the side of a trailing convertible with the top down and four young and fairly pretty girls sitting high with their feet on the seat, trying to keep their cowboy hats from tilting over their eyes as they waved energetically at the people on the sidewalk. They were a little shy and they were keeping up their spirits by nudging each other and pretending to spot dear friends in the crowd.

Benson turned away quickly. Three of the girls were scheduled to ride La Cañada colts in the grand parade, and he did not feel in a mood to be singled out for special greetings. The rodeo parade was always a useful experience for his colts, although they would have benefited even more with better riders. Once, two years ago, he had sold his entire string after that one exhibition at the Jaycee rodeo. Usually he had to send most of his horses to El Monte or Los Angeles or Las Vegas or

San Francisco before he got his price, but there had never been a year when he hadn't sold at least one good colt at the Rincon rodeo.

Probably he should be showing more civic spirit, he thought, but the hell with it. He was tired after a sleepless night in a dirty refrigerated hotel room. His nose felt stoppered and he couldn't draw in a good, satisfying lungful of air. The hotel barber had shaved him down to the blood, and there was a styptic-glazed gash under his ear. All told, a poor start to the day, and even an excellent breakfast had not set it right.

He had spent an hour in his office, disposing of his morning routine and reading through Burr's brief notes on the case of *People* v. *Arturo Campeón*. Now, as he walked toward the county courthouse, he was wondering where to begin his job. The fact was, he admitted to himself, that Burr had put his finger smack on the problem last night. He *didn't* want to make a jerk out of himself by mishandling a criminal case. But there was no way out that he could see—except one. Judge Groat might refuse to accept him as a substitute. Too much to hope for, probably, but a pleasant idea at the moment.

He crossed the street and went up the short flight that led to the courthouse grounds. It was a low building, square and white and elegant, designed after the kind of Moorish architecture that is usually called Spanish. The courthouse was a hollow square in the classic pattern, the sections at front and rear being four stories high and the connecting blocks just two stories. You entered by a low arcade in any one of the four sides and went through to a narrow, terra-cotta-tiled gallery that ran along the inside walls. Tiled walks led out to a circular pool and fountain in the center of a grassed courtyard. The grounds were kept green and very tidy; the robusta fan palms were never allowed to get droopy or go brown, and the transplanted flowerbeds were dug out every few weeks. There was always a dependable supply of local gardeners in the drunk tank, and if a big job had to be done, the cops always knew who was about ripe for a thirty-day jolt for wife-beating or petty theft or lewd and lascivious behavior. The Rincon county courthouse was included on all the lists of things to see.

Superior Court, Part One, took up the first floor of the north wing. Judge Bernard B. Groat had his chambers handily close to a side entrance but removed from the main traffic flow.

Benson tried the handle of the closed door, pushed it down and went in. The anteroom was small, bare, workmanlike. The walls were almost hidden by long racks of filing cabinets and glass-doored bookcases. There were a pair of oak benches just inside the door and a cluster of hard chairs around the single desk. The judge's clerk was seated there, hunched and frowning at his work.

He was Guillermo Rojas, veteran of some thirty years at his job and one of the few attorneys content with a career as clerk, which is customarily a job filled by a fairly intelligent courthouse hack. Many clerks are persuasive and voluble sea lawyers, but it is a rare clerk who is qualified to hang out his own shingle.

Guillermo's courthouse experience went back more than forty years to the time when, as a reticent, almost timid seventeen-year-old just out of high school, he had found a job as office boy, file clerk and dogsbody in the County Recorder's office. That he got the job at all was due to the growing importance of the Mexican-American vote in Rincon. That it was a minor post with small likelihood of advancement was due to the absent-minded but habitual scorn with which his people were then re-garded by the Anglo politicians who controlled the county and city of Rincon.

When—and why—he had decided to make a lawyer of himself even he could not remember now, for in those days there was neither future nor profit in the law for Mexican-Americans. But he had studied, doggedly and alone, had done his assigned work with persistence and apparent eagerness, and when he was ready to present himself to the bar examiners, he had friends enough in the county government to assure a sym-pathetic hearing. The examiners could see little harm in "those people" having a lawyer or two of their own. And they were right. There was no harm in Guillermo. He had realized his only serious ambition before he was twenty-five, and the effort it had cost him, the intellectual and emotional strain of reaching that peak, had apparently exhausted him. He was where he wanted to be. Now he wanted only to stay there.

In South Rincon he was Señor Licenciado Rojas, a man of known influence, of demonstrable power. He had early busied himself with politics to please and support his superiors. After he was established, he increased his political activity, to enjoy the taste of power for himself, and to make himself indispensable to Judge Groat, for any judge who looks to a long career needs someone to keep a sharp eye on the local politicians for him. Guillermo was good at that. He was also good at persuading his friends to vote the right way. He was especially good at keeping his mouth shut.

He was a short, thick-bodied man who moved as if he went on springs. He had a large head with a mass of wiry black hair that was only slightly touched with gray. From above he looked like a well-bred and placid Angus bull.

"Morning, Willie," Benson said as he came in the door. "Is the judge in?"

"Well, hi! Say, you're a stranger around here. I bet I haven't seen you for six months." Guillermo pushed away from his typewriter, spun around and came to his feet, hand stretched out, smiling in genuine welcome.

"Nice to see you again, Willie," Benson said. "No need to ask how you are. I can see. Taken off some weight too, haven't you?"

Guillermo laughed and patted his hard round belly. "Just getting in shape, Ben. Campaign coming up. Me and the judge will be out on the fiesta trail pretty soon, living on freehole beans and gorditas. I'll put it all back, don't you worry. Well, what can I do for you? Or is it something for the judge?"

"I'd like to see him. Any chance?"

"Sure, sure. Not right now, though. He's got a pack of soreheads from the Bar Association in there now. Grievance committee."

"How long will they take?"

"Who knows?" Guillermo shrugged vigorously. "Depends on how long the judge lets them talk. Why don't you try again in about half an hour, Ben? There's nothing much on his schedule for today. I'll get you right in."

"Thanks, Willie. I'll be back. You might mention to the judge that I was here, in case we miss connections again."

"Okay, Ben. Say, that's great news about Burr. Attorney General. Wow!"

"You said it," Benson agreed. "I'll be back."

B E N S O N closed the door behind him and went down the narrow hallway past the open double doors of Judge Groat's courtroom, where a mop-and-bucket brigade was lazing away the morning, getting the courtroom ready for the new term that would begin tomorrow. Benson nodded to the shotgun guard, detoured around him and turned left to climb the worn stone treads of the north staircase.

In that wing, most of the second floor—some dozen offices in all—belonged to the County Attorney and his deputy, his assistants, his investigators, his secretaries and his file clerks. Most of them didn't have room enough to shift around without careful planning, but the County Attorney retained a three-room suite in the corner. Benson entered the large quiet ante-room where a sharp-faced and warily suspicious secretary guarded the inner doorway.

"Mr. Kellogg!" she said brightly. "Mr. Sayer thought you might be coming to see him this morning. He isn't in just at the moment, but he'll be back quite soon. Can you wait?"

"Good morning," Benson said. He balanced his briefcase on a corner of her desk, noticed the name plate on a triangular brace and maneuvered unobtrusively so that he could read it. "Yes, Miss Latimer, I'll wait if I may."

"Won't you come inside? It's much more comfortable."

Frank Sayer had a handsome office. It was paneled with squares of mountain ash rubbed to a soft glow. The room had obviously not been furnished by the county; the brass-bound ebony desk was one of those big ugly pieces that Mr. Chippendale had made in his factory and then shipped out to Hong Kong for decorating, and it alone would have cost more than Rincon County paid its prosecutor for a year's work. A carved, openwork ebony screen shielded the windows behind the desk, throwing a busy, distracting pattern of shadows across the desk top, but hiding the tall air-conditioning unit that purred throatily, chilling the large room and muting the sounds of traffic in the street outside.

In an unbroken line across the inner wall hung matching black-and-gold molding strips arranged to frame a row of photographs that might have been used as cover illustrations on a series of books for boys: Frankie Sayer, Schoolboy Shortstop; Frankie Sayer at Rincon High; Frank Sayer, Class President; Frank Sayer, BMOC at Southern Cal; Franklin Sayer, USNR; Franklin Sayer, Attorney-at-Law; Franklin Sayer, Husband and Father; Hon. Franklin B. Sayer, Public Servant. In all the pictures his mouth was open.

Against another wall were some indistinctly engraved plaques mounted on a sloping display shelf. There was a thin parade of silver athletic trophies on a mantelpiece over an unused fireplace.

Frank Sayer entered his office silently and nudged the door shut with his foot. "Well, Ben, this is a pleasure. We don't see you down here very often." He came forward with his hand outstretched.

Benson stood up to shake hands. "How are you, Frank?"

"Never better," he said expansively. "Never better. Sit down, Ben. Just let me make a note and then we can talk." He sat behind his desk, took out a pencil and flipped up the leather cover of his desk pad.

He sat very straight and tall, even when he was bending forward. After three terms in office he would never be able to shake the feeling that he was always on public view. He had the sort of massive-bodied, big-headed joviality that is especially useful for politicians. His only handicap was his coloring, and that only in photographs. His was a wide, baby-pink face with thick hair that had once been a light reddish blond and was now smoothly, silkily gray. In a strong light, photographs of him registered as little more than a pale blur. Like most politicians, he dressed with sober circumspection, so that nothing would detract attention from that massive, flexible face.

He put his pencil down noisily and leaned back, dropping both hands flat on the desk top with a decisive, meaty smack. "Well, that's done," he said. "Let's talk. Burr called me on the phone last night, so I know what you're here for, but before we get into that, let me congratulate you on the way you handled that land-grant case. Old Andreas Leál was crying in his beer yesterday. It's the first time he's been clobbered since he started practicing law."

"The case hasn't been decided yet," Benson said.

"Andreas thinks it was decided yesterday," Frank Sayer said with a shrug. "I don't mind telling you that's why I agreed when Burr put up your name as his substitute. I had the idea you limited yourself to nonadversary cases. I didn't realize you were such a hot trial man."

"I'm not," Benson said.

"You're too damn modest, Ben. You won a tough case. Enjoy it. Now, about Burr's case. Okay. We'll cooperate, Ben. All the way. You can bank on that."

"That's good to hear, Frank. I'm not sure just what the situation is, though. I haven't seen Judge Groat yet. And maybe the defendant, this Campeón boy, won't want me for counsel."

Sayer snorted. "Don't worry about Campeón. He'll take whatever he gets. And Judge Groat will approve you." He looked away, tilting his head up and scratching his thumbnail along the fleshy ledge of his jaw. "He will ask you for one assurance," he said almost as an afterthought.

Benson stiffened in his chair. Here it comes, he thought. "What assurance?"

"Relax, friend," Sayer said with a wide, hearty gesture. "He's not going to ask you to job your client. No, he just wants to know that you won't try to stall. Every defendant is entitled to a speedy and impartial trial. That's all we're after. I've already talked to the judge this morning, and we see eye to eye on this point."

Benson shook his head slowly and firmly. "I couldn't agree to anything like that, Frank. I haven't talked to the boy yet. As a matter of fact, I don't even know what evidence stands against him. I might have to ask for a continuance, out of fairness to him. How could I say anything else at this stage?"

The County Attorney nodded smoothly. "I understand, Ben. I'm not rushing you. But you don't see my point. We've got this punk cold. I have his confession, signed and ready. I'll see you get a copy. Campeón doesn't stand a chance. When you've talked to him, you'll see there's absolutely no point in asking for a continuance. But I don't want to have to argue the point in open court. Here's what I want you to do. The April term opens tomorrow. Campeón is Number Fifteen, but there's nothing important ahead of him. Judge Groat will list Campeón's case first on the trial docket, so we can get started on the first jury day. That's next Monday. How about it?"

"I can't answer you, Frank," Benson said carefully. "I don't know enough about the case. Burr left me a memo and I read the story in the paper this morning, but it's all pretty sketchy stuff."

"I had the papers play it down," Sayer said blandly. "And for damn good reason. I'll explain in a minute. Let me put the question another way. If, after you have talked to Campeón, you see no purpose in applying for a continuance, will you agree to go to trial next Monday?"

"No," Benson said. "I couldn't even make a contingent agreement, Frank. I'm sorry I can't go along with you, but I don't have any idea what I'll want to do until I've seen the evidence. But while we're on the subject of mutual interests, how about a lesser charge for Campeón? If you're so eager for a quick trial, how about a deal?"

"I can't do that. I've got him dead to rights on murder in the first. I won't let him cop out. That's final. Forget it."

"I don't get this," Benson said quietly. "I simply don't see what's in your mind, Frank. I'm not begging for this case, you know. I'm willing to take it as a favor to Burr, as a favor to the court, but if you're going to try to tell me how to operate, then I'll have to turn it down."

Sayer smiled pityingly. "Okay. So you get sore and walk out. What happens then?" He leaned back and locked his hands comfortably behind his head. "I'll tell you what happens. Judge Groat sends word to Burr Kellogg, Esquire, that he is still attorney of record for one Arturo Campeón. And Burr hightails it back here, cursing at every step, and goes to trial next Monday because there isn't another single damn thing he can do about it, if you back out. Now I'm trying to be nice, Ben. This case goes to trial on Monday. With you or with Burr. You'd better decide fast, because Campeón's lawyer has to make an appearance with him tomorrow when court opens for the new term. Have you got all that straight, Counselor?"

Benson sat rigidly in his chair, his face very still. "You boys play rough," he said tightly. "What makes you think Burr will jump when you snap your fingers?"

Frank Sayer shook his head. He swung a foot up on a corner of his desk, being careful to place his shoe clear of the dark wood. "You don't know much about politics, do you, Ben? We're all members of the same party down here. Burr has our endorsement to run for Attorney General, but that endorsement can be reconsidered any time before the state caucus. And I can tell you this, he wasn't endorsed unanimously, not by a long shot. Most of us around here like Burr and we think he should have his chance, even if he didn't sweat out his time in the ranks. That's how we feel right now. We might change our minds if he didn't play ball with us."

"You're making this sound like the trial of the century, Frank. I know it's a murder case and this is an election year, but what is so important about it? You don't stand to gain that much from a conviction, do you?"

"Hell, no," Sayer said in a disgusted tone. "We don't stand to gain a thing. We're trying to keep from losing something. If this trial isn't handled fast and right, we could lose the county in the election. You don't think we're going to play with something that important, do you?"

"Spell it out," Benson said, tight-lipped. Frank Sayer's supercilious, insiders-only attitude was beginning to irritate him.

"Sure, I'll explain. We carried Rincon County by less than three thousand votes last time. And in the past four years some thirty thousand new residents have moved into the county, more than half of them Mexican-Americans. Those people are beginning to get together politically. And you don't know what we're worried about."

"I still don't."

"This kid Campeón is a Mexican citizen, we discovered, but that doesn't change the picture much. There is a feeling in the Southwest that Mexicans or people of Mexican descent don't get a fair shake in our courts. We both know that isn't true any more, but it's based on the same kind of historical background that makes Negroes afraid of the courts in the South. Your boy will get a fair trial all right. I'll even agree to a couple of Mexican-Americans on the jury, if that's what you want. But we've got to take him to trial fast and get him out of the newspapers."

"Why?"

"Because the Mexican-American Citizens Association is breathing down my neck, that's why. Dammit, Ben, don't you appreciate the position we're in? They're putting on a big membership drive among the new residents, and they just might get the notion to use Campeón's trial to dramatize themselves. They could stage a circus in that courtroom and I'd wind up looking like Simon Legree. And we would, sure as hell, lose the county on election day. Not only us, but Burr too. But if we go to trial fast, with a good lawyer to defend Campeón, we'll have that little bastard in the chair before the Mexican-Americans can get off the dime."

"It all sounds farfetched to me," Benson said coldly. "I know a lot of people in that association, but I don't recognize them from your description."

Sayer's thin-skinned face brightened angrily. He clamped

his mouth tightly shut for a moment until he was sure he could speak in a controlled tone. "I'm not being farfetched," he said thinly. "I know those people, too. Some of them are good friends. But this Campeón case is just what they need to draw attention to their program. As soon as I heard about Campeón, I knew they'd be after me. And they have been. One of their directors called me last night offering to furnish a lawyer for Campeón. You can guess what kind of a slob they had in mind. They got the address of Campeón's parents and they've written the family. I assume they have asked permission to represent the defendant. If they get permission before we go to trial, we're licked. Then this case will run on for two months with every stalling trick in the book, and when it's finished, we'll be the dirty villains who wanted to railroad an innocent Mexican boy to the chair, and the Mexican-Americans will be the Galahads who moved heaven and earth to stop them and save our hero. It's a corny routine, but it'll work, it always has. They'll wind up with ten thousand new dues-paying members. And we'll lose the election, because nobody, but nobody, my friend, ever votes for villains. Now that's all the explaining I'm going to do. If you don't understand the meaning of what I've said, then forget it. Just take off and I'll put in a call to Burr. I guarantee he'll know what I'm talking about."

Benson settled himself squarely in his chair. He crossed his legs and lit a cigarette with slow deliberation. Through the thin smoke he stared at the County Attorney, visibly speculating.

Most of my problem, he was thinking, comes of not knowing enough about Frank Sayer. He is sitting there, hard-eyed and tough, waiting for me. This is the kind of situation Frank has organized and handled often before, that's obvious. But what isn't obvious is whether he is being honest about his motives. He doesn't have the best reputation in the world, but you tend to expect a prosecutor to be a tricky fellow, so maybe a lot of that is propaganda. I don't know if he is really disturbed about the Mexican-American Citizens Association making a mockery of the trial, or whether he just wants to sweep it all under the rug fast before anybody gets the notion to investigate his charges carefully. I just don't know. I don't suppose anybody ever actually *knows* when it comes to a point like this. A certain amount of it you have to take on faith. And I don't know Frank Sayer that well.

"Let's have it," Sayer demanded. "What's the answer?"

"Let me make a couple of reservations first," Benson said slowly. "I'm not willing to rush this case to trial on your word alone, but I will agree not to request a continuance unless I'm convinced I need more time to prepare my defense. Don't interrupt, let me finish. If I find that further investigation would serve no purpose, then I'll go to trial next Monday. That's as far as I can go. If you want a sharper commitment than that, you'll have to get it from Burr. I won't give it to you."

"I could get it from him," Sayer said positively. "I suppose you know that?"

Benson shrugged. "You might," he conceded. "Apparently Burr is listening to politicians these days. But if you dragged him back here and upset his plans, you'd make an enemy of him. I know you've thought of that, but have you thought of this? You'd make an enemy of me too. I wonder if you want that, Frank. You're expecting a close election this year. And you hope to run for Mayor next year. I don't take much interest in local politics, but I could. And I might, if you gave me a good reason. Is that what you want?"

Sayer swung his foot down to the floor and turned to face Benson squarely. His big mobile mouth was pursed in a tight knot and his pale eyebrows rose, almost invisibly. Then, very gradually, his expression eased, the incipient scowl was gone and he seemed to be smiling inwardly at something that had just come to his mind.

"You may not be a politician, Ben, but you've sure got the horse-trading instinct. Okay. I'll buy it. You'll appear in court tomorrow with Campeón and you can tell me then what you decide. I'm not worried about it. If what you want is anywhere near reason, you'll get it. Is that all right with you?"

Benson nodded warily; he had expected far more opposition. "Yes, that's all right. I'll talk to Campeón today. I should know by tomorrow."

"Fine. It's better this way, letting Burr off the hook. He's got a lot of ground to cover in the next couple of weeks. He can't afford the time for a trial and—" Sayer looked up sharply —"he can't afford any more enemies behind him in Rincon County."

"That will be the end of that, Frank," Benson said tightly. "I took this case because of Burr. And I have made a contingent agreement with you because of Burr. But that's all. From now on he's out of it. You deal with me. Let's have no more threats, or you'll be hearing some from me."

Sayer made a covert gesture with one hand, as if to brush something off his desk. "Well, that's straight enough," he said briskly. "Now we know where we stand. Okay, let's talk about the trial. Burr says you're a little rusty on criminal procedure. He asked me to give you a hand and I'm glad to do it. The criminal information I filed should be returned this afternoon. I'll have a copy sent over to your office. And I'll include the names of my witnesses with a line after each one to let you know what I expect to establish with that witness. You'll get it all. Any of them you want to interview, you tell me and I'll set up an appointment. There's one area I'm not sure about yet. That's the California end. The Los Angeles cops are working on it and I should have something by this afternoon. That Rolls-Royce started out in Los Angeles. The owner was a man named Roderick R. Duquesne. I don't know anything about him yet. He must have been a wealthy man to own a Rolls, but his name doesn't ring a bell with the L.A. cops. Arturo Campeón does, though. He's got a petty criminal record. Four arrests, one conviction, all for theft."

"Nothing more serious?"

Sayer shook his head. "Not that I've heard. I may know more after I talk to L.A. this afternoon. They're checking on both of them. All we know about Duquesne is that he lived in a fancy apartment in Brentwood. The manager didn't know what his plans were, but from the baggage in his car, we figure he was headed for a couple of weeks in Mexico."

Sayer opened a manila folder on his desk and traced a finger down a sheet of notes. "Here's what happened, as we piece it together. Duquesne left for his vacation, driving alone. He had a Mexican tourist permit, and one of his neighbors saw him drive off by himself. Okay. Now Campeón was living in L.A. down in Mextown, been there a couple of years off and on. He was going home to visit his family in Chihuahua, he says, and Duquesne gave him a lift, picked him up just outside town. Maybe so. We don't have any reason to suspect a prior connection. We can't put the boy inside that car before he wrecked it north of town on Saturday night. We may turn up a witness who saw them together in El Monte or Palm Springs or someplace along the road. I'd like to prove it independently, but I don't expect it will be an important point. Campeón admits he came here from L.A. with Duquesne. If I should locate a witness, he'll be as much a surprise to me as he will be to you. I'll let you know. Okay so far?"

"Okay. Why did they stop at Lookout Point?"

"Just to take a break, Campeón says. It was getting on for daylight and they'd been driving all night."

"And Campeón confessed to the murder? Without any coercion?"

"Hell, yes. As soon as he was conscious, the sheriff's men took his statement. By then we knew enough so it didn't matter much if he confessed or not. But he didn't give them any trouble."

"What did you say? That he was unconscious?"

"Yes. He flipped that Rolls. I don't know how he managed it; that's the most stable car ever built, but somehow he turned it over. He broke an arm and a collarbone and he got a nasty gash on the head. He came out of it Sunday afternoon."

"And by then you knew about the murder. How?"

"Sunday morning the sheriff's office got a call from some kids who had spotted the body. It was lying on a ledge below Lookout Point. Papers in the guy's wallet said he was Roderick R. Duquesne. The sheriff already had the Rolls the defendant had crashed. The registration said the car belonged to Duquesne. It didn't take a lot of genius for the sheriff to figure out what had happened. He sent a couple of men to the hospital to talk to Campeón."

"And the boy confessed as soon as anyone asked him?" Sayer nodded.

"Why did he kill Duquesne? Did he say?"

"That's a little tricky, that part," Sayer said, pinching his rubbery underlip between two fingers. "The deputies found a cigarette lighter in Campeón's pocket, solid gold, very fancy. It was initialed 'R. D.' Worth about two hundred bucks. The deputies braced the kid and he admitted he'd stolen it from Duquesne. But when Duquesne's body was found he still had his wallet with some four hundred bucks in it, a pad of American Express checks for a total of five thousand, and about twenty bucks in bills and small change in his pants. And he still had his wrist watch, a beauty that would go for a thousand at least. And he had a gold cigarette case to match the lighter, a gold pencil and a gold belt buckle. He was a guy that liked gold. The deputies worked it out that Campeón tried to roll Duquesne when they made that stop, probably held him under the knife. He got the lighter, but then Duquesne kicked up a ruckus and Campeón sliced him. The body fell over that low guardrail and landed on a rock shelf about fifty feet straight down. Campeón didn't try to go after it. I guess he's no mountain climber. So that's why he didn't get anything but the lighter. The deputies put it to Campeón, and he admitted that's what happened."

Benson shook his head in a tired arc. "Is that all of it, Frank?"

"What more do you want?"

"I didn't need that much. There's one thing I'm curious about. You said Campeón is a Mexican national. Won't his government want to take a hand in the case?"

"I haven't heard from the local consul yet. I expect I will. To answer your question, yes, he'll want to make sure the kid gets a fair trial. He would probably furnish a lawyer if the court couldn't find one good enough. But the consul won't object to you, Ben. We're all right there. He'll very likely send someone to the trial as an observer so he can report that Campeón got fair treatment."

"I see," Benson said. "I hope that's the way it works out. Well, thanks for your help, Frank. I'd like to see that confession if you have a copy. I'm going over to see Campeón now. Where is he, county jail?"

"Rincon Hospital. We'll let him stay there till the trial. About the confession, let's see." He swiveled in his chair to face a table against the wall, lifted a telephone and spoke into it so softly that Benson could not hear what he was saying. He hung up and swung around. "Miss Latimer will have it for you when you go out."

"Okay, Frank. I'll phone you when——"

"Wait a minute," Sayer snapped. "There's something else I want to tell you."

His voice was domineering, arrogant. Benson turned warily, as if responding to a physical challenge.

"We haven't had a murder in Rincon for a long time. Did you know that, Ben? We executed the last killer and we're going to execute Campeón too. I want you to get that straight. He's a mad dog and he goes for the high jump. You'll be talking to him soon and you'll see a slick little punk who must have come from a nice family once because he speaks good English and that isn't the usual thing with Mexican kids. Somewhere along the line he went bad, but maybe you won't see that right away. He might fool you."

"So?" Benson said in a cold voice.

"So don't get any ideas about making an insanity plea, friend, that's all I wanted to say. I offered to cooperate and I will, but you've got to play ball with me. Campeón is sane, there's no doubt of that. As sane as any murdering punk ever is. Remember that lighter I told you about. That lighter in Campeón's pocket proves he was robbing Duquesne before the murder, because he couldn't possibly have done it afterward. There's premeditation, Ben. You'll never convince anyone he wasn't sane. Don't try it. That bastard carved the guts out of Roderick Duquesne and he's going to the chair."

"Maybe," Benson said tightly. "Let's let the jury decide about that. Good-bye, Frank. Thanks again."

BENSON was forced to wait ten impatient minutes in the anteroom while Miss Latimer chased through the County Attorney's offices trying to locate the confession of Arturo Campeón. She returned flustered, out of breath, full of apologies. The confession was a single sheet, certified as a true copy by a notary's seal in a bottom corner. Benson folded it and put it in his pocket without reading it.

"That's a nasty case you've got, Mr. Kellogg."

"I suppose all murder cases are nasty, Miss Latimer. Nice people don't commit murders. Now, could I ask another favor?"

"Of course, Mr. Kellogg," she said cautiously.

"I'm going out to Rincon Hospital to see Campeón. Will you phone and let them know I'll be over? There might be some confusion otherwise."

"Of course, Mr. Kellogg. Right away."

Benson thanked her and left the office.

He went down the stairs two at a time, turned right and put his head around the corner of the door to Judge Groat's chambers.

"Willie," he called. "Any luck?"

Guillermo Rojas nodded without looking up from his typewriter. He positioned a thumbnail on the page of notes he was laboriously transcribing, then glanced over his shoulder. "Go right in, Ben. He's expecting you. Got everything all set with Frank, hm?"

"News travels fast," Benson agreed. Frank Sayer had probably been on the phone to Judge Groat the moment he had left, he guessed. And trust Guillermo to hear all about it.

Guillermo chuckled and turned back to his typing. Benson

tapped on the closed door of the judge's inner room, waited until he heard a faint voice, then turned the knob and went inside.

The judge's chambers had been fitted as a workroom, not the auxiliary hearing room that many judges preferred. Half a dozen black leather chairs, biscuit-tufted on the backs, shiny and slick on the seats, made a loose circle around a low table that was just right for propping feet on and had deep scratches and nicks to prove it. There were pictures of former governors and judges on the neutral walls, a large one of Mr. Justice Holmes, another of a wispy rat-faced man in British scarlet and a ridiculous bag wig. A shifting breeze from two rotating fans kept dark rep curtains rustling at the windows.

Judge Bernard Groat sat behind a long dark mahogany table facing the door. Beyond him was an open rolltop desk crammed with papers. A narrow bookcase ran from floor to ceiling between two windows, close at hand so the judge could take down a book without leaving his high-backed chair. The judge's dull black silk robe hung under a protective pliofilm cover on an old and probably very valuable mahogany stand that had a series of little drawers down the center post and a melon-shaped bulb on top that had originally been intended for His Honor's wig.

The judge was wearing a loose black alpaca jacket. His high starched collar was pinching his neck, forcing him to hold his chin up sharply, emphasizing his old-man's reddened wattles and thin, corded neck. He looked drawn and sad, as always. Small suspicious eyes were shadowed under a thicket of coarse white eyebrows. He watched Benson cross the room toward him. Very deliberately he folded a blue-backed sheaf of papers and gestured for Benson to take the armchair beside him.

"Frank Sayer called me a moment ago," he said, wasting no time with preliminary amenities. "He says you are both reasonably in agreement about the Campeón case. Is that your impression as well?"

"Yes, sir." Benson leaned his briefcase against the leg of

his chair and took out a cigarette. "I couldn't flatly agree to take the case to trial next week, but I did say that I would not request a continuance unless it was absolutely necessary."

Judge Groat nodded brusquely, his thin-lipped mouth pinched down in a dry, bitter arc. "You have arranged to devote your full time to this case?" he said in a challenging tone. "You have nothing else pending?"

"Nothing important, Judge. If I find the case is substantially as Frank outlined it, then I'd say we can go to trial next Monday."

The judge smiled thinly, with no trace of humor. "Good. I can tell you I'm none too pleased with your brother at the moment. I realize he had a difficult problem, but I have been counting on having this case defended by an able lawyer with considerable experience on the criminal side."

Benson blew a plume of smoke toward the floor. He looked up and held the judge's eyes in a level, measuring gaze. You can go plumb to hell, Your Honor, he was thinking. I'm not going to beg you for this assignment. If you want me to take it, I will, but you'll damned well ask me.

Judge Groat was now the oldest active judge on the county bench, he remembered. Formerly he had been a trial lawyer, later County Attorney, but always he had been a politician of importance in Rincon and the state. He had a reputation for being fair but difficult, impatient with anything that smacked of quibbling, totally without interest in the legal complexities that charmed most judges. There was about him an air of the rough-and-ready sort of justice that had once characterized the courts of the Southwest.

Judge Groat's eyebrows knotted over his narrow, hooked nose. "Are you willing to accept complete responsibility for defending Arturo Campeón?" he demanded.

Benson nodded. "With the court's approval," he said quietly. "And at the court's request."

There was a brief moment of scowling silence before Judge Groat snorted in what might have been amusement. "You have both," he said finally. "It's all yours and God help you. A dirty case, Benson, a very dirty case. I'm not looking forward to it."

"Nor I, sir."

"No, I suppose not. Do you understand why we want to dispose of it as soon as possible?"

"I know what Frank told me. His reasons seemed valid enough, but of course they don't mean much compared to Campeón's right to a fair trial."

"Sir, do you suggest . . ." the judge's voice rose, dangerously shrill, almost snarling.

"No, I do not," Benson said bluntly. "I make no suggestions, Judge. Frank's reasons are acceptable, I suppose, but I cannot be guided by them. My first loyalty is to my client."

"Very well," the judge said slowly. "Very well. A proper attitude. Pompously put, but proper. Have you seen your client yet?"

"No, sir."

"Then you have a lot of work ahead of you. You will appear with him when the calendar is called tomorrow. We'll set the date for trial then." Judge Groat shifted the folded sheaf of papers an inch closer. "So far the newspapers have avoided any sensational reference to this case, but tomorrow, when the criminal information is offered, I expect to see a certain amount of comment. We can expect an aroused interest from the press and public. I don't want you adding to it, Benson."

"In what way, sir?"

"In any way," Judge Groat snapped. "Don't fence with me, Benson. This is the sort of trial that becomes a Roman holiday once it gets out of hand. I'm determined that it will not get out of hand. Is that clear?"

Benson nodded. "I understand."

"You haven't been before me in some time. Four or five years, I would guess. You don't handle much trial work, do you?"

"Not much," Benson admitted, determined not to show any sign of irritation.

"Would you like me to appoint a junior counsel? Someone

familiar with procedure? Are you worried about taking this case to trial by yourself?"

"No, sir, I'm not worried. And I don't want any court-appointed help. I'm rusty on criminal procedure, but it's not that different from civil work. I'll manage."

"You bristle just like your father used to," Judge Groat said with a trace of a smile. "Don't. Not with me, Benson. I want to help, not interfere. If you need anything, let me know. I'll do what I can for you."

"Thank you, sir," Benson said stiffly. "I'll remember that if I get in a pinch. I don't expect I will. The case seems fairly simple."

"Maybe," the judge said in a grudging voice. "Maybe it is. I won't venture a curbstone opinion on a case I'm going to try, but I can tell you that I've never yet seen a trial go just the way you expected it would. Remember that. All right, Benson. Many thanks for accepting the case. Do your best for your client." He nodded in curt dismissal.

"I will, Judge." Benson reached across to rub out his cigarette in the judge's bowl. He picked up his briefcase and got to his feet. He left the judge's chambers and closed the door silently behind him.

RINCON COUNTY HOSPITAL was the tallest building west of the business section of town. Benson walked slowly up the long curving driveway, climbed the low flight of steps and pushed open the glass door.

A rosy dumpling of a woman at the reception desk greeted him cheerfully, summoned a blue-striped probationer to escort him, and passed Benson through to the inner corridor opposite a row of elevators.

The fourth floor of the south wing of the hospital had the guarded ward for prisoners and other undesirables. Its windows were straitly barred, the doors were heavy metal. You entered along a corridor that was blocked by a glassed-in cubicle. The deputy on watch when Benson tapped the glass was a man with a bulky chest, short and stiff white hair, the tight, brittle-looking skin of a man in poor health, and that relaxed and fatherly manner that only the best cops develop.

"I'll have to see some identification, Mr. Kellogg," he said apologetically, hiding a sharp suspicion behind an easy smile.

Benson opened his wallet, laid it on the counter and turned the card holders until the deputy had seen enough.

"Should have guessed," he said, shaking his head. "You're the brother. I knew this Campeón kid was Burr Kellogg's client and when I saw you I surely knew you weren't Burr Kellogg."

"Burr asked me to take it on for him," Benson explained. And knowing it would be best to eliminate any hint of mystery, he added, "He has some political business upstate. He won't be free for a couple of weeks, so I'm stuck."

The deputy nodded, filing the information away until he found a chance to spread it. "Stuck is the word, all right, Mr. Kellogg. That boy hasn't said a word all day. One of those sullen kids."

"Maybe he'll talk to me," Benson said. "Where is he?"

"Go right in, Mr. Kellogg. He's got the whole place to himself. I guess you can find him easy enough."

Benson pushed through the swinging doors and went into a large barnlike room that was painted in two shades of bilious green and lighted by bare bulbs behind thick mesh screening. His shoes made no sound on the linoleum floor.

The ward was divided by portable canvas partitions into open two-bed sections. Benson walked toward the high windows, looking into each section. He found Arturo Campeón in the last bed, lying propped on two pillows, turned away to look out the barred windows at the harsh lunar landscape of the desert foothills.

He was a slight, small-boned young man, not tall, close to being skinny. His right arm and shoulder were buried in a thick white plaster cast that made his sallow skin seem darkly tanned. His hair was thick and solidly black, almost blue in the highlighted shadow. A fat pad of bandage was taped lopsided on his head like an old-fashioned bellhop's cap.

Benson dropped his briefcase on the empty bed beside Campeón's, picked up a straight-backed chair and carried it around to the windows, placing it so the boy could see him without moving his head. He sat down.

"I'm Benson Kellogg," he said. "The court has appointed me to defend you. How are you feeling?"

The boy shifted on the pillow. His eyes turned to Benson indifferently. He had a sharply handsome, almost a pretty face. The broad low forehead was smooth under a clearly defined hairline. Heavy eyebrows emphasized his very large brown eyes. He had a thin, high-bridged Spanish nose. His chin was roundly in proportion to his face, his mouth wide and shapely and so red it seemed to have been painted. Everything about him was sharp and emphatic, like a primitive portrait. He was lightly stubbled with a boy's beard that rasped softly on the pillow when he looked at Benson. He did not speak.

"You're Arturo Campeón," Benson said easily, giving the boy a chance to get used to his presence. "How do they call you? Arturo?"

The boy closed his eyes briefly. With just that and a slight movement of his mouth he managed to suggest an elaborately bored shrug.

"I grew up with a fellow named Arturo Penneccal," Benson went on. "We called him Turo. That what they call you?"

With another starkly economic movement of eyes and mouth, the boy indicated contemptuous laughter. He had the simple, natural power of a born mime, and Benson was impressed by his obvious talent, though this was no time to explore it further.

"What they call me mostly," the boy said in a voice gone husky and strained from disuse, "is greaseball. Sometimes pachuco. Sometimes Mex. Sometimes goddam greasy spic. Sometimes . . ."

Benson took out his cigarettes and put one in the corner of his mouth. "Go ahead," he said amiably. "It doesn't do any good, but once in a while it's a relief to snarl around and kick yourself in the head."

The boy's eyes opened wider as if he were seeing Benson for the first time. His wide, thin-lipped mouth twitched, less than a flickering movement, and Benson could see him laughing at himself.

"They call me Turo back home," the boy said. "What did you say your name was?"

"Benson Kellogg."

"Kellogg. That was the name of the other guy."

"My brother," Benson said. "He asked me to take over for him. Something has come up and he'll be too busy to handle your case himself."

The boy's mouth pinched in a faint sneer. "Sure he will. Okay, Mr. Kellogg. What can I do for you?"

Benson smiled gravely. "That's a hell of a way to put it," he said. "I'm supposed to do something for you."

"Now what could anybody do for me?" the boy asked in a tone of genuine curiosity.

"I don't know yet," Benson said. "Let's find out. The County Attorney tells me that you have been charged with murdering a man on Cobre Peak Saturday night. You signed a confession. I've got a copy, but I haven't read it. I wanted to get the story from you. Is it true? Did you kill that man? Roderick Duquesne?"

The boy narrowed his eyes, made his mouth a tight slit. Now, Benson could see, he had become the routine version of the hardened criminal, defiant, spitting. *You ain't gettin nuthin outa me*, he was saying in the universal, unmistakable language of the mimic actor.

"Let's get a few things straight between us," Benson said. "I'm your lawyer. Anything you tell me is confidential. Nobody can force me to divulge any of it. And if I go around shooting my mouth off, I can be kicked out of my profession, and I might even go to jail. That clear? If you can't trust me, just say so, and I'll withdraw from the case. You can get another lawyer."

The boy's mouth tightened with contempt. He made a

quick gesture with one finger that flicked Benson into the trash can.

"All right," Benson said with an edge of anger in his voice. "You're a tough guy. We both know you're tough. But don't play it with me. You've already spilled everything to the sheriff. Why stop now?"

For the first time the boy seemed unsure of himself. He closed his eyes again, but not from boredom; now he was retreating from a situation he did not want to face.

"Let's get acquainted first," Benson said easily. "I hear you're a Mexican citizen. Where did you live there?"

"Chihuahua," the boy said in a tired voice.

"What did your family do?"

"Tourist hotel. A little posada up in the mountains. Mostly for hunting and fishing. Not very fancy. Not much of a living."

That explained his good English, Benson thought. Any hotel man has to know the language of his customers. "Well, what did you come to the States for? Looking for a job?"

"I had a job." He opened his eyes and Benson could see a haze of tears. "I was a real bright boy. The Sisters of Santa Theresa passed me out first in the class, so I got a job with a company that imported Mexican stuff, pottery and baskets and glass and furniture, that kind of stuff. They brought me up to L.A. Apprentice, they called me. Flunky is what it meant." He moved his hand and he was mopping a floor. Another gesture and he was driving a truck.

"When was that?"

The boy lifted three fingers, tapped his thumb on each in a slow rhythm. The time was passing. "Three years," he said.

"Are you still working there?"

The hand turned over. A thumb poked toward the floor in the classic negative, then jerked slightly in a sketchy version of an umpire's decision.

"Fired?" Benson said. "Why?"

The hand moved stealthily, pinched up a fold of the covering sheet and moved it an inch.

"Stealing," Benson said. "You were fired for stealing?"

"That's what they said."

"Were they right? Did you steal?"

The boy nodded. "A lousy bottle of tequila. Two years there, and I get bounced for pinching a bottle. There were guys in the warehouse who used to glom a bottle a day and nobody ever bothered them." He turned his head to look directly at Benson. "It was my birthday. I gave myself a little present. Trouble was, I started drinking on the job and the boss spotted me." The hand sketched a tilted bottle, the eyes moved enough to suggest drunkenness. "So he called the cops and turned me in."

"What happened? Probation, I suppose?"

"Yeah, probation. First offense. Report every Wednesday for three years."

"Then what did you do? You stayed on in Los Angeles, didn't you?"

"Sure, why would I go home? I got six brothers, four sisters all sucking on the old man, and he's no prize, I can tell you that. A stooge, natural born." He bent his wrist, his hand hanging free, and he was a cringing peon. "Yeah, I stayed in L.A. Me and the other pachucos. I scraped along."

"What else is against you on the record?"

"Breaking and entering. Couple petty theft charges. They couldn't make anything stick, though. Not after the first time." The eyes were hooded now, the mouth bitter. A knowing hard guy was facing enemies he knew how to handle.

"Why did you leave Los Angeles? Were you going home?"

"Yeah, going home. Thursday was my birthday. I got stinking just by myself to celebrate. Then I came out of it and decided to go home and give the folks a treat, let them see what a big man I grew up to be. I was lonesome. I always get into trouble on my birthdays. Me, I'm a guy shouldn't have birthdays. I guess I don't have to worry about that. I won't be having any more, will I?"

"You can't tell," Benson said noncommittally, refusing to be distracted. "How did you meet Duquesne?"

The boy jerked his thumb in the hitchhiker's signal. "Highway."

"He just stopped and offered you a lift. You'd never seen him before?" When the boy shook his head, Benson went on to ask a question that might have critical meaning to his defense. "How did he treat you?"

"Huh?" The boy's eyebrows bunched in a hard frown.

"You were driving all night together. You must have stopped a couple of times for gas, maybe for a meal?"

"Sure," the boy said dubiously.

"Who paid the tab? Did Duquesne buy dinner for you?"

"Yeah. He was loaded."

Benson nodded. His face showed nothing of what he was thinking. "Why did you stop on Cobre Peak?"

"I don't know. I guess the guy was getting sleepy. He wouldn't let me spell him."

"What happened then?"

The boy's eyes closed. His face closed. He hardly seemed to breathe. The sharply incised outline of his face against the pillow was hard and lifeless, like the face on a coin.

"You'll have to tell me, Turo."

"No. No, I don't have to," the boy said tightly. "Who's going to make me?"

"Just you, Turo. You're the only one who can." When the boy buried deeper into his blind silence, Benson said, "You had a gold cigarette lighter in your pocket when you were arrested. Was it Duquesne's?"

"Yeah." Turo made the stealing gesture again. "I copped it."

"When?"

"In the car. The guy left it on the seat. He never did remember it, so the next time we stopped, I copped it."

"That was stupid."

The boy shrugged.

"The County Attorney has another explanation."

"For what?"

"For how that lighter got in your pocket. He claims you were trying to rob Duquesne on Cobre Peak. You got the lighter, but Duquesne put up a fight before you could get anything else. So you killed him. Do you understand what that means?"

"Who cares?"

"You do, if you have any sense. Without that lighter, the County Attorney wouldn't be sure of a conviction on a charge of first-degree murder. But the lighter in your pocket says you killed while you were committing a felony. That makes a clear case of first-degree murder."

The boy's eyes popped open. "That's crazy! I copped the lighter somewhere back on the highway. I already had it!"

"That might change things," Benson said. "But why did you kill Duquesne?"

"What difference does it make?" The boy's mouth pinched in bitterly and his chin came up. "You already got me strapped in the chair. What more do you want? You expect me to bleed for you?"

"Take it easy, Turo," Benson said quietly. "You're just supposed to tell me what happened. You've already told me something really important. If you stole that lighter sometime earlier than the time you stopped on Cobre Peak, then the County Attorney's theory is wrong. At the moment he honestly believes you killed Duquesne while trying to rob him. If I could tell him it didn't happen like that, tell him exactly what did happen up there, he might be willing to reconsider the charge."

"What does that mean?"

"If he believed me, it could mean a change to second-degree murder at the very least. Maybe even manslaughter."

"If he believed you," Turo said mockingly. "Hell, why would he believe you? He don't make a big name by letting people off the hook. He thinks he's got me cold and he's going to sock it to me. You know that as well as I do."

"No, I don't know it. He isn't hired to persecute you, Turo. A reduction of the charge is possible. You don't want to die; nobody does. It means death if you're convicted on murder one. It's a life sentence with a chance for parole on murder two. That's a hell of a difference, Turo. I say it's worth trying for. I'm supposed to be your legal adviser and you are supposed to take my advice. That's why the court appointed me."

The boy studied him carefully, and for the first time there was no mockery in his expression. He nodded soberly. "Okay, Mr. Kellogg. I guess I got no call to be giving you a bad time. I'm not going to take your advice, but I don't want you thinking I don't appreciate what you're doing for me. How much are you getting for the job?"

Benson almost smiled at the obvious attempt to sidetrack him. "I think the county allows fifty dollars. Now what did you——"

"And how much would you charge if I was loaded? Say I was Duquesne, dirty with dough, what would you soak me?"

"The fee would vary according to the work involved," Benson said patiently. It was clear that the boy was not willing to talk openly, but with a little time to get used to the necessity for it, he might become more tractable. "The basic fee would be twenty dollars an hour for my time. There would be other charges for other people's work. Plus as much as five hundred dollars a day for every day in court. Call it five thousand in all, if the trial didn't last beyond a week."

Turo whistled softly. "Five grand! And for me you get a lousy fifty bucks? What else do you stand to get out of it?"

"Figure it out yourself," Benson said amiably. "You were the bright boy of your class. What am I getting out of it?"

Turo tightened his mouth in a faint sneer. "Good publicity, huh? You gonna run for dogcatcher, Mr. Kellogg?"

"I'm not going to run for anything," Benson said. He looked at the hard, indifferent face of the boy and added softly, "Now just how do you figure it would be good publicity for me if my client goes to the chair?"

Turo flushed. He gave a grudging nod. "I see what you mean," he muttered. "So what do you——"

"That's enough about me," Benson broke in. "Let's get back to the subject. I'm assigned to defend you. I'll do the very best I can for you, but I have to know exactly what happened, and why it happened. Now listen to me, Turo." He leaned forward and spoke very soberly. "It's not my job to judge anybody. I'm just here to defend you. It might be easier for me if I could believe you were innocent, but it isn't necessary. I'd work as hard for you in either case. But you've got to level with me now. I won't go into that courtroom with my hands tied. I'm considered a pretty fair lawyer and I know how a case should be prepared. I want the whole story from you, Turo. Tell me and I can probably figure out some way to help you."

The boy closed one eye skeptically. "But you couldn't get me off, could you?"

Benson sat back. He dropped his cigarette to the floor and stepped on it. The boy's attitude was bewildering; he seemed genuinely disinterested, too controlled, not disturbed and frightened as you would expect him to be. That might be the result of an unusual maturity, Benson realized, but it was more likely to be the dull resignation that comes from despair.

"I can't promise to get you off, of course," he said slowly. "There is a strong case against you and we'll have to be ready with a strong defense."

"How do you know it wouldn't be worse for me if I did tell you what happened?"

"It couldn't be," Benson said simply. "Turo, plenty of boys in trouble react like you. Because you are ashamed of what you've done, you can't believe that anyone can ever understand what happened. You just want everybody to stop talking about it. But you can't have it that way. The County Attorney is going to be talking about it in complete detail to a courtroom full of people. When he's finished I'll have to answer him. And what can I say? That my client refuses to tell me what actually happened? Is that what you expect?"

The boy stared at Benson. His eyebrows pulled together in a puzzled line.

"If I do that, Turo, you'll be convicted. I can guarantee that. I'll leave that court like a fool and you'll leave it like a dead man. I can't allow you to do it. What happened up there? Was it something so bad that you can't bring yourself to talk about it? Something you just don't want to remember?"

The boy nodded silently.

Benson turned away. He looked out the window and spoke with his head turned from the boy. "I'm sorry to be pushing you, Turo. The court has appointed me your friend but I don't suppose you think it's very friendly of me to go prying into things you want to keep hidden. What did you tell the sheriff's men? They asked you, didn't they?"

"They asked me." The boy's fist flickered above the sheet like a pounding hammer. "They asked me, all right. But they didn't want anything but a confession. So I confessed. What the hell, I was shot full of dope and hurting like I never knew you could hurt. I'd have signed anything to keep them from banging on me."

"Banging on you? What do you mean by that? They kept insisting on answers, is that it? Or do you mean they actually hit you?"

"No, they didn't hit me. It was just that skinny old bastard standing behind me. Every time I didn't answer fast enough, he'd lean over and crack his knuckle on my cast." The boy's gesture was vivid. "I'd go off my nut for a minute. So I started answering real fast."

"I want to get this very clear, Turo," Benson said, deliberately calm. "Are you saying that your confession was extracted from you by physical violence? Is that what you want me to believe?"

"Who cares? I killed the guy. I told them I did it. That's all."

"That's not all," Benson said, coldly angry and very quiet. "That isn't all by a long way. But let's drop it for the moment. The sheriff's men wanted to know exactly what happened Saturday night. What did you tell them?"

The boy made his sketchy shrug. "I didn't tell them. They told me. Mad dog killer, they said. I said okay, where do I sign? They wrote down something and held it for me and I put down an X and they went away. That's all I wanted. I was hurting, man. I didn't give a damn. I just wanted them to get out and let me sleep."

"You didn't even read what you signed? Did anyone read it to you?"

"I don't know. Maybe. I was sort of dropping off while they were shouting at me. I don't know what all they said. I was doped to the balls. I don't remember what went on."

"I'm going to find out," Benson said, bleakly determined. "I can promise you that. But it doesn't help with our problem right now. Tell me about the weapon. Was it your knife?"

The boy nodded.

"What kind of a knife was it?"

Turo punched down his thumb, then flipped one finger out quickly from a loose fist. Benson could almost see the long switchblade springing up from its sheath.

"Why were you carrying a knife?"

"All us pachucos pack knives. You ought to know that."

"Tell me," Benson insisted. "Why a knife?"

"I thought maybe I'd need some protection, being on the road by myself."

Benson drew in a long slow breath. At every step the boy seemed to make the case against him more damning, if that was possible. "All right. Now tell me the rest. Take it from the moment you and Duquesne drove up on Cobre Peak. You saw the sign that said 'Lookout Point' and Duquesne turned off and parked near the railing. Then what? Did you both get out of the car?"

"I don't—I can't . . ." The boy rolled his head to one side and closed his eyes as if he could shut out Benson's voice and his own clamoring memory by an effort of will.

"You'll have to tell me, Turo. Take it slowly and see if we can't——"

The double doors of the ward swung open and back, sending a whisper of cool air along the floor. Benson looked around. A brisk, no-nonsense nurse came toward him in a rustle of starch, trailed by a jittery probationer who was balancing a loaded tray in both hands and walking with the tongue-biting concentration of a child trying not to spill a full glass of water.

"That's all for now," the nurse said sharply. "The doctor will be in to see the patient. You can come back later."

"How is he getting on?" Benson said, moving away from his chair beside the bed.

"Well enough," the nurse said with no interest. She jammed a thermometer in the boy's mouth and stripped down his covering sheet. "You'll have to leave now," she said in her brisk, no-nonsense voice.

"All right," Benson said. "I'll be back this afternoon, Turo. Think over what I've said to you. We'll talk again later."

The boy nodded. His wide, almost fearful eyes followed Benson as he moved down the long corridor and out the door.

WHEN BENSON came into his office, the small gilt clock on his secretary's desk was chiming softly. It was an irritating, insistent sound that he had tolerated since last Christmas when Mary's husband had given her the clock. And now there was no way he could suggest its removal without offending her sense of propriety, which in Mary's view equated with human decency. Benson was resigned to spending the rest of his professional life being musically reminded of the passage of time.

"Good morning, Mary," he said, going past to his own desk. "Is there anything I can't put off?"

"Nothing much, Mr. Kellogg," she said. "Did you take that murder case? I was reading about it. It sounds ugly."

"I guess it is. I don't know much about it yet, but it's all mine."

Mary shook her head slightly. She opened a ledger on her desk. "How do you want me to organize your attendance record? How do we charge your time?"

"Make an entry for Arturo Campeón," Benson said absently, thumbing over his mail. "Accent mark over the o. God knows who will pay the bill. Probably nobody, but at least we can deduct it on the income-tax return. I want to talk to my brother's secretary. That's Miss Harkins, isn't it? See if she's gone to lunch yet."

"I'll try. Also a man named Cook wants to come and see you whenever you're free. Shall I call him?"

"Cook?" Benson hesitated. "Oh, yes. About Burr. All right, Mary. Let's see what he wants."

The light on the base of his phone glowed red before he had signed the third of the letters on his desk. He finished his signature before picking up the receiver. "Miss Harkins? Can you—— Oh, Mr. Cook. Sorry. You wanted to see me?"

"I missed you this morning," Tim Cook said in a hollow voice. "Slept late. I think I'm coming down with a cold or something. When can we get together?"

"I'm pinched for time today, Mr. Cook. Couldn't we— how about lunch? Would that do?"

"For a starter. Where?"

"Let's make it the Stockmen's Club. We can talk privately there. In half an hour. Fine." Benson hung up and nodded to Mary. That was signal enough. She would see that a table was reserved. He went back to his letters.

The next time his phone light came on it was Miss Harkins, sharp and impatient as always.

"A few things I'd like you to do for me, Miss Harkins," Benson said, speaking with more forceful decision than he normally did. "I need a refresher course in criminal law. I want to read some up-to-date handbooks of criminal procedure. And there was a new book published last year by some lawyer in El Monte called, I think, *The Law of Evidence*. We should have a copy in the library. Then I want you to snoop around for me and see if you can find any transcripts of recent felony trials prosecuted by Frank Sayer. With special emphasis on crimes of violence, but I'll take whatever I can get. I want to get an idea of Frank's courtroom style when he's working with a jury. Can you do that?"

Miss Harkin's harsh voice said that she could, very easily. Anything else?

"That's all for the moment. Unless you can think of another book that might be useful. I'll be in for a conference with you in a day or so. We'll draw up a trial brief as soon as I see the problem more clearly. Thank you, Miss Harkins. Just put the stuff on my desk, please."

Benson finished his letters and carried the stack to Mary's desk.

"Gracie is just going to love running errands for you," she said with happy malice. "She was looking forward to a nice easy time with her boss off politicking."

"I'll probably need her help, Mary. You and I are not very sharp on criminal law. Soothe her feathers, will you? I'll be at the Stockmen's for lunch, if anybody wants me."

"Then where?"

"Back to the county hospital for another session with my nonpaying client. He wasn't quite ready to talk to me this morning. I'll have to squeeze him if he keeps being coy, but I'd rather he came out of it by himself. After that, I'm going out to the ranch. I'll leave straight from the hospital. Send those books and transcripts over to the Frontier Hotel Garage for me."

Mary nodded without looking up from her shorthand book. "You sound sort of excited, boss. Is it going to be an interesting case?"

"I guess I am a little excited," Benson admitted. "Murder cases are rare in any lawyer's life. God knows I never expected to be handling one." He took his briefcase from Mary's desk and went out into the corridor.

IN ALL TOWNS that are heavily dependent on tourist trade there are usually pockets of dark solitude reserved to the lo-

cals who have had all the tourist gaiety they can stand. The
Stockmen's Club was one of several such places in Rincon.
Originally, as its name implied, it had been a club for ranchers,
a place where the boss could have a drink, put his feet up and
talk business without being elbowed by his ranch hands. As
Rincon grew and ranchers became largely extinct, the club
shifted its focus to the town's professional men.

Benson came through the narrow bronze door into the cool
gloominess and stopped at the porter's desk, where the names
of members were kept in slots on a sloped panel. Old Matthew
shifted Benson's plaque from *Out* to *In* and held his hand up to
stop Benson from going past.

"Your guest is waiting, Mr. Benson," he said. He put his
head inside the foyer entrance and called, "Mr. Cook."

Tim Cook blew his nose and wadded his handkerchief into
his pocket before getting up from his chair near the pebbled-
glass front windows.

"Sorry you had to wait, Mr. Cook. Let's go into the
dining room." Benson took Tim Cook's elbow and led him
down the wainscoted hallway. The steward showed them to a
corner table and left them with menus and a silent, alert
waiter.

"Have a drink, if you want," Tim said. "I'd join you if I
could. Damn doctor says I have to cut down."

"I won't have one either. It just makes me sleepy in
the middle of a hot afternoon. See anything you like, Mr. Cook?
The beef is always good."

Tim Cook shook his head. "I'll have an egg salad on whole
wheat and a glass of milk," he told the waiter.

"Bring me the special, please," Benson said. "We'll think
about dessert later." He put his menu aside and looked at Tim.
"You wanted to talk about my brother?"

"You don't know much about a man unless you know the
place and people he comes from."

Benson lit a cigarette and leaned back in his chair. "You
know, I don't mind discussing my brother with you, Mr. Cook,
but it seems to me you're making quite a production out of it.

Burr's background is fairly routine. One paragraph would cover most of the facts anybody cares about. Why are you interested in anything more?"

Tim cocked one eyebrow and stared at Benson quizzically. He blew his nose on a damp handkerchief and snuffled until he could breathe clearly. "Excuse me," he muttered. He kept his handkerchief ready. "Your boss asked me the same question and I told him it was my job to see the state central committee was protected. And ready to protect your brother, if he needed it. When I know everything there is to know about him, I'll never be mouse-trapped if the opposition tries to make yardage against him with an old scandal."

"You make it sound plausible, Mr. Cook," Benson said, putting out his cigarette and folding his hands on the table. "I wonder why it isn't convincing."

"It convinced your boss."

"A great many things do. That isn't the recommendation you might think it, Mr. Cook."

Tim grinned. He sipped from his water glass. "Maybe I'm not playing this right," he said easily. "I'm feeling kind of thick in the head today. Let's start over again, okay? And maybe you better call me Tim. When you say Mr. Cook, I begin looking around for my father."

"Okay, Tim," Benson said readily. "Where do we start?"

"Burr Kellogg is still the subject," Tim said. "But let's get to him by the back door. What do you know about your state government, Ben? Is that what they say? Ben?"

"Ben is all right. I don't know much of anything, if you're speaking politically."

"Yes, that's how I meant it. Politically and personally. We control the state government now, our party does, and that means the state central committee is dealing the cards. The committee is Nathan Barstow and a few others, very damned few others. Maybe you're not particularly aware of them; you aren't supposed to be. But you do know one thing about them and right now that's the part I'm worried about. What is that, Ben?"

"I'm not sure what you want me to say. I know your committee raises money and runs campaigns. I suppose it has a lot to do with picking candidates, since Nate Barstow picked Burr."

"Right. It's the last point I'm talking about now. Picking candidates. The state committee has a lot to say about that, all right. Without its okay, you ain't a candidate. It's that simple. And right now, at a time when we can carry an election in this state almost without campaigning, we haven't got more than three good candidates in the whole bagful. It's a situation that has everybody worried, I can tell you. That's where Burr comes in."

Benson moved back to let the waiter put down his plate. "What's wrong with your other people? I don't know many of them, but I've met the Governor. He seems good enough."

"He's not bad," Tim said sourly. "But this is a funny part of the country, out here. History hasn't caught up with you people yet. You don't have the wide range of interests you find back East. Here it's about the same as it was fifty years ago. You still have just three sources of important money, just three: mining, railroads, ranching and farming. Some light industry has been coming in lately and things are beginning to change, but the change hasn't had any effect on politics yet. The three big interests are still in control. If a man wants to make a buck, he has to tie himself to one of them. The Governor now. You like him, huh? Well, I like him too. He's a likable man—that's his job, to be likable. But I wouldn't trust him with anything important, not unless I was a mining man. Up in El Monte, they call it 'wearing the copper collar' and the honorable Governor is about to choke on his. The others are just as bad in their own ways. Well, maybe bad isn't the right word. It's just the way things are out here. You have to choose sides early if you want to get any place. So what does all this mean to Burr Kellogg?"

Benson waited. He tried a forkful of roast beef hash and reached for the salt. "A rhetorical question?"

"Huh? Oh, rhetorical. Yeah, I guess so. Seen from El Monte, your brother looks pretty good. He isn't actually in anybody's pocket. He just might be a guy who could go all the way. I told you things are beginning to change. We can probably win a couple more elections without much sweat, but then we'll be in real trouble unless we find some good candidates. People are flocking into this state, I suppose you know. Rincon's population has just about doubled in eight years and El Monte is growing even faster. These are new people and they're mostly working in new industries. They don't give a damn about mining or railroads or ranching. They haven't begun to vote in large numbers yet, but when they do, some fur is going to fly, I can tell you that. An awful lot of clowns who've been sucking on the public tit for thirty years are going to have to go to work." Tim took a sip of milk. He picked up half a sandwich and waggled it in the air.

"So," he went on, eating as he talked, "before the big change comes, we have to develop some new candidates who don't have labels pasted on their butts. Maybe your brother is the man we want, one of them anyway. Maybe not. That's what I'm supposed to find out. We can't afford to spend any time building up a man who can't go all the way."

"I see. You are running Burr for Attorney General as a sort of trial heat, to see how he handles himself. Is that it?"

"Something like that. You can never be sure how the voters are going to react to a new face. Burr is making the rounds right now. We'll probably run him for Attorney General. But even that isn't as definite as it might look."

"I thought he had already been named."

"He will be named by the state caucus next week. Probably he will be named. Then he'll run in the primary for the party nomination. If anything should go sour between now and the primary, the committee could dump him and throw the nomination to someone else. Attorney General is an important job. It makes a fine springboard for the right man, so we can't let it go to a guy who isn't the right one. Nothing is actually settled."

"Did Burr agree to that?"

Tim Cook looked up in mild surprise. He shrugged. He

took another bite of his sandwich and chewed with obvious distaste. "That's the way things are done," he said. "Don't fight City Hall. I only mentioned it to let you know why I'm poking around in your family background. I figure you're a guy I can level with. I don't expect to find anything bad about Burr, but if I do, then the committee still has time to change its mind. Now forget that part of it. Let's talk about your brother."

"Did Burr agree to go along with this damn foolishness?" Benson said tightly, holding his voice low and even with some effort.

"Sure, why wouldn't he? Listen, Ben, you're looking at this all wrong. You think we're rousting your brother, huh? Putting him over the jumps just for the hell of it? Forget it. There's nothing in that. He wants a political career, and he's going to have one. The only question that hasn't been decided yet is how big a career he's going to have."

"But damn it——"

"Your brother's not beefing," Tim said sharply. "What have you got to complain about?"

After a moment, Benson nodded grudgingly. "I guess it's up to Burr," he said slowly. "I don't know why he would go along, but if he has . . ." Benson lifted his shoulders briefly and let them drop. "All right, Tim. What do you want from me?"

"I want to spend a little time with you and talk about your brother. That's all. Like what you did when you were kids, how it was at school, when you learned about girls, how you got your first job. That kind of thing. I want to talk to everybody around here who knew your brother, especially his enemies. I want to see the ranch where you grew up. And I want to hear about old B. Kellogg."

Benson snorted. "So you really are going to dig up the old boy and run him again?"

"Huh?"

"B. Kellogg. He's your real candidate, isn't he? Not Burr Kellogg."

Tim shook his head sadly. He finished his sandwich and

choked down a sip of milk. "The name is supposed to be an asset, they tell me. I don't believe it amounts to much, but I want to find out. Your brother is going on the ticket as B. Kellogg. I suppose you knew that?"

"I suspected he might."

"Yeah. The name's an asset, so he uses it. It's my job to find out if this asset is solid gold or just run-of-the-mine. And that," Tim said with a patient sigh, "is the sum total of my interest in anybody named B. Kellogg."

"All right, Tim. Maybe I was yelling before anybody hit me. God knows there isn't any secret about any of this. I can't see why I shouldn't answer any questions you'd care to put. I don't know much about politics and I don't like what I do know, but I'll help as much as I can."

"That's all I expected," Tim said. "When can we——"

The waiter soft-shoed to Benson's elbow and bent to speak softly in his ear. "A phone call for you, Mr. Kellogg. Are you here, or should I have them——"

"Who is it?"

"The County Attorney's office, sir."

"I'll take it," Benson said promptly. "Excuse me, Tim. This shouldn't take long."

Benson went out of the dining room quickly, turned left toward the glass door of a small cubicle and picked up the phone.

"One moment, Mr. Kellogg," a woman's voice said. "Mr. Sayer is trying to reach you."

"Ben, I'm glad I managed to find you," Frank Sayer said almost immediately. "We've got trouble."

"We have? What trouble?"

"I told you the Mexican-American Citizens Association was sticking its nose in the Campeón case. I thought they were going to write the boy's family, but they didn't. They moved faster than that. They telephoned."

"All right, Frank. What of it?"

"What of it?" Sayer was close to shouting. "Goddammit, Ben, where's your brains? The family is up here right now.

They got in an hour ago. They're in my office. And thank God they came here instead of going to the Mexican-Americans. With luck we may be able to stall them off."

"Why should we?" Benson asked coldly.

"Listen to me, Ben. This is important. You know what will happen if the Mexican-Americans take over Campeón's defense. Why, it'll be a damned farce. You don't want to see that happen."

"It's not up to me, Frank," Benson said patiently. "If the family wants another lawyer, that's their right. Do they want to make a change?"

"I swear, Ben, I don't understand you at all. Now how in hell do they know if they want you or not, when they haven't even seen you, or the kid. If the Mexican-Americans sell them a bill of goods, they'll switch. You can bet on that. But if you see them first——"

"Then I can sell them a bill of goods. Is that what you had in mind?"

"You're being awful hard-nosed," Sayer complained. "What's wrong, Ben?"

"I talked to the boy, Frank. He told me how the sheriff got that confession out of him. I wasn't very pleased with that. I hope you don't think I'll let you use it in court?"

"We can talk about it later," Sayer said hastily. "I don't know what you're talking about, Ben, but if something's fishy about the confession, we can straighten it out. Don't worry about that. Just get over here and take care of these two birds before the Mexican-Americans beat you to it."

"All right, Frank," Benson said. "Tell them to wait there for me. I'll take them out to see the boy."

Benson put the phone back on the table and returned to the dining room. He stood beside his chair and bent over to sign the check the waiter presented.

"I'm sorry, Tim," he said absently. "I'll have to leave right away. About your investigation, why don't you start with Burr's secretary? She's not very busy just now and she can brief you on his daily routine, tell you the kind of work he's been handling. Get Jason Blumberg to phone a man named Harold Judson and introduce you. Harold was Burr's best friend when they were in school. He's a real-estate broker and his office is in the Territorial Insurance Building. If he's willing to talk to you, he should keep you busy for the afternoon."

Tim nodded. "I'll try him. But what about——"

"I'll be going out to the ranch later on, as soon as I'm free. Would you like to come along and spend the night?"

"You bet."

"Why don't you meet me at the Frontier Hotel Garage about three thirty or four? I'll be there around then. If you can't make it, phone and leave a message. Will that do?"

"That'll do fine." Tim wiped his mouth and tossed his rumpled napkin on the table. "I'll walk along with you if you're headed back for the office."

"I'm going the other way," Benson said. "Sorry. See you later, Tim." He went out of the room with long quick strides that had left Tim Cook well behind by the time he had reached the front door.

MISS LATIMER signaled him urgently the moment he came inside the County Attorney's office.

"They are waiting for you in here, Mr. Kellogg." She opened the door and held it for him.

Benson stopped just inside the small room and looked at the three men who stood close together in front of the windows. Frank Sayer thrust out one arm in a wide gesture of relief.

"Ben, come in, come in," he said hurriedly. "I'm glad you could get here right away. Let me introduce Señor Campeón, Arturo's father, and Señor Darango, his grandfather. They just flew in from Chihuahua this morning."

Benson nodded. He shook hands with Señor Campeón, feeling the man's hand engulf his like a moist sponge. He was tall and heavy, only a few inches shorter than Benson, but overfleshed and out of condition. A shiny film of sweat made his pale skin glisten like wet lard. His vast collar and spread of white shirt under a spotted bow tie were already soiled and dappled with sweat, but he was wearing the coat of his suit buttoned all the way. Points of a limp handkerchief blossomed from his pocket, one petal slanting up toward the circular disk of a Rotary emblem in his lapel.

"You are Mr. Kellogg," he said in a throaty, barely accented English. "Mr. Sayer told us of you. We are pleased to meet Arturo's attorney. We have been very concerned, you know? We could not hope that——"

"Luis." The voice of the old man beside him was thin and light and brittle, like crackling twigs, but it silenced Campeón as if he had been slashed with a whip.

"Sí," he said hastily. "Sí, señor suegro. Mr. Kellogg, this gentleman is my——" he hesitated for a nervous moment, chewing his heavy underlip, then went on as the elusive phrase came to mind—"my father-in-law, Arturo's grandfather. He does not dominate English, but I can——"

"Let's speak Spanish, then," Benson said. He held out his hand to the lean old man, looking at him directly for the first time.

This was not the modern successful Mexican, not the plump, well-barbered businessman who came to all the weekly luncheon meetings at the Palacio Hilton and always remembered to call his friends by their first names, heartily, with the sound of empty laughter. Not this one.

This was the hot-blooded fanatic Spaniard who had conquered the New World with his sword and cross, had suffered and stolen, murdered and enslaved millions in the name of God and profit. The man was an alien in that room, would probably be an alien everywhere these days, Benson thought. He stood hunched a little, bow-legged and light-boned, his thin veined hands dangling from the too-short sleeves of his black, iron-hard coat. He was clean-shaven with a long underslung jaw. His hair was thin and white, freshly trimmed. His tight-skinned, dark and bony face was turned slightly upward so that he could look at Benson. Light from the window struck his hooded eyes and made a yellow glint. They were flat unwinking eyes, bitter as a wolf's eyes.

Frank Sayer moved quickly toward the door, speaking nervously, his voice shaded by caution. "You can go see the boy any time, Ben. I've fixed it for you. Well, I'll leave you alone. I guess you have lots to talk over."

"All right, Frank. I'll want to see you later."

"Any time, Ben. You know that." He shut the door behind him, still talking as he went out.

Benson turned back to the two men, feeling the challenge of their silence. He stood erect, hands locked behind his back. They were waiting for him to speak and he meant to let them wait for a while longer, until he had the feel of the situation. The father was a known quantity, a man worried and fearful for his son. But the old one was another question entirely. You could almost feel the menacing quality of the man; it seeped out of him like smoke.

"We have some things to settle between us," he said carefully in Spanish, speaking directly to the old man, knowing that he alone was important here. "Do you know why your grandson is in jail?"

The old man did not answer.

"He is charged with murder." When the old man's chin lifted in sharp arrogance, Benson went on before he could speak.

"He killed a man Saturday night, a man who had treated him well. He stole his automobile and a cigarette lighter, made of gold, an object of value. He later wrecked the automobile, injuring himself. He was taken to the hospital. When his crime was discovered, he was questioned by the authorities. He confessed. No, señor," he said quickly when the old man muttered angrily, "do not dispute me. These are the facts. Arturo will tell you himself when you see him."

"I do not believe you," the old man said thinly.

It was hard to believe he was an old man, Benson thought. That swift, hard truculence was more suited to a man able and eager to fight. The blunt, savage challenge of him could not be ignored. He would have to meet it head on.

"Then you are a fool, señor," he said coldly. "I do not lie. And I have no time to waste with fools."

The old man's eyes closed slowly. His thin high nostrils flared with the effort of restraint. Then he looked at Benson again and there was a dark promise in his eyes. He turned away on his heel and moved with the easy tight-coupled stride of a predator toward a chair against the wall. He hooked it to him with his toe and sat down. He cupped his rough, wind-darkened hands on his knees and, without looking at him, lifted a finger in signal to Campeón.

"Sí, señor suegro," Campeón said as if he had been prodded. He faced Benson and lifted his beefy shoulders in a quick, despairing shrug. "Señor Kellogg, we wish no disagreement with you. But if you believe my son guilty of this crime, how can you defend him? Would it not be best if we . . ." He raised his eyebrows and tilted his head eloquently.

"That's up to you," Benson said in a voice that was beginning to tighten. "I did not say he was guilty; that is for the jury to decide. I said he had done these things and that he had confessed. As for me, I have been appointed by the court to defend your son, not to judge him. The law requires that he be given legal assistance if he cannot provide it for himself. I agreed to take his case. But if you wish another attorney, you can hire one and petition the court for permission to discharge me. It's just a matter of form; there will be no difficulty. I can tell you, though, that you will not find any attorney prepared to say that your son is innocent. He has already confessed."

"But you said——"

"I said guilt is a matter for the jury. Arturo will get a fair trial and the jury will determine if he deserves to be punished."

The old man made a harsh sound in his throat, an animal sound of pain and rage.

"My—my father-in-law thinks that Arturo was compelled to make the confession. He thinks he was—" another moment of lip-chewing produced the magic phrase he was searching for, but he had to say it in English—"that he was brainwashed."

Benson shook his head. "I'm not pleased with the way the sheriff got that confession, but the facts are not in dispute. The boy admitted the same thing to me when we were alone. You can ask him yourself."

"We will be permitted to see him?"

"Of course. You heard the County Attorney. I'll take you over to the hospital. Or you can go alone."

"That would be all right? You don't insist on coming with us?"

"No, Señor Campeón, you can go alone." Benson turned and stared at the old man, seeing the flat yellow eyes fixed unblinkingly on him. "Provided you discharge me as Arturo's attorney. Otherwise I go with you."

"You still wish to be his attorney? Why?"

"No," Benson said, letting his voice go hard and rough, as insolent as the old man's. "Dismiss that from your minds, both of you. This case was assigned to me by the court. It will mean weeks of hard work, for which I will be paid almost nothing. I would be relieved to be free of it. I now require you to decide. I have no more time to waste on idle debate."

All right, he thought, watching the old man tightly, is that tough enough for you, Conquistador? You came here to find out something and now you know.

The old man got up from his chair. He walked across to a table near the door and picked up his stained and warped rancher's hat. He turned and his long wolfish jaw flattened in a tight smile.

"This is how the good ones are," he said to no one. "Firm and with decision. I remember B. Kellogg."

Benson frowned. The old man said it "Bay Kullock," in the fashion of North Mexico and it took Benson a moment to recognize the name.

"He was old then, as I am now, but muy macho as a good man always is." The flat yellowish eyes glared at Benson. "And always, he was a man for truth. I see him in you, Señor

Kellogg. Let us go now."

He jerked his head at the closed door, and his half-terrified son-in-law hurried to open it.

IN THE TAXICAB Campeón squeezed himself against the car door, sweating heavily now in the heat and beginning to smell. The old man sat in the middle, stiff and unmoving, dry as a lizard, showing no emotion or interest now that he had made his decision. Benson shifted to look at him.

I wonder what he was like in his young days when he knew old B., he thought. These light-boned little Mexicans can be very tough sometimes. Zapata had no size to speak of. Neither did Madero or Juarez. Size doesn't mean much to people who do their fighting with knives. And a flat white smear of scar tissue down the old man's eroded brown neck said that he was a man who knew about knives. Like his grandson, Benson thought suddenly.

"I will need your help," he said, speaking freely in Spanish, knowing the Anglo cab driver could not follow what he was saying. "Arturo and the man he killed drove here from Los Angeles on Saturday. They were tired and they stopped to rest outside town. It was then that the man was killed. But I do not know why. Arturo will not tell me. Something very bad happened then and he feels a sense of—shame, and something more. I did not want to force him when we talked this morning, but you will understand that I must know all that happened."

The old man nodded. The brim of his weathered hat tilted with the slight movement.

"Arturo will be pleased and relieved to see you. He is bearing himself well, very well, but he is frightened, as any young boy would be. He may be willing to tell you what happened."

A light snort from the old man was answer enough. Willing or not, Arturo would tell him. That much was clear.

"Good. It might be best, I think, if you and Señor Campeón saw him first by yourselves for a few minutes. I will wait outside, and you can tell me when Arturo is ready to talk to me."

The old man tapped Campeón's knee. He lifted one finger briefly and stabbed it at the floor. Campeón was to stay with Benson. The old man would talk to his grandson alone. It was easy to see, Benson thought, where the boy got his talent for the decisive pictorial gesture that saved so much talking.

At the hospital, Benson stopped to pay the driver, and the old man marched unhesitatingly up the low stone stairs to the entrance, sure without even thinking of it that someone would be there to open the door for him. Campeón just made it. Benson followed slowly. The old man had the quietly arrogant assumption that is usually associated with royalty. But more often these days, Benson thought, you find it in the military. The old man moved like a general officer full of years and honors, bored with all of living except the exercise of power. And maybe he had been a general. He seemed to have every general's quality except maybe technical knowledge, and a man like that would learn whatever he needed to learn in order to do whatever he intended to do.

Benson escorted them to the fourth-floor corridor, where the deputy's cubicle blocked them. He signed for them in the register and stood aside, knowing the old man expected him to swing the gate back for him, but refusing to make the one small deferential gesture that would have ruined their relationship. The old man stood in place until the deputy glanced up, blinked and reached down to open the lock. The old man marched through, his high boot heels making a muffled sound on the flooring.

"We'll wait here," Benson said. He moved across to the deeply inset window where you could stand and brace one foot high, or perch with the edge of your rump on the hard molding. He propped his briefcase on the sill and leaned against the wall, folding his arms. Campeón lifted himself wearily and sat on the narrow ledge.

"You speak Spanish very well, señor," he said in a tíred, diffident voice.

Benson shrugged. He would not have answered but he looked at the drawn, exhausted expression of the man beside him and he could sense the pain and dread that tightened in Campeón's mind, keeping him hunched, unmoving and fearful, but still with the politeness that had been bred in him, trying to make courteous efforts at conversation.

"It is good of you to say so," Benson said. "I was taught early and well, but I speak barbarously now through lack of practice."

He turned so he was facing Campeón. "Listen," he said gently. "Don't have so much fear. Or don't show it. Your son is in trouble. We'll have to help him now and it is no help to be afraid."

"I know," Campeón muttered. "That is why I brought el señor suegro. He is muy duro in all things."

Muy duro is right, Benson thought. That's a genuinely hard guy. No wonder Frank Sayer was beginning to get edgy by the time I showed up. He was probably thinking the old boy was about to cut off his ears.

"Why did you bring him?" he asked. "Why didn't you bring the boy's mother?"

Campeón shrugged helplessly. "She is not well. And someone must manage the posada. And besides, my father-in-law . . ." Another shrug completed the thought. His father-in-law was all the law in the Campeón family.

"We'll have to keep him out of the courtroom," Benson said. "One look at him and a jury would begin to get some peculiar ideas."

"It will be as el señor suegro decides."

"It will be as I decide," Benson said quietly. "But I'll take care of it."

He offered Campeón a cigarette and held a match for both of them. They seemed then to run out of conversation. Campeón was obviously worn out from strain and the journey, and Benson had much to think about.

They each smoked three cigarettes in silence except for the politenesses exchanged when matches were lighted. With the slow passage of time Benson began to shift restlessly, not because he had to wait but because of the presence of Arturo's father. It was as though the man gave off impulses of depression and hopelessness, and after a while Benson himself was feeling somber and despondent.

They could hear the soft sound of the old man's boots before he appeared at the deputy's gate. He hissed once, in the signal that is never insulting in Mexico but always makes an Anglo bristle. Benson remained where he was, not moving when Campeón leaped up.

"Please, Señor Kellogg, do not make difficulties now," he whispered. "El señor suegro is furious. Please, señor."

Benson allowed Campeón to push his briefcase under his arm and draw him toward the gate. He went with a strange reluctance.

This is no time to be getting twitchy, he told himself. You've hired out to do a job, so for Christ's sake get on with it. What are you scared of?

I don't know, Benson thought. I'm not actually scared. It's just that something about that old man's murderous face makes me leery. If I didn't know who he was, I'd want a gun in my hand before I went anywhere near him.

The old man turned away and went first through the double doors of the guarded ward. As he entered, Campeón could no longer restrain himself. He brushed past Benson and ran, almost waddling, along the lane between the canvas partitions, calling for his son. The old man slowed and stopped. He made a slight, demanding sound and Benson looked at him.

He looks about the same, he thought. It wasn't a face that would ever register much emotion. What made Campeón so sure the old man was furious? Then the old man lifted his head and Benson could see his hooded eyes. And he knew what Campeón meant. The yellow eyes had a light inside that made them glitter. Frightening eyes. Killer's eyes, Benson thought.

"In the trial," the old man said thinly, "is it required that an explanation be given?"

"Unless you want the boy to hang."

The old man turned away.

"What did he tell you?"

"Let him say it himself. Ask him."

What's got into him? Benson wondered. Ten minutes ago he wanted to fire me because he didn't think I was going to fight hard enough for his grandson. And now—now what? Did he want the kid to hang?

Benson went down the long ward toward the windows. Campeón was down on his knees beside his son's bed, holding the boy with both arms, crying with the hard, painful sobs that tear out of a man's heart. Turo was looking up at the ceiling, the tracks of tears clear on his face. There was a long, newly made red streak across his cheek, and Benson suddenly thought of the ring on the old man's hand. The boy heard Benson. He stiffened against his father and pushed at him with his free hand.

"Let go, Papá," he said. "Let go, now."

"Turo, Turo."

"All right, Papá. All right now. You go talk to el Dorado. I'll be all right. You go now."

El Dorado, Benson thought. Is that what the old man was? One of Villa's golden boys? By God, I'll bet he was. He's about the right age, and he sure as hell acts the part.

"All right, Papá," the boy insisted. "You go buy el Dorado some coffee or something. I'll talk to Mr. Kellogg by myself."

Just who is being comforted here anyway? Benson thought. Campeón came unsteadily to his feet, stumbled and almost fell against Benson.

"Turo . . ."

"All right, Papá. You can come back in a little while." The boy held his voice steady but now he was crying again. He rolled his head away so that Benson could not see. "For the love of God, Papá, go!"

"Turo, I can't . . ."

The boy shook his head, crying without a sound.

"Just for a few minutes, Señor Campeón," Benson said. "Turo and I will have a talk and then you can see him again." He put his hand flat on Campeón's heavy shoulder and leaned against him, slowly forcing the man toward the aisle. "It won't be long." Benson stood blocking any view of Turo's bed until Campeón finally turned and walked away toward the old man, who stood spraddle-legged and rigid where Benson had left him.

"What did you bring them here for?" the boy said angrily.

Benson smiled slowly. "Me? You don't really think I could make your grandfather do anything, do you?" He went around the bed and sat in the chair where Turo could see him. "All right, Turo, let's get at it. There's been enough shouting and crying around here. Let's get started. We've got a job to do, you and I. Get at it, and without any more crap."

The boy's eyes widened. "What are you getting so tough about?"

Benson moved his shoulders impatiently. "It's in the air. The old man brings it out in everybody."

Turo nodded. He wiped his face with a corner of the bed-sheet. He knotted his fist and waggled it in the air.

"Muy duro," Benson agreed. "He's hard, all right. But that doesn't help much at the moment. What did you talk about, Turo?"

"I told him."

"He looks like he was tromped by a crazy horse," Benson said. "Are you going to tell me, or do I have to ask him to repeat it?"

"No. No. Wait a minute." The boy lay back flat. The pillows behind him had slipped aside and he was looking straight up at the ceiling. He drew in long slow breaths, as if trying to find some extra strength.

"Jump right in, Turo. Get it over with all at once. Just give me the nubbin. You and Duquesne parked that fancy car of his on Lookout Point. You were pretty tired, driving all night. Then what happened?"

"He wasn't," the boy said in a thin half whisper. "He'd been gobbling bennies all night like peanuts. He wasn't a bit tired."

"But you were."

"Sure. The guy wouldn't let me drive that car, even to spell him, so why should I take bennies? I was asleep when he parked. I guess it was a while before he woke me up."

"He woke you up. Then what?"

"He——" The boy's throat made a dry click and he almost gagged. He turned his head to ease the tightness of his neck. His eyes squeezed shut. Tears made the lashes shine.

"Tell me, Turo. Say it in Spanish if that's easier."

"He had my pants down to my knees. He was kissing me, slobbering over me, trying to—to——" The boy's throat closed completely. He couldn't say it.

He didn't have to. Benson felt cold with the knowledge. He waited for a moment until he was sure he could keep his voice level and impersonal.

"Did you try to fight him off?" he asked quietly. When the boy did not answer, he said, still very quietly, "I have to know, Turo. Did you fight him?"

The boy nodded.

"Is that when you knifed him? In the car?"

"No." Turo's voice was a hoarse, strained whisper. "I—I pushed him off."

"You got away from him?"

"No. I fell out the door. He was right after me. I got my knife out and cut him."

"Why?"

"Why?" The boy's voice soared, almost cracking. "I told you. He was trying to——"

"You knifed him more than once."

"I don't know. I guess so. That's what the cops said. I don't know. I was kind of nutty right then. I was mad. I was pretty scared, too. I was bleeding like a bull and the blood in my eyes so I couldn't see and I—I——"

"Take it slow and easy," Benson said. "We've got plenty of time. You got that head wound while you were fighting in the car? How did it happen?"

"I don't know. He belted me a couple of times. I guess I cracked it on the dashboard." The boy drew in a long, ragged breath. "I couldn't see. The blood in my eyes."

"You got out of the car? How?"

"I put a knee in his gut. The door just kind of opened. I went out on my head."

"Then Duquesne came out after you?"

"Yeah, he was right on top of me, I tell you. He grabbed my arm and I rolled away from him. He kept coming after me."

"And you went for your knife?"

"It was right in my hand," the boy said. "I couldn't see anything but that—thing—sticking out of his pants. I remember that all right. It looked like a club, like a goddam barber-pole. I was trying to cut it off, I guess. I got in a couple of swipes but he went over the rail before— Before I could——"

"All right, Turo," Benson said heavily. "Hold it a minute. I'll be right back."

He got up from his chair and went out into the aisle. The old man and the boy's father were standing close together, just beyond the canvas partition that shielded the boy's bed. Benson motioned to them and kept on toward the entrance of the ward. He pushed back a wing of the double door and held it, waiting for them to go out into the hallway.

Both of them were stiff, grim-faced, sick with anger. The old man was trembling, but not from weakness. His dark hands flexed constantly, clenching into agonizingly tight fists, then extending slowly until his knuckles cracked. He was breathing in quick shallow gulps, like a man who has been working hard for a long time.

"You heard?" Benson asked.

They had heard; their faces held the knowledge.

"I have to ask him many questions," Benson said. "About every detail. It will be better for all, especially for Turo, if you will leave him alone with me until we have finished."

"Señor, that man—" the old man's voice was barely audible, a thin whispering tone like his grandson's, like a knifeblade—"that maricón who———"

"Let us not think of him now," Benson broke in sharply. "He is dead. Let us think only of Turo, who is still alive. You wish him to stay alive, do you not?"

"That is a foul question, señor," Campeón said, stiffening. "Foul."

"No, it's not that," Benson said. "There is only one person here who can help him." He tilted his thumb back toward his own chest. "Me. I can help him, but I must now speak to him alone. If you are in the same room, he will not speak openly. You understand that. He has been shamed and he does not want you to see his shame. Go away for a time, please, and let us talk alone."

"But how can I know that———"

"You don't understand," Benson said, holding his anger in check. He could have them both forcibly removed by the deputy if necessary, but he wanted to avoid that if he could. "Listen to me, señores. I am the boy's attorney, not yours. Our relationship includes no one else. Turo speaks to me as he speaks to his priest, alone except for God."

Campeón crossed himself nervously. He glanced at the old man indecisively.

"Downstairs is a coffee shop," Benson went on hastily. "On the ground floor. You will probably be glad of a cup of coffee and something to eat after your long journey. Please wait for me there. You can return for a while when I have finished."

The old man nodded. He settled the brim of his hat squarely across his heavy eyebrows and jerked his head for Campeón. He looked long and sharply at Benson before turning away. Benson watched them until they were out of sight around the bend of the corridor. Then he lit a cigarette and stood at the window, smoking with fast erratic puffs, waiting until he felt more quiet within himself. After a long moment he dropped the cigarette, ground it under his heel and went back into the ward.

"OKAY, Turo, let's get to work." Benson took the straight chair beside the bed and opened his briefcase. He took out a long yellow pad and searched his pockets for a pencil. "It's not easy for you to talk about it, I know. But we're over the hump now. From now on it won't be so tough. Just remember that everything you say is strictly between us. Clear?"

"I—I guess so."

"Aren't you sure?" Benson demanded. "Let's get it settled right now. Do you trust me or don't you?"

"Sure. Sure, I trust you."

"Are you going to level with me? All the way?"

"Okay, sure." The boy lifted his free hand in a slight gesture that was abandoned before it was well begun. "You know how it is," he said vaguely.

"Yes, I know. But we haven't got time for it. I'm going to ask you some questions and I want you to answer them without taking any time to think about your answers. Just spit it right out. Don't try to answer in gestures, or those one-word responses. Give me the whole story. Okay. First, did you kill Roderick Duquesne?"

"Sure. I told you I——"

"Answer the question, don't argue about it. Why did you kill him?"

"He—he was trying to—" The boy made a curious movement with his hand. "I don't know what to call it," he said in obvious confusion.

"Did you believe he was making a homosexual attack on you?"

"That's it, a homosexual attack."

"Why did you believe that?"

"Because he—he hauled my pants down, like I told you. And his fly was open and his dick was sticking out and he was trying to kiss me and feel me up and I—I——"

"That's all he did? Nothing more than that?"

"Mother of God! What more do you want?"

"Answer me," Benson said quietly. "Is that all?"

"Well, yeah, I guess so. I don't remember anything else."

"Did you try to get away from him?"

Turo nodded. "Yeah. I went wild there for a minute."

"It was during the scuffle in the car that you received that scalp wound?"

"Yes, some time around in there."

"It wasn't later? You're sure?"

"No, I'm sure. I was all over blood before I ever got out of the car. That's what made me so scared. I couldn't see very good. I was rolling around there on the ground trying to haul my pants up so I could get on my feet. The knife just sort of fell into my hand."

"No, you're going too fast," Benson objected. "Just stick to the question, don't try to anticipate me. How did you manage to get out of the car?"

"I don't remember. I guess I hit the latch with my elbow or my head or something."

"And Duquesne tried to restrain you?"

"He grabbed my foot, damn near pulled off my shoe. I was kicking with my other foot and I caught him a good one. He let go then."

"And when he let go, you fell out of the car and tried to roll away. Did Duquesne follow you immediately, or did he wait?"

"No, he didn't wait. He was right on top of me, I told you. I just gave my pants one pull, and he was right there, standing on top of me. I had to roll some more to get up."

"Did you get to your feet?"

"Not right away. I had to cut him first to make him give me room. I got up on my knees and my damn pants were still dragging. I just swung wild with the knife. I knew he was there somewhere, but I couldn't see him clear."

"All right," Benson said slowly. "Now take your time with this one. Think for a minute. Try to remember just how everything was, what you thought, how you felt. Why did you use your knife?"

"He was trying to——"

"Why didn't you run?"

"I don't know," the boy said with a bewildered frown. "I never even thought about it. Christ, Mr. Kellogg, he was trying to——"

"So you killed him. Did you intend to kill him?"

"Hell, I don't know. I guess so. How do I know? I wasn't doing a whole lot of thinking right then. That bastard had me down and he was going to slip it to me. So I kicked him off. He kept coming at me, so I stuck him. That's how it was."

"Had you ever met Duquesne, or even seen him, before the time he gave you a lift?"

"No."

"Did you know he was homosexual, or suspect it? Did he talk about it?"

"No, it was a surprise to me, I can tell you. Hell, I had him figured for a normal guy. He was all the time talking about how he was hot stuff with the girls. You know how they do, talk dirty and sort of give you the eye to see how you take it."

"And how did you take it?"

"How do you think I took it? The guy was giving me a lift. If he wants to tell dirty stories, I laugh. Hell, it was his car. I didn't want him getting pissed off at me. I had a long way to go."

"And his dirty stories were always about normal sex acts? There was no element of perversion in them?"

The boy shook his head.

"So until the moment you woke up with Duquesne trying to attack you, there had been no hint of perversion in anything he said or did?"

"I didn't notice anything. Hell, Mr. Kellogg, I'm normal myself. With sex, I'm strictly square. I go for the girls and that's all. Maybe he was trying me out to see if I was fruit. I wouldn't know about that."

"You're normal," Benson repeated with slow emphasis. "Is there anyone who might have a different opinion?"

"What does that mean?" The boy colored angrily.

"Don't fence with me, Turo. Answer the question. Is there any official record that shows you have been suspected of sexual perversion?"

The boy shook his head and said, "No," emphatically.

"Does anyone, anyone at all, have any reason to suspect you of abnormal tendencies?"

"Hell, no. I told you——"

"I heard you tell me, Turo. Now tell me something else. How did you manage to live during the two years you spent in Los Angeles after you lost your job?"

The boy moved his head in a restless arc. "I don't get what you——"

"Not always honestly, from what you have told me. There were times when you were in a bind for money, I suppose."

"Sure, plenty of times."

"Did you ever try to get money by making yourself available to homosexuals?"

"No! Damn it, I never——"

"Stop shouting, Turo. Just answer my question. You must have known boys in your neighborhood who did make money that way?"

"Yeah, sure. There's always some joy boys around, but I never hung out with them. You ask anybody."

"I'm asking you, Turo. Is that your final answer?"

"You're damn right it is. And you can . . ."

Benson put his pad aside and lit a cigarette. Seeing his momentary inattention the boy fell silent. He lay back on his pillow, a dark glower drawing his eyebrows close together.

"My questions are a little rough, aren't they?" Benson said mildly. "But they're nothing compared to what you'll be getting from the County Attorney. You'll have to hold your temper with him, and give full answers whether you like it or not, so you might as well start practicing with me. Let's move on. Tell me about Duquesne. What did he look like?"

"He looked okay," the boy said in a grudging voice.

"Get the chip off your shoulder, boy. Describe him to me."

"He looked all right. A good-looking guy. About forty. Maybe six feet. Heavy built. He looked like anybody else. Dark hair. Good clothes. You'd never figure him for a faggot. He looked more like a football player."

"A football player. Would you say he was in good physical condition?"

"He was soft, or I'd never have got away from him, big as he was. But he looked hard. He had a big chest and big arms, but his belly was mush. He ran out of puff pretty quick."

"When he came at you, did you feel frightened of him? Did you think he was capable of doing you physical injury?"

"I guess so. Fact is, I was so damn mad I don't know how I felt."

"Suppose he had not come out of the car after you. What if he had stayed there and you had managed to get away from the car. You would have pulled up your pants and got to your feet. Then what?"

"Huh?"

"What would you have done then?"

"I don't know. How can I tell? He was right there on top of me, I tell you. It wasn't him in the car and me outside. He was right there with me."

"I'm trying to get at something important, Turo. Let's say that Duquesne stayed in his car. You are outside alone. Your clothes are adjusted again. Your knife is still in your pocket. Duquesne is just sitting there looking at you. What do you do?"

The boy's fist knotted convulsively. "I'd bust him," he said with no hesitation. "Boy, I'd beat the shit out of him."

"What about your knife?"

"I'd want to pound on him first, I guess. Maybe not. Maybe I wouldn't even think of it."

"You would pull your knife and go in after him. Is that what you mean?"

Something cold and forbidding in Benson's voice made the

boy cautious. He swallowed heavily. "I don't know," he said uncertainly. "I don't know what I mean."

"You intended to kill him, didn't you? The only reason you tried to get away was to give yourself room to use your knife. You meant to kill him. Didn't you?"

"Hell, how do I——"

"Answer me, damn you!"

"Go to hell." The boy's chin came up sharply with that habitual, defiant arrogance. "I told you I killed him. Any sonofabitch who tried to stick it in me is going to get his balls cut off. What the hell do you think I am anyway?"

"All right, Turo," Benson said soberly. He blew a streamer of smoke with an audible pressure. "I didn't know what you were. That's why I had to ask."

But I know now, he thought. And I'd give a lot if I didn't. I am beginning to understand him—a little bit, at least. I grew up with boys like him and I remember how they were. But I wonder if anyone on the jury will know or remember? People like Turo Campeón don't often get called for jury duty. I don't believe a routine juryman will understand the boy, and right now I'm not sure I'll be able to explain about him.

For the first time since he had received it from the County Attorney's secretary, Benson took out the copy of the boy's confession. He spread it open on top of his scribbled notepad and read through it carefully.

"This is the confession you signed," he said when he had finished. "In it you admit killing Duquesne because he fought when you tried to rob him."

"I didn't say that!"

"Read it." Benson held the brief statement so that the boy could see it without moving. "Is that what it says?"

"Yeah, but I didn't——"

"Unfortunately you did. This is a certified copy of your confession. Don't argue about it. Just explain to me why you didn't mention Duquesne's homosexual attack when you were talking to the sheriff's men. Why did you confess to a lie? If it was a lie."

"It's a lie, all right. You're looking at this all wrong, Mr. Kellogg. Those bums didn't ask me anything. They told me. I don't remember all of it, but I know I didn't tell them I robbed Duquesne. Or maybe," he hesitated, eyes widening with a sudden recollection, "maybe I did."

"What!"

"The lighter," Turo said with a painful slowness. "I sort of remember something about the lighter. If they asked me about it, I most likely told them I copped it off Duquesne. I'm not sure. I think somebody did ask me about the lighter."

"Good God," Benson almost groaned. "Okay, Turo. Are you clear about one of the deputies hitting you on your cast while you were being questioned?"

"Boy, I'll never forget that. It was like somebody jabbing me with a hot poker. I think I blacked out a couple of times. You let a guy do that to you, and you shot full of dope, and then see just how much of it you can remember."

"Were you in the hospital when you were questioned?"

"I guess so. I don't remember that either."

"Was a doctor present with the deputies?"

"I didn't see any."

"No one but the sheriff's men?"

"Not that I know about."

"I see." Benson folded the confession and slid it into his briefcase. In his mind was a vividly sharp image of the scene the boy had outlined. He didn't dare allow himself to focus on it, or he would not be able to hide his anger. And anger at that moment was a luxury he could not afford.

Outside, a bulldozer went clanking and snorting along the berm of the highway, sending up a thick ragged plume of dust and a bellow of noise. Benson waited for it to pass. He looked absently out the window, watching the dust boil high. A crook-winged vulture soared over Cobre Peak, tilted with the wind and sailed in a long lovely arc into the dust haze.

When it was quiet again, Benson said, "Tell me about that cigarette lighter, Turo. Exactly where did you steal it? And how? I want all the details."

The boy blinked. He took a moment to adjust himself to the new subject. "The lighter? We stopped at a drive-in for coffee. It was somewhere in California, near the state line, I think. I had a piece of pie and Duquesne just had coffee. Duquesne started to light a cigarette and just then the girl came for the tray so he put the lighter down to get out some money and I guess he forgot it. He lit up with the dash lighter and then headed back to the highway. The lighter slid down in the seat and I sort of pushed it back. I waited for a couple of hours, but he didn't pick it up, so the next time we stopped for gas, I put it in my pocket."

"Duquesne didn't notice it was missing, then or later?"

"He didn't say anything about it. I figured I had it made. Maybe I was wrong."

"Why do you say that?"

"Well, you know. If he was a fag, maybe he figured me copping his lighter would give him some kind of edge over me. I don't know. These fags don't think like normal people."

"Tell me about your fight in the car. You couldn't have had much room to swing. I suppose it was mostly wrestling and shoving?"

"Yeah. I kept jabbing at him, but I couldn't get clear. He twisted around somehow and clipped me a good one behind the ear. That's when I cracked my head on the dashboard and got cut."

"Just a minute, Turo. You're going too quickly. Didn't either of you say anything? You weren't fighting in silence, were you?"

"There wasn't much talking that I remember. He was sort of mumbling at first, whispering. I pushed him off and told him to get away from me and he said, 'I'll pay you. Don't worry, I'll pay you.' He kept saying that over and over. I was just shoving at him, trying to get away, and he was moving in on me all the time, saying he wouldn't hurt me, something like that. 'Be quiet, I won't hurt you.' "

"And what did you say?"

"I must have said something, I guess. I don't remember

anything except, 'Get away from me.' I said that a lot."

"All right. Now skip to a later time, after Duquesne's death. You got back in the car. Was your head still bleeding?"

"You should have seen it," the boy said wonderingly. "Blood all over the place. Duquesne had a pack of Kleenex on the seat and I used it up trying to stop the bleeding. Finally I tied my handkerchief over it so I could see to drive."

"And when you had the bleeding stopped, you drove back down the mountain and headed for Rincon. How did you come to wreck the car?"

"I still can't figure that, Mr. Kellogg. The car was new to me. It had more power than I've ever tried to handle before, but hell, I'm a good enough driver. I don't know what happened. I was going along okay. I got around the big curve on the mountain and straightened out for town. Then I must have gone off my head. Next thing I knew, the car was all over the road and I never did get it back in control."

"Do you think your head injury affected your driving?"

"Must have. Duquesne didn't hurt me much. He got in a couple of good licks, but nothing to worry about."

"What did you have in mind when you took Duquesne's car?"

"I don't get you." The boy frowned, puzzled.

"Where were you going? Did you think you could drive it all the way to Chihuahua?"

"No. Christ, I was bleeding like hell. I wanted a doctor. I was kind of shook. For a minute there I was thinking I was going to bleed to death."

"You wanted a doctor. What about Duquesne?"

"What about him?"

"You slashed him with your knife. He backed away from you, I suppose, and fell over the guardrail?"

"Hell, he wasn't backing anywhere. I went at him head-first and got a couple swipes at him. I knocked him over. I damn near went over myself."

"Did you know you had killed him?"

"I knew he was dead," the boy said positively. "When you

give them the knife down there, they're always dead."

"He landed on a rock ledge on the side of the mountain. Could you see him?"

"Just a kind of a blur. It was still dark. He had on a white shirt and I could see that pretty clear."

"You didn't think of going down to see if he might still be alive?"

The boy moved his head irritably. "I knew he was dead. And I was bleeding like a bull. I wanted a doctor. I just took off as quick as I could."

"A doctor. Is that all you wanted?"

"What else?"

"The police, possibly. Did you think of that?"

"Yeah, I thought about it. But I sure as hell didn't mean to turn myself in, if that's what you mean."

"Why not? You claim you were just defending yourself against Duquesne. Why run away?"

The boy's mouth thinned with contempt. "Listen, mister. I'm a Mex, a pachuco, a greaser. I'm not a human being. You think I'm going to stick my head in some Anglo jail and ask them to chop it off?"

Benson ignored the boy's bitterness. "You were afraid that you would not be treated fairly because you were Mexican. Was that your reason?"

"Now you got the message, dad."

Benson put his pad down and looked at the boy, his eyes grave and impassive. He drew in a long careful breath. "Curl your lip at me just once more," he said softly, "and I'll give you a thick ear. Now you just mind your manners, if you ever learned any."

After a strained silent moment the boy nodded in awkward apology. "I was out of line, I guess. I got better manners than that, most times. I didn't mean it like it sounded."

"Okay. Just take it easy and try to help me. The questions are rough, but there's no way to make them easy. If you're trying to figure out what I'm after, I'll explain. You have been charged with first-degree murder and there are several elements the County Attorney will have to establish if he hopes to get a conviction. First, did you do it? We've got the answer to that one. Second, did you do it intentionally, knowing what you were doing? That answer is in too. Third, was there any legal justification for doing it? We're still exploring that one. Fourth, did any act subsequent to the crime indicate a sense of guilt or innocence? That's what the last question was about. Flight is commonly considered a sign of guilt."

"Guilt, hell. Excuse me, Mr. Kellogg, but I wasn't thinking about was I guilty. I was thinking about some big bum with a badge smacking me around in a jail cell like they do in L.A."

Benson turned a page of his notepad. "I guess that's enough for the first session, Turo. We'll be talking again tomorrow and I want you to think over everything you've told me. Every single detail. I have the general picture now, but I'll need lots more before we're ready to go to trial."

"When will that be?"

"Next week, probably. I don't see we have anything to gain from a delay. You haven't given me any reason for applying for a continuance."

The boy worried at his underlip briefly. Then he looked up and forced a smile. "Whatever you say, Mr. Kellogg. Kind of a tough case for you, huh?"

"For both of us, Turo," Benson said carefully. "We're in this together."

"For a while anyway." The boy's voice was little more than a low murmur. He cleared his throat. "Well, what do you think, Mr. Kellogg? How do we stand?"

Benson lit another cigarette, taking his time. How did they stand? It wasn't a question he could answer. Not yet. Too much hinged on the boy himself, not the evidence.

"You're in trouble," he began, feeling oddly hesitant. "You knew that. You've given me some idea of what happened on Lookout Point, and now I can start to plan our defense. Some of your story will be hard to prove, because a lot of it depends on your unsupported word."

The boy braced himself. "Can you do it?" Small knots of

muscle bunched along his jaw.

"We'll find a way," Benson said quietly. "But it won't be easy." He looked at the boy and smiled with more confidence than he felt. "Now I go to work and you stay here and bite your nails and hope to hell I know what I'm doing. Waiting is hard work any time. For you, right now, it's really going to be tough. Back in the old days, when you had to dig an arrow out of a man's back, you gave him a bullet to bite, to help him control himself while you whittled on him. That's what you'll have to do now, Turo. Bite on the bullet."

"Have I got a chance?" The boy was holding himself tightly.

"Yes," Benson said soberly. "You've got a chance. I don't want to speculate about the case, Turo. Right now all I can say is that we will put up a strong defense against the charge of murder."

The boy let out his pent-up breath in a long sigh. "I thought I was gone."

"You're not gone. But you're not out of the woods. We still have a lot of work ahead of us."

"What happens next?"

"You'll appear in court tomorrow. It will be just that, an appearance. The criminal information will be filed and the judge will set a date for trial. That's all there is to it. I'll order a wheel chair for you. The sheriff will take you to the courthouse and bring you back here afterward. Do you think you're up to that?"

"I'm okay. A little wobbly is all."

"Good. You'll stay here in the hospital until the trial starts. That will be next Monday. Then you'll be moved to a cell in the courthouse. But don't worry about that. If you still need medical attention, I'll see that you get it."

"By next week, I won't need much, I wouldn't think."

"We'll see." Benson strapped his briefcase and rose. "I want you to do something for me."

"Sure."

"I'm going to send someone to talk to you, some time today or tomorrow. He'll have a note from me and he'll ask you a lot of questions. I want you to answer him truthfully."

"Okay. Questions about what?"

"About you. I'll explain later. Just go along with me."

"Well, all right. I guess you're the boss."

"Except for that one man, I don't want you to discuss the case with anyone at all. Is that clear? And I include your father and grandfather. Talk to no one."

"Boy." Turo shook his head and for a moment he looked very young and unsure. "The Dorado is going to burn my butt."

"Let him. Just tell him you have orders from me. If he wants to argue, tell him to argue with me." Benson put out his cigarette. "Was he really a Dorado?"

"Sure he was." The boy's chin rose with pride. "You know about them, huh?"

"I was born the year Pershing broke the Dorados. I know about them all right. So do other people. Tell the old man I want him to soft-pedal that Dorado stuff. There's still some hard feeling around here. We just might wind up with someone on the jury whose father was scragged by Villa's boys. If the newspapers get wind of the old man, they'll be after him for a statement. You tell him to keep his mouth shut. Tight and all the time."

"I can see me telling him anything like that," the boy said shakily.

"Tell him it comes from me. If he talks to the newspapers, he just might manage to hang you. Make sure he understands that. I'll tell him myself, but you drive it home."

"I'll try. Okay, Mr. Kellogg, I'll tell him."

"And make it stick. All right, Turo, I'll see you tomorrow in court. Take it easy and don't worry." Benson turned away, then stopped and came back. "I forgot to mention it before. You have some credit down at the hospital coffee shop if you want to order some magazines or candy or anything like that. I noticed they have a pretty good-looking line of pies on the counter. The deputy on the gate will order for you. Just give a shout. See you tomorrow."

Benson left quickly, as if pressed for time. The boy's voice followed him to the door, quick and light, almost cheerful. Almost.

ALONG THE WIDE palm-lined streets in the center of Rincon a thin scattering of people moved listlessly through the heat of the afternoon. The sun was slanting and westerly now, and its strong unrelieved light struck dazzles and glints from shop windows and store fronts, from the worn concrete roadways and the tiny flecks of mica embedded in the sidewalks. Benson stopped under a shop awning, waiting in the pale hot shadow for the traffic light to change. He had walked back along the highway and over the stone bridge from the county hospital, usually a pleasant, leg-stretching distance, but this afternoon oppressively long and tiring for reasons that had little to do with the blast-furnace heat of the desert air.

When the light clicked and "Walk" signs appeared on each corner, Benson crossed diagonally to the entrance of the Medical Arts Building, pushed open the door and went inside. He climbed the stairs beside the bank of elevators, turned at the first landing and opened the pebble-glass door that carried the legend, "Laurence L. Cass, M.D."

Dr. Cass had a small well-furnished waiting room, with masses of clove-pink carnations and stocks to make a lively pattern against the ice-blue walls and give some life to the heavy, artificially cooled air. His nurse, a thin, tight-faced, deliberately moving woman with an attitude of inhuman detachment, was alone in the room, seated at a small desk, making entries in a leather-bound ledger which she closed carefully before looking up.

"Oh, Mr. Kellogg, how nice," she said with no change of expression. "Were you hoping to see Dr. Cass?"

Benson glanced at her quizzically. "You might put it that way," he agreed. "Is he free just now?"

"We have ten minutes before our next appointment, but

I'm not sure if . . ."

She came to her feet in a graceful spiral, making her stiff white nylon skirt swirl with motion. She smiled at Benson with the chill impersonality of a harried hostess and disappeared through the dark-blue door behind her desk. Benson clamped his briefcase under his arm, took out his cigarettes and lit one with the lighter on the desk.

The nurse made a soft sound in her throat. She beckoned to Benson and, as he passed her at the doorway, whispered, "Only ten minutes, remember."

Benson went into a large, quiet and gently lighted room. Two walls were solid with heavy, dark leather books in open shelves. The furniture was dark, austere and old, well-made and well-tended. The large carved desk was wax-rubbed mahogany that glowed like a faraway fire. Beyond it was a long padded leather couch with a sharp-nosed, heavy-chested man lying on it in his shirt sleeves with his collar sprung comfortably open. He had his eyes closed and he did not look up as Benson came in and sat in the straight-backed chair beside the couch.

Benson blew a thin cloud of smoke at the man's face and watched it disappear toward the ceiling with the soft suction of the air-conditioning system.

"Now then, Mrs. MacGillicuddy," Benson said. "Just where does it hurt?"

The man on the couch opened a dark and skeptical eye. It focused briefly on Benson, then closed again. "It's like this, Doctor," he said lazily. "Every time that door opens and someone comes in, I get a kind of a queer feeling. I don't rightly know what to call it, but it's sort of like a pain in the ass."

Benson grinned. He slumped in his chair and stretched his legs out straight. "I'll swear," he said easily, "I don't see how the hell you ever manage to keep any patients. Haven't you ever heard about the bedside manner?"

The man grunted. He sighed. He swung his feet to the floor and came up to a sitting position, propping himself on his hands. "What do you want, Ben?" he said in a slow growl. "No more donations, boy. I warn you."

"No donations," Benson said. "Or maybe it is, at that. I came to ask a favor, Larry. Have you got time to look at a client of mine?"

"Oh, God." Dr. Cass rubbed a hand vigorously across his face. He yawned and stretched his heavy blacksmith's arms wide. He was round-faced, strong-jawed, with a mottled line of smallpox scars along his cheek. His eyes were dark brown, set in whites so clear they seemed faintly blue against his sallow skin. He looked pleasant and ugly and very dependable. He had not changed noticeably since his boyhood days, when he and Benson had ridden their horses together through the barren foothill ranges of East Rincon to attend the consolidated township school. But he did look tired, Benson thought; the sharp lines around his mouth and eyes might have been cut with a knife.

"I figured you'd be around," he said. "I was looking for you yesterday when I heard what happened to Judge Turnbull. It's a damn shame, Ben. I know you and old Famous Amos were buddies, but I can't do anything now that he has been——"
He broke off in mid-sentence and his eyes narrowed in speculation. "But you didn't come here about him, did you?"

"No," Benson said honestly. He hadn't even thought about the judge all day, he realized. And he could not spare any time for him now. "I'll want your advice about him too, Larry, but I came here because of something else."

"No dice," Dr. Cass said flatly. They were old friends, and he could say it like that and know Benson would accept it. "I haven't got the time, Ben." He buttoned his collar and slid the knot of his tie up into position.

"I know, but let me tell you about it, Larry. Your dragon said I could have ten minutes. Maybe you can give me a useful tip."

"Sure. Ten minutes. Deep analysis in ten minutes. Any other headshrinker in town might need fifteen minutes, but not me." Dr. Cass snorted derisively. He pushed himself up from the couch and went slowly toward his desk. He took the coat that was draped over the back of his chair and put it on. He frowned at Benson for a long moment before he sat down. "Okay, Ben. Don't horse around. What's on your mind?"

"I was handed a nasty one by the court today, Larry. I've been appointed to defend a boy who killed a man up on Lookout Point Saturday night. Did you read about it in the paper?"

"The hitchhiker? That one? Young Mexican?"

"Yes. He's my client. I've just been talking to him. A lot of what he told me is outside my area of competence. Over my head too, probably. That's why I'm here."

"Okay, get on with it," Dr. Cass said sourly. He cleared his throat noisily, swallowed with a twisted grimace and lit a cigarette.

"The boy—his name is Arturo Campeón, by the way— admits the killing. He claims he was fighting off a homosexual attack." Benson leaned forward and sprayed some ash over an enamel tray on the desk. "That's the basic point. I don't have the professional background to test the boy's story. I don't even know what questions to ask or how to ask them. You do. I want you to ask them for me."

"Not a chance. I haven't got the time. What do you want to know anyway?"

Benson lifted his shoulders and let them drop. "I want to know if he's telling me the truth."

"Why? What do you care? If he's lying, you still have to defend him, don't you?" Dr. Cass let a gobbet of thick smoke sift toward his desk top. He stared at it morosely.

"It's not that simple. Goddam it, Larry, I need some help. If I base my case on self-defense, not knowing myself if the boy's story is true, I'll probably get clobbered. And you can guess what Frank Sayer is likely to suggest about my client's motives."

"I can guess," Dr. Cass said in a tired voice. "If Frank has any sense he will probably claim that they were a couple of bunghole buddies who had a little spat and one of them wound up dead. That sort of thing is not uncommon among homosexuals. What does your boy say? That he was fighting off a rape job?"

"That's about what it amounts to. Legally of course, rape is reserved for the girls. Boys don't qualify."

"The hell with the law," Dr. Cass said amiably. "I was speaking English, not law. In English, rape means to take something by force."

"Is that the way a psychiatrist would look at it? Can you equate homosexual attack with rape?"

"Why not? Where's the difference? You damnfool lawyers figure a girl has lost something valuable when a guy busts her cherry without permission. But what about the boy who gets his rectum ripped open and maybe winds up minus his marbles from shock? No legal loss there?" Dr. Cass scowled across the table.

"That's awful rough language for a learned doctor," Benson said mildly. "I thought you guys were supposed to talk politely about psychoses and syndromes and all that."

Dr. Cass waved an impatient hand. "I'm trying to make it clear to you. I've treated three homosexual patients and I'm pretty well convinced that the factor that determined whether each of them would develop as a homosexual was a childhood seduction or rape by a mature homosexual. The other factors have to exist to some degree, but this one is decisive. What about your boy? If he's telling a straight story, will you be able to get him off?"

"Maybe. The law isn't clear. It all seems to hinge on the degree of violence involved on each side. Rape is a felony and in defending yourself against felonious assault you would probably be justified in killing, if the surrounding circumstances were in your favor. But in this state, sodomy is listed as a misdemeanor, and in defending yourself against a misdemeanor, you are not justified in killing. That's the general rule. The thing I'm worried about is that the law doesn't say anything at all about this kind of offense. The statutes assume that sodomy is committed only by two equally willing adult males. It doesn't consider the possibility of homosexual attack. So I'm not sure where I stand. I'll have to study the authorities, if there are any to this point. I wouldn't be surprised to find that this is something new for courts in this state. So you can see why I have to be sure about the boy's story."

Dr. Cass propped his elbows on his desk and held his head in his hands. He glared gloomily at Benson through half-closed eyelids. "What you legal types need is a good psychiatrist, my friend. I never heard such goofy talk. I suspect all you guys are a little bit nuts."

Benson grinned in spite of himself. Trust Larry to cut through to the heart of his confusion. "It does sound nutty put that way. I was trying to explain that I'm worried about what appears to be an oversight in the statutes. In a general sense, we can say that everyone has a right to defend himself against attack, but the degree of violence used in the defense had better not exceed the degree of violence of the attack. Is that clear?"

"I get it," Dr. Cass muttered. "You aren't allowed to use a ball bat if I'm coming at you with my fists."

"That's about it. There are exceptions. If you were a professional prize fighter, I might be justified in using any weapon that came to hand, because I could assume that your power and skill gave you a dangerous advantage. In such cases, the court finds on a basis of intent, of mental attitude—and that isn't easy to determine, is it, Dr. Cass?"

"Nope. At least, it's never been easy for me. Have you figured where you'll stand if you find the boy is lying?"

"Sure. That's one of the things I'm worried about. He may be queer as a lead quarter. I have to be sure about him before I plan the defense."

"It's a possibility you'd better worry about. When most people lie, they tend to stay with familiar patterns. Your boy would hardly have invented a homosexual excuse unless he had some familiarity with the homosexual pattern."

"He could be telling the truth, of course."

"There's always that. Well, what do you expect me to do, Ben? You don't think I can just take a peek at him and give you the answer, do you?"

"No," Benson said. "I'll admit I'm ignorant about all this, Larry. I didn't think you could tell by looking, but I was hoping you could put a series of test questions that would give you a good indication."

"That's not the way it works," Dr. Cass said. "You can't identify a homosexual who doesn't want to be identified, not without a lot of exploration. There isn't any physical type. The passives, the ones who imitate women, are obvious sometimes, but the actives, the guys who play the man's part, are usually well disguised."

"Then how do you spot one?"

"It takes time. A homosexual identifies himself after a while. But you can't push people like that or they go dummy on you."

"I thought they were frank about it, most of them," Benson said. "God knows you see plenty of them prancing around. They don't seem to give a damn who knows about them."

"Only some of them. Only the ones who don't have much to lose. Hell, Ben, they're not just psychopathic personalities, remember. They're criminals too. That's one of the handicaps in treating them. The homosexual act is a crime in every state, so in addition to their other troubles, homosexuals are genuinely terrified at the thought of exposure. That constant fear makes them perfect targets for blackmailers. Most of them lie low when they can."

"I guess you're in a position to know, Larry. What is the best approach for me? Do you think you could tell me anything about my client if you saw him for an hour or two?"

"I might." Dr. Cass shrugged his thick shoulders. "Hell, you've got me curious now. I should never have listened to you in the first place. I'll talk to your boy, Ben, but I can't promise anything. You'd better realize that it's probably a waste of time. These guys are shifty; they have to be. They learn the hard way."

"That's all I wanted, Larry. Just let me know your reaction to him. Even if you don't have the whole answer, you can keep me from making a fool of myself."

"We'll see." Dr. Cass flipped up the cover of his desk calendar and ran a stubby finger down the page. "I don't see how I can fit him in, though. I'm booked straight through till eight o'clock today. When do you want me to see him?"

"As soon as you can, Larry. The kid's in the County Hospital, in the guarded ward on the fourth floor. How about stopping in tonight on your way home? I'll call the deputy and make sure everything's ready for you." Benson took a business card from his briefcase and wrote a short note on the reverse side. "Give this card to the boy when you see him. I've warned him not to talk to anyone, so you'll need this to identify yourself."

"Okay." Dr. Cass slid the card down behind the handkerchief in his breast pocket. "I'll call you after I've seen him. Where will you be, out at the ranch?"

"Yes, I'm on my way now." Benson picked up his briefcase and rose. "Thanks, Larry. I appreciate this."

"The hell with your thanks," Dr. Cass said. "Just send me a quarter of venison the next time you jack-light a buck. I haven't had any deer meat for a couple of years."

"I've got a side in the freezer, Larry. I'll bring in a chunk for you. But for God's sake, stop talking about jack-lighting deer. You'll have the sheriff down on my neck, and you know how my people like the sheriff."

"Your people," Dr. Cass growled. "Your damn clownish barbarians. Probably the whole lot of you comics would be in jail if anybody knew the truth. This is the twentieth century, bud, the beginning of the second half. You aren't supposed to be having any fun these days, don't you know that? Now get the hell out of here and let me get back to work." He looked up somberly at Benson. "I don't suppose anybody is going to pay me?"

"You suppose right," Benson said smiling. "Send me a bill if it will make you feel any better."

Dr. Cass pointed a blunt finger at the door. "Out," he said.

"I'm going. Thanks again, boy. Come on out to La Cañada when you get the time. I've got a fine crop of new colts this season."

"I'd like to, Ben, but I never get away." He lifted his telephone and held it midway to his ear. "I'll call you later, Ben."

Benson left by a side door that led directly onto the stair landing. Dr. Cass was speaking quietly into his phone as Benson closed the door.

THE DARK HOT CAVERN of the garage next to the Frontier Hotel was blaring with the overlapping and rhythmic echoes of a racing motor when Benson came down the grease-stained ramp from the street. The loud-ringing bell of the telephone in the small office near the entrance kept up a piercing shriek that eventually penetrated to the mechanic who was bent over, his head under the hood, tuning the motor. He switched off and came forward into the glare of light, wiping his hands on a wad of waste.

"Hi, Ben. With you in a minute." He rubbed the oily wad across his forehead as he went in to answer the phone.

"Is there anything in from La Cañada, Charlie?" Benson followed the mechanic to his cool, moist cubicle and propped himself on a corner of the scarred and nicked desk.

Charlie pointed to a wrapped package on his desk. "That's for you," he said to Benson. He picked up the phone and shouted, "Garage," in a thin belligerent tenor.

Benson turned the package until he could read the typed label. "From B. Kellogg and Sampson," it said across the top. The books and transcripts that Miss Harkins had collected for him. My homework, he thought sourly. He could barely get his arm around the fat package.

"No, we ain't," Charlie said angrily into the phone. He slammed the receiver down. "La Cañada," he said, turning to Benson. "Yeah, we got something. A five-ton Jimmy and that fancy Ford pickup. In the back on the left."

"You let Clemente hear you call it a pickup and he'll chew your head. That is a Ranchero, boy, and Clemente would rather have it than a Cadillac."

Charlie grinned, a quick, gape-mouthed grimace that caught him by surprise. He bobbed his head. "That is surely the truth. Old Clemente, he's just like a kid with a new saddle. And that's some pickup all right. They get fancier every year. You remember what they looked like when we was kids, Ben? My old man had one, and I swear it was all I could do just to turn the wheel."

"I remember them. And I remember that we had about twenty miles of paved road in the whole state when we were kids. A truck had to be a brute to stand up. How about the Ranchero? Is it loaded?"

"There's a roll of harness leather and a crate of horse-shoes in the back. Won't carry much more. You plan on takin' it, Ben?"

"I guess so." Benson hefted his load and went out into the dark garage. He inched his way between parked cars, skirted a spattered pool of oil and came up to the rear of a new white-and-scarlet Ford truck. The bed of the pickup was compact, neatly turned and low, with an eye to style as well as utility. Benson dropped his wrapped package in with the load and took his briefcase with him to the cab. The front seat and fittings were the same as those in a station wagon, except that the cab compartment was sharply cut off by a partition behind the seat. A truck behind and a cleanly designed, leather-padded section up forward. Old Clemente always put on his Sunday clothes whenever he drove it out of the garage at La Cañada. Benson got in and backed carefully out into the main aisle where he had room to turn around. He drove to the entrance and stopped.

"Charlie, tell Clemente to count noses before he starts home. I don't want anyone stranded in town."

"Okay," Charlie shouted. "Hey, Ben. If you see that crazy Limey, you tell him I can't find no goddam carburetor to fit that old heap he left here. They ain't made parts like that for fifteen years. Might be six months before I found one. Ask him what he wants to do with it, will you?"

Benson switched off the ignition and got out. "Fitz's old Duesenberg? What's wrong with it now?"

"Nothing much. That car was made to last, but the carburetor is shot. I can't fix it. You tell Fitz."

"Okay. What's the best thing for him to do? He's pretty fond of that old bus."

Charlie scratched his nose thoughtfully, pleased at being consulted and savoring the experience. "Well now," he said slowly, "I could sell it for him, I guess. People are always looking for Duesy parts. But maybe if he didn't mind laying out a little money, I could maybe find somebody to make him some new parts for that carburetor."

"How much? Any idea, Charlie?"

"Hell, I dunno. Fifty bucks, maybe. Could run more."

Benson nodded decisively. "Do that, Charlie. Get the old bus ready to roll. Fitz is talking about driving up to Alaska this summer. Put the carburetor on the La Cañada bill. Okay?"

"Yeah, it's okay, Ben," Charlie said dubiously. "If you say so."

"I say so. How is it otherwise, Charlie? I wouldn't want the old boy running around in a pile of junk that might break down on him."

"That car ain't gonna break down," Charlie said with belligerent sureness. "That ain't Detroit iron. Put you in a new carburetor, get some new plugs and grind the valves, and you can breeze along at a hunnert-ten, hunnert-twenny, easy. Best car ever built in this country, don't you forget that. Thirty years old and it's just broke in good."

"That's what Fitz says. Well, fix it up, Charlie, and send word when it's ready." Benson turned on his heel and started back toward the truck. He stopped abruptly and muttered, "Oh, my God," under his breath.

Tim Cook was waiting just inside the entrance, one foot up on his suitcase, leaning forward tensely, bracing himself with both hands on his lifted knee. "Forgot about me, didn't you?" he said in a deliberately neutral voice.

"For just a minute, I did," Benson said. "Sorry, Tim. This has been a rough day for me. Everything seemed to happen at once. I'd have remembered, but I might have driven halfway home before I did. I'm glad you were here to remind me. Ready to go?"

Tim Cook's narrow nervous face was set in long stiff lines of frowning suspicion. "Sure you want me along?"

"If you still want to come," Benson said easily, refusing to respond to the clear note of challenge. "Throw your bag in back."

Tim Cook made a snorting sound. He nodded with brusque assurance and straightened. He took a quick stride toward the truck and swung his light suitcase up into the open bed. He ran a slitted scornful eye along the bright red-and-white truck and shook his head.

"If you think that's gaudy," Benson said, "you should see what happens when the hands repaint our trucks to suit themselves. Pink and yellow, mostly, with red wheels and four-color saints' pictures on the doors. Very jazzy. Get in, Tim."

When the sour-faced fidgety man was settled beside him on the front seat, Benson started the motor, lifted a hand to Charlie and drove the truck up the ramp into the hard sunlight. He turned left with the one-way traffic, heading toward the highway.

Tim Cook wiped his forehead, folded his damp handkerchief and mopped under his chin. He let out a slow, noisy breath. "What a day," he muttered.

"Been hot, hasn't it?" Benson agreed. "Shouldn't be so hot this early in the year. How did you get on with Hal Judson? Get what you wanted?"

"We talked," Tim said with a shrug. "He was pretty busy, but yeah, he gave me a run-down on Burr. Nothing much I didn't have before. He's one of those loyal guys."

"Is that bad?"

"It's bad when they try to sugar-coat everything."

Benson put his hands on the top arc of the wheel and pushed back hard, stretching his shoulder muscles. It had been a long day, full of tension and uncertainty and unsavory discoveries, and it was by no means over yet. A sense of depression moved into his mind like a gloomy shadow whenever he considered the problem of Arturo Campeón. He was responsible for the boy's defense and he was afraid he might not be clever and persuasive enough to save him.

Every lawyer worries in just those terms, he told himself. When you're working hard for a long time, then of course you worry. It's part of the job. That's why so many lawyers have ulcers and hypertension and coronary troubles.

But not Burr, Benson thought suddenly. His mouth tightened and he sat erectly behind the wheel. Burr never worried about a case and he very seldom lost one, so where was your comforting generality now? But he was not Burr. He was different in many basic ways. Essentially, he suspected, he was a dull, slow-thinking man, whose only asset was a kind of implacable thoroughness, while Burr was quick and volatile, given to sudden and very sure insights, with an actor's sensitivity to the mood of his audience. Burr would never fret about whether Arturo Campeón was lying to him; he would know. And he wouldn't have to depend on Larry Cass to help him make up his mind. To Burr, Arturo Campeón would be a routine professional problem, nothing more.

Beyond the city, the highway was nearly deserted. An occasional car swept by from the east with a clap of thunder and disappeared into the dusty haze behind. A staggered pair of military jets lifted whining from the airbase to the south and blasted the sky overhead. Then they were gone beyond the mountains and the sky slowly closed up the wounds of their passage.

Far ahead, the raw purple mass of the Gritón range was softly, beautifully faded by the lowering sunlight, and the color of the jagged rock was lavender now, with touches of mauve and violet, outlined and sharpened by severe black streaks that were mountain fissures in deep shadow. The strong constant wind recoiled erratically from the mountain barricade, curled back on itself and scoured across the desert, sending a dust devil twisting high and angrily like a miniature tornado into the clear pale sky.

A gust of wind brought dust into the cab of the truck. Tim Cook sneezed explosively. He started to say something, changed his mind and covered his nose with his handkerchief. He turned to stare gloomily out at the bright, sterile landscape.

BENSON trailed a plodding farm wagon through the narrow, littered streets of Kellogg Junction, passing when the ambling team pulled up beside the abandoned freight office that still had the false front and the garishly lettered BANK sign left behind by the movie makers. Benson drove slowly, keeping his eyes on the road, not looking at the town. Probably he should explain to Tim Cook, he thought, but unless Tim made a point of asking, he knew he would not talk about Kellogg Junction.

Originally, when the town had been founded by his grandfather, it had been based on a spurline of the old Rincon-Alamos railroad, in the center of some fifty acres of holding corrals for the steers that half a dozen ranchers shipped out from here. Around and about were cantinas and cribs, crowded and blaring constantly during the shipping season. That was always spree-time for the hands, and a man who couldn't spend six months' pay in two days just wasn't trying.

All that was a long time ago. Now most of the ranchers had sunk deep wells, channeled irrigation ditches and put their land to price-supported cotton. The railroad was abandoned. Now the listless, unemployed men of Kellogg Junction stalked the streets like cut-rate conquerors in big hats and oilcloth boots from Monkey Ward, and posed against the collapsing front of the old hotel, picking their teeth with elegant, wristy precision, openly despising everyone that passed, and consulting in grunts with their peers on the great and shiny dream that was their only link with the present or the future.

The dream had been born when a pair of nameless saddle-tramps had drifted in from the desert and caught sight of all the ready money being flashed around by the cattle buyers. The bums got themselves brave on five-cent redeye and tried to stick up the hotel. One of the buyers had a fit of heroism and got shot in the rump. That shot emptied the cantinas. All the celebrating ranch hands came reeling out to get in on the fun. By the time it was quiet again, the two saddlebums were dead, a dozen riders were shot in various interesting places and everybody felt a lot better. They never did find out the names of those two visiting badmen.

That's all there was to it. But in Kellogg Junction they figured that fight put them right up there with Tombstone and Deadwood. Every year the leading lights of the town would practice up on their fast draws and stage a re-enactment of the famous shoot-out. It takes them two days, and during that time everyone in town has to be wearing three items of old-time Western gear or pay a fine. In Kellogg Junction they are very serious about it. What they are really praying for is television. That was the bright, secret dream. They all remembered the great days when the movie people plastered the buildings with false fronts and fake signs and put up a bogus calaboose and hid the telephone poles and covered the paved road with mud so everything would look authentic. Great days, and don't let anyone tell you different. For a month even the kids in Kellogg Junction had money to jingle in their ragged jeans. And the great days were coming back any day now. Some time soon, a gifted TV producer was bound to rediscover Kellogg Junction, maybe even plan on making a whole series right here in town, and then—hallelujah, brother. We'll all be riding around in white Jaguars and spittin' on ever' damn sonofabitch we see lookin' at us slanchwise.

Now, as he drove through the town, Benson Kellogg felt obscurely uncomfortable, almost ashamed, at what had happened in the place since his grandfather's time. There were flat, sullen eyes watching him from the porch of the dingy hotel, where indolent, slow-chewing men in big hats sat hunched like crows on a fencerail, following every movement. Tim Cook shifted restlessly, sensing the dull hostility in the watchful faces.

"What is this place?"

"An old town touched up by Hollywood," Benson said briefly. "Most of what you see is fake. It's a sort of rural slum.

Called Kellogg Junction."

He pulled the light truck quickly in a long arc to the left, accelerated rapidly and climbed the steep grade to the mountain pass that let onto the range of La Cañada.

Tim Cook drew in a long breath as they cleared the pass and started down the incline to the valley floor. He inhaled again, enjoying the cold clarity of the air. He put away his handkerchief. "Boy, it's like a different world up here."

"It is a different world," Benson said. "You're two thousand feet above the desert. You'll be wearing a coat if you go out at night."

"Suits me fine." Tim settled comfortably in his seat, turning his head slowly from side to side. "Is this your ranch? The whole valley?"

"Yes, plus a stretch on the other side of the pass. How do you like it?"

"I like it," Tim said, "but, by God, this country changes quicker than any place I ever heard of. Drive two miles with sweat on your face, and the next minute it turns to ice. Where do you live? Is that your house?" He pointed at B. Kellogg's old stone-and-adobe fort on the distant outcropping.

"That was the original house," Benson said. "We use it mostly for storage now. My father-in-law camps out in it when he stays here, but it's not very comfortable. Wait till we get around the bend, then you can see the house."

The road curved with the contour of the land, following the easiest line, swinging far out to cross a slight, culverted stream that trickled down from the spring near the old house. Its meandering route took it past a row of windowless adobe storage buildings that smelled sweetly of clover hay, and down the tidy, well-swept little cobbled street that divided lines of one-storey adobe houses with deep-shadowed terraces behind low shrubbery and flowerbeds. The road then gradually widened into a broad avenue, where the gravel was powdered by horses' hoofs and wagon wheels. Benson tipped his head toward Tim.

"This is our showpiece," he said, indicating a huge steel-

and-timber building set well back from the roadway. Double doors twenty feet high stood open at each end of a tanbarked aisle wide enough for a pair of boxcars to enter side by side. "Horse barn," Benson said. "Every modern gadget in the trade. We've just about got it paid for."

Beyond the great shelter, rolling grassland spread out in a wide pocket toward the mountains, separated into paddocks by fences that were low stone walls with a superstructure of white-painted timber. In each meticulous square of the checkerboard was a scattering of horses and colts. Mounted men moved like shadow figures, seen sometimes in miniature at a long distance, sometimes only as shoulders and wide-brimmed hats visible over a line of fences.

Benson slowed and waved at a barefoot boy in a big straw hat who was leading a fat-bellied chestnut mare along the side of the road. The boy swept off his sombrero with a wide bur-lesqued gesture that sent the mare skittering at the end of her lead.

The road circled the outer rim of a quarter-mile training track where a solitary horseman was walking a long-legged and jittery palomino in slow cadence. Benson tapped the horn once in warning and put his hand out the window as he drove past.

Turning south, the road dipped down into a half-mile canyon and then rose sharply to circle the large house that sprawled along the crest of a low knoll well out from the eastern mountain wall. The house was redwood and glass, single-storied, with the round butts of massive beams studding the roof line. Late sunlight struck the big windows and made a shimmer like a child's image of an enchanted castle. Benson pulled up beside a flight of stone steps that led up to a flower-edged flagstone terrace.

"Leave your bag. One of the boys will bring it in." Benson came around the truck and opened the other door. "As they say around here, 'This is your house, señor.' "

"I'll take it," Tim said quickly. He climbed down and stood squarely braced, hands on hips, surveying the wide, low house. Slowly he turned in a circle to take in the view of the long valley, the protective wall of shining mountain, the green fertile stretches of pasture. Not far down the rear slope was a line of a dozen children of assorted sizes, extending across one of the enclosures, each with a stick and a bag. All were waving at them, and Tim took off his hat and waved back.

"What are they up to?"

"Annual cleanup," Benson said. "Every spring the kids on the ranch patrol the pastures to make sure we aren't raising any larkspur or locoweed. The stuff is poison to horses. Those kids will be out every day after school. They make most of their pocket money that way. Up here, Tim. This is Margareta, who runs this house and just about everything else around here. Margareta, this is Señor Cook, who is visiting with us."

The broad-faced tawny-skinned woman who stood waiting for them at the head of the steps was dressed in a dark ruby velveteen dress that almost touched the floor. Over it was a stiffly starched white apron, like an adult version of a pinafore. Her dark lusterless hair was drawn tightly back to a severe knot. She stood solidly planted, hands locked at her waist, regarding them with serene impassivity. Then, very slowly, she smiled. As far as Tim Cook could see, she smiled only with her eyes. Nothing else changed, only the eyes. The skin around them wrinkled with cheerful good humor and a faint touch of mockery. Margarete bowed with an imperious dignity.

"Sí, patrón. Be welcome, Señor Cook. This is your house."

"I wish it was," Tim said quietly. "I wish it was my house."

"We'll have some drinks, Margareta, and lots of dinner. I'm starved. Señor Cook has a bag and I have some things in the truck. Have one of the boys bring them in and then run the truck down to the garage. Come on, Tim. This way."

Margareta plucked Tim's hat from his hand as he passed her on the steps. Benson led him across the flagstone terrace and through open glass doors into a big living room where a just-lighted fire of four-foot piñon logs was beginning to crackle in a high stone fireplace. The room was huge, some forty feet square, with a twenty-foot ceiling at the back stone wall. From there the ceiling sloped to a ten-foot height at the glass-walled western side that faced the sunset. Against one side wall, paneled in pale rowan squares, was a long bar with four high stools and a colorful shelf of bottles. A square-sided, very elderly Bechstein grand piano was set in an alcove, outlined against the sun-struck glass wall. Two matching leather couches faced each other across the hearth. An enormous sand-gray Navajo rug covered much of the tiled floor. Its central design was a primitively simple medicine-lodge pattern usually seen only in sand paintings.

Tim dropped loosely into a deep rawhide chair and whistled in admiration. "Boy, what a place! Did you fix it like this, Ben?"

"No, my father built it," Benson said. "He added this room when he married Burr's mother. She liked to watch the sunset. That's all she ever liked about the ranch. That's her piano over there." Benson turned away to the bar and rattled ice cubes into glasses, not giving Tim a chance to reply. "Bourbon all right with you?"

"Sure, anything," Tim said absently. He took the glass from Benson. "You didn't get along with her, huh? Your stepmother?"

Benson put his glass down untouched. "That's nothing to do with you, Tim," he said bluntly.

"Maybe not," Tim admitted. "It suggests something about you and Burr, though, and that does have something to do with me."

After a silent moment, Benson nodded stiffly. "Maybe I am making too much of it. God knows it's no secret. Don't get the idea you've stumbled onto the skeleton in the closet. I just have an overdeveloped sense of privacy. I didn't get on with my stepmother. I was six years old when my father remarried. My mother had died about a year before, and I still remembered her very clearly. I resented my father's new wife. I suppose that was a completely routine response for any boy. She was a little too young and high-tempered to be bothered with me. It seemed better for me to go away to school, so I never saw her very much after Burr was born."

"Didn't you come home for holidays?"

"Only in the summers. Burr's mother thought the desert country in summer was too hard on her son. They always went to California to get away from the heat."

"So you didn't see much of Burr either while you were growing up."

"Not much. As a matter of fact, I hardly knew him when I came home to stay."

"When was that?"

"A couple of years after the war."

"That's when you split up your old man's property, wasn't it? I heard about that."

"Now don't get any wild notions about that, Tim. My father left everything in equal shares. Burr didn't want the ranch, but he stayed here for a few months until I could raise enough to buy him out. He didn't like the ranch. His mother had brought him up that way. She was always going off somewhere for months at a time. It's no surprise that Burr grew up thinking that La Cañada was a kind of prison. That's about what it was for his mother."

"She didn't fit, huh?"

"She didn't want to. She'd been trained for a social sort of life, and if she had stayed in Virginia where she was born, she'd probably have been fairly happy. Out here she was lost and lonely. This isn't easy country for women, even now. They tend to get old before they should."

"So what became of her? Back home to old Virginny?"

"Yes. Burr sees her occasionally. She was out for a visit a couple of years ago, but she didn't come out to the ranch. It doesn't mean anything to her."

"Doesn't mean much to Burr either, I gather."

"It's just as well for you it doesn't," Benson said tightly. "A working rancher wouldn't have time to play with politics."

"Don't get sore, Ben. I have to ask questions if I'm going to find out anything. I want to get the background straight in my mind. What I still don't understand is how come you two were both named B. Kellogg. What about that?"

"Oh hell, Tim, figure it out for yourself. It should be obvious. A young second wife produces a boy baby and she wants to make sure the first son doesn't have any edge over her baby. Burr's mother wanted him to have the important name in our family, and that is B. Kellogg. The old boy always wrote it that way, you know. His name was Benson Kellogg but he never used it. There was no reason why Burr shouldn't have been given the name. In fact, there's no legal reason why he couldn't have been named Benson. His mother was overprotective, I suppose, and a little bit silly. But that's no reflection on Burr. Now let's drop it, shall we? It's not a subject I enjoy talking about."

"Okay," Tim said readily when he saw that Benson's patience was wearing thin. "I wouldn't want you to kick me out before I got a good look at your place. How about taking me on a tour?"

"Of course," Benson said. "I'll call one of the hands. I have some work to do, so if you don't mind, I won't——"

Benson broke off as a shrill two-note whistle sounded from the terrace outside the open glass doors. His rigid posture seemed to relax abruptly. He looked over his shoulder.

"Come in, Fitz," he called.

The man was visible at first only as a silhouette against the sky. He was very tall, unnaturally thin, almost emaciated with long skinny legs in frayed-cuff jodhpurs. His narrow high-held shoulders emphasized his height.

"Hullo, Benson," the man said in a quick, light and very English voice. "Saw you drive in. Just thought I'd see if—oh, sorry. Didn't realize you had guests. Very sorry to barge in. Excuse me, won't you?" He crossed to Tim and held out his hand. "I'm FitzAllen, this rascally fellow's father-in-law. You'll be one of Benson's riding friends, I take it? Come to the right place, I must say."

"Timothy Cook," Tim said, liking the man on sight. "I'm no rider, but I've come to the right place, all right. I was just asking Ben to take me on a tour."

"First visit, is it? You've a treat in store. Never forget my first look at the place. Three years ago, it was. I go away from time to time, but I always come back to see if it's as unbelievable as I remembered it being. Are you going to offer me any whisky, Benson?"

"Coming up," Benson said, busy at the bar.

FitzAllen said, "Cheers." He put his glass down empty and drew an immense silk handkerchief from the sleeve of his shabby tweed hacking coat. He scrubbed it vigorously over his deeply lined and bony face, then wadded it to brush over his short-cut white hair. "Been a filthy hot day, hasn't it? Clemente and I were giving the yearlings a taste of the saddle, but he buggered off to town after lunch. Too much for the old boy, I suppose."

"That'll be the day," Benson said, pleasantly scornful. "Clemente could run you and me into the ground and still have enough gimp left to go dancing all night." He made a second round of drinks and distributed them. "Fitz, why don't you take Tim on a tour? I have to go through some stuff from the office."

"Be delighted," FitzAllen said. "Shouldn't be surprised if I knew the place better than you, at that."

"Nor would I," Benson said soberly. "You spend more time here than I do. Maybe I can change that in a year or two."

"Let's hope," FitzAllen said briskly. "Well, come along, Timothy Cook." He surveyed Tim's square tightly held stance, his hard light-boned frame, and grinned at him. "Built just like Gordon Richards, ain't he? Don't tell me you're no rider, young fellow. This way for the roundabouts. Have your penny ready, please. Dinner at the usual, Benson?"

"Yes. Bring Tim back in time for a drink."

He winked at Tim and followed them out to the flagged terrace and stood there until the long-legged energetic Fitz-Allen had led Tim around to a dusty white-painted jeep. They made an odd but well-matched team, he thought suddenly— both nervously quick and impatient. Fitz was nearly seventy and Tim wouldn't be forty yet, but they might be brothers. Benson went back into the big quiet room.

He sat at the bar with his unfinished drink, half turned to

look out at the spectacular, familiar sunset that was beginning to streak the sky with the flamboyant burst of color that comes only over the desert country. From the corner of his eye he could see the square, once-ominous bulk of the old piano, and he remembered sitting in this room as a boy, stiffly proper, with a glass of flat ginger ale clamped moistly in both hands, watching, sullen and warped with a boy's bitterness, as his father leaned, blindly adoring, over the piano, turning pages of music while his new and darkly fragile wife tinkled out the syrupy ballads they both liked so well. They were unmindful of Benson and more than once he had stayed hunched in the too-big chair, staring at the sunset beyond them until the vast newly built room had grown somber and frightening with darkness.

That had been a bad time for him. He couldn't understand what was happening or why. He learned then how to live behind a protective barrier that formed like scar tissue over a wound. He learned so well that later bad times were never as hurtful or damaging as they might have been. And possibly, he suspected, the good times had never been as good as they might have been.

Benson went out of the room quickly, going down a narrow corridor that connected with the original house. This was a simpler structure, built of native stone with smaller windows and lower ceilings, large and comfortable enough for any family but with no rooms as impressive as the new living room his father had built later. Benson went into his study and turned on the light.

Spread across his father's old black walnut desk were the working records of La Cañada—the stud books, the veterinary reports, ledgers and account books. On top of it all was Benson's briefcase and the wrapped package that carried the label of B. Kellogg and Sampson.

Benson sat behind the desk, cut the string of the package and peeled back the paper. Inside were three heavy books and a bound stack of trial transcripts. These were the stenographic reports of two felony trials conducted by Frank Sayer as prosecutor for the county of Rincon. Benson riffled a few pages.

Reading them should give him a good line on Frank's style when he was pleading before a jury. He put them aside for the moment and opened his briefcase. He took out the yellow pad whose legal-size pages were cobwebbed with his penciled notes.

He leaned back and surveyed the collection. He would work his way methodically and conscientiously through it all, and when he was finished, he might know half as much as Burr knew right now. He snorted at himself and swung both legs up on a corner of the desk. He propped the pad on his knees. Arturo Campeón, he thought, looking at the top page. I'd give a lot to know if that boy was telling me the truth today. I hope Larry Cass can find out for me. And I hope to God I'm smart enough to use what he tells me to save that kid's neck.

But don't fool yourself, Counselor. Even if Turo Campeón did tell you the truth, you still haven't got a sound legal defense to offer the court. Just stop worrying about the boy and get down to your work.

Benson tilted the desk lamp so its light was directed at his pad of scribbled notes.

FITZ was in fine talkative form at the dinner table. He kept Tim skeptically fascinated with a long and fraudulent history of La Cañada, making his fictitious points with a grapeshot rattle of enthusiasm and noisy nonsense. He was flushed and excited from a busy day in the open and the drinks before dinner and the wine with dinner. And he was volubly quick, as always, enjoying the sound of his own voice and the play of his imagination. He and Tim were having a fine time, talking in a bogus Western-movie language they had just invented.

Except when he had to get up to carve the roast at the sideboard or reach out to pass a wine bottle, Benson was free to sit quietly, inwardly focused, reviewing in his mind the case he would have to present for Arturo Campeón. He was beginning to see the problem more clearly now. It was taking shape from a mass of chaotic impressions, and the shape was depressingly ugly. The simple truth was that the boy had committed murder, and Benson did not know of any justification that would be acceptable in court. Recognizing that, Benson dismissed any hope of proving him innocent. He would have to concentrate on destroying Frank Sayer's case, and with that decision, Benson sensed a faint glimmer of light for the first time.

". . . isn't that so, Benson?"

"I'm sorry, Fitz. I was woolgathering. Isn't what so?"

"Been trying to tell young Timothy that La Cañada makes its profit from horses, not cattle. He won't have it. Keeps asking about the bloody cattle."

"It's a ranch, ain't it?" Tim demanded, half seriously. "In the golden goddam West, ain't it? So where's the cow critters, podner?"

"Fitz is right, Tim. We found out some years ago that we could make a lot more money out of the kind of horses we raise. La Cañada is a small ranch for this part of the country. There's no way to expand it, so we have to make every acre count. We do run some beef, though. Just what we need for ourselves. About fifty head at the moment."

"So why horses, then? Horse eats as much as a cow, doesn't he?"

"More, when he's working hard. My big stud gets through eighteen pounds of oats a day, plus whatever hay he wants. But it's not the feed that counts, it's the profit. Beef cattle are profitable, but a well-trained young parade horse will bring in ten times as much for the same investment in time and effort. That's why La Cañada is a horse ranch now. To keep operating, we need more income than we could get from cattle."

"What's a parade horse? Are you talking about those palominos? I never saw prettier horses, but what makes them special? What are they, show horses?"

"Not exactly. A show horse is highly trained in either three or five gaits, and he needs a rider just as highly trained if he's going to look good in the ring. A parade horse is a big handsome horse trained to make a poor rider look great. There is always a shortage of parade horses, and they fetch a good price."

"Are they always palominos, these parade horses?"

"It's not required," Benson said. "Any color is good on a good horse. Palominos are spectacular, though, and most people prefer them, so we concentrate on them."

"How can you, though?" Tim demanded, frowning at him. "I thought they weren't a breed? How do you know what you're going to wind up with, if they don't breed true?"

"Well, you couldn't," Benson said mildly, "not if you bred palomino to palomino. In that case half your colts would be something other than palomino. The way to be sure of getting a palomino every time is to breed a chestnut mare to an albino stud. And not just any albino, either. You have to get the type called Albino-A that has the right genetic pattern."

"My Christ," Tim groaned.

"Old Clemente is the fellow you want to talk to, Tim," Fitz said through a mouthful of beef. "He's the foreman here. He and Benson have some trade secrets. All very hush-hush. That's why you never see a La Cañada colt go unsold."

"That right, Ben? You got a gimmick?"

"Hell, no," Benson said flatly. "That's a lot of bunk. Clemente is full of superstitions and he likes to shoot the bull when he finds a gullible sucker like Fitz. What we raise here are well-bred big-boned colts, healthy and well-mannered. The only trick we have is that we never let them trot."

"I guess that means something, but I'm damned if I know what. Are you going to tell me?"

"If you're interested, Tim," Benson said politely. "What I mean is that every horse has a natural gait in between a walk and a canter. Usually that intermediate gait is either a trot or a pace. Both are comfortable for the horse, but they are not easy for a rider. A pacing horse is especially rough to ride. Once in a blue moon you will find a horse whose natural intermediate gait is a slow rack, what the cowboys call a single-foot. It's smooth and rhythmic and anyone can sit a racking horse easily without any experience as a rider. So we train all our horses to rack. By the time they're ready to be shown, they have pretty well forgotten they ever knew how to trot or pace. They walk, they rack slow and fast, and they do a slow canter. That's all. And anybody sitting on one of them looks like the finest rider alive."

"You know, I reckon I might try one of those babies myself, podner. I never rode a horse in my life, but maybe I could ride one of yours."

"Be glad to teach you properly, young fellow," Fitz offered. "Best sport in the world when you know how. Wouldn't you agree, Benson?"

Benson had his head cocked toward the half open window. "Hear that? Listen to the wind."

"Hear what?" Tim asked. "It's been whistling like that since sundown, podner."

"Not like that. It's just veered south. Means it will rain tonight. By morning, it should be spring, Tim. Not this unseasonable heat, but the real thing. That's all we needed. A light rain tonight, and come morning you'll see the desert bloom. Ask Fitz. He comes back here every year just to see it."

"Quite right. Most extraordinary sight. There's the desert like a bleached bone, not a damn thing above ground but some scruffy cactus and dried bush. Then a little rain falls in the spring, and I tell you, it's perfectly amazing. There's a scattering of little wind flowers all over the bare sand, and the bushes come green and full of bloom, and the cactuses swell up and sprout a hellish big bunch of flowers, and all at once there are birds and small animals all over the place. It never lasts very long, a few weeks at most, and then it all seems to disappear. Very disturbing experience, I promise you."

Margareta came in the door on silent feet, followed by two pigtailed, large-eyed girls with trays under their arms. "It is the telephone, patrón," she said. "The Señor Doctor Cass wishes to speak."

Benson kicked his chair back. "Why don't you two have

coffee in the big room? This may take some time. Fitz, get Tim some brandy."

He left quickly and went down the hall to his study. The telephone was propped on the blotter of his desk. Benson drew a long yellow notepad close toward his hand, found a pencil and picked up the receiver. "Larry? What did you find out?"

"I saw your boy, Ben. I can see why you were worried about him. You should have told me."

"Told you what?"

"That is the handsomest kid I ever saw. He's damn close to being pretty. You'd expect Hollywood to be after him."

"So?"

"So if I was queer, I might go for him myself. He's just what the flits dream about. He looks like——"

"To hell with what he looks like," Benson said roughly. "I know what he looks like. I want to know what he is. What's the answer? Is he, or isn't he?"

Dr. Cass sighed. "It's not that easy, Ben. I put in an hour and a half with him, gave him a sampling of Rorschach and a little Machover and then just talked to him. He comes through pretty well. Good sense of reality, impulse control is okay. I'd like to give him a Wexler-Bellevue. I think he'd assay out with a pretty good IQ."

"Skip the professional jargon, Larry. I don't know what you're talking about. And I don't honestly give a damn if he's a genius or the stupidest kid in town. What did you——"

"Just listen, Ben. I'm looking at my notes right now and I'll give it to you the way it comes. He was belligerent at first and it took a little time to get him talking openly. I nailed him in a few lies, the usual stuff a kid will lie about. Erotic dreams, masturbation, sexual fantasies, all that. But on balance he was fairly honest, I'd say."

"Get to the point. Is he or isn't he? If you had to lay money, which would you pick?"

"I'd say no," Dr. Cass answered after a moment's delay. "But I think I'd want odds. That boy has led a rough life the past few years. He told me enough so I'm sure of that. He has associated with male prostitutes and he knows the classic routine of blackmailing the rich homosexuals. I don't think he is homosexual, but there is something fishy about his account of that fight on Lookout Point. Did you sense that too, Ben?"

"That's one of the reasons I wanted you to see him."

"Yes. He's leaving something out, I suspect. I won't go so far as to say he's lying, though. It occurred to me that he might have drawn a blank during the fight. He was cracked on the head and he just might have been knocked out."

"But wouldn't he know if he'd been unconscious?"

"Not necessarily. Temporary amnesia isn't rare after a bang on the head. I can't say more definitely than that, Ben. I suspect he isn't telling the complete story and I've been trying to account for it. Otherwise we'll have to assume that he is deliberately lying."

"You aren't giving me much to go on," Benson complained. "You're just tossing it back in my lap."

"You've got a complex problem, Ben. I've been wondering if it mightn't be easier to approach it from the other direction."

"What have you got in mind?"

"The victim," Dr. Cass said.

"Yes, I thought of that, Larry. But Duquesne has no record with the Los Angeles police, and if he was an active homosexual, he couldn't have been unknown to the police. Frank Sayer is expecting a detailed report from Los Angeles tomorrow. Maybe the answer will be in that. If not, I'll have to decide what to do about him."

"The answer lies with Duquesne, Ben," Dr. Cass insisted. "When you know what kind of man the dead man was, you'll know if the boy's story is credible. That's the simplest approach. But maybe there is another one just as simple."

"Have you got an idea?"

"A small idea. Let's just suppose your boy was had. He was knocked out when his head hit the dashboard, and while he was out, Duquesne raped him. The boy wakes up afterward, or even during, fights the guy off and winds up killing him. It could have happened that way and the boy could have blanked it out. If I had time I could find out, but I can't spare time for a deep probe. Maybe I could find out just by looking."

"Looking where?"

Dr. Cass coughed. "Up his rectum. This all happened Saturday night, if it did happen. It's now Tuesday night and we are talking about highly regenerative tissue. But if the boy was had, I should be able to tell. Want me to look?"

"I—I don't know, Larry," Benson said, instinctively cautious. "Let me think about it for a moment. Before we go into that, what about the boy's history? Would you say he might have a record of abnormal tendencies?"

"I said I'm not sure. I'm not even sure what an abnormal tendency is. I don't think he is homosexual, but I'm not going to take an oath on it."

"At least you're sure he's not one of the biological homosexuals, then?"

Dr. Cass snorted lightly. "There ain't no such animal. The evidence on that point is pretty clear."

"I read somewhere that——"

"You can read a lot of nonsense anywhere," Dr. Cass said firmly. "But forget it, Ben. There is only one gene to differentiate between the male and female, but the difference of that one gene is enormous and conclusive. Homosexuality is a pathological condition. It ain't physical. Is that clear, Counselor?"

"Don't get testy, boy. I'm sorry you have to spell these things out but I'm ignorant. Maybe you'd better send me a good textbook. Now, even if my boy is not homosexual, is it likely that he might have had some homosexual experience in the past, something he would conceal from me?"

"It's possible. You're getting into a very tricky area, Ben. Homosexuals can be made. It's a pathological state, and pathological states can be induced by pathological acts and circumstances. The best definition of a homosexual is the obvious one: a person who habitually engages in homosexual acts. But just as a matter of practical observation, we know there are boys who hire themselves out to homosexuals without having or developing any interest whatever. They are usually amoral and moronic, damn close to being animals. Your boy doesn't fit that pattern."

"So if I should find out that he has ever hired out to a pervert, I'd better assume he is actually a homosexual?"

"That's the wisest course, Ben. Anything else you would have to prove and I don't think you could, unless you had a jury made up of psychiatrists. Your boy might be a homosexual. It's an outside possibility. If he is, he's unusually well disguised. His instinctive response to the whole range is revulsion. He has an excessive response, I'd say, and I was dubious until I heard about his background."

"I don't follow that, Larry. Take it more slowly. You say the boy was revolted by the notion of homosexuality and that his response made you suspicious. How does that make sense?"

"He was excessively revolted, Ben. A well-oriented man is revolted by homosexuality, but his revulsion is usually little more than mild disgust. Sometimes, if he is sensitive to the social and moral status of the homosexual, it may even be a kind of pity. But when you find a man who goes all white and shaky and wants to kill a homosexual, or castrate him, then you should get suspicious. The chances are that you're dealing with a latent homosexual who is using up all his emotional reserves in an attempt to pose as a normal male. Clear?"

"I see your point. The guy who protests too much is a suspicious character. Okay. I might argue that on the basis of logic, but let it go. What about the boy's background removed your suspicion?"

"He's a Mexican," Dr. Cass said rather stiffly. "He speaks such good English that I didn't think of that until he told me. He was born in Mexico and he lives there most of his life. And his grandfather was a Dorado. You know what that means in Chihuahua?"

"Sure. Muy duro, to put it mildly."

"Right. And his father, he feels, is something of a jerk.

Nice enough, very good to the family, but not quite good enough as a man. Does all that suggest something to you, Ben?"

"I was just thinking about it, Larry. The myth of 'machismo,' eh?"

"And not such a myth as you seem to think. 'Macho' means manhood, among other things, and to a Mexican it can be the most important element of human character. It represents his sense of pride, of self-respect, of courage, even of honor. Your boy has an enlarged view of his macho, as you might expect. Having it, his excessive revulsion to the idea of homosexuality is understandable. A lesser response, as a matter of fact, might be suspicious, coming from a boy with that emotional background. Using a knife to fight off Duquesne is logical, too, in that context, for a knife to such a boy is merely the extension of his manhood. In knifing Duquesne, he would be justifying his own idea of himself, living up to his grandfather's example, excusing his father's incapacity. Yes, macho could explain the boy's response, Ben."

"I follow. It does fit, doesn't it? I don't think I'd care to explain it to a jury, though. Would you think his exaggerated sense of macho would also tend to keep him from homosexual contacts?"

"Don't lean too much on that one, Ben. The focus on macho doesn't mean that Mexicans are less inclined toward homosexuality than any other people. It merely explains why they are as a group more violently contemptuous of homosexuals than most. Just a minute." Dr. Cass covered the phone briefly. "Sorry. Time for dinner, I'm told. Well, that's it, Ben. What about that physical examination? Want me to set it up?"

Benson took time to consider before he answered. "No, I think not, Larry."

"Why not? You want to know, don't you?"

"I'd like to know, but it's not a vital point. What I'm really concerned about is whether the boy has been telling me the truth as he knows it. If, as you were speculating, he was had by Duquesne, he obviously doesn't know or remember, so he wasn't lying to me about that. I have to think of the boy himself, Larry. This trial is going to be an ordeal for him. I can't let him go into that courtroom so damaged in his own estimate of himself that he can't put up a vigorous, sustained defense. Then there is another reason."

"I'm listening. What other reason?"

"You would have to examine him at the County Hospital, and there is no way in the world to keep Frank Sayer from finding out what's going on. He might even be able to find out the results, but that's not as important as the fact that he would know I had an examination made. He could guess why and I don't want him guessing. I'm not sure that what I have in mind is the best defense to offer in court, but until I decide, I don't want Frank to know I'm interested in homosexual possibilities. I'll want to spring it as a surprise."

"We-ell," Dr. Cass said dubiously. "I guess you know your own business, Ben. I have to go now. Let me know how it turns out."

"Just a minute more, Larry. I don't know if I'll want to go into much detail about the homosexual side of this case, but if I do, will you come and help me explain to the jury?"

"No! I told you before, Ben. I can't spare the time."

"I won't ask you unless it's important. This is new ground for me. I'm not sure I understand it well enough to——"

"I can't do it, Ben. I didn't make the kind of examination that would justify formal testimony. And I haven't got the time. I tell you what, Ben. I've got some useful books on the subject. I'll send you a good basic text. At least you'll have the terminology. But leave me out of it."

"Okay, Larry. I won't push you. Be sure to send the book, will you? Many thanks. I'll have one of the hands drop off that venison at your house. We've got a ten-pound fillet in the freezer. Will that do?"

"Sold. Keep in touch, Ben. Good night."

Dr. Cass hung up. Benson sat with the receiver in his hand for a long quiet moment, thinking of a dozen questions he could have asked. Preparation for Turo Campeón's trial was giving him more trouble than it should. He had never been involved even casually with the homosexual fringe, and to him it was a dim and incomprehensible area of experience. But to Larry Cass it was merely another of the emotional aberrations he dealt with as capably as a good surgeon would deal with an inflamed appendix. It was going to be hard to manage without him when it came time to put the boy's case before the jury.

Benson swung his chair around to face the stack of books on a corner of his desk. He pushed the first two aside and picked up the third. The faded gold letters along the spine, hardly legible in the artificial light, identified it as a handbook of criminal law.

He opened the thick volume to the index and traced his finger down the listing of "admissibility." There were three pages of references. Benson sighed. It was going to be a long job. He sat up straight and reached for a pencil.

THE STRONG MORNING SUN lifted clear of the barricade made by the Rincon National Bank Building and struck the turned-back leaf of the window outside Benson's office, breaking a glitter of reflections across his desk. For a while he worked on, with one hand across his eyes to bar the light. Then he rose irritably, kicked back his chair and went to the window. He wound the panel in flush with the wall and reluctantly turned on the air conditioning. Another searingly hot day was beginning, and it would be far more uncomfortable than yesterday because last night's brief rainfall had brought a steep rise in humidity. In the arid world of the high desert, a mere ten per cent humidity can make for a stifling day. Benson's shirt was sticky against his back.

His secretary made a small smothered sound when she came in the door. "Oh, Mr. Kellogg. I didn't expect you so soon." She made a flustered gesture. "Will you be going to court this morning?"

"Yes, I'm leaving right away," Benson said. He slid a sheaf of notes inside his briefcase. "Now, what else do I need?

My formal appearance. What about that, Mary?"

"I sent one of the boys down with it yesterday, Mr. Kellogg. It's been filed. The receipt is in your center drawer."

Benson pulled out the drawer, picked up the flimsy county receipt form and put it in his pocket. "Then I'm all set." The red light on his phone came on with a flickering glare. Benson took up the receiver.

"It is Señor Cook, patrón," Margareta's placid voice told him. "He has injured himself this morning. Already Señor Doctor Ricardo has come to attend."

"Good God. What happened?"

"He stepped from the terraza, patrón. Would you wish to speak with him? He has asked——"

"Yes, yes," Benson said hastily. "Take the phone to him, please, Margareta."

Benson lit a cigarette during the time he waited. He held the phone pinched between his shoulder and neck and used both hands to strap his briefcase.

"Hi, Ben. Hear what happened to me?" Tim Cook's voice was slow and slightly fuzzy, as if he had something in his mouth.

"Margareta said you fell off the terrace. What happened, Tim?"

"Hell, I didn't fall. It wasn't even that sensible. I was walking out there with a cup of coffee in my hand, looking up at the mountains. I just walked off the edge. Like that. I didn't even break your cup."

"Were you hurt badly?"

"Your doctor thinks maybe I broke a bone in my foot. All I know is that my knee is about the size of a football. I won't be moving around for a while, it looks like."

"I'm glad it wasn't more serious, Tim. How are you feeling?"

"I feel just like I fell off a cliff. I'm okay. Thing is, I have to keep still for a while. I've been thinking, Ben. I don't want to put you out, but . . ."

"Don't worry about it. We've got plenty of room. You know that. Glad to have your company."

"I'll have to do a lot of telephoning. I'm going to be a real bother around here. I was thinking maybe we could fix up some kind of arrangement to——"

"You're a guest, Tim. Forget it. Just tell Margareta if you need anything. There'll be somebody coming into town today. Did you get my note?"

"Yeah, thanks. What's this box of papers you left in my room?"

"It's a sort of daybook that old B. kept off and on. It doesn't have much continuity and it isn't very detailed, but it gives you an idea of what it was like to live out here in the early days. Be careful with it, Tim. I've been meaning to get it copied but I haven't gotten around to it yet."

"Okay. Thanks, Ben. I'd like to look at it. I'm going to have plenty of time for reading for the next week."

"Well, take it easy, Tim. Call me if you need anything. I'll see you this afternoon."

Benson hung up, shaking his head. Tim Cook was welcome to stay at La Cañada as long as he liked, but he was going to be a miserably unhappy house guest, Benson suspected. The man simply wasn't geared for a sedentary life. Maybe he should get the ranch kids to hitch up that old pony cart so Tim could move around by himself.

"Will you be coming back after court, Mr. Kellogg?"

"Yes, but I don't want you making any appointments for me." Benson clamped his briefcase under his arm and went toward the door. "You might tell Miss Harkins I'll want her to help me outline my trial brief this afternoon."

"You had some calls yesterday, Mr. Kellogg," Mary said quickly before he could leave. "The Mexican consul wants to talk to you. And Mr. Lanning Lathrop called."

"Tell the consul he can come in any time. Or I'll call him back, whichever he prefers. What did old Lathrop want? Another will?"

"I think so. He said something about his daughter."

"Put him off," Benson said. "He just wants to cut her out of his will again. Or put her back in. I forget where she stands at the moment. He changes his mind every year or so."

"But I don't think I can——"

"All right. Tell him I'll call him when I get back. But don't make an appointment for him. I want to keep my time free unless there's a real emergency. I've got a lot of studying ahead of me."

THE UNIFORMED GUARD swung open one wing of the double door to the courtroom and touched his cap in a lazy half salute.

"Thanks, Eddie," Benson said. "How's the leg?"

"Who cares?" The guard shrugged and pursed his mouth as if to spit. "I can't ride with her no more, so I just don't pay her no mind. You're lookin' good, Ben."

"You've got me confused with someone else." Benson went down the long center aisle toward the mahogany railing. There were only a few spectators, all sitting along the first row of seats, as close to the working area as they could get.

Four old-fashioned evaporation coolers were making a low humming sound. Lank strips of faded ribbon tied to their grilles fluttered half-heartedly to show they were functioning, but the long high-ceilinged courtroom was already oppressive with the growing heat. The bailiff stood on tiptoe at the farthest window, fiddling with the blind cords, trying to find an adjustment of the slats that would cut off a bar of sunlight that lay across the court reporter's desk.

A dozen lawyers stood about restlessly inside the railing, all of them hoping to buttonhole Frank Sayer for a last-minute conference. Any moment now the court would be gaveled to attention, the pending criminal cases would be called and listed for trial. If you were a lawyer thinking of making a deal with the County Attorney, this was the last chance you were likely to get.

Benson came in through the gate. He sat in a chair at the table usually assigned to defense counsel. Several copies of the court calendar were scattered across the table. Benson turned one to face him. Arturo Campeón's was the fifteenth name on the list. Three others followed his. It looked like a long morning ahead.

Judge Groat entered silently from his chambers, narrow-shouldered and stern in his black robe. He climbed the short flight to his high-backed chair and stood there stiffly until the bailiff sensed his presence. The judge remained standing while the bailiff scuttled awkwardly across to his gavel and banged it hastily.

"All rise, all rise," he called in a breathless mumble. "Superior Court for the County of Rincon is now in session. Honorable Bernard B. Groat presiding."

Judge Groat bowed to the lawyers. "Welcome back, gentlemen. Take your seats, please." He swung around in his chair and stood again to adjust his robe. "Mr. Sayer, are you ready? Call the criminal calendar, if you please." He opened the leather folder on his desk and read the first name. "People against Loyal Lee Hanna. Housebreaking."

The April term had begun.

Frank Sayer took the first file from his deputy, drew in a slow breath and identified himself as the County Attorney in and for the County of Rincon who was acting for and in behalf of the People of the State in advising that honorable court of Loyal Lee Hanna's grave offense against the peace and dignity of the People of the State. His words were only occasionally audible. None of the lawyers seemed to be paying attention, although one of them stepped forward at the proper time to make the proper response. Loyal Lee Hanna was an unshaven string-bean in levis and a skin-tight yellow rodeo shirt with two-pointed pockets and snaps instead of buttons. Loyal Lee, what a name, Benson thought. Get two rabid never-say-die Confederates on the jury and you could get him off even if he shot the Governor. Loyal Lee stood slouched with his big hands in his hip pockets and grunted when his lawyer told him to plead not guilty. His case was scheduled for trial, and he shuffled off between two deputies toward the jury conference room where the prisoners were being held. That was all there was to it, very little worth watching, certainly no apparent element of drama, but Benson could feel one of the spectators breathing on the back of his neck. The man was bent forward over the rail, intent as an aficionado at the barrera. Benson shifted his chair to one side and tried to wait patiently for his turn.

The proceedings were desultory, scrupulously correct, but carried forward in a quiet, almost lackadaisical routine that could be interesting only to someone directly involved. Benson repressed a yawn. He was thinking of the stories his father used to tell about the early Territorial courts, when every trial session was high, stark drama. In those days a handful of lawyers rode the circuit and they were known and awaited far more as actors in familiar roles than as lawyers. Each could be identified by costume, stance, gesture, emotional attitude and by the degree of fervent conviction he could develop. The anticipated characterizations were never varied. Old B. Kellogg, in frockcoat and fine Spanish boots, was the wild, untamable bull whose voice bellowed in habitual outrage. Another who had once been noted as a gunfighter, wore a thonged holster under his white linen coat, empty when court was in session but never at any other time. He spoke with the slow, bewildered voice of a man appalled by man's inhumanity and he won more cases than his legal capacity justified. The judges were chosen from among themselves and they knew what their audiences expected of them. Ranchers and farmers and townspeople from fifty miles around attended every court, standing usually, rapt and critically admiring, in the back of a saloon, a schoolhouse, a church, a warehouse, nudging each other when the florid rhetoric reached a fervid peak, shaking their heads pityingly when an involved process of logic missed the head of the nail. Among such demanding judges, an indecisive mumbling lawyer was a lawyer without clients. He soon ceased to be a lawyer at all.

It was all different now. Probably better, Benson was willing to admit, but damn dull most of the time. He ticked off each case as Judge Groat droned through the calendar. Several were disposed of promptly by guilty pleas, the rest were remanded for trial. The first date assigned was Monday week, which meant that Frank Sayer was reserving a full week for Arturo Campeón's trial, beginning next Monday. That was a long time by local standards, especially in view of Frank Sayer's eagerness to get through it quickly.

Benson was half dozing when he heard Judge Groat say, "People against Arturo Campeón. The charge is murder."

Benson scrambled to his feet, red-faced, kicking his brief-case across the floor toward the bench. Frank Sayer retrieved it and handed it back with a sly grin.

"Your boy will be here in a minute, Ben," he said. "I had him called out of turn because the hospital people don't want their ambulance tied up for long. Don't mind, do you?"

"No, of course not, Frank. I just wasn't expecting it."

A fat-jowled sheriff's deputy opened the door from the hallway and held it back while another deputy pushed a wheel chair through the opening. Arturo Campeón sat in it, hunched sideways to protect the cast over his arm and shoulder. He was wearing a loose hospital gown that covered the cast, a sheet wrapped around his legs. He had his head against the wicker backrest, his eyes closed. He was pale and tight-faced.

"Morning, Turo," Benson said, coming forward to meet him. "Are you feeling all right?"

"I'm okay," the boy said in a tight, belligerent voice. "Just sick of these monkeys, is all."

The deputy behind him reddened angrily. One hand lifted, balled into a fist. He made a low growling sound.

"Don't try it," Benson said in a savage whisper. "Just look cross-eyed at that boy and I'll pull that badge off your shirt and make you eat it. You hear me?" He moved in one long stride, putting his shoulder roughly against the deputy, pushing him back from the wheel chair.

"My God, Ben, slow down," Frank Sayer said. "What's the trouble?"

"Ask your fat-assed deputy," Benson said tightly. "He likes to talk." He rolled the wheel chair through the gate and eased it toward the judge's bench.

« *163* »

"For the defense?" Judge Groat asked dryly.

"Benson Kellogg, Your Honor."

The judge nodded and made a notation on his calendar. "Well, Mr. Prosecutor," he said. "Please proceed."

"Your Honor," Benson said. "The defense will waive the reading of the information. We stand mute."

The judge smiled briefly. "Your elocution is not admired this morning, Mr. Sayer. No one wants to hear you. Very well, enter a plea of not guilty. Is the defense ready for trial, Mr. Kellogg?"

Benson hesitated. "May I have a moment, Your Honor?"

"For what purpose?" Judge Groat eyed him suspiciously.

"I wish to consult with the County Attorney."

"Very well."

Benson touched Turo's shoulder. The boy was sitting erectly rigid, his mouth thinned with tension. He was still angry because the deputies had given him a rough time on the trip from the hospital. And he responded well when he was angry, Benson noted. That was worth knowing. In anger the boy was less conscious of himself; he focused on what was happening around him and less on himself. Before he let Turo take the stand, Benson thought, he would have to make sure he was like this, cold and controlled and well able to stand up for himself.

Benson crossed to Frank Sayer at his station beside the court reporter's desk. "I haven't seen your list of witnesses yet, Frank. You were going to send me a copy."

"Oh hell," Sayer muttered softly. He ran a hand over his smooth hair and made a distracted gesture. "Sorry, Ben. We've been swamped the last couple of days. Here you are." He gave Benson a copy of his list. "There aren't any surprises, Ben. Just the official witnesses you would expect. The first two are the boys who found the body."

Benson scanned the names quickly. "It's okay, Frank. I'll want to talk to some of them. Today, if possible."

"Come have lunch in my office at noon, Ben. We can set up a schedule then. Will that be all right?"

"Fine. Thanks." Benson turned to face the bench again. "The defense is ready, Your Honor."

"Mr. Sayer?" the judge inquired.

"The People are ready, Your Honor."

"Very well, gentlemen. We will schedule People against Arturo Campeón for the first jury day. Next Monday at nine A.M. Call the next case, Mr. Prosecutor."

Benson wheeled Turo's wheel chair to the gate, pushed it back and went up the aisle toward the door.

"Is that all there is to it?" the boy asked.

"That was just the beginning. You've made your appearance and from now on you belong to the court. We go to trial on Monday." Benson motioned for the guard to open the door. As they went through, the two deputies ranged themselves alongside.

"Where is the ambulance?" Benson asked.

"Right out front."

"All right. You fellows go ahead. I want to have a private talk with my client."

"Why, we couldn't do that, Mr. Kellogg," one deputy protested. "This boy here is a county prisoner. We can't just go off and let him——"

"He won't run away," Benson said. "How in hell could he? I'll be responsible. Now just give us a little room. You can trail along behind if you want to."

The deputies looked at each other uncertainly, then shrugged and dropped behind as Benson pushed the wheel chair toward the courthouse entrance.

"Did those deputies ride you very hard, Turo?" Benson turned the wheel chair just inside the door and braced himself in a window embrasure.

"Nothing I couldn't handle," the boy said. He looked at Benson and cocked his thumb out defiantly.

"You don't have to handle anything at all. Just be sure you don't let them egg you into hitting them. If they get rough, let me know and I'll burn their tails for them. Tell them I said it wouldn't be fair for you to hit one of them. How did you get on with Dr. Cass last night?"

The boy made a quick, expressive gesture. Contempt. "We got on swell," he said with a twisted mouth. "He asked me was I fruit, I told him to take a flying fuck at the moon. We got on real fine. Dandy."

"I told you once before about curling that lip at me," Benson said softly.

The boy flushed. "What the hell do you expect, sending that prick around to——"

"To see if you were telling me the truth," Benson said, to finish the sentence.

"I didn't lie to you." The boy's face was white and strained. His lips pulled back hard against his teeth. "Damn you, I didn't——"

"Good," Benson said. I wish I could be sure, he thought. But I can't let the boy know I'm not sure. I can't take the chance of tearing down his confidence. "I didn't think you lied to me," he said. "But I wanted to be sure. Dr. Cass thinks your story was pretty straight."

"Screw Dr. Cass," the boy said.

Benson straightened and took out his cigarettes. He lit one and blew a fat cloud over the boy's head. "I was about to ask you if you felt jittery about the trial. But I guess you don't."

The drawn tension of the boy's face softened for a moment, then he frowned. "I'll be damned if I can figure you out. Half the time I don't know if you're . . ."

"If I'm what?"

The boy shrugged. "Forget it."

"Sure. Just don't get the notion I'm not on your side, Turo. This is going to be a hard case to win. It'll be a lot harder if you fight me too."

"You think we got a chance, Mr. Kellogg?" His voice had altered subtly. The harsh, almost strident sureness was gone. He was young and frightened now and trying to hide the dry chill of his terror.

Benson nodded and smiled with more confidence than he felt. "We've got a chance, Turo. I'm going to give it a strong charge. For the rest, we'll have to see how it shapes up. How is your family taking it?"

The boy looked away. "Papá went home. He was crying all the time. He made me nervous. The Dorado told him to beat it."

"The Dorado isn't doing any crying, I suppose?"

"Not him. He wanted to come here with me this morning, but I told him he better not."

"Right," Benson said flatly. "I don't want him in the courtroom. Do I have to explain that again?"

"Just because he was a Dorado? That was an awful long time ago, Mr. Kellogg."

"Not if you look at that old bandit," Benson said. "You'd swear it was only yesterday. Listen to me, Turo, and don't argue. We can't afford to give the prosecution any advantage at all. I don't want the newspapers writing about a Dorado's grandson who is going on trial for murder. If they write about you at all, I want them to refer to a young Mexican boy, alone and friendless in a strange country. People around here just might be inclined to think that a Dorado would train his grandson to kill. Nobody would waste any sympathy on a boy like that, and we can use all the sympathy we can get. Do you understand what I'm saying?"

"I guess so, but . . ."

"Just follow my lead on it, Turo. Make damn sure the Dorado stays under cover. I'll leave that to you. There's something else I want you to remember."

"What's that?"

"Hold on to your temper. Don't let anyone goad you into talking about the case. Get that chip off your shoulder. Whenever you open your mouth, just think that everything you say will be reported directly to the County Attorney, who is the guy who means to cut your throat. Keep your mouth shut. The same goes for the Dorado. The newspapers will be trying to get comments from both of you. Be careful. Don't talk to anybody."

"Okay, I guess we can do that."

"Good boy." Benson signaled to the waiting deputies.

"Just try to ride with the punches, boy. It won't be long now. How are you making out with the bullet?"

"Bullet?"

The boy grinned suddenly. He sat up straight in the wheel chair and almost laughed. "Still biting hard, Mr. Kellogg. I'm really bearing down."

BENSON was moving briskly down the office corridor a few feet from his open door when a stiff finger prodded him in the spine.

"Good morning, Mr. Blumberg," he said. He turned, resigned, and forced a polite smile.

"Full of the old vinegar, aren't you?" Blumberg said cheerfully. "I saw you come bouncing in. Nothing like a good tough case to set you up, right? I've been meaning to talk to you about it. Be glad to give you some help if you need a hand with your trial brief. I'm terribly busy these days, but I'll make time for you, my boy." His pudgy hands rubbed across his stomach and patted it approvingly.

"I haven't got that far yet, Mr. Blumberg," Benson said cautiously. "We don't go to trial until Monday."

"Well, you'll have plenty to do between now and then, won't you?" Blumberg bobbed his head up and down rapidly. "Don't let me keep you, Benson. Call on me if you need help. Remember, we all want you to make a good showing. That young fellow Timothy Cook phoned me this morning. Said he's going to be staying out at your ranch." Blumberg cocked his head up at a painful angle and peered at Benson. "Why is that? The man a friend of yours?"

"You might say that." Benson returned his stare coldly. "He hurt his foot this morning, so I suppose he'll be around for a while."

"So he said. So he said," Blumberg muttered in a dubious tone. "Well . . ." He lifted one hand in a vague, dismissive blessing and pushed past. He went down the carpeted corridor with quick bouncing steps, looking in each open door as he moved by.

Benson waited until he was out of sight. Blumberg was the senior partner, Benson's unquestioned superior, but he was not a lawyer, or a man, who commanded Benson's respect. The prospect of Blumberg interfering with his trial preparation was chilling to Benson. He wouldn't make an issue of it unless Blumberg brought it to a head, but privately Benson promised himself to see Blumberg in hell before he let him fiddle with his case.

He went inside his office and nudged the door shut with his foot. He had a scant half hour before he would have to leave for his appointment with Frank Sayer. Not much time for work, but without interruption he might get something done.

His secretary sat with her shoulders hunched secretly over his daybook, entering yesterday's report. She looked up and smiled hazily, marking her place with an inky fingertip. At Benson's desk, Miss Harkins was sitting in the customer's chair, holding his telephone to her ear with one hand and scribbling industriously with the other. Benson looked at her swift pot-hooks, detoured around her and put his briefcase on the window sill. He shifted his desk chair toward the window before he sat.

"He's here now," Miss Harkins said into the phone. "Yes, Mr. Kellogg. Do you want to——"

Benson swung his chair around. "Is that my brother you're talking to?"

"Yes, sir." She held out the receiver.

"Burr?" Benson reversed the phone and balanced it in the hollow of his shoulder. "What's up? Have you been trying to get me?"

"Morning, Counselor. No, I wasn't chasing you. I just had a hot flash last night and I thought of a few ideas that might help you plan your trial. I was going to dictate a memo to Harkie, but now you're on hand, we can do it straight. How've you been, boy? Had any trouble with Frank yet?"

"No, not a bit. He's been very cooperative, as a matter of fact."

"I'll bet," Burr said skeptically. "Well, he can be a nice guy when he puts his mind to it. He needs your help, so he's probably on his best behavior. I was feeling a little guilty about you last night. I wouldn't want you thinking I'd sandbagged you."

"No fear," Benson said easily. "This is pretty new stuff for me, but Frank is not one of my worries. What's on your mind?"

"Just a general-type suspicion, Ben. Frank can be a dirty fighter. I'd thought maybe I'd better tip you off to some of his tricks so you'd know what to expect, in case he reverts to type."

"I'm not afraid of Frank, Burr, but I can use any advice that's lying around."

"The basic point is that Frank likes surprises. He always has a couple of rabbits to pull out of the hat. What's your opinion of him as a lawyer?"

"I don't have any basis for an opinion. I read some trial transcripts. He's good and very careful. He's made mistakes."

"Forget the mistakes, Ben. Just assume he's the best lawyer you ever went up against. He isn't, but he's a demon for hard work. He claims he wins most of his cases because he prepares them better than the defense people ever do. And he's right. Most of our colleagues in Rincon are too damn lazy to fight him on criminal cases, so Frank has a pretty easy time. And he has a lot of experience, of course. The average attorney doesn't handle a dozen criminal cases in a lifetime, but Frank is in there all the time."

"I know. I'm not likely to underestimate him. I've been sweating over the books lately."

"Yeah, well that's another thing I wanted to warn you about, Ben. Those tricky cases you've been trying. They were full of nice legal points, classic cases damn near. But a criminal trial is nothing like that. You won't be pleading before a judge who knows more law than you do. You're going to have a thick-skulled, witless jury that doesn't know anything about law and doesn't want to be told. You keep that in mind."

"Yes, sir," Benson said mildly.

Burr laughed, snorting. "I was giving you the old lecture, huh? Well, I've been worrying about you, Ben. Lately you've been concentrating on nonadversary cases, and you've got into the habit of playing it subtle. But you can't be subtle with a jury. You can't say anything by implication. You have to spell everything out in capital letters and say whatever you have to say as if you were explaining it to a child. You don't mind my talking like this, Ben? I'm not trying to tell you what to do."

"I don't mind, Burr. What else?"

"That's okay, then," Burr said in a relieved voice. "You're a better lawyer than I am. We both know that. But I'm trickier and that's what counts in a criminal court. I always tell myself I'm putting together a jigsaw puzzle and I pick up each piece and tell the jury what it means and what it adds to the complete picture. Then I show them the whole pattern in my summation. That's all routine organization, but in a murder trial you have to make it dramatic as well. Build it up. Juries like a show. Give them one."

"That's not as easy as you make it sound, Burr. The prosecution controls the trial, after all."

"I know it's not easy, but it's what wins trials, Ben. Put on a show, let them see you're fighting tooth and nail for your client, and you'll win trials you've got no business winning."

"I guess you know what you're talking about, Burr. What else?"

"Tactics," Burr said, his voice momentarily muffled by transmission. "I imagine you're planning a few surprises for Frank. Just be careful you don't tip your hand when you're cross-examining his witnesses. It's always tempting to ask too many questions. You'd be better off to find some independent witnesses to the same fact, then lie back and wait for your turn. Get what I mean?"

"Yes. I've been thinking of some problems that fit in that picture. It works out to be a tricky problem of alternatives, doesn't it?"

"Amen, boy. But if you're going to slug the prosecutor, there's no point in warning him first. Sock it to him just when he's beginning to think he's got it made. Well, all that stuff is just common sense. What may be a little more useful is Frank's preferences in selecting a jury. I don't suppose you've ever watched him?"

"No."

"I have. All told, I've locked horns with Frank more than twenty times, and in every case he tried to get the same kind of jury. He'll excuse every man over sixty if he can afford to use a challenge, and every woman under forty. He doesn't like the truckdriver type, and he won't touch anyone with a sub-standard income. If you want to get rid of someone like that, don't waste a challenge. Let Frank do it for you."

"What does he like best? The blue-ribboned mob, I suppose?"

"Sure. Just what you'd expect. Solid, middle-class churchgoers with good incomes and big mortgages. People like that hate any guy who tries to cut corners. Frank is also very fond of skinny old women, if they look mean enough. They'll convict anybody, any man especially, just for the hell of it. He'll be going for people like that and he'll have a good background report on the whole panel, so he'll know all about them. I used to waste a lot of money investigating the venire before I figured out Frank's system. Now I save my money and let Frank tell me about them. And I guess I don't have to tell you why Frank is going to select that kind of jury, if you let him?"

"The knife," Benson said. "I've been worrying about it, too."

"Boy, you have been doing some woodshedding, haven't you?" Burr said admiringly. "That's it, all right. The knife. You've got reason to be worried. If I had Frank's job, I'd be rehearsing in front of a mirror with that switchblade knife. And when the time came, I'd wait until I had the jury's attention and then I'd walk slowly over to the table and pick up that knife and swing around. I'd hold it up and watch the eyes. When they moved up to the knife, I'd raise it a little bit and then push that button, and that long wicked blade would snap open. And every juror would let out a gasp and then look over at the defendant, sort of measuring his neck for a rope. And your case would be lost right there."

"I don't know how I could stop him, Burr. He'll have the knife to present in evidence, and he can display it to the jury as dramatically as he likes."

"The hell he can," Burr said. "Not if you're ready for him. When he gets that hand moving with the knife, you break up his pattern. Distract the jury somehow so they don't follow what he's doing."

Benson chuckled. That's just what Burr would do too, he thought.

"And don't get the notion this is a question of ethics," Burr went on persuasively. "It's merely a matter of timing. Frank has the right to introduce evidence, but no law gives him the right to present it in a way that is more damaging to your client than the weight of the evidence itself. It's your job to stop him if he tries. Make a good loud objection when Frank is turning to the jury with that knife. Get the jury's attention off him for a moment, and his effect is ruined. And don't worry about old Judge Groat. He'll know what you're up to, but he won't be able to stop you. Ask him for permission to open a window because your poor client is about to suffocate. Ask for the blinds to be raised or lowered. Drop a handful of change on the floor. Do any damn thing. But for Christ's sake, Ben, do something, or Frank will crucify your boy with that knife."

"He could just wait me out, Burr, and then try it again when he had the jury's attention."

"Then interrupt him again. Stand up and ask the judge if the County Attorney has any intention of introducing the knife as evidence. Frank will have to turn away to answer and when he takes his position again, even the jury will see that he's trying to pull something. But whatever you do, stop him before he gets a chance to build up to a big production. A knife is a frightening thing in itself. I guess it's something in the genes— we're all a little bit scared of cold steel. You be careful, Ben. Don't even mention that knife if you can help it. And you'd better go all out to get one or two Mexicans on your jury. At least they can look at a knife without getting queasy."

"I agree. I have to get some jurors who can understand the boy's background."

"Frank will block you if he can, just out of habit," Burr said. "What are you going in with? Self-defense?"

"Maybe. I have some ideas that haven't jelled yet. There's a tricky point of law I haven't got clear. I wish you were around so we could talk it over."

"Hell, you don't need any help from me on the law. All I'm good for is the in-fighting. Just keep on your toes and be ready to shift around. Don't let Frank catch you flat-footed or he'll make you look sick. Ben?"

"Yes?"

"You're not really worried, are you? I mean, hell, nobody expects you to get the kid off. Frank's got the case sewed up tight. You just want to give him a good fight. You're not worried, are you?" Burr's voice was uncertain, strained with a meaning he could not put into words.

"No, I'm not worried, Burr. I'm just afraid I might goof it, forget something so obvious I just can't see it."

"Not you," Burr said confidently. "Not old Steady Ben the Beefeater. But you'll be getting plenty of offers to help with the preparation of your case. Jake Blumberg will stick his nose in if you let him."

"He tried just a moment ago."

"Yeah. He's not worth listening to, but it wouldn't be smart to brush him. Just remember that everything he knows he'll spill to his buddies at the Bar Association. He likes to show them he still knows what's going on. So if you want to sucker Frank, just let old Jake spread the word for you. Slip it to him in confidence and Frank will have it by morning. I've tried it a couple of times and Frank always bites. I wish I could be there for the trial, but I don't guess there's much chance."

"Are your political friends keeping you busy?"

"Busy? My God! I haven't had a minute to myself since I left. I give about forty speeches a day to the damnedest bunch of mutts you ever saw. They let me take five minutes to shave and go to the can in the morning, and from then on, I'm running. Right now there's a mob in the other room waiting for me to show up and say a few words so they can make up their stupid minds whether they want me for Attorney General. They don't know what in hell an attorney general is, but they sure do like to walk in little circles around me and shake their heads like I was a spavined old mare that wouldn't fetch the freight charges. Boy, it's dispiriting, I can tell you."

"Are you still set on running, Burr? No second thoughts?"

"No, I'll play out the hand. Simple fact is, I'm getting to like it. Beats working, anyway. Well, I've got to get moving again, Ben."

"When are you coming back?"

"Week or two, maybe. It takes a long time to run down some of these people. Why, I've been through stretches the size of Connecticut where there isn't a damn soul but a couple of Navajo sheepherders. A county chairman just has to figure out how to swing three or four votes and he's won an election. I should be finished by the end of next week. Maybe not. We'll see."

"Keep in touch, Burr. And thanks for the advice."

"Welcome, Counselor, very welcome. Hope you can break it off in Frank."

"I mean to try. So long, Burr."

Benson hung up and sat looking at the phone with a slow smile. It was good to hear from Burr, he thought, good to hear the irreverent practicalities that were as much Burr's trademark as full-throated determination had been old B.'s. It was too bad, in a way, that Burr wouldn't be trying this case himself. He obviously enjoyed fencing with Frank Sayer, and he would not be plaguing himself with anything tangential to the trial itself.

"Will you want me to type these notes, Mr. Kellogg?" Miss Harkins tapped her pencil impatiently on her notebook, eying Benson with the veiled distrust of a competent and busy woman who will have no truck with dreamy people during business hours.

Benson skinned back his cuff to look at his watch. "Yes," he said. "I'll want to see them, Miss Harkins. And you'd better have lunch early today. I'm having a conference with the County Attorney at noon and I'll want to start on my trial plan when I get back."

"Don't you want me to—" Miss Harkins bit her lip and looked away.

"Don't I what?"

"It's not important, I suppose," Miss Harkins said with an unexpected hesitancy. "I was just thinking you might want me to come to the conference with you."

There was about her an anxious intensity that made Benson frown. She had a law degree, he remembered, though, as far as he knew, she had never practiced. A good legal secretary lives well and vacations in Hawaii. A beginning lawyer eats beans and vacations in the law library. Miss Harkins had made her decision long ago, but Benson could sense something in her manner now that suggested a renewed ambition. What did she expect from him? he wondered. Was she hoping that he would accept her as surrogate for Burr and let her have a hand in decisions that were life-or-death for Arturo Campeón? The possibility struck him so sharply that his voice in reply was abrupt and harsh.

"No, that won't do," he said bluntly. And you would never have dared make the suggestion to Burr, he thought. "Thank you, Miss Harkins. I'll manage. Please meet me here at one thirty."

Benson got up quickly. He left the office without speaking to Mary, who had listened to everything, wide-eyed, and was now staring in awe at Miss Harkins. A thin shrill squeak, half admiring, half in shocked protest, would spill out of her at any minute. Benson went out fast.

FRANK SAYER got to his feet with stiff formality when Miss Latimer ushered Benson into his office. His big rubbery politician's face was fixed with a strange rigidity and his hand was cold in Benson's grasp.

"All right, Miss Latimer," he said. "No calls until I tell you. Except from Los Angeles. You can send in the lunch tray when it comes. Sit down, Ben."

He lowered himself fussily to the outer rim of his chair, shot his starched cuffs and put both hands flat on his desk blotter. He pulled his lower lip to a petulant line and scowled at the far wall, pointedly not looking at Benson.

He seemed to be nerving himself to something, Benson thought. He took the chair beside Sayer's desk, conscious again of the strong antipathy between them, instinctive and irrational, a dislike based on unknown and unconscious motives but tangible as a wave of cold air. He waited, wary and ready.

Frank Sayer shifted restlessly. When he spoke his words came slowly, carefully enunciated, as a man will speak when he expects his words will be precisely remembered later.

"We had a talk yesterday, Ben," he said. "We laid out some ground rules for the Campeón trial. Right?"

"We talked about a lot of things, Frank. What's on your mind?" Benson took out his cigarettes and drew an ashtray to the corner of the desk.

"I told you why I wanted this trial to come off smoothly. Remember what I said?"

"I remember," Benson said. "You were concerned about the Mexican-American Citizens Association."

"Right. Well, they've been very decent, I will say that for them. I talked to the chairman last night, and we agreed that harmony in the community is more important for everyone than any advantage they could gain by making a stink about Campeón." Frank Sayer looked at Benson directly for the first time. "They knew you were handling the boy's defense, so they weren't worried about him getting a fair shake."

"What are you getting at, Frank?"

The County Attorney drew in a quick breath, bracing himself. He squared his shoulders and pulled his chin back. His eyes slid away from Benson again. "Things have changed, Ben. We don't have to worry about the Mexican-Americans, thanks to you. I'm grateful for that, Ben, don't think I'm not. But we've got a bigger problem now." He locked his hands together in a hard double fist. "I just found out who the dead man was. I've been talking to his father. Long distance from New York. He's flying out tomorrow."

Benson blinked. He waved a cloud of smoke away from his face. "What do you mean? Wasn't he Roderick Duquesne?"

"That's the name he was using in Los Angeles. It's not his real name. Roderick Duquesne, for Christ's sake! It even sounds phony. I should have spotted that myself."

"Who was he?"

"His name was—" Frank Sayer hesitated for added emphasis— "Robert Caine."

"Okay," Benson said. "Lots of people change their names, especially in Hollywood. So what? He's still dead."

"So what?" Frank Sayer swallowed to keep his voice from going shrill. "Well, I'll just tell you so what. His name was Robert Caine. C-a-i-n-e. His father is H. L. Caine."

"The hell you say." Benson sifted cigarette ash into the tray. "Is that the old pirate, the one they used to call Hurricane? I didn't know he was still alive."

"None other. And he's alive all right. You'd never doubt that if you'd talked to him. He's coming tomorrow to claim the body." Frank Sayer shook his head. He let out his breath noisily. "I wish I could start all over with this one. I just figured Duquesne for a dead Californian, who didn't mean anything much in this state even if he was rich. Who in hell could guess he would turn out to be old Caine's son?"

"Nobody could, Frank. But what's bothering you?"

Frank Sayer scowled. His hands tightened with a nervous

spasm. "I wouldn't have to explain to Burr," he said, quietly bitter. "He'd know what I meant without being told. That's one of the things that's bothering me. Don't you know who the old man is?"

"Caine? Sure. Railroad man. Southwestern Belt Line. And he has something to do with mining, too, I think."

"Something to do with mining," Sayer repeated as if he couldn't believe what he had heard. "I should just think he does have something to do with mining. He's just chairman of the board of Consolidated Copper, that's all. Half the miners in the state work for one or another of his companies."

"So he's an important man," Benson said equably. "And I suppose he's important politically, too. I can see you have to consider that, Frank, but what does it have to do with the trial?"

Sayer pulled his hands into his lap. He swung his chair so that he was facing the row of pictures on the far wall. "You've been drawing up your trial plan," he said, "so you've been thinking about Duquesne. What do you know about him?"

Benson put out his cigarette. Watch yourself now, he warned himself. You know what he's getting at. He has heard something about Duquesne, but he isn't sure if you know. If he wants to look at your cards, make him put his on the table.

He sat back, waiting until Frank Sayer turned his head. "I don't know much about him yet. I haven't had time to check. You were going to get a report from Los Angeles, remember?"

"Yeah, so I was." Sayer's voice was a low mutter. "Before we go into that, let's talk about something else. I can see that this trial is going to be a damn nuisance for you. You'll be wasting a lot of time on something that doesn't interest you very much. How would you like to be excused as defense counsel? I think Judge Groat would approve your application if we both went to him."

Benson made a noncommittal sound. Frank is scared of something, he thought, and if it's what I suspect, he's right to be scared.

"You'll have to explain that, Frank," he said. "I took the Mexican-Americans off your back when I accepted the case.

But they'll be after you again if you switch lawyers, and they'll be twice as hard to handle because they'll be suspecting collusion. And another thing. You were twisting my arm yesterday to get me to agree to an early trial. But we both know that no other lawyer would take the case unless he was given time to make his own preparation. So you must be willing to postpone the trial. Is that what you want?"

"No, I don't." Frank Sayer looked bleakly at Benson, waited for him to figure it out.

"You just want to get rid of me. And you'd rather have the Mexican-Americans gunning for you, and take the rap for an unnecessary continuance, rather than see me defend the case. All that is clear enough. Do you want to explain?"

"No."

"That's my answer too," Benson said. "I'm committed to my client. I won't throw him over. And only a natural-born shit would ask me to."

Benson's voice had been so level and controlled that a long moment passed before Frank Sayer appreciated what had been said. Slowly, painfully, his big face reddened. "Goddam you," he said thickly, almost choking. "You sit there like you were the only honest man in seven counties. Don't pull that crap with me, friend. I'm not——"

"You're a shit," Benson said, angrily quiet. "You've been trying to sucker me and you're so damn clumsy about it, a six-year-old child could guess what's on your mind. You've heard something about Duquesne, haven't you? The Los Angeles police couldn't find a record on Roderick Duquesne, but I'll bet they had a fat file on Robert Caine. What did they tell you about him?"

Frank Sayer shook his head. His face was flushed and damp with sweat in spite of the air conditioner at his back. He was drawing in shallow, harried breaths.

"Don't try to con me any more, Frank," Benson said. "If you want to talk about the case, let's talk like sensible men. Give up the tricks. And you can forget about me selling out my client. There's no chance. Now do we talk or do I get out?"

Frank Sayer squeezed one hand over his face. Large rubbery hillocks stood out between his gouging fingers. He took his time, not looking at Benson until he had himself under control. "I'd like to kick your ass out of here," he said hoarsely, "but this is too important. You just watch your tongue, friend. I guess we rub each other the wrong way, but we haven't got time for personalities. You don't know what I have to contend with in this office, and I don't have any way of knowing what goes on in your mind. But if we're going to try this case—and I guess we are—then we'd better get together. Let's talk. Did you really know anything about Duquesne, or were you taking a stab in the dark?"

"A little of both," Benson said. He noticed a flicker of relief move across Sayer's harassed, apprehensive face. "But now that you've told me there is a police record on Robert Caine, you might as well tell me what's in it."

"I didn't say he had a record."

"Knock it off, Frank. What did the police say?"

Frank Sayer lifted his heavy shoulders in a half shrug. "He doesn't exactly have a record, nothing official anyway. His name just pops up now and again in confidential reports."

"What for? What offense?"

Frank Sayer stared at Benson for a long thoughtful moment, his eyes shadowed by the bony ledge of his forehead. "No," he said flatly. "You tell me."

"Sodomy," Benson said with no hesitation.

Frank Sayer winced. "My God, no," he said hastily. "It's just—well, he had an interest in a couple of blue joints the cops raided. The chief of the confidential squad knows about him, but nothing much, nothing very definite. His name just crops up in a kind of suspicious repetition, but nothing—" he squared his shoulders confidently—"nothing you could use in court."

Benson snorted quietly. "Don't tell me what I can use, Frank. If you thought I couldn't use it, why are you scared?"

"You damn fool," Sayer said. "If I'm scared, which I'm not, it isn't because of Duquesne. It's his father. I told you who he was."

"You told me. What about it?"

"H. L. Caine. He's rich, he's important and he's no man to have for an enemy. All that is obvious, but you can't see anything more, can you, Ben? You think I'm ready to roll over and play dead because H. L. Caine has twenty million dollars or whatever it is. You're wrong. It's not like that. Mr. Caine is one of the very important men in this state. He's something more, too. He's a father."

Frank Sayer's voice deepened to an oratorical organ tone. "He's a father who invested all his pride and love in one worthless son. And now his son has been brutally murdered. Isn't that enough, Ben? Do we have to pile filth on that dead body? Think of what Mr. Caine must be going through right at this minute. Just think."

"I'd rather think about you, Frank. You're the one who interests me. Did old Caine tell you he wanted a cover-up, or did you think of it yourself?"

"Damn you, I'm not trying to cover up anything," Frank Sayer said angrily. "Duquesne's past record has no bearing on the fact that he was murdered."

"You don't know that, Frank. You just hope it doesn't have any bearing."

"What do you mean?" Sayer demanded.

"You didn't even bother to question the boy when you had the chance. It was Sunday and you were taking a day off. So nobody asked him what happened. And it's too late now. You booted that one, Frank. And now you want me to take you off the hook." Benson shook his head decisively. "No."

"Is that the way you're going to play it? Dirty and mean, rubbing a fine man's pride in the dust to make yourself look good?"

"Did it ever occur to you that Arturo Campeón comes from a proud family too? That he has a right to defend himself by telling the truth about what actually happened between him and Duquesne?"

"The truth! That murdering little punk never told the truth in his whole filthy life. He doesn't even——" Frank

Sayer stopped himself with a visible effort. After a moment he said, "Are you going to do it, Ben? Smear innocent people who never hurt anyone?"

"I'm going to defend my client the best way I can."

"Goddam it, Ben! Don't you realize what H. L. Caine can do to you if——"

"Don't threaten me," Benson said. "Mr. Caine has nothing to do with this. I've never met the man and I don't expect to. This is between us, Frank. Let's keep it that way."

"You're getting in over your head, Ben," Sayer said in an ominous growl. "I'm warning you."

"You know what you can do with your warning. But I don't believe you're worried about old Caine at all. I think you've just begun to realize what happened on Lookout Point on Saturday night. I think you've got a pretty good idea of how Duquesne came to get killed."

"How?"

"I'll tell you in court at the same time I tell the jury," he said. "But you know already, don't you?"

Frank Sayer squinted with a shrewd eyebrow. "You couldn't make it stick," he said slyly. "Hell, even if you could, it's only a misdemeanor anyway, so you still haven't got any defense. Why do it, Ben? You'll just make it worse for your boy. No jury likes to see a dead man smeared."

"I think you're wrong about the law, Frank," Benson said steadily. "We'll let the court decide if it's a valid defense."

"It won't work," Sayer said with an increasing confidence. "Just explain to me this, Ben. If you think you can introduce a new element into the trial, how are you going to explain that the boy didn't say anything about it in his confession?"

"I warned you about that confession yesterday," Benson said, his voice sharpening. "You'd better talk to the deputies who squeezed it out of the boy. It's fraudulent, Frank. You know it. I won't let you offer it in evidence."

"You won't let me?" Sayer repeated incredulously. "God, you're comical. That confession is the foundation of my case.

Just try to knock it out. The judge always likes a good laugh. Do you know how many confessions I've had thrown out since I've been County Attorney? None. Exactly none. And you think you can keep this one out?"

"I'll keep it out," Benson said. "You can get ready for a fight on that one, Frank. If you had any sense, you'd keep it out yourself."

He pushed back his chair and got slowly to his feet. "You know you don't have a sound murder charge, Frank." He walked to the desk and watched Sayer lift his head. "You offered to let me read your trial brief. And you were going to set appointments for me to interview your witnesses." Sayer's mouth widened in a tight, complacent smile that was close to a sneer.

"Let's finish talking about Campeón first," Sayer said blandly. "I want to be sure you aren't going to drag in any dirty rumors about Duquesne just so you can——"

"His name was Caine, Frank," Benson said sharply. "And I'll run my defense program as I see fit. What about the help you promised me?"

Sayer made a brusque, impatient gesture as if he were brushing something off his desk. "We'll discuss it another time. Come back when you've had time to think."

"Some other time," Benson said. "How about the day after the trial, Frank? Would that suit you?"

Frank Sayer's smile stretched slowly wider.

"Spit it out, Frank," Benson insisted. His voice sounded thick in his ears. His face felt stiff. "I've known people who said you were a lying, conniving sonofabitch whose word wasn't worth a fart in a high wind. But tell me yourself, Frank."

Frank Sayer rose in a swift lunge. He leaned over the desk, supported on arms that trembled under him. His pale eyes bulged at Benson. "Get out of here," he whispered. "Now."

"There's a sign on your door," Benson said, openly contemptuous. "It says, 'Honorable Franklin B. Sayer.' You should get a new sign, Frank."

He turned on his heel and walked stiffly away. The long muscles of his legs quivered with tension, with a primitive readiness. His fingers locked together, making each hand a tight, aching hook. He was breathing quickly in shallow gulps, as if he had run a long distance. He pulled open the door and let it swing back against the wall. Miss Latimer looked up, startled, as Benson went past her desk and out into the courthouse corridor.

THE LIGHT came mistily through the restaurant window behind Joss, softened and strained through the low palms so that it was a strange and gentle blue, like the sea. It made a halo around her head, and Benson found himself watching the movement of light as she shifted. Her eyes were fixed on his in hard childlike focus.

Benson took a moment to trim out the last bite of steak on his plate, lifted it and then put it down. He took a long gulp of water, seeing the glass shake slightly. His throat was very dry and his voice still came hoarsely.

"I haven't been that mad since I was a kid in school," he said. "That's strange, isn't it? I've had some fights since then. I went through a war that was anything but fun. But Frank made me mad. And I can't even pretend I was surprised. From what I knew of his reputation, I'd have expected Frank to cross me if he had a chance."

"Or a reason," Joss added.

"I suppose so. He really got to me. I'm an even-tempered guy. You know that. I used to take a certain pride in it, but I was wrong. By God, I haven't got any more balance than any other jerk where Frank Sayer is concerned. Do you know I had to walk around by myself for an hour before I could talk sensibly? If anyone had said hello to me, I'd have hit him in the chops. I was wild. And what for? Why?"

"Moral indigestion?" Joss offered. "Lost illusions?"

"Probably," Benson said, shaking his head. "It's a sad and

cautionary tale, isn't it? There should be a moral to it somewhere. Put not your faith in princes, something like that."

"You're making too much of it, Ben. According to his
lights, Frank Sayer is acting honorably, as politicians go. As
long as you and he were working together, he would have kept
his end of the bargain; but when you went against him, you just
ceased to exist. Politicians don't keep bargains with the dead."
Joss pushed aside her salad plate and rummaged in her bag
for a cigarette.

"You've got a mighty low opinion of politicians," Benson
said. He held his lighter for her, then signaled the waiter for
more coffee.

"I don't have any opinion at all," Joss said indifferently.
She looked at her reflection in a hand mirror, stroked her napkin along her lower lip and took out her lipstick. "Anyway," she went on, "Frank Sayer isn't the important question.
You are. It's in your lap now, not Frank's."

"I know."

Joss smoothed her lipstick expertly, blotted the fresh
glossiness with a tissue. She shook her head when the waiter
bent to pour her coffee. She was silent until he had filled Benson's cup and they were alone and private in their corner of
the large busy restaurant.

"I don't believe you do know," she said with a sharp and
brittle clarity. "You are pretending to be furious with Frank
Sayer but I think you are furious with yourself. Frank didn't
invent this mess, Ben. He merely brought it out into the open
and made you look at it."

"Joss, what are you——"

"You are going to ruin yourself for that worthless boy
and you are trying to make yourself believe it is Frank
Sayer's fault. It isn't, Ben. It's yours."

"That's a hell of a thing to say to me, Joss."

"Dear God, Ben, I've seen you put yourself in a dozen
positions like this. I used to think it was because you didn't
know better, that you were striking a posture, but I know that's
not the answer. You're not a masochist and you aren't fanatic.

I don't know what brings it on. You always take the short end of everything. And you don't even get angry about it, or not very often. You sat quietly while Burr took all the cash in your father's estate and you nearly lost La Cañada because you didn't have enough money to operate. Oh, don't shrug it off, Ben. You know it's true. You let that old fraud Blumberg saddle you with all the difficult, unprofitable work in your office. You even let Burr sucker you into taking this case in the first place. Why wouldn't Frank Sayer think you were a safe man to double-cross? If you act like a patsy, people are going to treat you like a patsy."

Benson didn't say anything. He watched a slow-moving gardener pick his way through the twelve-foot poinsettias in the patio—huge, flowering, tree-like plants, unlikely as basketball players.

"I'm sorry, Ben," Joss said in a voice that suggested she wasn't at all sorry. "I didn't mean to go shrill. But I just can't stand it, seeing you put up with second best all the time when you could have anything if you'd just reach out and take it."

"I'm sorry, too," Benson said gently. "But my character or lack of character doesn't have much to do with the Campeón case."

"Yes, it does," Joss said flatly. "You just won't face it. Tell me this, Ben. What exactly did Frank Sayer ask you to do?"

"I explained all that," Benson said.

"He wanted you to leave out all the homosexual business. Isn't that right?"

"Yes."

"Will the judge let you bring it in?"

"He might. It depends."

"But you admitted it probably wasn't a legal defense. So even if you can get it in, the judge will have something to say about it, won't he? When he talks to the jury, I mean?"

Benson nodded. "He could tell them to disregard whatever I said, if he thought it wasn't a valid defense."

"And what would the jury do?"

"It's hard to say. A jury is supposed to accept the judge's

ruling on the law. Most do. Some don't."

"So even if you could prove the dead man was a working homosexual, it probably wouldn't win the case for your client, would it?" Joss leaned forward urgently. "Would it?"

Benson sighed and closed his eyes and rubbed them with his fingertips. "It isn't that simple, Joss," he said patiently. "I can't omit one element without destroying the whole fabric of my defense plan. Unless I show them the complete picture, the jury will never understand what happened. I have to do my best for that boy, Joss. His life hangs on it."

"But he'll be convicted anyway," Joss said fiercely. "No matter what you do, he'll be convicted. He deserves to be. You know that. He did kill that man."

"You don't mean that, Joss."

"Oh, I don't know what I mean. You make me so mad I can't see straight. But I do know it is absolutely senseless to go out of your way to make an enemy of one of the most power-ful men in the state. It isn't as if you stood to gain any-thing, even if you could win. A week afterward, all that any-body will remember is that you were the lawyer who smeared H. L. Caine's son. Do you think anyone will want to hire you after that?"

"I'm Arturo Campeón's lawyer," Benson said quietly. "He is the only client I'm thinking about right now."

"But you can't get him off, Ben. Why ruin yourself too? It might be different if you had a chance, but you don't. It's hopeless and I think you know that, even if you won't admit it."

"None of that matters, Joss. The boy has to be defended."

Joss tapped her cigarette in erratic rhythm on the rim of the ashtray. "Some kinds of mud don't just stick to the man who touches them, they rub off on everyone who is close to him. If you aren't worried about your own future, what about Burr's? Do you intend to ruin him too?"

Benson blinked. The smoke from Joss's cigarette was mak-ing his eyes water. He picked up his coffee cup and drained it quickly. "What about Burr?"

"You know who runs this state, Ben. The same men who

run the mines and the railroads and the big ranches. H. L. Caine is one of them, maybe the most important one. His political contributions must be half the party's income. Do you think Burr could go anywhere in politics without Caine's approval?"

"Possibly not." Benson squared his shoulders against the back on his chair.

"And what about me?" Joss added soberly.

"You, Joss?" Benson asked gently. "Are you involved in this too?"

"I'm trying to understand you, Ben," she said, forcing herself to calmness. "I want to understand, but all I can see is a futile, quixotic gesture that will ruin you. And it would ruin me too, if I——" She sat back abruptly and looked at Benson squarely. "You've asked me to marry you, Ben. Half a dozen times. Why do you think I've refused?"

Benson shook his head. "Tell me."

"Can't you figure it out for yourself? I like you better than any man I know. Maybe I love you. You're a good man and you'd make a good husband. But I want a man who thinks I am important, as important as his career, or his horses, or all the extraneous people he has filled up his life with. And I don't want a man who would throw up his whole future—and mine too—for a wooden-headed, sentimental gesture like——"

"Please, Joss." Benson reached out and touched her hand.

"Don't try to soothe me," she said tightly. "I don't want to be soothed, damn you. I want to be *first* with you. Just once, I want to be first." She turned her face away from him.

Then, with a sudden, decisive movement, she stabbed her cigarette out in the ashtray and got up from the table. "Stay here, Ben," she said. "Just stay here. I don't want you with me right now."

Benson rose, rigidly stiff. He waited until Joss had come around the table and walked away toward the door. Then he sat again.

In the patio the gardener lowered a canvas shield against the afternoon sun. Thick shadow made a mirror of the window, and Benson could see wavering movement in the restaurant behind him. People were vague shapes, dim figures like an uncertain memory. The high, tinted plate-glass doors opened for Joss and closed behind her. And closed against Benson, with a thin whisper of sound. He sat very still, watching, remembering another time the doors had closed against him. He had been six then, when Burr was born, and through the large open house the doors were suddenly closed and he was told to keep out, to be very quiet, to go play somewhere else. The chill of loneliness and rejection had touched him then. As it did now.

Beside him the waiter coughed discreetly. He twiddled Benson's check in his hand, hesitant. Benson took it from him and dismissed him with a nod. He swung around in his chair. Better give Joss another few minutes, he thought; she'll have to get the doorman to flag a taxi. Benson crossed his knees and looked out blankly across the restaurant.

When he was a boy, this had been the Chinaman's chili parlor. The building was an adobe shack with a pressed-tin roof and splintered wooden floors and it smelled wonderful, even with the Chinaman's chickens running free underfoot. The food was terrible, he remembered; Cantonese peasants cook no better than peasants from anywhere else, but Benson could think of it now with the sharp pleasure a man finds in a boyhood memory that comes back to mind in clear, vivid detail. I wonder what happened to all the chili parlors, he thought. I haven't seen one since my high-school days. The current restaurant was a considerable improvement, he recognized. The Levantine gentlemen from Chicago who owned it had brought in a famous decorator and a chef who deserved to be famous. It was called "The Girl of the Golden West," now and it was done up in an aggressive gay-nineties style that was bright and expensive and self-conscious and probably amusing. It sometimes got an honorable mention in the gourmet columns and it was actually a very good restaurant. But it had precise duplicates in almost every city, and no one was likely to remember it with either clarity or pleasure.

Benson got up and took out his wallet. He left a tip for the waiter and walked across to the cashier's booth to pay his check. He asked for a pack of cigarettes and he scanned the headlines of the *Rincon Record* while he waited for his change.

LOOKOUT POINT MURDER TRIAL SCHEDULED FOR MONDAY, the banner said. And under it, MEXICAN YOUTH STANDS MUTE.

Benson picked up a paper and dropped a coin on the counter. He went outside, gave his parking stub to the doorman and stood on the curb, skimming the long, packed column on the front page. Frank Sayer, "hard-hitting veteran County Attorney," was quoted as saying Duquesne's death was a "vicious, inhuman crime." He said Arturo Campeón was a "brutal fiend" who had robbed and killed his benefactor, stolen his car and attempted to escape to Mexico. "Prompt and admirable police work" had resulted in his speedy capture. "The cold and callous killer with a long record of previous crimes" had not even tried to deny his guilt. The Honorable Franklin B. Sayer confidently predicted a verdict of guilty in the first degree. Benson was identified as "brother of Burr Kellogg, well-known Rincon attorney." And Duquesne was, throughout the story, Duquesne. Benson folded his paper, tipped the doorman and got into his car.

AT THE TRAFFIC LIGHT guarding Apache Drive, Benson stopped. He leaned his forehead on the top of the steering wheel. The sun was hot brass on the back of his neck, and he thought vaguely of putting the top up and then did nothing. After a moment he straightened again. Far to the right he could see the sharp and massive outline of Cobre Peak against the hard sky. When the light turned, Benson abruptly twisted the wheel to the right and drove north out of town toward the mountain road where the man who had called himself Roderick Duquesne had been killed.

The road was stark, bone-white in the sun and crowded with traffic. The cars in each of the three northbound lanes were segregated as distinctly as sprinters on a cinder track, with the

slow rattly old ranchers' Fords and the dusty tired tourists pulling overloaded house trailers puttering along in the outer
lane, in the center the routine law-abiding citizens bound for
El Monte or Palm Springs holding the speedometer reading
steadily at the limit, and speedsters in sports cars and souped-
up fenderless inventions slashing along the inner lane, swoop-
ing daringly like questing eagles into the southbound lanes to
pass a car that just wasn't moving fast enough. Huge diesel
double-trucks roared and sang and belched greasy smoke
from their high stacks when they hit the foothills.

In the center lane, Benson adjusted his speed to the
traffic and settled himself squarely. He drove past the long glittering mile of motels with flickering neon signs that were almost invisible in the brilliant sun, past the board fences of the
drive-in movies, past the cinder-block shanties that were liquor
stores or restaurants with signs that said EATS! or night clubs that
had signs that said, WHOOPEE! or WELCOME, PODNER! and
promising CHAR-BROILED STEAKS, and BIGGEST DRINKS IN THE
WEST! Then he was in the barren, lifting range of foothills.
And the traffic, for some unaccountable reason, was not speeding up as it always did at the city limits, but was gradually
slowing. Benson rode his brake, keeping a safe distance from
the car ahead.

Behind him a bright new convertible hugged his bumper,
growling and surging with impatience. In his mirror Benson
could see a crop-headed young boy behind the wheel, wearing a
snarl on his face and a nestling little blonde like a chrysanthe-
mum on his chest. The girl pushed up to look out the windshield, said something to the boy and snuggled down again.

And now he comes, Benson thought. His perilous manhood has been challenged, so here he comes. He saw the convertible lunge toward the inner lane, wiping the nose of a fast
sedan whose driver squealed brakes and swerved briefly into
the southbound traffic to avoid a collision.

And that's how it works, Benson thought sourly. Any
challenge will do. Christ, the things men will kill for. Not for
crusading causes, but for an affront to the fat flatulent ego, for

getting out of the way too slowly when the sick little creature wants to go by.

And you watch yourself, friend, he thought, aware of the danger. You are in a foul mood right now and you don't even need an excuse. Benson slowed and worked his way over to the outer lane where the traffic was drifting more sedately.

The highway narrowed slightly to squeeze through the pass that was halfway up the flank of Cobre Peak. The cars ahead of Benson's moved slowly. On the northern side was the entrance to the parking space at Lookout Point, and that was where the traffic moved slowest of all.

Benson inched along. He glanced down at the newspaper beside him, and then he could guess what was happening. The *Record* was a morning paper, delivered to home addresses at six o'clock, with a fresh edition on the street by eight. The trial of Arturo Campeón was big news today, dominating the first page. Benson suddenly had a vivid and bitter picture of the *Record*'s readers bugging their eyes at the headlines, gulping their coffee and bundling wives and children and picnic lunches into their cars and all hitting the trail for Lookout Point to see the splashes of blood where the "vicious and inhuman crime" had occurred. It would give them something to talk about for weeks. Rincon was really getting to be a big city when it could produce a murder as good as any you'd ever see in New York or Chicago.

Three sawhorses end to end blocked the access road to Lookout Point. A county patrol car was parked behind the fence and three deputies were strung along the highway, waving the cars on, letting none stop. Benson drifted with the traffic until the nose of his car was between two deputies. Then he cut his wheel sharply right and rolled to a halt beside the barrier. The cars behind him, driven by men who weren't about to let any sonofabitch get away with a damn thing, followed him bumper to bumper, stopping when he did, blocking two lanes of the highway solidly. In five seconds the horns began to blow, slammed down into the steering posts by angry fists.

The deputy closest to Benson almost ran toward him. He was old for active duty, scrawny and juiceless with a pinched face and a worried scowl. He wore shapeless khakis and a rain-warped hat with the county insigne dangling from a bent pin. He moved in short, choppy, finicky steps. A bronc-stomped ranch hand, Benson thought. And he looked to be mean as a molting snake.

"What do you think you're doin'?" the deputy snarled. His thin hand slapped his belt holster and hooked under the butt of his pistol. "You git that car out. Go on, move!"

"I want to go up to Lookout Point," Benson said. He switched off his motor.

"Closed," the deputy snapped. "The public ain't admitted. Go on out of here. You got a hunnert cars backed up."

"Wave them off," Benson said. "I'm not the public. I'm an attorney. My name is——"

"I wouldn't care was you the goddam Governor. Git moving or I'll run you in. I mean it, now. You're fixin' yourself for a mess of trouble, you don't git." The deputy half drew his sixgun.

The noise of the horns was piercing, nearly deafening. The deputies closed ranks along the highway. One of them intercepted the car immediately behind Benson, said the appropriate and threatening words, pointed demandingly at the highway and waved it ahead. The trailing cars followed slowly, still honking. Benson opened the door of his car and stepped out. He took one slow stride forward. His hands were shaking.

"You're under arrest," the deputy shouted in an ugly voice. "Damn you, you're gonna git what——"

"Now what in hell is going on here, Shriner?"

Another, younger and quieter deputy approached Benson with the languid and arrogant step that all policemen adopt when they're demonstrating the majesty of the law.

"This sonofabitch here is some kind of privileged character, he thinks," the deputy said. He prodded a thin and dirty finger at Benson's shirt. "He don't have to move on when he's told, not him. He's a——"

"I'm an attorney," Benson said to the second deputy. "My name is Benson Kellogg. I want to go up to Lookout Point."

"It's closed. Sorry, but we can't let you up. Now just move along before you get into trouble." The deputy put a hand on the old man's shoulder and pulled him gently away from Benson. "Slow down, Shriner. You get along, mister. Unless you want me to run you in?"

The shaking was gone from his hands now and Benson felt, except for an edge of bile on his tongue, well and ready, almost eager. He half smiled at the deputy.

"I'm going up to Lookout Point," he said, angrily quiet. "If you want to arrest me, go ahead." He held up his hand to stop the deputy before he could answer. "I told you my name, Deputy. I'm here on official court business and you will find yourself in contempt if you interfere with me in any way. Now it's in your hands. Arrest me, or move that fence out of my road. And do it now." He looked at the old man and smiled into his bitter eyes. "I'll give you ten seconds," he said softly. "Move!"

Benson got back into his car and started the motor. He nosed forward slowly until he was nudging the fence. Then he turned his head and leaned forward expectantly, looking at the hesitant deputies.

After a cautious, silent moment, the deputies conferred in undertones, nodded wisely at each other. They dragged one section of the sawhorse barrier away and waited until Benson had driven through and up the narrow road. Then they replaced the fence and went quickly toward their patrol car.

Benson watched them in his mirror, one reaching into the car for the radio microphone, holding it to his mouth and speaking into it, waving his arm in short, stabbing gestures. Calling the sheriff, Benson thought. And the sheriff will call Frank Sayer and Frank will hesitate for a minute and then, reluctantly, tell them to let me alone. And when I come back down they will pull the barrier aside and salute as I go by. And aren't you proud of yourself, you nasty bastard? You're as bad as that stupid kid in the convertible and you don't even have a girl to show off for. A few sensible words, and there would never have been a problem, even with that mean-eyed old man. But no, you had to handle it like a hard guy with his brains in his biceps. You outbullied a bully and isn't that a fine, useful exercise for a civilized man?

Benson grinned privately. It was stupid and childish and damn bad manners, but by God, he felt better because of it. Everybody's got a primitive streak in him and maybe it needs to be taken out for an airing once in a while, if only to remind yourself that no man has ever been entirely civilized.

He drove up the steep curving incline onto a wide, natural plateau that lay level with the desert below and looked directly toward the west.

A low peeled-log railing ran along the open side, with a narrow graveled walk just inside it and with concrete hard-stands behind the walk, marked with white-painted diagonal guidelines.

This was where you came with your girl late at night, after the movie let out, and parked for another low-voiced, muttering, squealing, pleading battle with buttons and hooks and snaps and zippers. Here in the mountain dark you tried persuasion and force and tears and laughter and kisses that shook your soul, and then, when you were both worn out, you gave up and kissed her some more gently and longingly and drove her home and kissed her and tried a little more but not very hard because you knew it wasn't any use and then you drove home and put the car away and walked by yourself in the night for a while and talked to the stars. You were never tired and never discouraged in those days. You lived on peanut-butter sandwiches and hope and the feel of girl flesh and Technicolor dreams in which you never had to fight because the girls were all so eager. Those were terrible days and it's a wonder you ever lived through them. But you did, and now, Benson thought, it isn't so very different except that sometimes you get a little tired.

He opened the door and got out and walked over to the log railing. He braced one foot on it, leaning forward. The harsh mountainside broke sharply down to the highway below. Jagged boulders as big as houses thrust forward and seemed to hang in midair, unsupported. It was easy to see where Duquesne had landed. A rough shadowed outcropping sixty feet below rose almost straight up, tilting back into the mountain to form a tight pocket that was still smeared from peak to base with dark flakes of color that could only have been blood.

Benson moved along inside the railing until he was directly over the place. Here the raked gravel was pocked with the holes left by camera tripods and with the crazy scratchings of birds that had come scavenging for the picnic scraps thrown out by visitors. The railing was scored deeply by ropes that had been tied here to support whoever had gone down for the body.

And that was all there was to see. The body was gone, the blood nearly worn away. The police had taken their pictures, had measured distances and angles, and they would be preparing a chart that would show just what had happened here on Saturday night. It was very quiet on Lookout Point now. The sun was hot, but the breeze through the mountan pass was sweet and cool. Benson lit a cigarette and sat on the railing, his back to the steep drop. He stared blindly at the rough worn face of the mountain, trying not to think of anything.

Coming here had been a mistake, he realized. Until now he had not allowed himself to visualize the explosion of violence that had resulted in Duquesne's death. And that had made it easier for him to accept the boy's story. Now, in the hard sun, and alone, it all seemed incredible.

Of course it had been dark then, and deserted, with a cold wind whistling from the mountain. What had happened then could only have happened in darkness. But—had the boy told him the truth?

Overhead a shifting black shadow soared across the sun-bright concrete. It seemed to veer directly toward Benson and he ducked in reflex, then grinned at himself and turned to watch a great raw-necked white-shouldered buzzard sail through the pass, beating once before he caught a rising thermal updraft in his huge wings, then coasting, tilting with the air currents and sailing high over the mountain. Benson turned back and looked up along the jagged slope where sparse clumps of oak and cedar grew in tiny, precarious pockets of earth. The buzzard nestlings would be up there somewhere, he suspected, but probably too high for anyone ever to see. He quartered the mountain carefully before he gave up.

He rubbed his cigarette out against the railing, stripped the paper with his fingers and let the loose tobacco drift away on the wind. Then he got in his car and drove down the steep road to the highway and back toward Rincon.

BENSON backed his car tightly into a metered parking space near his office, got out and took his briefcase from the back seat.

He rode up in a crowded elevator, silent, unhearing, and went past the receptionist's desk with aimless speed, unaware that she had called his name. He pushed back the half-open door of his office and went inside.

"Oh, thank goodness," Mary said. "I've been trying to find you everywhere. Mr. Blumberg is very anxious to see you. Shall I . . ." Her hand hovered over her phone like an anxious hummingbird.

"No," Benson said sharply. Now why did I say that? he wondered. I'll have to talk to Blumberg sometime. But not now. Not just yet. He was aware of a deep reluctance to talk to anyone. There were a dozen problems that had to be faced and solved; he could not hope to put them off for long. But for a few hours, why not?

"No," he said again, more quietly. "I don't want to see him just now, Mary. Tell him . . ." He looked down at her thin, worried face. He could not give her a brusque message to be relayed to Blumberg because Mary was flatly incapable of blunt harshness. She would soften it somehow, with a charming, fearful censorship, and make a worse mess for him. "Tell him you gave me his message, Mary," he said. "But wait until I've left. I'm going out to the ranch. I want you to phone for me and have someone tell Clemente to saddle the stud and send a boy with him to meet me outside Kellogg Junction in about an hour. Will you do that, please?" Benson leafed quickly through a pile of papers on his desk.

"Of course, Mr. Kellogg," Mary said mechanically. "But, your calls! The phone has been ringing every five minutes. Mostly it was Mr. Blumberg. Then your brother called twice. He wanted——"

"I know what he wanted," Benson said shortly. As Joss had warned him, the pressure was reaching Burr too. He went across the room to Mary's desk, took the list of calls from her and held it to the light.

All of them had tried at least twice to find him. Burr's name was first on the list. Then came the *Rincon Record* with three tries. The County Attorney's office twice. The Associated Press twice. Tim Cook had three strokes after his name. The last notation was "L.A." with two check marks. Benson put his thumb under that one and showed it to Mary. "No name for this one?"

"The second time, yes," Mary said, nervously brisk. "The man said he was calling for Mr. H. L. Caine. Isn't that the man who——"

"Yes," Benson said. "It probably is." He put the list in his pocket. "They'll call again, I suspect. Tell the newspapers that a plea of not guilty has been registered for Arturo Campeón. I will have no other comment until after the trial. Tell the others that you gave me their names."

"But aren't you going to——" Mary caught her lower lip between her teeth and worried at it gently, watching Benson with large fearful eyes.

"You don't know what this is all about, do you, Mary?" Benson asked curiously.

She shook her head. "No." Dubiously, she added, "Grace Harkins said it was probably something about your client."

"It would be Miss Harkins," Benson said. "She's wrong this time. I would tell you, Mary, if there was any way you could help. I want you to hold off the wolves for me. I'm going riding for a while. I want some time to think about what I have to do. Just tell everybody you don't know where I am. And don't let them fluster you, Mary. We'll take care of it all tomorrow."

"That—that is very wise, Mr. Kellogg," Mary said. "My father always said that problems will work themselves out, given time."

"A wise man," Benson said cheerfully. "You might also tell Miss Harkins that I will want a dozen John Doe warrants for the Campeón trial. Ask her to pick them up for me and leave them on my desk. Then she can get on with her own work. I've decided I won't ask her to help me after all. I'll prepare my trial brief by myself."

Benson left before Mary could ask the question that was shaping itself on her lips. There was no need to explain anything. Miss Harkins would understand what he meant. Her loyalty was reserved for Burr, and Burr could no longer be considered a sure and dependable ally.

Benson went down the corridor with long strides. He caught an elevator just before its door slammed shut.

THE DRIVE to Kellogg Junction took far less time than it should have. Benson drove fast down the center lane west toward the high sun-bright Gritones, through the downtown district of department stores and expensive shops and narrow cramped movie houses and new-car dealers, past the green palm-lined grounds of Rincon High and through the city's oldest residential district, where the Iowa-Moorish fortresses were shouldered aside by supermarkets and drive-in movies and used-car dealers. Then he passed the city limits and the road widened and the traffic thinned. Here were isolated clumps of new, pastel-plastered houses clustered like children's building blocks around a shopping center or a new school that always sat far back behind a cyclone fence on a treeless stretch of raw, bull-dozed sand. There were still a few old adobe-and-frame houses little better than shacks with rubber-tire swings hung from the old mesquites, and pepper trees and straggly rows of budding flowers in the bare yards where chickens scratched at the soft ground.

Benson slowed for the approach to Kellogg Junction. He turned left onto the gravel road to La Cañada, accelerated into the lifting range of foothills. He cut his motor at the top of the hill and let the car drift to a stop beside a giant saguaro that cast a thick, drowning-man's shadow across the gravel.

He took out a cigarette, punched in the dash lighter. The reflection of his face in the tinted windshield was blank and pale, and there was a slight tremor in his hands as he held the lighter to his cigarette. He was full of a tight senseless anger, di-rected at himself as much as anyone. He had let himself be trapped in a situation that offended the few convictions he still held strongly. It was too late to get out of it now, and knowing that only increased his anger.

You'd better cut that out, friend, he warned himself. The only thing you can do now is to get such thoughts out of your head. The thing to remember is that a boy is going to be tried for his life. Even your fumbling defense will be better than none at all. And if the details of the case make you want to vomit, then you can damn well do your vomiting in decent privacy and stop bothering people.

Benson grinned bleakly at his reflection. You're a delicate fellow, you are, he thought. The trouble with you is that you've been protected all your life. Just because you went off to war and got shot up, and found a fine wife who went and got killed, you had an idea you must have lived a crowded and varied life. And now you know how wrong you were, don't you? It's a little late for you to be learning the facts of life, and it's going to be painful, but you'd better start learning fast because right about now you are about as well equipped to handle this case as an acned schoolboy who still hasn't figured out how the he-and-she business really works when you get between the sheets.

Behind him he could see a high-sided yellow county school bus come groaning up the low grade, rattle along the summit and swoop down to pass him in a cloud of pale dust. Through the windows he saw the dark laughing faces of the La Cañada kids shrieking at him. He waved his hat out the open door and grinned as they swept by. There went one of the best investments La Cañada had ever made, he thought. The ranch had bought that bus, furnished one of the hands to drive it and given it to the county school board. The county paid for operation and maintenance, paid the driver a small salary and put aside a sum for depreciation. So from now on the ranch kids would be picked up at their doors and delivered home every day and there would be no more of that miserable, jolting, dusty ride in an open truck from the ranch down to the highway at Kellogg Junction. Benson could remember it well, and what he remembered most clearly were the rainy days and the cold days and the days when the sky was red with dust or gray and streaked with the clouds that sometimes brought snow to the upper reaches of La Cañada. Buying the bus had been Burr's idea, a damn good one. And because of an insane tax structure, the ultimate cost to the ranch would be exactly nothing. It took a smart and tricky lawyer like Burr to figure out a deal like that.

The yellow bus rumbled inside its pale plume of gravel dust, rose above it briefly at the mountain pass and disappeared beyond the peak. The dust went very quickly, blown high and dispersed by the wind, but before it was completely gone, Benson saw his white stud come through the high pass, shimmering like a new pearl in the haze.

Benson got out of the car. He stripped off his coat and tossed it on the front seat. He pulled his tie loose, rammed it into a pocket of the coat. By then the white stallion breasted the last rise and came ambling toward the car. The rider unstrapped a pair of jodhpur boots from the cantle and swung down.

He was short and thick with a barrel chest and heavy mountaineer's thighs. His black mustache was thin and long and drooping at the ends like Genghis Khan's. He thumbed his sweaty hat back from his forehead, smiled beautifully and reached out to take the cigarette from Benson's mouth. He gave him the boots.

"Holá, patrón," he said deeply from the chest. "You look lousy. Why in hell you want the Caballo Padre?"

"To ride," Benson said. He sat in the open door, shook the spurs out of the boots, kicked off his shoes and smoothed his socks before putting on the boots. He strapped them tightly at the ankle, cinched the blunt spurs and tossed his shoes into the car. He tugged at his hat and looked up with a half-smile. "All right, Clemente," he said. "What's on your mind?"

Clemente burned up half the cigarette in a long, powerful drag and spoke with streamers of smoke sifting from mouth and nostrils. "That big old Dolly mare," he said. "You remember when she foaled?"

Benson frowned, counting back. He moved around the front of the car, walked quietly up to the stallion and stroked his hand flat along the high hard curve of his neck. He lifted the near stirrup, measured its Gibson Red leather against his arm and slid the buckle down two notches. "Must have been five, six days ago," he said in a casual voice, "but from the way you're glaring at me, I guess it was more." He came forward, ducked under the stud's neck and fixed the other stirrup.

"It was eight," Clemente said positively.

Benson nodded. Clemente would be right, as always. He had the infallible memory of an illiterate man. Also he was foreman of La Cañada, and it was his job to be right about things like that. He was foreman, minority stockholder, sales manager, purchasing agent, veterinary technician specializing in horse obstetrics, farrier and designer of horseshoes that cured all acquired and congenital defects of gait, talented and sometimes inspired trainer of nervous colts, eager and gifted brawler with fists, knives, guns, ropes or rowel-spurred boots, braggart, man of honor and composer of romantic ballads which he played on a pearl-faced guitar and sang in a shrill and piercing tenor that was amazingly effective in the seduction of plump young females.

"I guess it probably was," Benson said. "So you've scheduled our old boy to leap the Dolly mare tomorrow and you don't want me bringing him home so tired that he won't have any interest in his work? That it?"

Clemente's wide mouth tucked in wryly at the corners. He pinched the coal from his cigarette and shredded it onto the ground. "Not as young as he used to be," he said.

"Nobody is, except you," Benson said. And it was true; Clemente was sixty-seven, and his day was sixteen active hours long every day except on those days when he went to town, and then he never got to bed at all—not to sleep, that is. Under his tight hat he was almost bald and that was his secret shame, but since he never took his hat off in public, hardly anyone knew. He looked now just the same as he always had and always would, probably. "Don't you ever get tired, Clemente?"

"No time, patrón. Too much to do. You too, huh?"

"What do you mean?" Benson gathered the double reins and pulled the stud to him.

"Margareta says the goddam telephone rings all day. She gave me this." Clemente held out a twisted spill of paper. "You want it? Names of people?"

"No." Benson twisted the stirrup, balanced the ball of his foot in the iron and swung up with a quick leap. He kicked his toe into the off stirrup, settled himself hard in the saddle and signaled for the stud to collect himself. The small faceted Arabian head drew in tightly and nosed toward the ground.

"Gracias, Señor Caporal," he said with a half-salute. "Until later, eh?"

Clemente nodded soberly. He started the car, lurched forward, spraying gravel. He ground his way slowly up to the pass, staying in low gear because it was safer to go slowly where stock might be wandering out on the road.

Benson let the big stud find his own route along the moraine of foothills until they had passed the great dry arroyo that carried the flash floods down from the Gritones.

Then they turned north, away from Rincon, away from the people and the problems that were beginning to close in like damp fog in Benson's mind. Decisions had to be made, and soon, Benson knew, but he also knew, or suspected, that any decision made under outside pressure might well be disastrous. He reined the stud toward the last stretch of low hills and leaned forward slightly as they worked their way down into the magic desert.

It was so that Benson thought of it to himself. A magic land with magic animals, magic plants, with a history like no other part of the country.

This land had been desert for a long time and man had not yet learned how to live in it, though many men in the past had accommodated themselves better than any in recent knowledge. There had been the Pueblos who had irrigated stretches up to a quarter-million acres with primitive tools. The wild tribes had finished them. Then came the Spaniards, and for a long time everything went plumb to hell, because the Spaniard was a conqueror and what conquerors do best is wreck things. They were all gone long since, and what they left behind was also a part of the current magic.

Wherever a man is born and grows is a magic land, and no other will ever touch him in quite the same way. England in April has a magic for Englishmen that no visiting member of the Browning Society will ever feel. And only the Sherpas know the magic of Everest. A man knows and relishes his home and is cheered by the memory. And a man who knows no home is lost to man.

Here, for Benson, was the magic of place, and of time.

This was the upper Sonoran desert, the American part. Here giant saguaro cactuses lived for centuries, branching out arms to celebrate golden anniversaries. They weighed a ton in dry winters and could absorb as much as two tons of water whenever water was available. The enormous ribbed stalks were protected from evaporation by dense, impermeable waxy coats and stood solidly on wide and shallow root structures that spread a hundred feet around. The saguaro grew nowhere but in this magic land.

And the animals, the magic animals. The sidewinder, which was often confused with the common rattler, and the kangaroo rat, tiny, big-eared, made for a child's toy. A small salute for them, please. They are the ones who have solved a problem that no man can understand. They create their own water. Say it again, and tip your hat. They need no water. They share a secret and they can manufacture water as easily as a lank-haired high school chemistry teacher manufactures water in the lab, taking two of H and one of O and giving the test tube a shot of power and then holding up the single, magical, glistening drop of water—pow! But the kangaroo rat and the sidewinder don't have tanks of H and O from the Du-Pont warehouse and they don't have a direct line to the Mountain States Light and Power Company. They do it all by magic, from the air, because of their need. They are free as no other animals are free. They are magic creatures and they live in the desert and they make the desert a magic place.

Benson breathed more deeply and easily here. When he rode alone through this land he was at home and his spirit sang. This rough, barren, broken, abandoned country was the only world he loved.

The magic desert was beginning to disappear now. As a boy Benson had traveled the fifty miles from the mountains to Rincon seeing few fences and only an occasional ranch house that was always miles from its nearest neighbor. It was not like that now. People were crowding into the towns and spilling over into open land. The largest population increase in recent years had been measured in the desert, all from the restless migration that is America's unbreakable habit. Expanding towns were sinking new and deeper wells to find water for the new people and industries. They were mining fossil water that could not be replaced, and in another few generations the desert would be a bleak and arid world worse than the Sahara. Already a section of the northern suburbs of Rincon had sunk half a foot due to the lost water. Some time fairly soon the magic plants would die, except the ones preserved in open-air museums, and the magic animals would move along somewhere else as they always had; they have an instinct for knowing when to take off. Especially the scorpion, who will manage to tough it out somehow. He is still here and he may be the oldest living creature on earth. His ugly tracks can be seen in the fossils of primordial ooze in just the same shape as they are visible outside the back door where the evaporative cooler drips and softens the hard surface of the desert. He is not indestructible, as any kid knows; he isn't highly poisonous and he scares nobody, but he endures. He has escaped being crushed by dinosaurs and by men. Another magic creature that lives in the desert and makes the desert a magic place. And he too will move along when it is time for him to go.

But not just yet.

Benson put the stud to a low knoll, drew him in a circle and halted for a breather. He swung down, keeping the bights of the reins over his arm.

From the knoll the desert sloped to the south with the fall of the waterline. The stone-hard earth was no longer bare and dusty since the last brief rain. Now little pastel anemones grew in riotous, multicolored sprays, following the erratic pattern of the winds that had scattered their seeds. Mesquites and cottonwoods along the banks of the dry streams were heavily green. A distant canyon, sloping quickly up into the mountain and angled like a greenhouse tray tilted to the sun, was completely blanketed with a startling mass of scarlet and gold poppies.

Benson watched a cactus wren poking her head timidly out of her ramshackle nest in among the savage spines of a spindly cholla. The wren eyed Benson beadily for a long moment, then decided she had no pressing business and ducked back out of sight.

The big stud moved in a restive circle. He lowered his head, butting Benson lightly between the shoulders. Then he put his soft velvet mouth to Benson's collar and lipped at the loose fabric. Benson reached up and back with one hand, running it gently along the big crushing jaw. Champion Nur Hafiz, in the official registry. El Caballo Padre of La Cañada, known to the hands as *the* stud. It had taken a thousand carefully bred generations to produce him and four solid years of daily training to give him his skill and manners.

Benson drew the stud to him and went up smoothly into the old Stubben saddle. A desert thrasher ran busily through a patch of hollyhocks, whistling an impudent trill like a street-corner bum watching the girls go by. The stud skittered nervously, almost rubbing against a scarlet-tipped ocotillo. Benson steadied him, then turned him south from the knoll.

The desert was beginning to glow with the soft light of late afternoon, and Benson could see pale tinges of color that until now had been bleached to nothing by the overhead sun. With each step, the fast-walking stud crushed a dozen wind flowers that bloomed in thick bright patches between sagebrush and mesquite and greasewood. The desert in the last brightness of the day was full of color and frail, dusty, scent. The shadows were not so sharply black and white now and the wind from the mountain was no longer hot.

Benson brought the stud up to the bit and angled away from a high thicket of flame-tipped cactus. They were heading in a wide easy arc back toward the bright Gritones, and their long purple-black shadow reached out far ahead.

ONCE THROUGH THE PASS, Benson rode down into the cold darkness of the mountain valley, feeling the chill through his thin shirt. The stud moved with an eager surge toward the lights of the ranch below.

They went along the graveled road in a slow collected canter, with the stud changing leads at Benson's signal, moving with high elegant action that gave them both great satisfaction. He and Benson knew that what they were doing was difficult and precise, and beautiful when it is done properly.

Short of the small cluster of houses, Benson pulled the stud down to a walk so that he would not be tempted, through tiredness, to break his slow, perfect rhythm.

From the steepled shadow of the chapel, a dark horse with a thick-bodied big-hatted rider moved out into the road with a soft jangle of chains and fell into place like a guidon-bearer behind Benson, half a length to the rear. Benson did not turn his head. That would be Clemente, he knew, and Clemente would speak in his own good time.

They moved in tandem past the great horse barn, past the training track and up into the lifting curve that ended at the ranch house. Benson reined in below the terrace, dismounted and held the big stud's head warmly in the crook of his arm. Clemente got down, ground-tied his horse and came stumping toward Benson in the short, stilted steps of a horseman in tight boots.

"A little moment, Benito, if you can favor me?"

Clemente's heavy voice demanded attention. But more than the tone caught Benson. The foreman was speaking Spanish, strongly inflected and overcareful. When Clemente spoke Spanish it was best to listen closely, for he was proudly a Norteamericano by birth and inclination and English was the language he preferred. He often thought in Spanish, however, and when he wished to say something precisely, with no possibility of confusion, he spoke in Spanish. And always slowly, gravely, in the tones of judicial pronouncement.

"Command me, Don Clemente," Benson answered formally. He took his cigarettes from his shirt pocket, shook one free of the pack and offered it to Clemente. "It's been a long time since you called me that," he said with a slight, puzzled smile.

"I say Benito as I used to say Benito before you became patrón. The patrón of La Cañada is a man of much importance and must be respected. But I speak now to Benito." He took a cigarette, hung it in a corner of his mouth and scratched a match on the seat of his pants. In the sudden flare of light his strong dark face was somber, unsmiling. "With your permission, patrón?"

"What troubles you, Don Clemente?"

"Not me. You." Clemente drew in on his cigarette and his

face seemed to glow like wet bronze in the faint light. "Today
came an old one to La Cañada. Such an old one as I have not
seen since my father's day." Clemente crossed himself with
the hand that held the cigarette. "A light-boned hard man of
much anger, like an eagle. With a face like an eagle. Such men
are not often seen in our time. There is no longer a place for
them, or a need." Clemente tilted his massive head and
squinted at Benson. "You know this old one, eh?"

"Yes," Benson said.

"A killer, is he not?"

"He was once a Dorado, I have heard."

"Ah!" Clemente's indrawn breath made a soft hiss. "Of
course! It becomes clear. One of Villa's golden men. I knew
some. Not this one, but others. Men whose hats and saddles
were heavy with stolen gold. Savages. Men like wolves. Yes,
now I understand. This is a strange old one, Benito. Dangerous."

"I believe it, Don Clemente. Why did he come here?"

"Because of you." Clemente made a sharp gesture in the
darkness. "He knew of B. Kellogg. He knew of La Cañada.
But he came to see with his own eyes."

"To see what?"

"That the seed was strong still, that the land was held and
prospered. This is not a man to be told. He must see for himself."

"What did you do with him?"

"I showed him," Celemente said easily. "All things. The
land, the mares in foal, the new colts, our people and the
places where they live. You understand why he wishes to see
these things?"

"I can imagine why. His grandson has great trouble with
the law. It is for me to defend him. I suppose the old man
wanted to find out what sort of man I was."

"That, yes. And more. He is suspicious, you understand.
He trusts no one. He must see for himself that you are a man
who will fight for his grandson as you would for your own."

"It does not rest with me, Don Clemente," Benson said

with slow, controlled patience. "A jury will decide. I will defend the boy as best I can."

"So the old one now understands. He has talked to the women and learned that our children are schooled as well as any Anglo child and may choose for themselves whether they stay at La Cañada or leave for another life outside. He spoke with the men who are trained in the arts of the horse and also in machinery so they could work and make a living anywhere. He has seen that all of La Cañada's people share in the patrón's prosperity. So he can now believe that in the court his grandson will be well defended." Clemente finished his cigarette and rubbed it out against the steps.

"Listen to me, Don Clemente," Benson said seriously. "You must explain to the old man that his grandson's life is not in my hands, but God's. I will defend the boy in court, but it is the jury that will decide."

"No," Clemente said quietly. "That is what I have been trying to tell you, Benito. It is the old one who will decide. You know how a man like this is, within himself? What does he care for the law, for the courts? He will decide."

"Decide what?"

"If the boy will live or die."

Benson shook his head. "You must have misunderstood him, Clemente. No man would wish to——"

"I do not misunderstand," Clemente broke in sharply. "Attend to me, Benito! I know this man. I know him in my bones. He cannot be sure the boy is innocent. He does not entirely believe what the boy says. So he will listen to you, listen and decide for himself. You speak to two judges, Benito, the one in court, and the Dorado."

"Clemente——"

"I tell you he is a killer, patrón. He will kill the boy. No matter what happens in court, he will kill the boy, unless . . ." Clemente shrugged.

"Unless I convince him the boy is innocent," Benson said mildly. "All right, Clemente. And I suppose he has threatened to kill me if the boy is convicted?"

"You are listening too quickly, patrón," Clemente said stiffly. "The old one has not made threats. He does not need to. I feel something about this man. He is accustomed to killing, yes. Killing is nothing to such a one. But more than that, he is a man of honor. If he should kill his grandson, it would be because of the dishonor the boy has brought to his name. Now I speak no more of this. I have said what needed to be said. Do you understand, patrón?"

"I understand," Benson said soberly. "Many thanks, Don Clemente."

"Ah, Benito," Clemente sighed. "As always I am easily angered when you do not listen. Forgive me. You know what must be done. I leave it in your hands. In God's hands." He took the stud's reins from Benson and caught up his own reins. He pulled both horses toward him and turned them to face down the driveway. "Is the boy in danger, Benito?" he asked abruptly. "I cannot believe he is. I am not schooled in these matters. I see only that a boy has killed a corrupt man who would pollute him. Is it not allowed for him to defend himself?"

"The law is not clear on that point, Don Clemente. I could explain, but it might take more time than you would care to—"

"Enough," Clemente said quickly. "I am an ignorant man. I put stud to mare and expect to get a colt with the qualities of each. I do not put stud to gelding or mare to mare. I geld a horse so that he will be more gentle and easier to manage, but I know he is no longer a horse when he is gelded. A man who would make of himself a gelding, a mule, is an abomination. Such a man I might kill myself. I do not believe this boy will be punished for killing such a one. If you say it is difficult and not clear in the law, then I know that is so. But you will save him, Benito. With the help of God."

"With the help of God," Benson said. And some shifty footwork in the courtroom.

"But the old man will not believe that all rests with God, Benito. He looks also to you. Remember that. If things go badly, you must tell me at once."

"All right, Don Clemente. Many thanks. Good night."

"May God walk with you, Benito."

Clemente turned and went slowly down the slope, his spur chains ringing softly against the paving. Both horses moved after him on long leads.

Benson stood at the foot of the steps for a long moment, watching until even the vague, moving shapes were lost in darkness. He turned then and went up the stone treads to the terrace.

When the lazy voice spoke behind him, he whirled suddenly, dropping his cigarette.

"Sorry, Ben, I didn't mean to scare you," Tim Cook said in quick apology. "I was just sitting here when you and Clemente rode up. You seemed to be having a serious talk, so I didn't want to butt in. Didn't think it mattered, me being out here. I don't understand Spanish."

"It's all right, Tim," Benson said slowly. He kicked the cigarette toward the edge of the terrace. "I'm a little jumpy today, I guess."

"Got reason to be, from what I hear," Tim said dryly.

Benson did not answer. He crossed toward Tim's long canvas sun couch and sat on the corner of a redwood table. "Where is everybody?" he asked. "Are you alone here?"

"Me and a bottle of brandy," Tim said. "Jest a-settin' here and a-gettin' mildly stoned and a-waitin' for that ole desert moon to come up."

"Long wait," Benson said. "Three or four days, anyway."

"I can wait."

"How's the leg getting on?"

"Not bad. The pain's gone down. Maybe that's the brandy. Paula found me a pair of crutches and I can get around a little bit. She and Fitz took me on a trip this afternoon. Out in the desert. Mighty purty country, podner."

"Yes, it is," Benson said absently. "Is Paula here?"

"She went home. Said you wouldn't want her around right now, the way Burr has been acting."

Tim waited for Benson to say something. When he was

sure there wasn't going to be an answer, he said, "Fitz went off to the airbase. Some three-star is retiring and they're having a ball. Fitz was really dolled up. You knew he was a soldier, I guess?"

"Brigadier," Benson said. "Retired."

"That's what he said. Christ, he looks like the Roxy doorman in that fancy uniform. He ought to go to Mexico. They'd make him president."

"Not these days." Benson reached behind him for an ashtray, touched the brandy bottle and picked it up. He pulled the cork, sniffed the bottle and then tilted it up for a long swig. He held it out to Tim.

"Just a touch, since you push me," Tim drank and corked the bottle. He put it down carefully beside his couch.

Benson sat quietly, and the growing silence made Tim fidget. He cleared his throat noisily. "I'm beginning to like your country, Ben," he said. "I never saw so much open land before. Or if I did, I never had time to take a good look at it."

"Takes getting used to," Benson said. "It's too bright for most people, and too dry."

"I know what you mean. I can't say I'm used to it yet, but I'm trying. You know, I grew up in Chicago and the only open space we had was Lake Michigan and a one-block park that was paved with tar. I never saw anything like this country when I was a kid. It feels good. You know? I feel like I belonged here."

Tim put his head back against the canvas cushion and looked up toward the dark circle of mountains.

We are simpler people by night, Benson was thinking. Maybe even better people. "You're likely to become one of those old desert rats, if you keep it up," he said.

"You bet," Tim said lazily. "Me and old B. Kellogg. Now there was a genu-wine, blowed-in-the-glass hard case for you. I was reading his diary this afternoon. Is that all straight stuff, Ben, or did the old fellow shade it some to make himself look better?"

"It's hard to say, Tim. There's no way to check most of it."

"How would you bet, if you had to lay money?"

"I'd give old B. the nod. He was a remarkable man in a time when you had to be a pretty good man just to stay alive out here."

"Hell of a guy, all right," Tim said. "He wrote an awful elegant kind of English. I guess most people did in those days. He could be tough, but he was always nice about it. He sure didn't care much for preachers, did he?"

"Not much," Benson said. "If he'd ever bothered to decide on a religion, he would have been a Deist, probably."

"Him and Tom Jefferson, huh? 'The only gods of meaning and endurance have been invented by men who lived in the desert.' That's B. Kellogg for you. Sticks in your mind, doesn't it?"

"He was romantic about the desert," Benson said. "You get that way if you stay long enough. The Arabs call the desert the Garden of Allah. The Land of Goshen in the Bible is the desert. The Arabs say you can find Paradise on earth in the pages of a book, in the arms of a woman, on the back of a horse in the desert."

"Who did you say was romantic?" Tim snorted. "Help me up. I want to show you something I found in that diary." He swung his legs to the stone surface of the terrace, propped the crutches under his arms and waited for Benson to lift him. He crossed to the doorway in careful, short lunges, moving smoothly as long as he went slowly. Benson pushed the door back and held it for him.

Tim hopped on one foot to a deep chair, turned cautiously and dropped down into the cushions. He picked up the top sheet of a sheaf of loose papers on the table near his elbow.

"I liked this one too, Ben. Listen. This is old B. talking. 'The climate of this territory is excessive. Most of man's vital energy is consumed in his effort to remain alive. One must live here as a wary, hunted beast, for a man may easily be drowned and swept away in a torrent from exactly the same place where, a day earlier, he might have died of thirst. Such an immoderate climate makes for immoderate men. It ratifies convictions of superiority and pride in men whose only achievement is that they have contrived to stay alive in this inhospitable, this cruel land.' That's pretty good." Tim put the paper aside and looked up sharply at Benson. "I've been wondering what made people around here so damn stiff-necked."

"Now you know," Benson said shortly. He poured a small drink from the brandy bottle. He held up an empty glass and glanced at Tim.

"Not right now," Tim said, speaking now with his customary sharp quickness, as though by coming into the lighted room, his mood of reverie and quiet had been broken completely. "I have to talk to you, Ben."

Benson tossed off the drink and put the glass down on the bar with a sharp tap. "About what?"

"Pretty obvious, isn't it?" Tim said. "You've been ducking the phone all day, I hear. Most of those people called here, too. I took some of the calls. Paula took some. And I got a call from my boss. You remember who I work for, Ben?"

"Nate Barstow," Benson said tightly. "What about it?"

Tim Cook sighed. "I'd like to sit around and talk some more about old B. Kellogg. I like him and his country and I'm glad I got a chance to look around for myself. That's what I'd like to do and that's what you'd like me to do. But I've got a job too, Ben. I'm just an errand boy. I do what Nate Barstow tells me to do. What he tells me to do right now is try and talk some sense into you."

"About Mr. H. L. Caine?" Benson stood stiffly with his back against the cold wall.

"That's it. About H. L. Caine. My boss has got himself a goose that lays golden eggs. And now you're about to clobber his goose. It's reasonable that Nate should want to get you to change your mind, isn't it?"

Benson said nothing. His long face was gaunt with strain but he held himself in hard control.

"Isn't it?" Tim insisted. "Isn't it reasonable, Ben?"

"I don't know Nate Barstow very well," Benson said. "I don't know what he thinks is reasonable. I do know that I will not discuss the Campeón case with him or with anyone he sends. Is that clear, Tim? Now let's drop it, please."

"Are you going to let that little punk of a murderer smear a man like H. L. Caine? Why, damn it, Ben——"

"I said, drop it, Tim. I won't discuss it."

"Listen, Ben. Think it over. You don't know what this means. A lot of people are going to get hurt if you drag Caine into this mess."

"Another threat?"

"Another?" Tim said quickly. "Who else has been threatening you? Frank Sayer, I suppose?"

And a savage old man who will probably try to kill me if his grandson is convicted of murder, Benson thought.

"Never mind, Tim. You can tell your boss that I haven't got time to worry about him or H. L. Caine. I've got a client to worry about."

Tim Cook leaned back in his chair. He braced his elbows on the arms and made a steeple of his fingers, looking at Benson over the apex. "The way I hear it, your punk is going to hang, no matter what you do. What's the good of hurting a man like Caine when it can't do your boy any good?"

"You're not competent to judge that, Tim. I won't——"

"Listen just a minute, Ben." Tim said hurriedly. "I know you've got a lot on your mind these days. But just give me a minute. You know, for a politician, Nate Barstow isn't much of a crook. At least he always remembers people who do him favors. That's why he's going to bat for Caine right now. And he'd go to bat for you, if you were one of his friends. Wouldn't you like to be a judge someday, Ben? Wouldn't you like to be general counsel for Consolidated Copper with a fifty-grand retainer every year and a bonus on Christmas?"

"You're not making a serious offer, are you, Tim?" Benson said, thin-lipped, tautly angry.

Tim broke the tension with a quick laugh. "No, I'm not in that end of it. Just something for you to think about. Nobody is bribing you. I wanted you to think about what it could mean to have Nate Barstow and H. L. Caine for friends. Then there's the other side of it."

Benson said nothing.

"I mean," Tim went on blandly, "what if Barstow and Caine didn't like you? What if, for some reason, they wanted to do you dirt? Have you ever thought about that, Ben? You've got a brother in politics. He'd be out, I guess you know. And these days a lawyer doesn't get much business thrown his way if people know he has powerful enemies. All that's worth thinking about, Ben."

"You're wrong," Benson said in a slow, thick voice. "It's not worth thinking about."

Tim Cook put his head back and studied Benson. "You're not very sure of yourself, are you?" he said in a puzzled voice. "You don't know what in hell you're going to do. I can see that." He rubbed his locked hands along the edge of his jaw. "If you were really sure, you'd tell me what you had in mind, and then you'd tell me to go to hell. If you did that, I'd pass the word along to Nate Barstow and everybody would get off your back because we'd know there wasn't any point in trying any more. But you aren't sure, are you, Ben? You just can't make up your mind."

"That's enough, Tim." Benson opened the door that led into the corridor.

"I guess it is," Tim said with slow reluctance. "You'll have to decide sometime, Ben, and you'd better decide right. Well, I've said my piece and now I'll shut up. I'm in a kind of funny position here, being your guest and all. It would be a lot easier if I was just some guy who walked in off the street. Easier for me, anyhow. As it is, I can't push you. I can't keep talking after you tell me to shut up. But you'd better be braced for the others. They won't let up on you, Ben. In the next couple of days you're going to find out what pressure means. You'll think a house fell on you."

"All right, Tim," Benson said heavily. "You've said your piece. Leave it at that. Will you have a drink?"

Tim shook his head. "No, thanks. I think I'd better get to bed. I've had a busy day and I have to get up early tomorrow.

I'm going back to El Monte."

"There's no need to leave, Tim."

"I think I'd better. Anyway, I'm expected at the capital tomorrow. We've got a state caucus coming up and I'm supposed to do some work. I hired a guy to drive me up. He'll be here pretty early. Don't mind if I hang on to your crutches for a while, do you?"

"Of course not. I'm sorry you have to leave, Tim."

"So am I, in a way. This has been something new for me." Tim pulled his crutches into position and levered himself upright. "You're a hell of a nice guy, Ben, you know that? It's been a real pleasure knowing you. But you haven't got enough wolf in you. Maybe you ought to read old B.'s diary again; he could straighten you out. You're just not with it, Ben. You're going to get run over by a truck and you won't even spot the license number."

"Good night, Tim."

"Don't get sore at me, Ben. I'm just an errand boy. Nobody asks me what I think. I just do what I'm told. Good night, Ben. Thanks again. I'll be seeing you, maybe."

Tim hobbled awkwardly toward his bedroom, keeping his head down, watching the floor, not looking at Benson again.

THE RANCH HOUSE at La Cañada was very quiet, almost hushed. All the lights were out except for the goose-necked lamp in Benson's study. In the crisp predawn chill of the mountain meadows, horses were beginning to shift and stamp, waking from their last short sleep. In an hour the hands would come stumbling, gummy-eyed and clumsy, to haze the horses toward the feed lots. But for the moment everything was unnaturally still and Benson became oppressively aware of the silence. He lurched back in his chair, his concentration broken, and lifted his arms wide overhead, hearing the tendons grate as he stretched. He was no longer tired; he had passed that point. His mind was numbed, his eyes tender from long reading in the closely printed pages of the law books that were spread across his desk. Two legal-size yellow notepads were filled with his scrawled notes, a collection of references that would support him from the bailiff's initial "Hear ye, hear ye," to the final gavel that dismissed the court.

An attorney experienced in criminal procedure would not have needed that close review, but Benson, knowing his limitations, had forced himself to an abecedary approach and now, leaning back and yawning, he felt fairly sure of his command of the rules that governed criminal trials. But sound procedure is only a minor part of any trial. His father used to compare it to spelling, Benson remembered—something that conferred no honor when correct but was slightly shameful when wrong. Probably it would be more accurate to compare it to the paperwork done by the military, Benson thought. Slipshod staffwork can ruin a campaign in a hundred ways, but the best paperwork in the world never won a battle. But at least, he felt, he had done something useful, even if it was merely a beginning.

He had not yet had a chance to interview the witnesses listed by the prosecution and he was not now likely to get the chance, but from what Turo Campeón had told him, he could anticipate the line their testimony would follow. From his night's study and his own observation, he had prepared a few ugly little surprises for Frank Sayer. The County Attorney was going to get a battle on several points, including the matter of the confession that had been forced from the boy. With what he had in mind now, Benson knew he could throw several slippery rocks under Frank Sayer's feet.

But that was all he could see in front of him. And no lawyer could hope to win a case with a negative approach. The law in its solemnity declares all defendants innocent until proven guilty. But in practice, said defendant had damn well better be prepared to prove his innocence. Merely contesting the prosecution's evidence is never adequate.

So the bigger and more important hurdles were still in front of him. Benson folded his arms on the desk and put his head down. He knew what had to be done now. And he knew exactly what he needed. But he had no idea of where or how he could get it. There might be some hope for——

The phone rang, softly insistent, in Benson's ear. He lifted his head and picked it up without thinking. All night long it had been ringing at intervals and Benson had ignored it each time. And now, forgetfully, following the reflexes of long habit, he picked it up with no hesitation.

"Mr. Benson Kellogg?" a woman's voice asked. "Hold on, please. Mr. Burr Kellogg is calling you."

Benson coughed to clear his throat.

"Hi, Counselor," his brother's voice said briskly. "I've been telling the boys you'd probably be in about now."

"What?"

"I figured you'd be out prowling around the desert on that white stud. That's where you always head when you've got a problem, isn't it? How've you been, boy?"

"Just a minute, Burr." Benson put the phone down. He shifted books and papers until he found his cigarettes. He lit one and went out of the study, going down the hall to the big living room, turning on lights as he went. He stopped at the bar cabinet, poured two inches of bourbon in a glass and splashed it with a little water. He took a long sip, then crossed to the far end of the couch near the fireplace and picked up the extension phone that sat on a small table. He swung around and stretched out flat on the couch. "All right, Burr," he said, "let's have it."

"People are giving you a bad time, I hear," Burr said cheerfully.

"I guess so," Benson said. "You too, Burr?"

Burr laughed easily. "No, I'm no hatchetman, Counselor. But I won't say I'm not curious. I've got a certain stake in this, too, remember."

"I remember. Tim Cook suggested you'd be politically dead if I didn't roll over for Nate Barstow."

"Tim Cook is a jerk," Burr said sharply. "I've been telling all these guys that you aren't anyone they can push. I've seen you stick out your jaw too often to make a mistake about that. Don't worry, Ben. I'm not trying to push you and I won't go along with anybody that does. But it is pretty important, Ben. You can see that. A lot of things hang on your decision. I'd like to know how you're going to play it. Do you know yet?"

Benson let out a slow relieved breath. He had been avoiding Burr's call because he had dreaded getting from Burr the same kind of thick-headed interference he had already had from Frank Sayer and was due to get from Jake Blumberg and others. Now, hearing Burr's voice, knowing he was the same man as before, was like a weight lifting from Benson's mind.

"Not yet," he said honestly. "And thanks for putting it that way, Burr. Tim Cook seemed to feel I was betraying the republic by not making a decision right now. He's no lawyer, of course. I didn't try to explain to him."

"I'm a lawyer," Burr said. "Explain to me."

"It's simple enough, Burr. This is a very tough case. I'm not sure I have the law on my side. I don't know just what appeal I'm going to make to the jury. I haven't set a central theme yet. I'll probably need to use every emotional appeal I can get away with, so how in hell can I promise to eliminate the one emotional appeal that is a central element of the case, something that has been put right in my hands?"

"I can see it's a tough problem, Ben. But how does H. L. Caine fit into this emotional appeal?"

"I don't know that he does. I suppose I might show the jury a rich man's son who tried to corrupt a poor man's son and got killed for trying. That's an approach that might work with the right kind of jury."

"Or the wrong kind," Burr amended. "I see the point, boy. I don't think much of it."

"It's a decision for me to make, Burr."

"I know, Counselor, I know. Don't get testy, boy. You've got to think of your client first, last and always. I know that."

"Then why ask me?"

"Well, Counselor, let me spell it out. Wait till I close the door. Those guys in the other room are getting noisy."

During the short intermission, Benson sat up and wedged

himself in the corner of the couch. He threw the stub of his cigarette into the fireplace.

"Okay, this is how it works," Burr said. "In a couple of days there is going to be a state caucus up here. All the wheels are going to make some decisions they won't be able to change. Mr. H. L. Caine, being a damn big contributor, is going to be asked for his opinion on some of those questions. So far he hasn't said anything, apparently he doesn't interfere very often, but the word is that he's boiling. Around here, people are trying to guess what he wants so they can butter him up in advance. Whatever he wants he'll probably get. If he wants my neck, these guys will serve it up thin-sliced and french-fried."

Benson took a long drink and put his glass down empty. He waited to be sure that Burr was finished. Then he said quietly, "Do you know what Caine's son tried to do, Burr? Do you know why he was killed?"

"I know, Ben," Burr said wearily. "And I hear the note of outrage in your voice. But I've got a suspicion that you're outraged more for yourself than your client."

Benson said nothing.

"Outraged innocence is a boring pitch, Ben. All this dirty business comes as a shock to you, I guess. You've come a little late to the world. But this is the way the world is, boy. People like Duquesne have fathers like H. L. Caine. And you have to concentrate on the father now, not the son. You understand what I mean, Ben?"

"I follow," Benson said coldly. "What I don't understand is why these people are putting the pressure on you. Do they really expect you to control me?"

Burr made a deep-throated, patient sound. "I'm the only one they can reach, Counselor. Another lesson in practical politics for you. They don't do much thinking in this racket. Mostly they work on a set of conditioned reflexes. When they get mad, they think first of cutting off somebody's balls. I'm the closest somebody. They're all pretty mad at you, Ben, especially Frank Sayer. You've made him look like a man who can't control things in his own county. That's bad. He's lying awake right now trying to figure ways to clobber you when he gets you in that courtroom."

"And he's the man who promised me all the cooperation of his office, just a couple of days ago," Benson said with an edge of sour distaste to his voice.

"A couple of days is a long time in politics, I've learned," Burr said casually. "Everything is different now. I guess you know that Frank isn't going to let you see any of his witnesses before he puts them on the stand? Try to find them and you'll hear they're off on a visit somewhere, due back Monday morning, or whenever Frank wants them. And that's only the beginning. Frank is really sore, Ben. You're making him look bad."

"The hell with Frank Sayer," Benson said. "Are you asking me for something, Burr?"

"Boy, you really lay it on the line, don't you?" Burr said mildly. "I guess I am asking for something, Ben. At least I would if I thought you wouldn't get pissed off. I've put a certain amount of time and effort into this political stuff. I'd hate to see it go down the drain."

"So would I," Benson said. "Do you think it's in my hands?"

"Part of it, Counselor," Burr said persuasively. "I want this chance to run. You can't give it to me. We both know that. But you can sure as hell take it away from me."

Benson coughed and swallowed a bitterness. Outside, enormous headlights swept along the rocky face of the mountain, swung right and lighted the glass wall of the room where Benson sat. The deep roaring pulse of a motor in low gear made echoes against the mountain. Benson watched the lights move away as the car straightened out and began the climb to the ranch house. He could hear Burr's voice vaguely in his ear, but his mind would not focus on what he was saying. Burr had said enough already. Benson brought the phone close to his mouth, said, "Good night, Burr," and hung up.

He was sitting there stiffly with the phone base in his lap, his thin strong hands locked around the cold angular mass, staring sightlessly down at the floor. When hard-shod feet made a clatter on the flagged terrace, he blinked. He turned when he heard knuckles rapping a tattoo on the glass door.

He could see Fitz's long narrow head, white hair shining like thin silk in the lights from the room. The face seemed to hang, disembodied, in the darkness, because he was inclined forward from the waist and his body was still in the dark. With one hand he made a questioning gesture. Benson nodded. Fitz pushed back the sliding door and came inside.

"Saw your light, old fellow. Thought we might have a nightcap."

Benson put the phone aside and got to his feet. He stared at Fitz and smiled in slow admiration. "My God, you are a vision, Fitz. Too bad we don't have uniforms like that."

"Merely mess kit, old boy," Fitz said complacently. "Nothing to compare with full dress, you know." He rotated gracefully, arms crooked comically away from his body. Basically his uniform was a lively dark blue, but it was flashed and striped with scarlet, braided, looped and fringed with gold lace. His high stand-up collar was scarlet with a bordering of gold. Even now his boiled shirt was brilliantly white, unwrinkled, and his square black tie was precisely and perfectly tied.

"Jesus," Benson breathed. "And a triple row of miniature gongs. You must be the very hell of a martial type."

"Am I not," Fitz agreed.

"Well, let me make you a drink, General. No, you're not called general, are you? What do we call a British brigadier anyway?"

"Get on with that drink, man. You may admire me later." He took a full glass from Benson, drained it in a long thirsty swig and then retreated to a chair near the fireplace. He sank into the cushions, shoved his long legs out straight and propped his patent-leather half-Wellingtons up on their short gold spurs. Then Fitz put his head back and let out a long noisy sigh.

"Tim said you were on the town tonight," Benson said. He brought a freshly filled glass to Fitz, picked up his own and went back to the couch. "Must have been a rough night."

"Oh, God," Fitz groaned. "Oceans of grog but hours of the dullest damn speeches I've ever heard. Nothing like my retirement party, I can tell you. Can't imagine what's got into the young officers these days; they just don't seem to have any fun. They were all so sedately polite they damn near put me to sleep." He stretched lazily, looked at Benson and added in a deceptively innocent tone, "I saw your girl at the party."

"What girl?"

"Tall blonde one. Came with a flying type who got pissed early on and spent the rest of the night puking his eyes out in the gents'. Naturally, I—ah—did what I could to cheer her up. Lovely girl, I must say. What's her name—Jess?"

"Joss," Benson said mechanically. "I don't think you'd better call her my girl, though."

"Heard all about it," Fitz said with a languid lift on his hand. "Poor girl made a dead set at me just so she could cry out her sorrows on me manly bosom. I wasted the hell of a lot of time with her before I found out she wasn't having any, thank you. Merely wanted to talk about you. Ah, you're the one, dear boy. Nothing is forgiven, mind you, but if you were to present yourself groveling, decently clad in sackcloth with a tasteful sprinkling of ashes, why, something might come of it." Fitz put his glass down, produced a magnificent square gold case and gave himself a cigarette. He tossed one to Benson. "Bit too good for you, that girl," he said with a blandly fierce smile. "You worry me, young Benson. You should be married, I suppose you know. You're the type to make a go of it. You made Liza very happy, the short time you had together. She wouldn't like thinking you were letting her training go to waste. You aren't sitting back mournfully, mumbling your sorrows, are you?"

"I don't think so, Fitz," Benson said uncomfortably. "I had the best time of my life being married to Liza. I'd like to marry again. You're right about me being the type. I'm not running from it. I just haven't managed to get around to it."

"Well, I won't poke. That girl Joss would do very well, I

think. She might give you a worrisome time, but even that is better than glooming about by yourself. I waited too long for it. Liza probably told you. Never was a good husband, I'm afraid. Never particularly wanted to be. Liked doing too many things that can't be done in a well-ordered household." Fitz clamped his cigarette at a high angle and squinted at Benson through a haze of smoke.

"Your girl told me about your argument," he said abruptly. He lifted one thick eyebrow and waited.

"Oh, Christ," Benson said sourly. "Skip that one, Fitz. I'm sick of talking about it."

"I dare say you are," Fitz said crisply. He drew a handkerchief from his tight sleeve and mopped his bright red face. "I suppose it's all far more complicated than she made it seem. But I did think, from what she told me, that you might be on rather a poor line. Is it true that your client killed a fellow who was trying to bugger him?"

Benson nodded.

"Do you actually hope to convince a jury that he was justified in killing? That's the way Joss put it. Don't suppose she had it right?"

"Right enough," Benson said slowly. "But, as you said, it's more complicated than that."

"My word," Fitz muttered. He put his handkerchief away and sat back with his drink in both hands. "Well, I dare say things in the legal line are rather different here. I don't think that you would be likely to get far with that sort of defense in a British court. Not saying you wouldn't, mind. Just my opinion it wouldn't wash."

"Why not?"

"My dear boy," Fitz said, "you can't go about killing for such a reason. Not saying the lavender boys aren't offensive. Stench in the nostrils, as a matter of actual fact. But if buggering a boy were a killing matter, half the people I went to school with would be dead long ago."

"What the hell are you talking about, Fitz?"

"Well, it's all very nasty, I agree, but there aren't many

boys who've gone through a British public school without being pounced upon one time or another by a brace of larger boys. Sort of thing you have to expect in a monastic society. Rather the sort of thing that happened to Grecian boys during their school days, wouldn't you say?"

"No," Benson said. "No, I wouldn't say that. Are you serious?"

"More or less. Just wanted to make a suggestion, dear boy. Hate the thought of interfering, you know. But in my life I've seen a lot of boy-lovers at one time and another. Quite decent men, many of them. Remember the Pathans, for instance. Finest soldiers anywhere. Never been conquered. Almost all of them are homosexual, though. 'A woman for business, a boy for pleasure' is what they say. Same as the Arabs and Turks."

Benson sat up squarely and put his glass down. "We aren't Pathans or Arabs or Turks," he said slowly. It was hard for him to speak in a quiet tone.

"Realize that, dear boy. Different cultures, of course. But, dammit, rogering never hurt a boy yet, that I've noticed. Didn't hurt me."

"You?" Benson said thickly.

"Nothing to cry about. Happened to most boys. Not much you could do about it when half a dozen muscular louts catch you out."

"I don't agree," Benson said stiffly. "A great deal could be done about it any time. I don't believe you went through such an experience as calmly as you pretend. And I don't believe it is as common an experience as you say."

"Possibly not," Fitz said gently, eying Benson with curious intensity. "Possibly not. It was a long time ago. One forgets. I do recall I thought it a fearful indignity at the time."

"And what do you think about it now?"

"Dear boy," Fitz said with an attempt at lightness. "Not anything I'd care to go through again. I merely question if it would justify killing."

"If you had been taught as a boy to believe it would

destroy your integrity as a person," Benson said in a voice like stone. "What then?"

"Might be different, I can see." Fitz put his glass on a table and got to his feet. "Well, it's not a subject one cares to discuss endlessly, is it? Just thought I'd give you my views. Mustn't keep you any longer. Damn near daylight already."

The brigadier stood tall and adjusted his brilliant uniform, watching his reflection in the night-backed glass wall. He tweaked his tie into perfect alignment and turned to smile at Benson. The smile dwindled as he met Benson's eyes.

"Well, see you at breakfast, eh?" he said in a tone that was a shadow of his former jauntiness.

"No," Benson said flatly. He turned away to get rid of his cigarette. "No, I won't be here tomorrow. Talking to you has given me an idea, Fitz. I'll be taking the first plane to Los Angeles. Tell Margareta for me, will you? I'll be gone before she gets up."

"Glad to, dear boy. But why Los Angeles? What idea did I give you?" Fitz paused with his hand on the door latch. His smile was more confident now.

"You didn't give it to me, Fitz," Benson said. "But after talking to you, I can see that I'll have to present the jury with another view of the homosexual world. A view different from yours. Good night, Fitz."

"Yes," Fitz said uncertainly. "Good night."

Benson waited unmoving until Fitz's car had turned and disappeared down the long curving driveway. Then he turned abruptly on his heel. He stopped in the doorway with the empty glass in his hand. He looked down at it, his mouth pinched in a hard line. Suddenly he took a stride forward and threw the glass as hard as he could into the stone fireplace. It went off like a grenade, scattering bright splinters across the pale rug. Benson turned and went down the corridor to his bedroom. He took a small leather kitbag from a closet shelf, pulled open drawers of his dresser and began to pack.

BENSON was the first passenger up the narrow staircase when the TWA Constellation bound from the Dallas-Fort Worth airport to Los Angeles stopped at Rincon to pick up passengers. He dropped his bag and kicked it under an empty seat near the door, tossed his hat on the rack and sat down beside a fat, snoring man. He tilted his head toward the hovering stewardess, gave her his name, declined coffee, magazines and pillows and was left alone. He leaned back, let the seat down one notch and closed his eyes.

The plane would bring him into Los Angeles shortly before noon, not a good time but the best Rincon airport could offer today. There was something slightly ludicrous, Benson was aware, in the picture of him rushing into town at daybreak, stopping at the office to pick up the John Doe warrants he had applied for, scribbling a hasty memo for Mary, and then phoning the airport to learn that he would have to wait more than three hours for a plane.

He had spent a restless hour in the office, cleaning up routine work he had ignored the day before. With the stack of mail on his desk was a bulky package containing a book from Dr. Laurence Cass's library and a short note. Benson crammed the book in his small bag. Then he had gone down to the quiet hot street and walked, carrying his bag, to the county hospital.

Turo had been awake when Benson came into the long prison ward. He was having his face washed by a young, flower-faced girl in a blue-and-white striped uniform. He was complaining to her about the soft beard that had grown to a dark bristly shadow over his lower face.

"We'll have a barber sent up, miss," Benson said, dropping his bag beside the bed. "Morning, Turo. I'll join you in a shave. I left so early this morning I didn't have time to scrape the beard off."

Turo smiled warily. He reached up to touch the pad of bandage on his head. His eyes flickered toward the girl. "It's about time for breakfast, Mr. Kellogg. How about some coffee or something?"

"Sure. Good idea. How are they feeding you?"

"Okay. Nothing to brag about." He inspected Benson closely. "You don't need a shave very bad. You blond guys got it lucky. I can't even see your beard except against the light. Me, I've been shaving every day since I was fifteen."

They spoke of nothing important until the barber had shaved them both and had trimmed Turo's long hair. "Short," Benson had insisted over the boy's objection. "And get that ducktail off him. Raise the hairline in back an inch or two. And you shut up, Turo. That pachuco haircut wouldn't do you any good with a jury." Benson took out his notebook and jotted a memo to himself so he would not forget to make sure the boy had some decent clothes to wear in court. With that big white cast, he wouldn't need much, but Benson was not going to let him appear in a ratty prison bathrobe. The clothes he had been wearing when he had wrecked Duquesne's car had been cut off him at the hospital.

"You don't look so hot, Mr. Kellogg," the boy said during breakfast. "You feel okay?"

"I'm all right, Turo. I've just been doing a little late studying. Like the night before exams. How are things going with you? I suppose the County Attorney has been after you?"

"Yeah. Some guy that said he was from the D.A." Turo made a quick, expressive gesture with his spoon. "A jerk. He wanted me to give him a new confession. Said the first one didn't do me justice." The boy formed his mouth as if to spit. "He said!"

"And what did you say?"

Turo shrugged. "See my lawyer, is what I said. A couple other guys come up. Sheriff's men, they said. Same answer."

Benson smiled tightly. "There may be more of the same. Keep yourself braced, Turo. Don't say a word to anybody." He looked down the long empty ward. "They'll be moving you to the county jail some time before the trial. You may be put in a cell with someone else. You'd better assume that he is a police stool pigeon. Just tell yourself that everything you say will be reported to the County Attorney. Until this trial is over, you have no friends. Except me. Remember that, Turo. You talk to me, and no one else."

"I get it." Turo nodded. "Don't sweat." He pushed his cereal bowl aside and dipped a triangle of toast into a dish of stewed fruit.

"All right, Turo. That's all for now. I've got to make a trip to Los Angeles today. I may not see you again before the trial."

"L.A.?" The boy's eyes brightened with sharp curiosity. "Got a line on something, Mr. Kellogg?"

"Maybe," Benson said. He put down his coffee cup. "That's another item you can keep to yourself."

"You bet." The boy leaned back against the pillows and nodded once, self-possessed. He lifted one hand in a half-salute as Benson went out.

The kid had plenty of guts, Benson was thinking. A horse breeder would be inclined to look for a powerfully good bloodline somewhere in the Campeón strain.

Before sliding his bag under the seat, he flipped the catches and took out the book Larry Cass had sent him. A plain wrapper, he noted, and probably just as well. He snapped on the tiny overhead light, settled into a comfortable position and opened the cover. He read with the speed and concentration of a lawyer accustomed to extracting nuggets of information from complex, technical writing.

The book was not the basic text he had expected, but a wide-ranging collection of essays that considered the homosexual in his historical, social, criminal and clinical aspects. For the most part its language was chilly and dispassionate, though not always.

When the plane lurched inside a pocket of turbulence over the brown and fuzzy California mountains, Benson riffled quickly through the last few pages. He drew in a long unsteady breath and bent to put the book away. He sat back and lit a cigarette. It's a good thing I read that book, he was thinking. I'm not quite as ignorant now as I was, but by God, I really didn't want to learn that much about homosexuals.

The plane circled slowly and nosed smoothly down into its approach. From his window Benson could not yet see the ground. Then, with the plane only a few hundred feet up, visibility broke upon them like a shower of light. A second later the plane's wheels touched, lifted once, touched again and settled. The plane taxied slowly around to the terminal building, and the stewardess broke silence to warn everyone to remain seated until the engines had stopped. Benson pulled his bag from under his seat and got his hat from the rack. He was not the first at the door, but he was among the first five.

He walked quickly across the graveled tarmac to the gap in the woven-wire barrier, and through the terminal to the cab stand outside.

He signaled a cab forward, got in and told the driver to take him downtown. "Police Headquarters," he added.

THE POLICE BUILDING was almost new and handsome, designed in long clean lines. It was set back from the street, with a patch of flowerbed in front and a high shapely tree making an airy oriental pattern against a pale brick wall. The office of the confidential squad was on the second floor, in the back where there would be no view and very little air. The offices of most confidential squads are usually the worst available because they are reserved for the cops who get the strange, unwanted assignments from the commissioner; one of these is to watch the other cops, and there are no cops anywhere that care to be watched as closely as another cop knows how to watch them.

The chief of the squad was Captain C. G. Valentine, according to the directory. The name was repeated on his door. Inside, another sign beyond the secretary's desk said, CAP'T VALENTINE, PRIVATE. And the stern face of the captain's secretary had an almost visible sign that said, "Keep Out."

Benson took off his hat, smiled politely and gave her one of his business cards. "I'd like to see Captain Valentine," he said. "I think he can help me in a case that involves two former residents of Los Angeles. Will you ask him if he can spare a few minutes, please?"

The secretary looked at him steadily and blankly while he was talking. "Is he expecting you?" she demanded in a thin, reedy voice.

Benson stretched his smile a little wider and nodded. "He just might be," he said easily. "He has talked to other people about this case. I don't think he'll be surprised to hear from me. Would you ask him, please?"

"It's about lunchtime," she said dubiously.

"I won't take much of his time," Benson said on a note of youthful eagerness. "This is very important to me."

The secretary retrieved her pencil and poked at Benson's card with the eraser tip. "Well, I'll see," she said after a judicious, lip-pursing hesitation. "But I don't think . . ."

She got up and drifted backward as she was talking. She opened the captain's door and went inside. The door closed behind her with a sharp, flat click.

When she reappeared, she held the door for him and waited with her blank stare until he realized that he was now expected to come forward.

"Thank you," he said hastily. He went through and pivoted on his heel immediately. Even so, the closing door caught his shoe a glancing scrape.

"Good morning, Captain," he said. "Thanks for giving me a minute. I'll be as brief as I can."

Captain Valentine grunted. He put down a pencil, pushed aside a big thundermug of a coffee cup with a pale pattern of dribbles down the side and levered himself up from his chair just long enough to touch Benson's hand with two fingers. He sat again and pointed toward the chair beside his desk.

"Have a seat, Mr.—ah—" he took a moment to look at Benson's card—"Mr. Kellogg. What can I do for you?" The captain screwed a short soggy stump of cigar into his mouth and rolled it around with his tongue. He was a big man, as most cops are, thick and heavy now with aging, well-larded muscles. He had a strong face, full of integrity and marked by thought as much as by combat. He was nearly bald and his eyebrows were thick and irregular, misshapen by the scar tissue around his eyes. A battler at one time, Benson could see, but he had the air of a man who has fought often and hard because he had to, not because he had purposely developed a taste and an ability for fighting.

There was an angled sign on the captain's desk that said, "C. G. Valentine, Captain," and Benson stared at it briefly, collecting his thoughts. He wondered vaguely what the "C. G." stood for. If the "C." represented one of the unhappy names such as Cyril or Claude or even Cecil, he could understand why the captain had so many knuckle scars on his face. The "Valentine" alone would make a cop's life a kind of hell. He had probably had to fight since his first day at school, just for the right to stay alive and grow up and become a ranking cop who could hide his shame behind his initials.

"I wonder if you know why I'm here, Captain," Benson said abruptly.

"I'll know when you tell me," Captain Valentine said. He was clearly a man of patience, and he had long ago learned there was no profit in playing the other man's game. He sat unmoving and waited for Benson.

The captain's cautious, noncommittal attitude answered Benson's question. He felt reasonably sure Captain Valentine knew exactly what had brought him here.

"I'm the court-appointed defense counsel in the case of People against Arturo Campeón," he said formally. "My client is charged with the murder of a man known as Roderick Duquesne. Both Campeón and Duquesne lived in Los Angeles. That's why I'm here, to find out what I can about them." Benson sat back, put one knee over the other and looked into the captain's dark impassive eyes. "I believe you have already discussed the case with the Rincon County authorities?"

The captain nodded grudgingly. "The D.A.'s investigator called me, some detective lieutenant by the name of Jurgens." He took the cigar out of his mouth, picked a shred of tobacco from his teeth, using his little fingernail in a delicate prying gesture. "And your D.A. phoned me this morning," he added.

"It's safe to assume then," Benson went on, "that you don't need any information from me. Arturo Campeón killed Roderick Duquesne because——"

"You admit it?" the captain said with some surprise.

"The facts aren't in dispute, Captain. The trial will hinge on the point of motive and justification. I'm hoping the jury will agree that a boy has the right to defend himself against homosexual rape."

"Rape?" the captain muttered. "Jesus!"

"A good psychiatrist said the term is justifiable," Benson said sharply. "I believe it's proper."

"Maybe so." The captain rolled his cigar to the other corner of his mouth. "What about it?"

"I will have to convince the jury that Duquesne was the kind of man who was capable of such an attack, possibly that he was a man who had committed such an offense before. That's why I've come to you, Captain."

"On the door it says, 'Private,'" the captain said heavily. "That *could be* the label on my files too, Mr. Kellogg. They aren't for publication."

"You have already published the information, Captain," Benson said, quietly firm.

"What's that?"

"When you gave the information to our County Attorney, you made publication."

"The hell I did. It's my job to cooperate with official investigators anywhere in the country. Whatever I give them is confidential. It stays confidential."

Benson rocked his chair back, supporting it with the toe of one shoe. "I appreciate your position, Captain," he said soberly. "And I think you realize that I can't accept that answer. I'm prepared to subpoena you if I have to."

The captain made a low growling sound behind his cigar. "You can't make it stick," he said flatly. "That's already been decided."

"It's been decided both ways at different times, Captain. I suspect you know that. But I'll admit that you are probably right in this case. Confidential files are not considered to be in the same category as other public records. I don't expect I could force you to testify. But I still have to get that information somehow, and you are the key to it. I'll either get it from you, as the County Attorney did, or I'll have to use you to force the County Attorney to divulge what you told him."

"Just take that one a little slower," Captain Valentine said. His cigar twitched in his mouth as if he might have started to smile and then thought better of it.

"If you make it necessary," Benson said calmly, "I will serve you with a subpoena. Then I'll explain to the newspapers that I did so because you have joined with the Rincon County prosecutor in an agreement to suppress evidence bearing on Arturo Campeón's defense."

"Suppress?" the captain said with an edge of anger. "What the hell do you mean, suppress?"

"That's what the County Attorney has done with the information, Captain. And that's all he plans to do with it. He wants to lay before the jury an image of Roderick Duquesne as a decent, kindly man who was murdered by a boy he had befriended. But we both know that isn't a true picture, don't we, Captain?"

"Go on," the captain said in a tone of growing interest. "So you tell the papers. What does that get you?"

"I can't be sure, of course," Benson admitted. "I think it might put the County Attorney in a difficult public position. He just might think it was wiser to share the information you gave him rather than create the impression that he was trying to railroad my client. I think that's what might come of it. Maybe not. I'd rather not have to put it to the test."

The captain grunted. "Be a kind of a dirty trick, wouldn't it? Make things kind of rough on me, too."

"I agree," Benson said. "But I don't see a useful alternative. I'd like to point out, Captain, that I am not the one trying to suppress evidence in this case. I want the jury to have all the pertinent information. I'll rest my case on full revelation. The County Attorney—with your help—is trying to distort the truth by suppressing part of it."

Benson leaned forward and let the legs of his chair hit the floor solidly. He had so far maintained an even, equable tone of voice, but the strain was beginning to make him sound anxious and slightly belligerent. "That's my position, Captain. I need your help. I don't know of any other source of information. Will you help me?"

The captain swung around to face Benson squarely. He pulled the cigar from his mouth, flicked a cylinder of ash in the direction of a tray and stared at it morosely. Benson could sense an uncertainty in him, an indecision that, he suspected, was not usual in Captain Valentine.

"I don't like coming to you like this, Captain," he said quietly. "I've been under a lot of pressure because of this case, and I haven't enjoyed it. I don't like to pass it on. But I have a responsibility to my client and to the court. I have to do everything I can to discover the truth. I will take any steps I'm forced to. I've outlined some of them. If they don't work, I'll figure out something that will."

"I'll just bet you will, too," the captain growled.

"I don't have any choice," Benson said. "My client killed a vicious, corrupt man. Whether he was justified depends largely on the record of the dead man. You know what that record shows, Captain." Benson stared at the captain's hooked, secretive profile. "You know who Duquesne was, don't you, his real name?"

Captain Valentine gave a loud snort. He whirled his chair toward Benson. "Hell, yes. I know all about him. I put in a rough two hours yesterday with his old man—H. L. Caine himself. He was right there in that very chair you're sitting in. Him and his two lawyers and a private cop."

"Caine," Benson said hoarsely. "What did he want?"

"Same thing you want, to see what we had on his son."

"Did he get it?"

Captain Valentine's eyes slid away from Benson's. He shifted his heavy shoulders a scant inch. "Sure," he said in a tone of smothered anger. "The Commissioner phoned me before he came in. Sure he got what he wanted." He pulled out the center drawer of his desk and picked up a yellow folder with a large red "Confidential" printed on the side. It was a bellows folder tied with faded cord. The captain put it down on his blotter and held it there with the flat of his hand. He looked up frowning, and seeing his narrowed, bleak eyes, Benson had sense enough to hold his tongue.

"That crap you were giving me before," the captain said tightly, "that's the kind of stuff that gives me a big fat laugh. In my job, everybody hates me, even the cops. A couple more squawks from your hometown would bother me like water bothers a duck. I've been taking it all my life. I don't even think about it any more. My wife is dead, so it can't touch her. My boy is in the regular army. I'm up for retirement at the end of the year. I don't have to butter anybody." He glared at Benson. "It was a damn good thing you didn't push that one any harder or I'd have kicked your ass out of here." With an abrupt, awkward gesture, he shoved the file across to Benson. "I don't like being put in the middle. I don't like people trying to use this office. I don't like big operators like Godalmighty Caine telling me what to do. Caine got what he wanted. Okay, you can have it too."

"Thank you, Captain," Benson said with a deep sense of relief.

"Don't thank me, thank Caine," the captain said heavily. "You can use that table over there. And snap it up. I want my lunch." He picked up a stapled sheaf of papers and pointedly swung his chair away from Benson.

Benson moved quickly, taking the file and crossing the dusty, heel-marked floor to a small table that stood between two smog-darkened windows. He untied the cord, and dumped the contents of the file on the table. He took out his pencil and notebook and sat down.

A spring clip held the file in an organized unit. The top item was a large printed card headed, "Caine, Robert Lawrence, alias Duquesne, Roderick." The upper half of the card listed routine statistics. Caine had been thirty-nine when he was killed. He had been six feet even, weighed one ninety, had d. brown hair and eyes and a fair complexion, was white, native born and had a long scar on his left arm and a cluster of three moles on the right side of his chest. He had graduated from college in Los Angeles, with a major in Fine Arts, had been 4-F in Selective Service records, though no reason was given for his deferment. He was a professional set designer and lighting consultant, whatever that was. The lower portion of the card was half filled with abbreviated dates and coded groups of letters and numerals.

Benson slipped the clip off, put the card aside and looked at the pages underneath. Each was an excerpt from local police records, probation investigations, anonymous letters and phone calls and testimony given in court. The sheets were arranged chronologically. Benson began with the first page, reading slowly and taking notes.

Robert Caine had first come to the attention of the police in 1937, when he had been questioned in connection with a riot outside a suburban house where a high-school fraternity was giving a dance. A gang had stoned the house and assaulted a man who had tried to stop them, kicking him and breaking three ribs with their boots. Caine was not held. Soon afterward he was named as the boy who had stolen a car from a man who had later refused to press charges. In 1940 Robert Caine was one of seven men arrested during a noisy party at a Malibu beach house. All of them were naked at the time and drunk. They were fined for disturbing the peace.

There was a gap for the war years, when Caine had worked as a clerk in an aircraft factory and apparently attracted no attention. He next appeared when a night club called "The Grecian Mood" had been closed for violation of the state licensing laws. The club had been raided and padlocked for selling liquor to minors. It was described as a rendez-vous for homosexuals, and on the list of men thought to be co-owners was the name of Robert L. Caine. He denied any connection and no charges were brought.

Benson lit a cigarette and shook his head wearily. The picture was shaping in his mind, but so far there was little he could use. He turned the page.

Two years later Caine had been identified as the financial backer of an espresso-and-poetry club called "Via Romana." He was proved to be owner of the building, but he denied any interest in the club, which had catered exclusively to homosexuals. No connection was proved and, after questioning, Caine was released. Another blank.

During the trial of a homosexual accused of murdering his male mistress, Caine was named as one of many who had been enjoying the mistress' favors. Caine, however, had not been called as a witness and nothing but the accused's uncorroborated statement stood against him.

There followed a collection of petty complaints for disturbing the peace, creating a public nuisance, drunkenness and gambling. All were disposed of by fine or dismissal.

A young and unsuccessful movie actor in 1953 had accused a man named Roderick Duquesne of homosexual assault during a drunken party at a ski lodge. Duquesne was identified as Robert Caine. Before Duquesne could be traced by the police, the actor had dropped the charge.

Then, in 1957, Caine, who was now calling himself Duquesne, had been questioned by the police in connection with an aggravated assault upon an elderly and well-known homosexual. Duquesne and his victim had previously and often quarreled about the victim's association with a young man who called himself Harald Elsinore. Elsinore was described as a part-time artist. His only known employment had been with a door-to-door sales company. The victim had withdrawn his complaint the next day, denying that Duquesne had been responsible for the broken collarbone that had sent him to the hospital.

A young boy named Billie Bayonne who had been arrested for soliciting homosexuals had identified Duquesne as one
of his regular customers. He had offered a convincing array of
details and dates, but nothing could be proven in the face of
Duquesne's flat denials.

After that, Duquesne had been very careful, it seemed, for
Captain Valentine's file ended there. Benson closed it with a
faint sigh.

"Not much to go on, is there?" the captain said.

"Not much," Benson agreed. "Duquesne was pretty shifty,
and lucky too."

"Not lucky," the captain said with bitter bluntness. "He
was rich. He bought off witnesses, or sent someone to scare
them. People like Duquesne learn how to spend money to cover
themselves."

"Why did he change his name, Captain? Do you know?"

"His father told him to," the captain said. "He didn't give
a damn what his son did; he just didn't want his own name
dragged in the mud. He tried to get Duquesne to make a legal
change, but he couldn't sell that one. I think Duquesne liked
the idea that maybe sometime he'd get hooked on a really bad
rap and the old man would get smeared along with him. There
was no love lost between those two, I can tell you."

"I suppose not. I don't imagine it would be very pleasant,
having a son like Duquesne."

"Don't waste any sympathy on the old man. He's not much
better than his son, except maybe in the sex department. He used
to live in town until a few years back. I know all about him.
He's ruthless and mean as a snake, in his own way. I know for a
fact that he drove his wife out of her mind. She was in and
out of nuthouses for years. She finally killed herself when the
kid was fourteen, cut her wrists and crawled into the kid's bed
and bled to death. He found her."

"My God," Benson said softly.

"Yeah," the captain muttered. "That's a way to live, huh?
No wonder he turned out rotten. Well, you've got what you
wanted. Now if you——"

"Just a minute more, Captain," Benson said quickly, "if you can spare the time. I copied a list of names from your file. Can you tell me if any of these people are still in Los Angeles?" He turned a page of his notebook and laid it on the captain's desk.

Captain Valentine picked up a pencil with slow deliberation. He put a check mark beside two names and pushed the notebook away. "Billie Bayonne is the kid picked up for hustling fairies. He's done some time since, but he's out now and still working the same side of the street. He lives in a dump near the railroad station, the Parma Hotel, a dollar a night and all the fleas you can catch. Harald Elsinore is private stuff. Duquesne's kept boy. And that is a very unusual relationship, if you know anything about homos. The average homo never manages a long-term relationship. Half an hour is routine for most of them. But Elsinore and Duquesne stayed together for four or five years. He's the one Duquesne had that fight about. He lives in the apartment right under Duquesne's, if he's still in town." The captain looked up with a scowl. "You don't expect to find any of them now, do you?"

"Why not?" Benson asked, puzzled.

"Now what in hell do you think old man Caine came here for? And brought a private cop with him?"

"He's going to get them out of town? Is that it? How do you know? Did he say so?"

"He didn't have to tell me," the captain said. "That's the kind of a guy he is. A cover-up artist. You won't get to first base, Counselor. You're just wasting your time, but by God, I hope you hit it lucky. Just once I'd like to see a man like Caine walk into a left hook."

"You sound like you've got a stake in this too, Captain," Benson said.

"Maybe I have," the captain said in a low, hard voice. "Maybe I have." He kicked back his chair and heaved himself up. "You still going to hunt for them? Bayonne and Elsinore?"

"Yes. I have to try."

The captain crossed the room, limping slightly but moving with a lumbering swiftness. He took a rumpled-brimmed hat from a hook near the door and looked back at Benson. "I'm going out to lunch," he said. "I think I'll get a sandwich at that place near where Duquesne used to live. Can I give you a lift?"

"Yes," Benson said readily. "Yes, sir, you can."

CAPTAIN VALENTINE maneuvered his small car through the noontime traffic with scrupulous, sedate regard for the regulations. He drove a private route down narrow alleys and one-way streets, then turned onto an elevated approach lane and along it to a wide and busy eight-lane freeway. He thumbed his hat back off his forehead and glanced at Benson.

"I let you get away with something today," he said heavily. "I hope you know that." He turned his head so he could watch the road and still see Benson out of the corner of his eye.

"Yes, I realize that. I'm grateful, Captain."

Valentine made a growling sound and rolled his dead cigar in his mouth. "I've been a cop for some forty years," he said. "Cops learn to follow the rules. But once in a while we don't. Like today. You know anything about sex perverts?"

"Not much. I'm learning."

"I hope you got a strong stomach. I've been dealing with them all my life and they still make me sick. I'm writing a book about sex criminals, so I've been gathering a lot of——"

"A book?" Benson said incredulously.

"What's wrong with that?" the captain said, turning to glare at him.

"Nothing, not a thing," Benson said hastily. "It's just that I've never met a book-writing policeman before. In Rincon we don't have that kind."

"Well, I guess it's not the common thing anywhere," the captain said graciously. "But a man's got to do something with his time when he lives alone. I used to go to college at night, just to keep busy, but I found out I'm not much of a student. But I know plenty about sex crimes, so I started collecting material. I'm going to use Duquesne as one of my case histories. He's a classic type."

"Of sex criminal?" Benson asked. "Do you classify homosexuals as sex criminals?"

"What else are they?" the captain demanded testily. "I'll grant you they aren't always listed that way officially, but they should be. We went up to the state legislature a couple years back and tried to get them to include the five acts of sodomy in the sex-crime list of felonies, but we couldn't convince them. They aren't a very sophisticated type of legislator, I guess you know. You take a hot-shot real-estate salesman who never did get through high school and some illiterate apple farmer who can't read Bugs Bunny without help, and you aren't likely to get much in the way of high-quality laws. Why, half those people up there didn't even believe there was such a thing as sodomy. Figure it died out in Bible days, I guess."

"I see your point," Benson said, half smiling. "Would it make your job easier if you had such a law?"

"Of course it would," the captain said. "But speaking as a practical cop, I'd have to say that probably all that would happen would be that the perverts would take off for some other state. That wouldn't solve anything. But you have to start somewhere. These people aren't real bad criminals, not the passive ones anyway, but they live outside the law's protection and they attract criminals the way honey attracts flies. But the active homo, the one who takes the male part, he's always a bad actor, like Duquesne. He's the one who commits the assaults and murders. He's vicious. The passives mostly just get into hair-pulling fights and all that."

"Do you have many of them here, Captain?"

"Too damn many," the captain said. "Nobody ever took a head count, but we've got more than a fair share, I'll say that. This is screwball country out here; we get all kinds. We've got a pretty good line on the homo crowd, though. They put out a magazine here and we've got the mailing list, so that gives us a check point. Your friend Duquesne, by the way, supported that magazine and he contributed to the one in San Francisco, too.

The editors are supposed to be anonymous, but a homo is an awful gossip, you know. Can't keep a secret for ten minutes. Duquesne wrote a lot of stuff for both magazines, poetry mostly, from what I hear. Can't say I ever read any of it."

Valentine leaned forward to wipe the heel of his hand across the moist inside of the windshield. The smog was thicker now, trapped in a low valley, eye-stinging and dense. "This is going to be a bad night," the captain muttered. "We get a hell of a lot of sex crime when the smog rolls in. Perverts like to hide in it. They are very responsive to weather; all compulsive criminals are. Rain or hot steamy weather or smog or the nights of a full moon, and they all come out from under their rocks looking for trouble."

Benson lit a cigarette and cranked down the side window to let the smoke escape. Then he rolled it up again. The smog was harder to breathe than the captain's cigar smoke.

"Do they give you a lot of trouble, Captain?"

Valentine snorted. "Hell, yes. I just said so, didn't I? Mostly they get in trouble because the average man just can't stand to have them around. A woman homo, a Lesbian now, she isn't much trouble. She keeps everything quiet, but a male homo likes to advertise. You take a male homo who goes into a taproom in some working-class neighborhood. I'll lay you ten to one there'll be a fight inside of twenty minutes. An educated man will maybe just laugh and get the hell away, but a working stiff just naturally despises a homo. And don't give me any of that latent-homo crap, either. I know what the books say. There's nothing in it, or damn little. It's a natural instinct to be leery of a foreigner, history proves that. And a homo is just about as foreign as they come. I hate them, too. I despise every one of them. I've seen what they can do and I tell you there isn't a single one of them who ought to be let walk the streets. They are either criminals or they are sick people. Whatever they are, they ought to be locked up."

"Are they your specialty, Captain? Sex criminals?"

The captain shook his head angrily. "Nobody specializes in sex crimes," he said. "There aren't many cops who can get it through their heads that most arsons and assaults and robberies and murders are actually a kind of sex crime. A cop just sees that some guy killed another guy or set fire to a schoolhouse or snatched a ring from a jewelry store. He can't see the sex motive and he doesn't even think about it. We don't do a good job there and that's a fact. We have different squads to handle the different crimes, but you know something? We don't have a sex-crime squad, just a team of men working out of the vice squad who roust the homos when there's nothing else to do. We don't have any specialists. We don't even know we need any. How do you like that?"

"I'm not qualified to judge, Captain," Benson said. "It doesn't sound very sensible."

"You're damn right it's not sensible. But that's the way we do things, and hard-headed old cops aren't guys who like to make changes in the way they do things."

The captain turned right onto a long curving road that swung away from the freeway and led them to a suburban boulevard. He turned at the second corner and parked in the middle of the block, not far from a palm-bordered restaurant entrance.

"Duquesne's apartment is just down the street and a block to the right," Captain Valentine said. He switched off the ignition. "I'll leave you here, Mr. Kellogg. I'm going in and get some lunch." He slid from his seat, slammed the door and looked at Benson over the top of the small car. "But first," he added, "I'm going to make a phone call. You go on over there. It's the only apartment building in sight. You can't miss it. Ask for the manager. She's a tough old trout, name of Fallon. She'll be expecting you."

"Many thanks, Captain," Benson said.

"Never mind," Valentine growled. "I don't want your thanks. I'm not doing this for you, Counselor. I just don't like the idea of some kid being executed for knocking off one of those scummy perverts. I'd hate to see anyone hang for that. I'd like to kill a couple myself." He came around the car and put out his hand. "Good luck."

"I'll need it, I suspect."

"Yeah. Did you ever try to talk to a homo?"

Benson shook his head.

"They look human. They act human most of the time. But they're scared of normal people. Just go easy with them and don't ever let them get the idea that you think they stink. They get real sensitive then and they'll clam up. Just act bored and kind of matter-of-fact and you'll do all right. Good luck to you."

Captain Valentine nodded abruptly and brushed past Benson, as if he were already beginning to regret having done anything to help him. He limped quickly up the path to the restaurant. Benson watched him until he was inside.

Benson dropped his cigarette and put it out with his shoe. He blew out his breath, long and slow. Captain Valentine was strong and unsavory meat on an empty stomach. He turned away, walking toward the corner up an easy rise. He went slowly, allowing time for Captain Valentine to telephone.

THE APARTMENT HOUSE sat back from the corner. A cramped half-circle of driveway led uphill toward the entrance in the central portion. It was some eight stories of pale brick decorated with Moorish tiling inlaid to simulate open-air filigree. Benson went up the driveway, pushed back one wing of the high glass door and went into the foyer. A small, soft, tired man at the reception desk pulled a plug from the switchboard and swung around. He wore a fixed glossy smile and he looked up vaguely, focusing on a point in midair over Benson's head.

"Mrs. Fallon, please," Benson said.

"Miss Fallon," the clerk said in a faraway voice. "Is she expecting you, sir?" He turned back to the board.

"I think so. My name is Kellogg."

"I'll see." He plugged in a jack and leaned over the fixed speaker so he could whisper without being overheard. He nodded vigorously while he was talking. "Miss Fallon will see you, sir," he said after a moment. "Will you go straight back? Just past the elevators. Suite A."

Miss Fallon was a raffish knowing old girl, rosy and round, with blue-gray hair recently set in cast-iron ridges and a translucent skin like a baby's. There was a careless spray of grease spots down the front of her scarlet-and-yellow dress. She took a step forward and wobbled on high open-work gold sandals that seemed to have been made for someone else— someone younger and less tempered by experience. She surveyed Benson with a cocked eyebrow, silently, with an air of good-humored suspicion.

Benson took off his hat. "Miss Fallon? I believe Captain Valentine . . ."

"In!" she said quickly, making a peremptory gesture. "In!" She closed the door behind him and stood with her back against it, pointedly not asking him to sit. "I don't like to talk with the door open," she said, tipping her head back so she could frown directly at Benson. "I don't want everybody and his brother knowing my business."

"Of course not," Benson said uncertainly. "Did Captain Valentine mention——"

"He said you wanted some dope on Roddy and his boy. That Valentine." Miss Fallon shook her head sadly. "He just can't stand the sight of those people. He's a little bit queer himself, if you ask me."

Benson gave no indication he had heard her. Captain Valentine was not the person he had come to talk about. "Is Harald Elsinore still living here, Miss Fallon?"

"Harald? Childe Harald?" Miss Fallon hooted. She rocked back against the door and shook with laughter. "You should have seen him last night! He went out of here like somebody in the funny papers, clothes every which way, suitcase under his arm."

"Where did he go, Miss Fallon?"

She patted her rigid hair with a meaty hand. The burst of laughter had gone, but it left traces in her eyes. She plucked at her lower lip. "I don't know if I should . . ." she began hesitantly. "They told me . . ."

"Who told you, Miss Fallon? Elsinore wasn't alone when he left here, was he? Who was with him?"

"Don't push me, young man." Miss Fallon edged away from the door, skirted Benson who stood unmoving in the center of the room, and sank into a chintz-covered wing chair. "Sit down," she said absently.

Benson carried a straight chair across and put it down facing Miss Fallon. "It is very important for me to find Harald Elsinore," he said soberly. "Can you help me?"

"What are you?" she asked. "Don't tell me you're a cop, too? I never saw a cop like you before."

"I'm an attorney, Miss Fallon. I have been appointed to defend the boy who killed Roderick Duquesne. You can understand that I have to find out what kind of man Duquesne actually was. Harald Elsinore is the best source of information I know about."

Miss Fallon nodded, her eyes widening. "Well, I wouldn't say Roddy was any kind of a man, if you mean it the way I do."

"He was openly homosexual, you mean. Without trying to conceal it?"

"Oh no! My goodness, no. He and Harald were little tight-mouths. But everybody knew, I guess. Harald used to come and talk to me when Roddy was away. He was a nice boy. Not everybody wants to waste time talking to an old bag, but Harald was nice, like a little girl who minded her manners. He made these drapes for me, sewed them himself." Miss Fallon fingered the sea-green fall of silk over the windows. "He was a sweet thing, gentle as a lamb."

"I want to talk to him, Miss Fallon. Can you tell me where he is?"

Miss Fallon looked away. "He didn't say, he left in such a hurry. Some men came from a storage company this morning and packed up everything in his apartment, so I don't think . . ."

Benson bit the inside of his cheek angrily, forcing himself to patience. Miss Fallon was a rambler and there was no point in trying to cut her off. In fact, there might be considerable profit in letting her run on freely.

"Harald Elsinore had the apartment immediately under Duquesne's, I believe," he said. "Who paid the rent, can you tell me?"

"Oh, Harald paid it," Miss Fallon said lightly. "He always brought me two one-hundred-dollar bills the first of every month." She eyed Benson obliquely and her mouth twitched. "Roddy always liked to carry hundred-dollar bills," she added slyly.

"Did Elsinore have a lease?"

"Yes, of course. It still had eight months to run."

"And when he left here last night and ordered his things stored, what did you do about his lease, Miss Fallon? Did he pay you?"

Miss Fallon shook her head. "The—the man with him paid it."

"Do you know who that man was?"

"He—he didn't say."

"But you know who he was?"

"I've seen him around," Miss Fallon admitted. "It was Manny Blue. He used to be on the cops. He does private work now, I hear. And he sure won't like the idea of me telling you he was here with Harald."

"I'll keep it to myself, Miss Fallon. How is it you happened to know him?"

"I know just about all the cops in the district, young man. Even bad cops like Blue. I used to have a business—well, I know a lot of cops, is all."

Her meaning was completely clear, even without the cocked eyebrow and the meaningful tilt to her mouth.

"Blue paid off Elsinore's lease? How? In cash, Miss Fallon?"

She nodded.

"And then he left with Elsinore?"

"Yes."

"How? In a car? A taxi?"

"Blue had a car."

"And you have no idea where they were going? No idea at all?" Benson leaned forward urgently. "I'd appreciate any kind of a lead at all, Miss Fallon. Can you make a guess?"

Miss Fallon hesitated. "Blue did say something about talking to his boss, but he didn't mention any name."

Benson looked at her silently for a long moment. "I wonder," he asked quietly, "if you know what Roderick Duquesne's real name was?"

Miss Fallon snickered. "No, I never heard. Childe Harald used to talk up a big mystery out of it, though. He always claimed Roddy's old man was the richest man in the country."

"I doubt if he's that, Miss Fallon, but he's rich enough. And yesterday he called on Captain Valentine. He had a private detective with him. That would be Blue, I assume. Duquesne's father is anxious to keep his own name out of this case. I think he forced Elsinore to leave here so I wouldn't get a chance to talk to him. I have to find him, Miss Fallon. Do you have any idea where he is?"

Miss Fallon pursed her lips and closed one eye. She squinted at Benson and licked her tongue across her lipstick. Then abruptly, she said, "How about a beer? I just got a case of Bohemia. You like Mexican beer?"

"A little later, if you don't mind, Miss Fallon," Benson said, patiently persistent. "To get back to Elsinore, have you any suggestion for me? Would he be likely to go home, for instance? Are his parents still living?"

Miss Fallon chuckled. "God knows. People like Childe Harald don't have parents, that I ever noticed. They usually get kicked out pretty early and then they take off somewhere and change their names to something fancy like Elsinore and set up business in the other alley. No, he didn't have any home, except here."

"No friends?"

"You don't know much about people like Harald, do you? Pansies don't have friends. They just have one lover-boy. Everybody else is an enemy. I guess I'm the only friend Harald had, and God knows I'm not much of a friend."

Benson sat back, looking at her and wishing he knew more about her, knew what questions, what attitudes would induce her to talk to him openly. She smiled as if she understood his problem and sympathized.

"Roddy was always a kind of a bad boy," she said slowly. "You know what I mean? A cheater. He never let poor little Harald go out alone, but all the time Roddy was on the town, sleeping around. It used to get pretty bad up there sometimes, with Harald screaming and banging his head against the wall and Roddy slapping him around like he was some hysterical dame. Little Harald would come down and cry on my shoulder. We'd sit here and talk and drink some beer and poor Harald would just cry and cry." Miss Fallon smiled at Benson with a sad, innocent sprightliness.

"He was lucky to have you for a friend," Benson said gravely.

Miss Fallon shrugged. "You go to your church, I'll go to mine," she said casually. "Pansies don't bother me. It takes all kinds, I always say. Live and let live. Love and let love. Mind your own damn business, that's what I always say."

Benson nodded.

Miss Fallon stared up blandly at the ceiling. "Roddy used to have a little apartment downtown where he took boys he didn't want to bring here. A love nest, you might say."

"Where?"

"Then after they'd just had a terrible ruckus, and poor Harald was just about to give up and cut his throat, why, Roddy got a change of heart and made it up with him. He promised he wouldn't cheat any more. And he gave Harald a key to his other place so Harald could check up any time. It made Harald very happy."

"I'm glad," Benson said soberly. "Where is the other apartment?"

"I've got the address in my little book," Miss Fallon said.

"Maybe I'll look it up in a minute." She leaned forward and smiled roguishly at Benson. "Now how about that beer?"

"Sure," Benson said promptly. "I'd like some beer."

THE BEER had not been a good idea. Benson slid low in the back seat of the taxi and let his head rest on the cushion with his hat tipped over his eyes. Three cold bottles and a handful of peanuts made an adequate substitute for lunch, but that much beer after a night of no sleep was making Benson heavy-eyed and sluggish. He dozed off briefly and was jolted awake again when the driver hit his brakes hard for a traffic light.

"This Parma Hotel," the driver said out of the corner of his mouth. "It's way downtown. Be a seven-buck haul anyways." He looked at Benson in the mirror.

Benson rolled up on his hip, pulled out his wallet and riffled the the bills inside. He drew out a ten and put the wallet away. He draped the bill over the back of the driver's seat. "Just hold that for me till we get there," he said.

"Sure. You bet." The driver brushed the ten forward and moved off when the light changed. "Reason I mentioned it," he said with a self-justifying whine to his voice, "that Parma Hotel is in a rough neighborhood. Know what I mean? Bums and winos and all kinds of queers. You get a long haul to a place like that and you got to make sure you're gonna get paid. Now I can tell by lookin' at you that you wouldn't be the kind of a guy to live in a dump like the Parma, but a guy's gotta be careful. You can get in trouble down there. You're a stranger here, I guess. Am I right?"

"Sort of," Benson mumbled, half asleep.

"Skid row, that's what they call it here. A bad place, mister. I could tell you some . . ."

Benson drifted to sleep with the incessant murmur of the driver's voice rolling against his mind like the surf. He woke with the driver shaking his shoulder.

"Parma Hotel, mister. You want me to wait?" He handed

Benson his change.

"I don't think so." Benson separated a tip and put away some coins. "Just a minute, though." He took out the slip of paper on which Miss Fallon had written the address of Duquesne's hideaway apartment. "Where is this place? It's around here, isn't it?"

The driver read it, moving his lips. "Be two, three blocks over, third street to the right. You don't want to walk it, mister. I better wait, huh?"

"If you want to," Benson said. "I may be right out."

"I'll take a chance." The driver got back in his seat, leaving the flag up and the roof light on.

The Parma Hotel began at the second floor. The entrance was a smeared glass door with flaking black-and-gilt lettering, squeezed between an army-and-navy surplus store and a barber shop. The door opened onto a dim, bare flight of splintery stairs. Each riser carried a stenciled message and by the time Benson had reached the top he knew where to find two "Fine Foods" beaneries in the neighborhood, knew who would give him "Highest Rates, Lowest Interest!" if he wanted to hock his watch. He also knew what to ask for if he felt rundown and listless. "Men! Feel Dragged-out? Lost Your Pep? Get Peppo!" The Parma Hotel has raised its rates since Captain Valentine had last checked it. Rooms were a dollar and a half a night now, but there were also weekly and monthly rates worth investigating, a sign said. The upper hallway smelled close and warm and rank, like a lion house.

The first door on the right had been cut off just above the knob and a shelf had been nailed there to serve as a registration desk. The space above was protected by cyclone-wire mesh. The room beyond was a shabbily furnished bedroom with a cluttered table just inside the door. There was a bell outside the wire. Benson tapped it twice.

The clerk was a thin, lank man in a heather-mixture coat sweater, baggy pants and a pair of horn-rimmed glasses tinted faintly blue. He held his head cocked up and to one side, like a bird twisting his neck to watch for enemies. He had a gray canvas ledger in his hand, but after one look at Benson, he put it down as if he could tell that this was no customer for the Parma. He made an inquiring sound and moved forward, resting his thin-fingered hand on the wire but making no move to unlatch the wicket.

"Billie Bayonne?" Benson asked. "He lives here?"

"Billie? Little Billie?" The clerk tipped his head up higher and his mouth quirked in a faint leer.

"Is he here?" Benson said impatiently.

"Out," the clerk muttered. His eyes squinted in the shadows behind his glasses.

"I want to talk to him," Benson said. "Do you know when he will be back?"

The clerk shook his head. "You don't look like one of Billie's—customers," he said.

Benson could feel his face tightening, but he kept his voice even. "I'm not," he said. "Do you know where I can find him?"

The clerk shrugged. "Worth anything?" he wondered, almost to himself.

Benson took out his wallet. He laid five dollars on the shelf outside the wire and watched the clerk hook it through with his little finger.

"I could ask around maybe," the clerk suggested. "You want me to say it's worth anything to Billie?"

"I'll ante another twenty if you get him here within the next couple of hours," Benson said, putting his wallet away. "I'll be back. Tell him to wait for me."

The clerk lifted his thin shoulders. "Depends if he's busy, if you get me."

"No," Benson said stiffly, "I don't get you." He turned away toward the stairs.

"You want I should give a name?" the clerk asked.

"The name wouldn't mean anything to him," Benson said. "I just want to talk to him. I'll be back."

He could hear the clerk speaking in a rising tone, but once on the grimy steps, Benson did not stop.

THE THIN ACRID BITE of smog in the street outside seemed clear and refreshing after the Parma Hotel. Benson went down the street looking for the waiting taxi, spotted the open space where it had been parked and walked on to the corner, following the driver's directions through the narrow old-town streets that from the signs were originally Spanish and were now the world of Chinese laundries, Mexican restaurants, Syrian groceries and unlabeled shops with strips of crepe paper masking their windows.

The address he was looking for was an old commercial building with offices on the lower floors and storage lofts above. The narrow lobby was lighted only by a bare bulb over a staircase at the far end. Benson went through to the elevators and pushed the button. Either the elevators had been given up or they worked only by appointment. He went past and up the stairs. He had five flights to go and he started slowly, pacing himself. This was hardly the sybaritic hide-out he had expected.

Each flight of stairs had one dim, naked bulb. The steps themselves were barely visible in the gloom. Each landing had a rustling accumulation of newspapers and paper bags and other junk left behind by bums who had sneaked in to get out of the rain or cold. Benson was breathing heavily when he reached the sixth floor.

There was only one door in sight, a high set of glass double-doors that still had commercial lettering vaguely discernible behind tightly stretched panels of scarlet silk. Benson tried the knob, then knocked. The doors vibrated noisily against the frame, doubling the effect of his knuckles. After a moment he knocked again, harder.

Even with his ear close to the silk-shielded door, he could hear nothing from inside. He twitched in nervous reflex when a thin, almost shrill voice came quavering through the crack between the doors.

"Who is it?"

Given a chance to decide for himself, Elsinore would not let him in, Benson suspected. He knocked again, making the loosely mounted doors dance against the lock. "Open up," he growled in a stern, officious voice. "Open up in there."

The voice inside tried to argue, but Benson kept the doors rattling noisily until he heard the lock turn back with a grinding click. He propped his shoe against one wing of the door, slid it in when the leaf moved back, and left it there, blocking it solidly.

The boy who had opened the door stepped back to let Benson come inside. He was slim and neatly built, like an athlete who specializes in quick, graceful things like swimming or jumping. His head was small, wide at the temples and tapering to a pointed chin, with tight ears and dark hair shaped in a cap of lazy curls. He wore a shirt and trousers of mustard flannel cut with the formality of a uniform. He had a paisley scarf knotted at his neck and another for a belt. In the soft light Benson could not see him clearly, but he was aware of an elusive familiarity and he stared for a moment until he could bring it to mind. Of course—this boy could be Turo Campeón's brother. They both had the same high coloring, the same sharp definition of feature, the same animal alertness. Obviously Duquesne had a strong preference for the type.

"You're Harald Elsinore," he said. It was not a question.

"Ye-es," the boy said nervously. "What—I mean, who are you?"

"Let's go in and sit down," Benson said. "I want to talk to you."

"But I'm leaving," the boy said urgently. "I just came here to get some things. Then I'm leaving. Right away. You don't have to——" He backed slowly away from Benson.

They stood in a small, cramped foyer, and when Elsinore stepped back, an overhead light made hard shadows on his face, broke glitters from his wild, evasive eyes. The boy was close to terror, Benson could see. And he wasn't as much a boy as he had thought at first; the marks of time and use were clear now. His eyes were moist and red as if he had been crying, and there was a lumpy dark bruise on the left side of his jaw, about where a fist would hit.

Elsinore's response was pretty damn excessive, Benson thought. He could guess what had caused it. Elsinore probably assumed that Benson was one of the men who had ousted him from his apartment last night. He would have been told to get out of town and been given a few stiff punches to make the message sink in. That would explain his fright. It might be useful, Benson thought, to let him stay fearful for a while longer.

"What did Manny Blue tell you?" he asked roughly.

"To—to get that train last night. But I couldn't!" Elsinore said in a voice that almost wailed. "He gave me a ticket and a hundred dollars, that's all. What could I do in San Francisco with just a hundred dollars? I came here to get a few things. Roddy used to keep some money here. I—I was hoping—but I can't find it!"

"Let's go inside," Benson said. "You can tell me then."

Beyond the dark foyer Benson could see an arched tunnel-shaped entrance barely large enough for him to walk through upright. It was formed by panels of canvas dyed in alternate scarlet and white stripes. Elsinore backed down it warily. Benson followed.

The tunnel let onto a blaze of color, the same scarlet and white stripes, but here the fabric was draped from the twelve-foot ceiling, where a varnished mast held it tautly. It came swinging down in long folds to meet the walls six feet from the floor. The walls were white, hung with circus posters and stylized masks and portraits of clowns. The light came from a hidden source, but it was bright as the full moon. The floor was covered with scarlet broadloom and the room was focused around a huge circular white couch that surrounded the base of the tall mast.

"Good God," Benson muttered under his breath.

"It—it's supposed to be a circus tent," Elsinore said in a wavering voice. "Roddy designed it. He—he had a clever mind."

"I can see he did," Benson said. "I'll bet he had funny hats and putty noses for visitors, too?"

"Roddy had clown suits," Elsinore said eagerly, pleased to find a subject that distracted Benson. "In white satin, with scarlet pompoms and . . ." His voice dwindled to nothing when he saw Benson turn away.

There were two other runways leading from the tent, and they divided the big room into three sections. One was an alcove formed by a ring of low scarlet-painted cabinets with two zebra-hide chairs on either side of a low table that had begun life as a bass drum. Benson led the way over there, sat in one of the chairs, lit a cigarette with a lighter from the table and motioned for Elsinore to take the other chair. He offered his cigarettes.

"No. No, thank you. I don't smoke."

Benson put his hat on the drum table and sat back. "Don't you want to go to San Francisco, Harald?" he asked.

"I—I don't mind," Elsinore said. "It's just that I don't know anyone there. You know how it is in a strange town."

"What if you didn't have to go? What would you do then? Stay here?"

Elsinore hunched forward with his elbows on his knees, his hands clasped tightly, staring down at the scarlet carpet. "I don't know," he said in a barely audible tone. "I haven't had time to think. I don't know what to do. I've been so upset since —since Roddy—died."

"Yes," Benson said noncommittally. "How long had you been with him?"

"Been with him?" Elsinore looked up, startled and frightened again. "I haven't been——"

"Come off it, Harald," Benson said with a tired and very bored lift of his eyebrows. "We aren't talking about secrets, after all. I just wanted to know when you met Duquesne, and where."

"Four, possibly five years ago," Elsinore said after a hesitant moment. "We met on the beach at Laguna."

"And you struck it off right away, did you?"

Elsinore nodded. He dropped his eyes shyly. "Roddy was

getting a divorce and he wasn't working just then, so we . . ." He shaped a graceful arc in the air.

"I didn't know Duquesne had been married," Benson said, making a question of it.

"He never worked at it." Elsinore's wide mouth twitched with secret knowledge. "That was when he was doing a lot of work for the movies. You know how some of the studios are—" he flicked a glance at Benson's impassive face—"so Roddy got married. He used to see the girl once a month regularly, to give her a check. Then she wanted to go back to New York and Roddy thought it would be best to divorce her."

Elsinore's voice was coming more easily now. He had regained a certain confidence by talking about the things he knew well—himself and Duquesne and their quality of relationship. He had a strange voice, flat and without resonance. It made a sound that might have been produced by a robot, brittle and metallic and very clear.

"I'm surprised you and Duquesne got along so well together," Benson said. "From what I've heard he wasn't your type. He was a rough customer and he was too damn fond of using his fists."

"He was virile," Elsinore agreed modestly. "Like a little boy who liked to break things."

"Especially heads," Benson said. He smiled at Elsinore. "I can't imagine what a sensitive boy like you would see in a guy like Duquesne."

Elsinore's eyelashes flickered. His mouth parted moistly. "You are so very understanding," he murmured.

You are so very right, Benson thought wryly. I am also a hell of a tricky fellow when I put my mind to it. Aloud, he asked, "Did he hurt you?"

"Roddy? Hurt me?"

"When he forced you," Benson said bluntly.

"Roddy? But he didn't——"

"Knock it off, Harald. We both know about Duquesne. In your circle he would probably pass for a very tough fellow. He liked to hurt people. You know the term for him, don't you?"

Elsinore made a strangled sound. "He—he had some problems," he said. "He wasn't exactly a——"

"I hope he didn't hurt you badly," Benson said more softly. "You got over it all right, did you?"

He held his breath, watching Elsinore, and let it out in slow relief when he saw the tight head of curls move up and down.

"It was just his way," Elsinore said thinly.

"Sure," Benson agreed. "It must have been hard to live with. Anybody as sensitive as you would be looking for a little more gentleness, I would think. Have you stayed with Duquesne ever since then?"

Elsinore looked up in momentary bewilderment. "No," he said reluctantly. "No, I went—away—for a while."

There was an element of strain in Elsinore's attitude, as if saying that had been painful for him, maybe even shameful. Benson studied him silently, trying to guess what it meant, knowing he had accidentally touched another sensitive area that might be critically important.

"It's easy to see why you would," he said encouragingly. "Tell me about it."

"I—I don't want to talk about it," Elsinore said. He looked at Benson with a tight frown. "Why should I? Why are you asking me all these questions? Who are you?"

"Never mind," Benson said easily. "We'll go into that later. I was asking you about——"

Elsinore half rose from his chair. Benson leaned forward quickly. He put up one hand and pushed him back. "Take it easy, Harald," he said. "I'm not going to hurt you. Just answer my questions." He could see Elsinore's chin lifting in defiance and he added sharply, "Don't argue, Harald. You don't want to argue with me."

Elsinore's eyes wavered. He sank back into the bristly, hide-covered cushions, shoulders slumped, as if the very limited menace presented by Benson was more than he was able to face.

"Why did you leave Duquesne?" Benson said again. "You had a fight, I suppose? He got rough with you once too often and you walked out. Right?"

Elsinore nodded gloomily.

"Where did you go?"

"To Phoenix," Elsinore said in a low voice. "I took a position in a dance studio."

"I thought you were a dancer," Benson said warmly, as if he admired dancers. "So you went to Phoenix and found a job. Good for you. And you were fighting the good fight?"

It was a phrase that carried special meaning in the homosexual world, Benson knew, and he watched Elsinore closely, seeing him look up quickly with a harsh glint in his eye, his mouth tight.

"Everybody always says that with contempt," he said angrily. "Is it something to be ashamed of?"

"I didn't mean it that way, Harald," Benson said soberly. "I think it takes a lot of courage to break away from everything Duquesne represented and try to work yourself back into the normal world."

"Normal!" Elsinore said waspishly. "That's another word I hate. I'm normal, I'll have you know. I was born this way. This is normal for me."

The old whining bleat, Benson thought sourly. I'm normal, I was born this way. So is a two-headed calf born that way, but that doesn't make it normal. He smiled apologetically at Elsinore.

"Things didn't work out for you in Phoenix, I gather. What happened? How long were you there?"

"Six months or more," Elsinore said in a sullen, resentful tone, his head averted.

"That's a long time. Shows strength of character. What happened then?"

"The—the man I worked for," Elsinore said, shrugging helplessly. "He kept after me and after me. Finally he forced me to——"

"Sure," Benson said as if he understood completely. "I can see how that would happen. So then you decided to come back to Duquesne?"

Elsinore nodded.

"And when he had you back, Duquesne let you know who was boss, didn't he? He kept you short of money, he didn't let you have any friends, he never took you out and he wouldn't let you go out by yourself. He was harsh and overbearing and arrogant and he put you through a hell of a life."

"Did—did you know him?" Elsinore asked wonderingly.

Benson laughed softly. "No, I never saw him, alive or dead."

"It's true," Elsinore said. "Everything you said is true, but it wasn't like that at all. I don't think you do understand Roddy, not the least bit. We didn't go out much, that's true. Roddy wanted me at home. He liked to find me home when he got there. Naturally, living at home, I didn't need much money. You are completely wrong about Roddy." Elsinore sat up straight and his voice grew sharp with a vehement conviction that Benson had not heard from him before.

"Roddy wasn't like me." He gave a small guilty laugh as if he took forgiveness for granted. "I'm not really a very strong personality, I'm afraid. But Roddy was very forceful and sure of himself. He hated the fraudulent world he had to live in and he rebelled against it. Only a strong, determined man would do that. But he wasn't always a rebel, you know. He came from a very important family. He didn't have to rebel. He was born into a life that was smooth and lovely. And then, when he was sixteen, do you know what happened to him?"

"I heard his mother killed herself," Benson said.

"No, I didn't mean that," Elsinore protested. "Oh, that was terrible, too, a really frightful shock for Roddy. But a year or so later when he was at school, Roddy felt feverish and he went to the infirmary and they put him to bed. It took them three days to find out what was wrong with him. He had syphilis. He was only sixteen! He had touched only one girl in his life. And he had syphilis!" Elsinore almost shrieked the word.

"Tough," Benson said. "It happens."

Elsinore looked at him sorrowfully, not quite sneering. "You wouldn't understand. It ruined Roddy's whole life. He was a very sensitive boy. He was desperately hurt and frightened and he couldn't go to his father for help. His mother was dead and Roddy had no one in the world. It wasn't until he met me that he ever found peace, ever had a home. We had a wonderful relationship, warm and close and full of tenderness. He took care of me. He was a great, unappreciated artist, a poet of real genius. But he had been restricted so long to mere embroidery and decoration that he had grown resentful and rather bitter. Sometimes he would lose control of himself. One needed patience and understanding to handle him at such times, but underneath it all, Roddy and I . . ."

Benson lit another cigarette and forced himself to listen patiently to that flat, toneless voice reciting the long and fictitious litany. He did not listen to the words. Before he could reach Elsinore's understanding, he would have to shatter that glowing mirror-image, but it was probably wiser to wait for a while and let Elsinore finish at his own pace. There was a genuine and disturbing quality of human distress in Elsinore's voice and manner as he spoke of Duquesne and remembered their days together with a deceptive, speak-no-evil-of-the-dead gloss that obscured but did not entirely hide the dreadful sense of loss and dispossession that had come to him after Duquesne's death. In the face of that distress Benson could not bring himself to interrupt.

". . . see for yourself," Elsinore said on a strained note of triumph, "that Roddy and I were very lucky, very happy."

"Except about this," Benson said brusquely, making a quick, contemptuous gesture to indicate the flamboyant tent overhead. "And the street boys that Duquesne brought here."

"But that was over long ago," Elsinore said. "Roddy promised me he wouldn't——"

"What else did he promise?" Benson wondered aloud, riding over Elsinore's protest. "Did he promise to give up Billie Bayonne? I'll ask Billie. I'm going to see him when I leave here. I suppose you know he lives just a couple of blocks down the street from here?"

"Billie Bayonne?" Elsinore repeated in a strident shriek.

"He'd throw himself at anything in pants. I wouldn't believe a word he said if he swore on his mother's grave. If he had a mother."

"Good for you," Benson murmured. He waited until Elsinore had settled back again. Duquesne's boy was very alert now, he realized, watchful for all traps, and that was a pity. It would be much more sensible to wait, to let him cool down before asking the next question, but Benson did not have time to waste. He smiled at Elsinore, calmly, and without animus.

"How did you hear of Duquesne's death?" he asked.

Elsinore blinked and made an impatient gesture. "I don't remember. Someone told me. Then I read the papers. What difference does it make?"

"Do you know how he came to get killed?"

Elsinore shook his head. "Some dirty little guttersnipe murdered him," he said tightly, "and stole his car."

"You read an early edition," Benson said casually. "Duquesne was killed because he tried to rape a Mexican boy who didn't care for the idea. The kid knifed him." He smiled grimly at Elsinore. "I guess you probably felt like knifing him, too, when he raped you?"

"Raped me?" Elsinore's voice broke like a boy's. "But he didn't——"

"Drop it, Harald," Benson said sharply. "We know what Duquesne was, you and I. If you had wanted to kill him, and of course you did, it was a perfectly natural reaction. Why try to hide it?"

"I'm not——" Elsinore began. He shrugged. "Well, maybe. Just for a minute. Not seriously. Not murder . . ." He swallowed heavily. "Are you absolutely sure that Roddy was trying to——"

"It'll all come out at the trial," Benson said.

"I don't believe it," Elsinore said shakily. "I simply don't believe it. I won't listen to——"

"It's true, Harald. You know that Duquesne made a habit of raping boys. This time he didn't get away with it."

Elsinore brought his head up achingly slow. His reddened

eyes were blank, dull. Then, as Benson watched, they filled, and overflowed, with sudden tears. He did not try to wipe away the tears or choke down the harsh, suffocating sobs.

Benson sat back. His toes curled with embarrassment. He let himself show no sign of it. He lifted his cigarette to his mouth, drew in smoke and let it out with every appearance of composure. Gradually Elsinore's wild self-indulgent sobs grew less noisy, then subsided to helpless, exhausted weeping.

"I'm sorry I was the one to tell you, Harald," Benson said gently. "News like that should come from a close friend. What do you plan to do now?"

Elsinore made a distracted gesture. "I don't know," he gasped. "What can I do? Where can I go?"

"Don't you have any family?"

"No."

"Didn't Duquesne provide for you in his will? Didn't he leave you anything?"

"No."

"After five years," Benson said with a forceful calm, driving it home. "Five years of devotion and he just forgot you, let you go off by yourself, like a cat he'd picked up in an alley somewhere."

Elsinore lifted one hand and let it drop.

"Duquesne was a very rich man. Did you know that, Harald?"

"Yes," Elsinore said resignedly. "We never talked about it."

Benson eyed him thoughtfully. "Did he tell you who his father was?"

Elsinore gulped audibly. He swept his hand across his face under his eyes, rubbing away tears and powder smears. He did not look at the mess on his fingers. His face had fallen apart.

"I won't tell," he said in a voice that slurred with panic. "I promised Mr. Blue. I gave my solemn word. I won't ever mention his name. Never!"

"His name is H. L. Caine," Benson said evenly. "It's easy to remember."

"But I won't remember it," Elsinore said hastily. "You can trust me. I've forgotten it already. You can tell Mr. Caine——"

Benson made a peremptory gesture that cut Elsinore off in midsentence. He had allowed the pretense to continue too long, he realized.

"I've never met the man," he said.

Elsinore sat up very straight, staring with shock. His loose mouth clamped in upon itself and his nostrils flared. It took a long moment for him to swallow the tension in his throat.

"You—you said you were . . ."

"No. You said it." Benson took out his wallet, thumbed a card from one of the compartments and held it out to Elsinore, who took it mechanically, not thinking to look at it until Benson told him to.

"Benson Kellogg," he read in an unbelieving voice. "Attorney-at-Law."

"I have been appointed to defend the boy who killed Roderick Duquesne," Benson said.

Elsinore looked at him, too startled to speak.

"I need your help, Harald. I want you to come and help me explain to the jury what kind of person Duquesne really was."

"No! No, I won't." Elsinore backed into a corner of his chair. "I won't! Why should I help him? You—you must be mad to think I would——"

"I'm not asking you to help him, Harald," Benson said. "I'm asking you to tell the truth about Duquesne."

"I don't know anything," Elsinore said wildly. "I don't believe those things you said. I won't——" His soft full mouth twisted. "You want to hurt me. You're trying to get at Roddy through me. I won't betray him. I'd die first!"

"Don't be so goddam dramatic about it, Harald," Benson said wearily. "I'm not trying to get at you or Duquesne. I'm trying to get at the truth."

Elsinore's eyes were wide and staring. He face was blank, masklike, unheeding. Benson leaned forward and spoke to him with a slow, strained patience.

"I want you to think about your position, Harald. You're intelligent and you understand the world. I know the kind of life you've had with Duquesne. Outside of your personal difficulties, it's been furtive and half criminal, full of secrets. Why was it like that, Harald?"

"Because—because . . ."

"Because the world doesn't understand people like you and Duquesne. It treats you like criminals instead of sensitive, tortured people. That's right, isn't it?"

Elsinore nodded. He swallowed heavily. Some of the tautness of fright was beginning to leave him and Benson went on, gently and carefully.

"It's not fair, is it?" he said insistently. "People like you don't harm anyone. All you want is a chance to live your lives quietly and decently, like anyone else. You don't think of yourself as a bad or dangerous person, do you, Harald?"

"Of course not," Elsinore said indignantly.

"Of course not," Benson repeated. "But the world treats you as if you were, because of people like Duquesne. Just for a moment put aside your personal feeling for him and try to look at him as he actually was. He was bad, Harald, and dangerous. But you're not like that. You're a good and decent citizen and you wouldn't approve of a man like Duquesne in any circumstances whatever. It's only someone like you who can explain Duquesne, Harald, because you knew him. He was a mad dog, Harald. He was never worthy of your trust."

"That isn't true! You don't know——"

"Stop it, Harald," Benson said sharply. "We both know Duquesne had a long record of violence. He raped you and he tried to rape my client. I expect when I talk to Billie Bayonne, I'll find that Duquesne raped him, too."

Elsinore pursed his mouth as if to spit.

"I've never seen Bayonne," Benson said, "but I've seen you and I've seen my client. I'll bet you, Harald, that I can describe Bayonne well enough to pick him out of a crowd. He has dark hair and sharply cut features, a highly colored complexion, very smooth skin and he's the general build of a junior welter-weight in good condition. Am I right?"

"He's fat now," Elsinore said pettishly. "He doesn't look like that any more. What if he did?"

"It's not an important point, Harald, but it's something for you to think about. How did I know what Billie Bayonne looked like? I've never seen him."

"Someone told you, then. What of it?"

"Nobody told me. Nobody had to tell me. I know because that's the type that Duquesne went wild about. You know, Harald, when I first came in here, I thought for a minute that you were my client. You and he look that much alike."

Elsinore closed his eyes. His face was set with petulant stiffness.

"My client is a young boy, Harald. He was going home to Mexico, hitchhiking. Duquesne gave him a lift. They drove all night and the boy fell asleep. He woke up with Duquesne try-ing to rape him. He had a knife and he used it."

Elsinore said nothing. His mouth opened slightly.

"He fought Duquesne, Harald," Benson went on. "He was lucky. He had a knife. If you'd had a knife when Duquesne raped you, wouldn't you have used it?"

Elsinore turned his head away on the cushion.

"Wouldn't you, Harald?"

"Why do you ask me these things?" Elsinore burst out. "I don't know! It was so long ago. I can't remember if——"

"Of course you remember, Harald. You've blotted it out as much as you could because nobody wants to live with a thing like that in the front of his mind, but you can remember all right. If it had been you, Harald Elsinore, five or ten years younger, in that car with Duquesne, if you had been awakened that way, if you had a knife in your pocket, you would have killed Duquesne too. Wouldn't you, Harald? Wouldn't you?"

"Leave me alone!" Elsinore said shrilly. "You have no right to say such things. I wouldn't have——"

"You're wrong," Benson said sharply. "You would have killed him. You admitted it before. Listen to me, Harald." Benson leaned forward and tapped Elsinore's knee. "I don't know if my client was justified in killing Duquesne or not. The law is not clear. But he does have a right to explain what happened. He does have a right to present a picture of Duquesne as he actually was—a corrupt, brutal man with a record of violence and rape. He has a right to that, Harald. And you are the only person who can give it to him."

"I—I couldn't," Elsinore said thinly. "Mr. Blue told me . . ."

"He threatened you, didn't he?" Benson asked in a grim, tight voice. When Elsinore nodded, Benson sat back. He took a folded sheaf of papers from his inner pocket, separated one and put the rest away. He took out his pen and wrote on the face of the paper. "Is Harald Elsinore your real name?"

"No, but——"

"Is it the only name you are known by?"

"Yes. Why do you want to know?"

Benson folded the paper and passed it across the table. "This is a subpoena, Harald. It orders you to appear in Rincon on Monday morning as a defense witness in the case of the People against Arturo Campeón." Benson raised his hand before Elsinore could say anything. "You are now under the court's protection, Harald. If Caine or Manny Blue should make a threatening move toward you, they will be in contempt of court."

"But—but what about—after?" Elsinore asked plaintively.

"I don't know, Harald," Benson said. "Let's figure it out. You don't plan to stay in Los Angeles, I gather. Have you decided where you want to go?"

"No, I—I haven't had time to think."

"Of course not. Well, the trial may last for a week. That will give you time to think. You will be appearing as an expert witness, so for your special experience and information, I will pay you an expert's fee of fifty dollars a day. And after the trial I'll see that you get a chance to make a fresh start. How's that?"

"It sounds all right," Elsinore said dubiously. "Are you sure . . ."

"I'll take Caine off your back, I promise that," Benson said firmly.

"But, I don't want to——"

"I know it won't be easy for you," Benson said. "The prosecution will give you a bad time on the stand. You'll have to expect that. But you'll be giving a boy a chance to live, Harald. You'll be giving him the chance that no one ever gave you."

Elsinore drew in a slow breath that expanded his chest. He was seeing himself in a new, attractive light. A hero. Selfless and wise through suffering.

"You've been subpoenaed now, Harald. That means you have been ordered to appear in court. If you don't, if you should run away or hide, you would be hunted down by the law. If I had reason to think you might run away, I could ask the police to arrest you and deliver you to the courtroom." He saw Elsinore go tense with alarm. "But I'm not going to do that, Harald," he said quietly. "Do you know why?"

Elsinore shook his head.

"I want you to come into that courtroom and testify honestly about what you know of Duquesne and his background. I could have you brought there by the police. And you could, if you were that kind of person, lie about Duquesne, or refuse to testify. I couldn't do anything about it if you did, and my client would probably be convicted. He would be better off, in such a case, if you didn't appear at all. Do you understand, Harald? You have to come willingly, as an honest citizen doing his duty."

"I see," Elsinore said softly.

"You hold on to that subpoena, Harald. It's your protection against Caine or anyone else who tries to interfere with you. And here," Benson took out his wallet and counted some bills onto the table. "Here's a hundred dollars as an advance against your expert's fee, in case you need it for expenses. If you're all packed and ready to leave, why don't you catch a train for Rincon right away? You'll find my address and phone number on that card. Call me when you get in." Benson pushed the money across to Elsinore, put his wallet away and got to his feet.

"I'm counting on you, Harald," he said, resting a hand on Elsinore's shoulder. "I know you won't let me down."

Don't overdo it, Benson warned himself. Elsinore was not used to people depending on him, and the weight of responsibility might frighten him. Benson looked down at the thin raddled figure in the gaudy chair and offered a confident and reassuring smile.

Elsinore lifted his chin and settled his shoulders back squarely. "I—I'll try," he said in a wavering voice that gradually steadied. "I'm not sure I can do as you ask, but I'll try, Mr. Kellogg. I'll think about it."

"You have my client's life in your hands," Benson said very soberly. "Keep that in mind, Harald. Every time you look in the mirror, think of him. You're his only hope. You can give him a chance to live, Harald. And maybe," he added quietly, "maybe that will give you another chance."

THE SKY was growing dark and ominous when Benson came out of the old building. Dirty granite clouds had drifted in above the smog, and what little light was left to the day reached the streets through a moist and polluted haze.

Benson walked quickly away, turning back toward the Parma Hotel. He was uneasy in his mind about the way he had handled Harald Elsinore. There was not much more he could have done, but he could not convince himself that he had not overlooked something.

Elsinore was an awfully weak reed to hang a defense on, he realized. Frank Sayer would chop him to raw hamburger when he got him on cross-examination. But he was the only person available to Benson who could testify about Duquesne's background, so there was no point in bleating about it. He could, at least, be grateful that Elsinore was not one of the defiant, hard-core homosexuals he had been reading about in Larry Cass's book, for he would probably not have been able to find an effective approach to one of them. In his four or five years with Duquesne, Elsinore had lived almost as a recluse. He had not been part of the strident, self-advertising community of homosexuals who would have shrieked themselves hysterical at the thought of testifying in support of a boy who had killed one of their own. They felt too clearly the aggressive hostility of the world; they thought it cruel and hypocritical and they resented it with a bitter intensity. No appeal on the basis of humanity would have been useful, for they had betrayed their own humanity. The tragic essence of their lives is that they know it, and punish themselves.

Being removed from that society, Elsinore was not so deeply frozen in passive fantasy, but he was no one Benson cared to depend upon. It was very good luck for Benson that Caine's private detective had mishandled Elsinore so badly. If he had pretended sympathy, given Elsinore time to pack his clothes and personal gear and seen to it that he had a comfortable amount of money, he might have succeeded in removing a witness that Benson needed very much.

Billie Bayonne would be a different matter entirely, Benson suspected. Judging from his record, Bayonne was not likely to respond to any persuasion. A subpoena would probably be the only solution.

Benson hesitated at the foot of the hotel staircase, reluctant and mildly nauseated at the prospect of another interview with still another homosexual, this time one who promised to be difficult and unresponsive. He pulled in a long breath of the soggy air and climbed the steps.

A light was burning in the upper hallway and the wicket of the wire-screened door was standing open. The clerk was leaning on the shelf, stringy hair down over his tinted glasses. He ducked back when he saw Benson.

"Kinda late, ain't you?" he called. "I thought you wasn't comin'."

"I was delayed," Benson said. "Did you locate Bayonne?"

In the poorly lighted room behind the clerk Benson could see another man who was only a vague outline as he moved past. The door swung open and the man came out into the hallway. He leaned against the wall languidly, folded his arms and grinned at Benson.

"Looking for little Billie Ringtail, are you?" he said with a deprecatory shaking of his head. He turned to the clerk. "You're right, Petie. He's no Mr. Brown, not this one."

"What I tell you, Manny?" the clerk said excitedly. "What I say, Manny, huh? I said he dint belong around here. Right? Who is he, Manny? You make him?"

"Sure," the man said cheerfully. He winked at Benson. "You've got a very fine eye for quality, Petie boy. This gentleman is the Sagebrush Kid, the two-gun terror from the high lonesome. Am I correct, Counselor?"

"And you would be a man named Blue, I suppose?" Benson said dryly.

The man moved in one lithe step to block the stairs. He was big and young and confident to the point of cockiness. His shoulders were wide and thick, their dreadful symmetry emphasized by three little pleats in the sleeves where they joined the shoulder of his shaggy gray sports coat. His face was heavy, lined with sardonic humor. His teeth were very large, very white and very prominent when he grinned, which obviously was most of the time.

"Manny Blue, that's me," he said. "You know me, eh?"

"By reputation," Benson said.

"That could be, you know? I have a rep around here. Okay, Counselor, let's take a little trip. The boss wants to see you."

"Does this boss have a name?"

Manny Blue regarded him with a serene, untroubled smile. "Sure, but why bother Petie-boy with our private business? You know his name, but let's not mention it here, Counselor."

"I want to see him," Benson said after a thoughtful moment. "But first I want to talk to Billie Bayonne. You can wait, if you want to, but I'll see Bayonne by myself."

Blue's laugh was deep, effortless, full of high good humor and self-esteem. "Now, Counselor, give me some credit. You've been rattling around town all day, trying to find people, and not finding them. You don't expect to find Bayonne, do you?"

"I see," Benson muttered. "It's like that. He was gone all the time but the clerk told me——"

"Sure. Petie told you what I wanted him to tell you. I've been looking for you all afternoon, Counselor. So when Petie slipped me the word, I hustled right down. The boss wants a word with you. All set now, Counselor? Got everything all straightened out in your mind, have you? Then let's get moving."

Blue pushed himself away from the wall and put out one hand as if to take Benson's elbow. Benson knocked it aside casually.

"You meant to invite me, didn't you, Blue?" he asked tightly. "Or do you plan to drag me?"

Blue stood very still. His bright dark eyes made a close and careful survey of Benson, and then he smiled again, slowly and pleasantly.

"You and me could go round and round, Counselor," he said amiably. "We'd break a lot of furniture, I'll bet, but I'd take you."

"It wouldn't be easy," Benson said. "I'm not even sure it would be possible."

"I'd take you," Blue said confidently. "That's my line of work. Tell you what, Counselor, let's just figure we had a little scrap and it came out a draw. So we clean ourselves up and go along and see the boss because he wants to see you and you've maybe got a thing or two you want to say to him." Blue spread his big hands and shrugged. "Why not save ourselves all that trouble?"

Benson laughed in spite of himself. "You've got a logical mind, Mr. Blue. Very well. Lead the way. I'll be right behind you."

Manny Blue grinned confidently. He lifted one hand in a cheerful salute, turned and went down the stairs with a swaggering bounce. Benson followed him. The clerk leaned out behind them, calling to Blue, "Don't forget me, Manny. 'Member where you got it."

"See me tomorrow, Petie-boy," Blue said. He waited on the street for Benson. "That Petie," he said casually. "A very dependable-type guy. You never have to worry about will he sell you out; you know damn well he will." He directed Benson to the left. "But at that he's not as bad as those punks you've been looking for. Lucky for you I got them out of the way, Counselor. Saved you many a grisly experience."

He seemed sure that Benson had not been successful in tracing any of Duquesne's associates. Benson saw no reason to set him straight.

"How many did you chase out of town?" he asked.

Blue pointed to a large white convertible parked at the curb around the corner. He opened the door for Benson, went around and got in under the wheel. "Seven, all told," he said. "A scummy bunch, Counselor, but every one got his hundred bucks and a ticket to nowhere."

"A hundred dollars," Benson said. "That won't last for long."

"Long enough," Blue said with a slashing grin. "Just a few days would be long enough, eh, Counselor?"

"I was wondering if you knew those people were potential witnesses in a murder trial," Benson said quietly. "I see you did."

"I might admit it to you, in private, Counselor," Blue said easily. "But not to anyone else. Forget it. You got outsmarted. Tough, but there it is, old bean."

He was a cheerful, amoral scoundrel, likable in a way that did not allow of approval. Benson watched him putting the big powerful car expertly through miniscule gaps in the traffic with an effortless confidence that marked everything he did. Blue was whistling softly to himself.

"How did you know I was in town?" Benson asked.

"Tricks of the trade, Counselor," Blue said with a shrug. He glanced slyly at Benson, tongue poked at his cheek. "Hell, it's no secret. That hick D.A. in your home town is always try-ing to crawl into Caine's pocket. He phoned this morning. I figured you'd head straight for old Valentine, and sure enough, you did. The captain wouldn't tell me where you went after you left. I don't think he likes me much any more. But you weren't hard to find, were you? Too bad you had to waste a day, Counselor."

"Yes, it was too bad," Benson said tightly. "I didn't like it. I wonder how you'll like it, wasting a day with the state commissioners, trying to persuade them not to revoke your license?"

Blue cocked an eyebrow. "In some circles," he said in a low growl, "it's considered impolite to holler copper."

"I wasn't being polite," Benson said. "We could talk it over, if that's what you want. Pick out a spot and stop the car."

Blue looked at him speculatively. He pursed his lips and whistled a soft tune, slowly shaking his head. "I never play the other man's game. Some other time, Counselor. Right now you've got up a full head of steam. I guess it's natural. You've had a frustrating day and you'd feel better if you could tear my head off. You could maybe do it, too, if you got mad enough. The hell with that noise. You're not mad at me, Counselor; you're mad at Caine. Save it for him. Sit back and enjoy the ride."

The big car rolled smoothly with a silent rush along the wide and busy boulevard. Gradually Benson relaxed and settled back squarely in his seat, realizing only then that he had been holding himself tensely upright. Blue glanced at him and grinned easily.

"Caine's staying at the Chancellor until after the funeral," he said. "I guess you know he's burying his kid tomorrow."

"No," Benson said with no interest.

"Yeah. Somebody was bound to murder that bum sooner or later. How's the betting, Counselor? Think you can get your boy off?"

"Maybe. Why do you ask? I thought you worked for Caine?"

"He just rents me, Counselor, he didn't buy me. I still do my own thinking. I don't figure anybody ought to hang for scragging dear Roddy."

"If Caine hears you say that, you won't be working for him much longer, I suspect."

Blue laughed. "Screw him," he said. "It was only a job, Counselor. It's about over anyway."

"You haven't helped my client much by chasing his witnesses out of town," Benson said. "I suppose you know that?"

Blue shrugged lightly. "Tough. Just doing my job. Nothing personal."

It was finished for him. It had no meaning. Just another job. Tomorrow there would be still another job, and that one wouldn't mean anything either.

BLUE'S BIG CONVERTIBLE swept between low stone gates and up a broad driveway lined with date palms and robustas. A high, square, ocher-toned hotel with bright-blue awnings sat on a low rise a hundred feet from the entrance. Blue turned right where a narrow drive met the first. Here, in a staggered row along the edge of a barranca that overlooked the freeway below, were small two- and three-bedroom bungalows kept for guests who wanted all the hotel's services without any of the bother and who could pay a hundred dollars a day. Blue drove to the last one, a pink stucco box ringed with bare jacarandas. He parked beside a black Cadillac, led the way along the path between dense crotons, holding back tendrils of bougainvillea that swung loosely away from a wire fence bordering the barranca.

Blue rang the bell and pushed open the solid redwood door without waiting. He ushered Benson into a small room and bowed him to a chair.

"Be a minute, Counselor. I'm going to tell the boss you're here. Can I get you a drink?"

"No." Benson sat in the low stiff chair and dropped his hat on the table at his elbow.

Blue shrugged and went into the next room, closing the door behind him. He was gone three minutes, and in that time

Benson had lighted two cigarettes and scrubbed them out after a puff. He had looked through a display of magazines on the table without focusing on any of them. He had crossed his legs and uncrossed them and was now thoroughly annoyed by the delay and even more annoyed at his own restlessness.

Blue opened the door. He made a gesture with his head. Benson got up and crossed toward him.

The inner room was very large. Two walls were glass, and if it had not been a smoggy day, there would have been a fine view of the opposite bank of the barranca. The glass was double thermopane and it muffled the sound on the heavy freeway traffic. It was meant to be a cheerful and comfortable room, and it would have been except for the lightweight gray metal desks and chairs that took up the central part. Beside the door was a big gray metal case shaped like a steamer trunk. The wings were spread apart, and inside Benson could see a filing cabinet, cased pieces of office equipment and drawers for supplies. It was a neat self-contained office, the sort of thing a man like H. L. Caine would have built for himself and would always take with him, along with his secretary and his checkbook.

The secretary was seated with her back to Benson, legs folded to prop up her notebook. She had smooth black hair and she was holding her head stiffly. She did not look around. The man at the desk stared past her at Benson, stonily.

"Mr. H. L. Caine," Blue said in a voice that was not as easy and confident as his normal tone. "Benson Kellogg, Mr. Caine."

Caine moved his chin an inch, up and down. His expression did not change. "Very well, Blue. That's all."

"Should I check with you tomorrow, Mr. Caine?" Blue asked hurriedly. "Maybe you still got some——"

"That's all." Caine did not look at him.

Blue made a smothered sound. He lifted one hand vaguely and let it drop. "Well, okay," he said. "Okay, Mr. Caine. You know where to find me."

Caine did not answer. He waited until Blue had left, then said, "You may finish that in the other room, Miss Enders." He did not look at his secretary either. She put down her pencil, took off her glasses and went out, walking with a long and interesting stride that Benson watched appreciatively. When she was gone he turned back and looked at Mr. H. L. Caine.

He had a grim, square face with no extra flesh, but with a suspicion of bagginess under his chin. His hair was stiff and gray, cut short. It matched the small, cropped and almost invisible mustache under his big nose. It also matched the tone of his skin, which was dry and gray, and the light worsted suit he was wearing, which was drab gray and cut loosely. There was nothing colorful about him. He looked like a man who has been trying for a long time to subdue a natural flamboyance— and not succeeding. He never would succeed. No matter how long he tried, he would never make himself inconspicuous; he was too big. His chest was enormous and his arms were the size of a normal man's legs. He was big and even at his age he looked to be hard. He had been called Hurricane as a young man. It was not hard to see why.

He sat stiffly in his hard metal chair, his head tilted back slightly so he could look directly at Benson. His voice was cold and flat and very positive. He spoke quietly because he was used to people listening closely when he had anything to say. He would never raise his voice these days. He would never need to.

"Do you know why I had you brought here, Mr. Kellogg?"

Benson took out his cigarettes, put one in his mouth and struck a match. His hand held the flame steadily and he looked over it at Caine. "You didn't," he said. He lit his cigarette, blew out the match and dropped it in a crystal bowl on Caine's desk. Then he pulled out the secretary's chair and sat in it, facing Caine.

Caine's expression did not change. "I didn't what?" he said coldly.

"You didn't have me brought here, Mr. Caine. Your man delivered an invitation. I decided to come because I wanted to see you. I think it's time we had a talk."

"You're wasting my time," Caine said. "We have nothing

to discuss. I had you brought here to tell you that I have learned that you plan to involve my name in a disgusting murder trial. I intend to see that you don't."

Benson stared into the slitted, unblinking eyes and felt the cold menace that Caine meant him to feel. He was angered by his response and by the nervous tension that now made his hand tremble when he lifted his cigarette. He gave himself a moment to make sure he could control his voice.

"I heard about your intentions," he said tightly. "I heard from your tame County Attorney. I heard from my senior partners. I heard from my family and friends. I heard from the politicians you control in my state. And now I hear from you." He made a slicing gesture with the hand that held his cigarette, and a spray of ash hit the desk in front of Caine.

"No one is authorized to speak for me," Caine said in a low growl. "I have sent no messages."

"I got them just the same," Benson said. "You don't have to tell people what to do, Mr. Caine. The minute they heard your name mentioned, they began working on me. I've had about all of it I intend to take. That's what I wanted to tell you."

"You've had nothing yet, Mr. Kellogg," Caine said indifferently. He picked up his secretary's pencil and held it between two fingers. "I prefer to live very quietly, Mr. Kellogg. I spend a good deal of money to keep my name out of the public eye. If you attempt to drag me in—" with two fingers he snapped the pencil and put the pieces down on his desk—"I'll break you. You'll be finished as a lawyer. You'll be finished with everything. You'll be finished so completely that no one will even remember your name. That, Mr. Kellogg, is what I wanted to tell you."

Benson's hand clenched painfully. His fingernails cut into his palms. His face was stiff with restraint. "I'm not a pencil, Caine," he said angrily. "You won't break me with two fingers. Why, goddam you. I'd cut my throat before I'd let you scare me."

"I have nothing more to say to you," Caine said. He

pushed his chair back slightly.

"You're a fool, Caine," Benson said roughly. "In Rincon we've got the notion you must be smart because you've managed to make twenty million dollars, or whatever it is. We've just about forgotten that you got your start cracking skulls in the copper fields. You haven't learned a damn thing since then. I came here to talk to you, thinking you were a sensible man." Benson laughed shakily. "Why, I was even feeling a little sorry for you. I must have been out of my mind. Nobody can talk to you. I'll bet nobody has tried in twenty years." Benson got to his feet abruptly. The chair skidded away behind him. It fell with a quiet thud.

He turned away very carefully, moving with small, even steps to control the imbalance that came from the rigid tension in his legs. He went slowly toward the door. He forced his hands open, feeling the dull ache of cramp in his fingers. He opened the door.

"Just a moment, Mr. Kellogg," Caine called in a thin, strange voice.

Benson looked over his shoulder, waiting.

"Sit down, please," Caine said heavily. "I think I may have made a mistake about you. I'd like to hear what you have to say."

Benson drew in a long breath and let it out silently. He came back, picked up the chair, and sat again.

"You don't frighten easily, do you?" Caine said. He offered the thin edge of a bleak smile. His eyes watched Benson with the same stony stare.

"I can be scared," Benson said. "But I've had too much of it lately. I don't respond much any more. Anyway," he said coldly, returning Caine's level gaze, "you don't scare me much, Caine. A man like you must have a lot of enemies. I wouldn't be surprised if a lawyer could make a very good living just handling litigation for people who don't like you."

Caine's tight mouth twitched at the corners. He took a large handkerchief from an inner pocket and opened it with a flip. He blew his nose, taking a long time about it. Benson suspected he might be smiling, but when he took his handkerchief away, Caine's face was just the same.

"Why did you try that scare technique with me?" Benson asked curiously. "Does it always work for you?"

"Usually," Caine said absently. "It's merely policy, Mr. Kellogg, an obvious beginning. It takes time and effort and sometimes money to reach an accommodation with any man. It is often quicker and cheaper to sink the iron in him first and see what color his liver is. In the old days we never bought a man's claim until we were sure he couldn't be run off or scared away."

Benson looked at him blankly. The man was serious and, because of that, very dangerous, he realized. There was probably no genuine emotion in him at all. What Benson had been thinking of as an unusual degree of self-control was the essence of the man himself—cold, remote, utterly focused. He would never be upset by any setback because there would never be a moment when he considered defeat to be possible for him. And that inhuman resolution put him beyond the area of normal response.

"You're not like your father," Caine said.

"I didn't know you knew my father."

"I thought of hiring him as my counsel at one time. I visited your ranch for a few days when you were away at school. Nothing came of it, but I remember your father clearly. A soft man."

"Only by your terms," Benson said sharply.

"Of course," Caine agreed, as if there were no other terms worth considering. "He would have been good enough in normal times, but we were looking forward to a bare-knuckle fight in federal court, and your father wasn't man enough for the job." His old cold eyes studied Benson dispassionately. "He wasn't like you. Too bad."

"I don't imagine he gave a damn what you thought," Benson said. "Do you?"

"We're wasting time," Caine said. "And I don't care for your tone, young man. Alter it. Now let's get to the point."

"I'll be go-to-hell," Benson said softly. "You are a sure-enough hard case, aren't you? What do you plan to do now, offer me some money?"

"Would that be attractive, Mr. Kellogg?" Caine said with a thin smile.

"No." Benson lit another cigarette. "No, I'm not looking for a bribe, Mr. Caine. I came to Los Angeles this morning to find out what kind of man your son was. What I learned makes me a little sorry for anyone who had anything to do with him, even you."

Caine glared at him, his thin mustache emphasizing the hard line of his mouth. There was something vicious in his eyes. "Your sympathy is offensive," he said.

"I'm not sympathizing," Benson said. He exhaled a cloud of smoke. "I don't feel a damn bit of sympathy for you. As a matter of fact, I don't have any interest in you one way or the other. Do you want me to finish what I started to say?"

Caine nodded tightly as if he did not trust himself to speak.

"I told you why I came to Los Angeles—to find out what kind of man your son was. It didn't take me long, Mr. Caine. Your son was well known around here."

Caine's gaunt face hardened. He said nothing.

"I want to be able to tell the jury about him. A man like your son, Mr. Caine, was bound to get himself killed sooner or later. The jury has to understand that."

"Get to the point," Caine said.

"I'm going to defend my client, Mr. Caine. I'm going to do my damnedest to get him off. I've managed to locate a witness who is qualified to testify about your son's background."

Caine's knotted hands shifted slightly. Benson smiled into his bleak eyes.

"You sent your hired thug around town last night to frighten away every prospective witness he could find. But Blue is not as efficient as you and he seem to think. I found my witness, Mr. Caine. His name is Harald Elsinore. I've already served him with a subpoena. I wanted you to know that. Maybe Blue will hear that he is still in town and try to interfere with him. Don't let him. That is a flat warning, Mr. Caine. Don't let him."

Caine nodded. "You have been resourceful, Mr.——"

"I don't want your opinion," Benson said. His voice was rising and he stopped for a moment to control himself. He took a last drag on his cigarette and scrubbed it out in the bowl.

He got to his feet slowly, putting both hands on the desk and leaning toward Caine.

"I don't like you, Mr. Caine. I don't like anything I know about you. I don't want to have anything to do with you. I told you about Elsinore for just one reason. If he doesn't show up in Rincon for the trial, I will know you are responsible and I will swear out a warrant for your arrest and come myself to see it served on you. Whether I can send you to jail, I don't know, but by God, you will explain in open court just why you interfered with my witnesses. I'll see to it that every newspaper in the country knows who Roderick Duquesne really was. Don't interrupt me, damn you! I'm not going to be bribed or scared or wheedled. I'm going to defend my client. The jury is going to learn what kind of man Roderick Duquesne was. I'll establish his background through Elsinore's testimony. But if you stick your nose in once more, I'll subpoena you and let you tell the jury about Roderick Duquesne. That's the way it is, Mr. Caine." Benson pushed himself erect. "I hope for your sake you believe me."

Caine's face was still and tight. He closed his eyes briefly, as if he had been staring for a long time into a hard light.

"You've got a nasty way of speaking, young man. Keep your tongue off me or you'll regret it. I'm not interested in your personal problems. You know what I expect from you. I'm not concerned with your motives. Just be very sure that my name is not mentioned in that courtroom."

Benson let out a slow breath. "You don't give a damn about your son, do you? You don't even care if my client is innocent or guilty."

"I'm sure you can protect your client without my help," Caine said. "You are right, Mr. Kellogg. My only concern in this matter is to protect my name. It means something to me. My son does not. He shamed and disgusted me many years ago. He began his filthy practices very early. His perversions killed his mother and sickened me. I do not propose to let his record pollute mine. I am proud of my name. It is all I have to leave behind me. I am speaking very frankly to you, Mr. Kellogg. I want you to understand that I will stop at nothing to protect my name."

"Your name," Benson repeated slowly. He turned with his hand on the doorknob. He felt an angry, bitter lump in his throat. "If using your name would help my client, I'd use it, Caine, and the hell with your threats. Harald Elsinore's testimony should be good enough, but if it isn't, you get ready for a trip to court, Caine. I'll let you know."

He opened the door, went through and closed it sharply behind him.

BENSON came awake slowly in the dark fusty atmosphere of the Pullman compartment. He could hear someone knocking on the locked door. He licked his dry lips and tried to swallow. He reached out awkwardly and slipped the latch.

"El Monte in forty minutes, sir," the porter said in a quiet voice. He pulled his head back and closed the door.

Benson rolled from the bunk and got to his feet. He stumbled into the tiny toilet cubicle and ran a basin of cold water. He closed one eye and studied his face in the dazzling mirror.

You're a sad, beat-up character, friend, he told himself. Look at the sore red eyes and the cracked lips and the rat's-nest hair. You were dissipating, weren't you?

Dissipating, hell, he muttered—I was drunk. He put his head down under the water as long as he could hold his breath. He drank long and deep, then rubbed his hands vigorously over his face until the skin began to tingle. He came up gasping for air, pulled the drain valve and turned on the hot water. He went back into the compartment for his shaving gear, moving very carefully with the rocking motion of the train.

He soaped his face and stood sleepily working up a lather with his long-handled brush. It had been a long, dreary, drunken and tiring night—good therapy probably, he realized, for after a day such as he had spent in Los Angeles, something drastic and thorough had been required to get the bad taste out of his mouth.

Still it had been damnfoolishness of the second-lieutenant variety, and at forty-two he was too old, too experienced and too conscious of himself to enjoy an evening drinking in a strange barroom full of strangers. Some of it he could blame on the airport management, if he needed to blame someone else. With all flights smogged in and no improvement likely before morning, the airport people had refused to cancel outright, insisting that there might be a change soon. So the bars in the terminal building were jammed and stayed jammed until the would-be travelers got tired and went home or, as in Benson's case, phoned for a reservation on the next train. And another two-hour wait in the Union Station had completed the damage. Benson had no clear recollection of having eaten dinner, though he must have, he thought, because drinking always gave him a fiendish appetite and he was not at the moment aware of being hungry.

He dressed awkwardly, balancing himself in the tight space between the bunk and the wall. By the time he had rammed his soiled clothes into his bag and closed it, the train was slowing for the El Monte station. Benson found his hat wedged under the bunk, banged it against his leg and put it on. He picked up his bag and went out into the corridor. He gave the porter a dollar, allowed him to flick his whiskbroom in a ritualistic pass as the train inched into the weathered old station.

Benson went through the open shed in long strides that left the other passengers behind. He checked at the ticket counter, learned that the first train to Rincon would leave at four o'clock that afternoon, and bought a seat in the club car. He put his bag in a coin locker and compared his watch with the enormous overhead clock. Six hours until train time. He could probably get a plane before then, he suspected, but the difference wasn't worth the effort, in his present condition.

He bought the thick Sunday edition of the *El Monte Independent* and went out to the cab stand, reading the headlines as he walked.

The train station was in the old section of town, as it always is in that part of the country, because towns on the east-west lines grew quickly after the trains came, spreading out from the station sites. The main approach street had recently been widened and was two divided lanes now with a center strip that would have flowers and grass and little pastel cactuses when the planting was finished. The oldest—also the smallest and loveliest—church in El Monte was a block from the station. Its old tile-protected adobe wall was almost on the edge of the new roadway. People had to walk in single file to reach the entrance and Benson watched them from the cab window, thinking that they made a beautiful pattern as they moved in the sunshine along the old pale wall in their Sunday clothes, the men dark and solemn, the women with small dabs of lace on their heads because they were going to church, but their eyes dancing and shifting because going to church was only a part of the special grace of Sunday. Their parade was slow and rather stately, and they made Benson think of the stylized figures in Minoan friezes.

The cab stopped at the side entrance of the Jefferson Hotel. Benson paid the driver, got out and went straight through the big lobby to the almost deserted dining room. He took one of the corner tables that overlooked the garden and a corner of the swimming pool, and spread his fat newspaper over the table.

He drank two whiskey sours very slowly, with several glasses of water. By then he was able to smoke a cigarette without feeling dizzy. He ordered a large breakfast, and the young and bouncy waitress giggled at the size of it. He worked away at it with no haste, his appetite sharpened now by the drinks and by the knowledge that he had the whole day before him.

At nine o'clock the following morning he would rise from

his seat at the defense counsel's table when Judge Groat made his entrance, and from then until the verdict was rendered he would never have a moment as free and relaxed as this. He had done all he could to prepare his case, and after a last-minute review tonight, he would be ready. It would be best now to put it out of his mind, and he tried, focusing on the big illustrated paper as if he had no other interest.

It was a very fat paper, full of advertisements, thickened by boiler-plate sections from the feature syndicates, with only an outer skin of news which was divided according to the ritual of American journalism with the first emphasis on crimes, deaths, disasters, fires and airline crashes. A local bank had been robbed last night and that took three columns, with pictures of a smirking manager showing just how horrified he had been at getting the news. The trial of Arturo Campeón was mentioned on page three, as if Rincon news could not possibly be worth page-one attention in El Monte. The story said the boy had murdered Roderick Duquesne and had confessed. It predicted his speedy conviction. There was no question of his guilt in the reporter's mind, no careful use of "alleged," no suggestion that people accused of murder had a right to be tried by juries, not newspapers.

Nathan Barstow, the paper said, had yesterday arrived in El Monte to preside at the state caucus scheduled for Wednesday. Which meant, Benson knew, that Burr would be in town, too. Benson thought briefly of trying to chase him down, then dismissed the notion. He didn't much want to talk to Burr. They didn't have much in common right now.

But thinking of Burr being in El Monte made him remember someone else who was here. Benson sat up and put out his cigarette. It wasn't a name he wanted to remember, but it had come knifing into his brain and settling like a dog bedding down in high grass, turning round and round until it had worn a hard-packed nest. Judge Amos Turnbull was in El Monte, at the Mountain View Sanitarium, where Burr had taken him last week. Pretending he wasn't aware of it would not work any longer.

Benson signaled for the check, went outside, flagged a cab and directed the driver to the northern section of the city, along the wide boulevard that passed the capitol grounds and led directly toward the great snow-streaked, softly rounded old mountain from which El Monte took its name. Here, some few miles from the original walled village, the prosperous first families had built their houses, on ground high enough to escape the desert dust but not so high that they could not bring in a well.

The street paralleled an unfenced cement irrigation ditch. These ditches cobwebbed the city, with narrower channels draining off for commercial watering. What had been an arid desert town was now fertile, always humid, sometimes steamy as the tropics, so that vegetation grew thick and rank and people had a hard time getting a satisfying breath of air.

Mountain View Sanitarium was surrounded by a tight redwood fence in a design that looked to be woven. The main building was an old colonnaded hacienda three stories high, built with blank walls to the world and all the rooms opening onto the center courtyard. At one side was a low brick structure, clinically austere.

The wire gate on the road was open and the cab turned in, climbed the short steep grade and stopped in front of the main building. Benson told the driver to wait, gave him five dollars on account, and got out.

He stood indecisively for a long silent moment, knowing he had to go inside and inquire about Judge Turnbull. The cab driver put his head out the window and stared at him from the parking lot. Benson swung on his heel, pushed back the wrought-iron gate, went through toward a door marked RECEPTION. He identified himself as Judge Turnbull's attorney and was directed to the medical director's office in the next room. The orderly led him inside the bleak, deserted, fluorescent-lighted room, slid a straight chair up beside the desk and told him it would just be a few minutes. Benson lit a cigarette, crossed his legs and stared blankly at the blank wall, thinking of nothing except that he wished he could get up and go away.

The doctor entered behind him, crossed the bare floor in

rubber-soled shoes that squeaked softly, and sat at the desk, putting square-fingered hands flat on the top and looking at Benson with an odd intensity.

He was young and pale and very tired. The skin under his eyes was dark and wrinkled. His eyes were bloodshot. I wonder why the good ones are always so tired, Benson thought. You'd expect a doctor to take better care of himself; but maybe when you're good you have to take on all the work the second-raters aren't able to handle, so you never get any rest.

"You're Mr. Kellogg," the doctor said in a thin, hoarse voice. "I'm Dr. Sotomayor. You wanted to see Judge Turnbull? What about?"

"We're old friends, Doctor," Benson said. "I just wanted to see if he was all right, if he needed anything."

"He's getting everything he needs," the doctor said stiffly. "We're taking care of him."

"I'm sure you are," Benson said politely. "But maybe I can do something a little more personal."

"Why didn't you think about that before you brought him here?"

"I didn't——" Benson began. Then he stopped and looked sharply at the doctor. "I'm not that Kellogg," he said quietly. "My brother brought him here. But I'm curious about your attitude. Why do you——"

The doctor lifted one hand and silenced Benson with a brusque gesture. He rubbed his hand over his face, pushing the palm hard against his eyes, first one and then the other, as if the pressure eased him.

"I'm sorry, Mr. Kellogg," he said. "Unprofessional conduct, I'm afraid. I could say I was tired and I got a little careless. My apologies, sir."

"That's all right, Doctor. There's no need to apologize to me. I'm not very happy about Judge Turnbull being here, either. I gather you think he——"

"He should never have been brought here," Dr. Sotomayor said, savagely quiet. "What kind of a goddam family does he have anyway?"

"Routine kind," Benson said carefully. "They were frightened, Doctor. Most families would——"

"Most families don't have people like Amos Turnbull. Don't they know who he is?"

"Yes, they know."

"Then why can't they take care of him? A man like that. Damn it, Mr. Kellogg, he is the closest thing to a great man we've ever had. I've known about him since I was a kid. My grandfather was his friend, my father was one of his law clerks. All my life I've looked up to him. So have most of the people in this state. Why can't his family——"

"That's enough, Doctor," Benson said patiently. "Judge Turnbull is a friend of mine, too. I know his family well. I'm sorry about what happened, but they are a hell of a lot sorrier. They know him better than you do, better than I do, and love him better, too, if that is a word you can use in a place like this."

"You can use it here," the doctor said with a slow, slanted smile. "Sorry, Mr. Kellogg. I'm too tired to make sense, I suppose. You want to see him, do you?"

"If it's all right."

"Sure. There's nothing wrong with him. He could leave tomorrow as far as I'm concerned."

"Then why——"

"Because some stupid court said he was mentally incompetent, that's why he's here. And because Judge Turnbull committed himself."

"You're sure there's nothing wrong with him?"

Dr. Sotomayor shrugged. He got up wearily from his chair. "He's senile. That's not a curable condition, but it doesn't justify sending him here, in my judgment. We'll take care of him, of course, but we can't do anything his own family couldn't do better."

"They were frightened, Doctor. I told you before. Judge Turnbull loses control sometimes, from what I've been told. Maybe they were afraid of publicity that would damage him as well as themselves."

"I suppose so," the doctor said hoarsely. "Hell, it's none of my business, Mr. Kellogg. I shouldn't be talking like this, I guess. Mountain View is a profit-making operation, after all, and there aren't an awful lot of people who can afford our prices. But I hate to see a man like Judge Turnbull come here. What we get for the most part are the rejects—old people whose families can't stand looking at them any more. Judge Turnbull shouldn't be put in a position like that. He's old and he needs care. But my grandfather is even older. He dribbles and spits food like a baby. Half of what he says doesn't make any kind of sense. He has to wear rubber pants. But he lives at home with us and when he has lucid moments, he knows where he is and he knows his family is there taking care of him. That's what Amos Turnbull needs too, Mr. Kellogg."

"I can't speak for his family, Doctor," Benson said, touched by the tired vehemence of the man. "Maybe in a little while we can arrange for him to go home again. I know they want him. They were afraid he might hurt himself."

"He couldn't hurt anybody. His periods of tension are cyclic and never last long. During one he needs light sedation and tranquilizers, nothing more. Except the item you mentioned before. Love." The doctor closed his eyes for a moment, bracing himself with one hand on the desk. "He's all right now, Mr. Kellogg. He gets tired very easily and he doesn't concentrate well, but he's as sane as either of us."

Dr. Sotomayor came around the desk and waited for Benson to rise. He was six inches shorter than Benson and he had to cramp his neck back to look at him.

"Get him out of here, Mr. Kellogg. Take that old man home where he belongs."

"I'll try," Benson said quietly.

"Do it. Don't just try." He took Benson's arm above the elbow, drew him out to the corridor and hustled him along to the door that let onto the inner courtyard. It was a big place, with narrow tile walks and thick smooth grass. It was shaded with pepper trees and acacias, and in each patch of shade was at least one bathrobed patient, some in wheel chairs, some in long reclining chairs of woven rawhide. Many of them had nurses attending them.

"Down at the far end near the wall," the doctor said in a low voice. "See him?"

"I see him," Benson said. "Thank you, Doctor."

Dr. Sotomayor dropped his hand from Benson's arm. "We'll take care of him, Mr. Kellogg. Don't worry." He turned away abruptly and went inside.

BENSON stood under the shadow of the high colonnade, reluctant to go out into the brightness of the sanitarium garden. He could see the back of Judge Turnbull's graying, half-bald head, and the sharp point of his shoulder in a dark blue bathrobe that was a lighter, glowing color where the sun touched it. The judge was leaning back in a long chair, his head tilted as if he were looking up at the huge, folded mountain that dominated El Monte.

From there he looked much as Benson had always remembered him, a slender, strongly muscled, slow-moving man, quiet and reflective but never somber or pedantic and, most of all, never too busy within himself to share actively the life around him. For two years during the school terms Benson had stayed at the judge's house in Rincon. In those days the ranch could be reached only by a poor road, and commuting would have been impossible. The judge had taken him in as a favor to his father who was the sort of man people did favors for. Benson probably knew the judge better than anyone except members of his own family, but he did not pretend he understood him. Amos Turnbull had always been a solitary man, deeply focused, and by the time Benson knew him, he was already becoming a legend, so that he was always seen through a haze of historic meaning that tended to distort the quality of the man himself.

Benson went slowly down the tiled path, purposely not

looking at any of the listless patients in their patches of shade. He moved around in front of Judge Turnbull. The judge was holding an unlighted cigar in his thin mottled hand and Benson, elaborately casual, took out his matches and struck one.

"Care for a light, Judge?"

Judge Turnbull blinked. He looked at the match and then at Benson, blankly and without recognition. For a brief, panicky moment, Benson was afraid the judge did not know him. He was tragically changed, with dull eyes and dry sunken cheeks and a bright yellow scarf knotted with frightful jauntiness under his chin. Then he smiled, very slowly. He lifted the cigar, turned it between his lips and bit down on it. When Benson held the flame close, he drew in long even breaths, being careful to get a good light. Then he blew the flame out and leaned back with the cigar cocked up in the corner of his mouth.

"Thank you, Benson."

"How are you feeling, Judge?" Benson asked in a shaky voice.

The judge shrugged frail, bony shoulders. He attempted a light, companionable smile. "Let's not talk about it, Benson. I have just discovered I am an old man. It's not a discovery worth discovering. I was hoping I'd never make it."

He shut a thick book on his lap and put it down beside the leg of his chair. It was the first volume of the state statutes had compiled long before Benson had been born. He saw Benson craning his neck to read the title on the spine and he turned it so it was easier to see.

"They should have been revised long ago. I've been thinking of getting some young men busy collecting recommendations. I might even try my hand at it if——" He took the cigar out of his mouth and made a vague gesture. "An old man's pipe dream," he said softly.

Benson frowned, hesitant. He did not know what to say. There was so much he wanted to say, but he couldn't think how to begin. The judge looked at him curiously.

"Don't be embarrassed, Benson," he said dryly. "This is a frightful place to come visiting, but let's forget that."

"Yes, sir," Benson said uncertainly. "How—how are you getting along?"

"Who knows, my boy, who knows? I am dying, of course. That's what people like me come here for. I had a bad day or two, but I'm over it now and I'm trying not to be rebellious. I've had a good long life and I suppose I should be more grateful than I am. No one ever is, Benson. No amount of living is enough. But now I have to prepare myself for the end. I'd like to do that with some dignity."

"You?" Benson said thickly. "You don't have to think about that, Judge. Why, you practically built the law in this state. If that isn't dignity, what is?"

"Be quiet, Benson. I hired out as a judge before you were born. I worked at being a judge for a long time. Don't you think I'm capable of judging myself?"

He let a thin streamer of smoke sift from his dry lips and coughed slightly.

"I have an enemy inside me, Benson. Can you appreciate the peculiar horror of that? To know that your mind is not your own any longer?"

"But Judge, the doctor said——"

"Nonsense," Judge Turnbull said with unexpected vigor. "Young Sotomayor is embarrassed, that's all. I make him feel guilty, for some reason. Well, he's a good boy and a fine doctor, but he's sentimental. He's wrong about me. I'm better off here. I don't want to think about leaving, Benson. I couldn't face another change, so don't get involved in any quixotic campaign to liberate me. I have a certain amount of pride, boy. I don't want to be a laughing stock. You don't let infant children run the streets alone and you shouldn't let senile old men out alone either."

Benson turned away quickly. He stared blindly out over the wall, seeing nothing.

"Stop it, Benson," the judge said. "Sending me here was a wise move. I'm glad Burr had the courage. It was a decision the family should have made some time ago, but it was hard for them, I realize. When you see it happen over the years, the gradual erosion of character and strength and intellect never seems quite to reach the peril point. But I had reached it, and passed it. Only an outsider could see it clearly."

"Judge, I don't believe——"

"Don't interrupt, Benson. I'm trying to look at it honestly, to accept it and resign myself. Now let's not talk about it any longer. The subject sticks in my throat. I am not so philosophical about it as I would like to be. Tell me about yourself, Benson. I see by the papers that you are defending in a murder case. Is it something you can sink your teeth into? I recall I always worked twice as hard on murder trials as any other. There is something about capital punishment that makes us want to be very sure. I suppose you find that true?"

"Yes, sir," Benson said. "It—it is a difficult case to prepare." He lit a cigarette to give himself something to do with his hands. "The papers don't have the complete story, by the way. It's more involved than they know. I wonder if you'd care to hear about it, sir? I'd value your advice."

Judge Turnbull smiled at him with a mocking twinkle. He took the cigar out of his mouth. "Buttering the old man, aren't you?" he said with a soft roupy chuckle. "All right. Tell me about it, boy. Nobody has asked my advice in a long time."

"I can use some advice, Judge," Benson said honestly. "I'm not trying to butter you. It's a long story, though, and pretty messy. Are you sure it won't be——"

"Nonsense, my boy. Pull up one of those chairs and get at it. Go slowly and make sure I understand the complex points. If my attention seems to wander, just repeat it. I get tired very easily these days and they've given me some sort of pill that keeps me drowsy, but I'm reasonably alert at the moment. Here, have a good cigar and throw away that coffin nail."

Benson did as he was told. The judge leaned forward with his elbows on his knees, watching Benson with a slight, intent frown and nodding encouragement.

Benson smoked his cigar gingerly, in short shallow puffs, trying not to taste the heavy smoke that was beginning to make him slightly sick. Before he was halfway through his abbreviated account of the case, he realized that the judge was starved for just this kind of mental challenge. He was taking it in hungrily, totally concentrated.

Benson deliberately slowed and went into more elaboration, taking out his notebook from time to time to refresh his memory. The judge seemed to be sharing Benson's search for a sound legal approach. He scowled when his vaguely written statutes were referred to, smiled grimly as Benson told him of H. L. Caine and his interference, clamped his thin hard mouth in a bitter arc as Benson spoke of his distasteful investigations in Los Angeles and laughed angrily and softly when he heard of Benson's interview with Caine.

"I don't know how I'm going to make the jury understand all that," Benson said finally. He held the cigar down at the side of his chair where he could not smell it.

Judge Turnbull sat back wearily. He lifted one bloodless hand and wiped it across his chin with a faint rasping of dry skin. "An unsavory mess," he said thinly. "From every aspect." He looked at Benson sharply and speculatively. "What troubles you most?"

"The felony-misdemeanor problem," Benson said promptly. "Sodomy is a misdemeanor in this state. Homosexual assault is not mentioned at all in the statutes, except as it may be included in the general category of child molestation, which does not apply in this case. I can't ask a jury to free my client because he was defending himself unless the law has given him the right to defend himself. And I don't know how . . ."

Judge Turnbull shook his head slowly, tiredly. He closed his eyes and pulled in a long breath. "I see," he said in a strained tone. He opened his eyes again, and they were surprisingly bright against the gray pallor of his skin. "It is a pity that young lawyers are not trained in the common law. Do you know anything of the history of the problem, Benson?"

"No, sir."

"In the common law, which is the basis of all our statutory law, homosexual acts were originally considered to be ecclesiastical offenses and left to the church to punish—which it did, quite severely. It was Henry the Eighth, as you will remember, who broke the ecclesiastical power and in the process the power of the church's trial process. Homosexual acts became felonies and subject to criminal jurisdiction."

"Yes, sir, but how does that——"

"I'm not quite sure it is the answer, Benson. I would want to study the arguments, but I would say that it shows you where to look for the answer. Statutes, after all, are laws written by the various states to clarify confusion and assist in the orderly regulation of the community. They aren't meant to be a hindrance. They take their weight from the sovereign authority of the state, but their massive influence stems from their roots in the common law."

"Is that the answer for me, then, to invoke the common law?"

"I would think it might be. I remember once writing in an opinion that the common law should prevail wherever there is no specific provision in the constitution against it. Go back to the common law for your basis, Benson. And don't be overly concerned with the distinction between felony and misdemeanor. I have often thought that was a point that sometimes merited more spirited argument in the courts. In the common law, the offenses originally listed as felonies were arson, burglary, larceny, manslaughter, mayhem, rape, robbery, and sodomy. Many of them have since been universally—and wisely —downgraded to misdemeanors, but in writing and codifying their statutes, not all states have agreed which should rest in which category. Here we have left it slightly vague, and we may discover that is the best course. At least, it leaves an opening for argument and that is all you need. I think you might be justified in presenting a plea of self-defense, if you can establish your facts."

Judge Turnbull shifted his high, thin shoulders against the chair. His voice was light and brittle and very tired and he spoke with a slow, hesitant precision as if he had trouble concentrating. When he finished he lay back, breathing heavily through his mouth. He screwed his eyes shut as though to escape the light.

"Thank you, sir," Benson said quietly. "That was the only basis I could think of. I'm glad you feel it's worth trying. Now I'll have to convince Judge Groat."

"Barney Groat," Judge Turnbull said in a weak, sighing voice. "He studied in my office in his early days. I never liked him, I'm afraid, so I was not able to guide him. He became a forceful prosecutor, but he had little insight, I felt. He is limited as a judge because he tends to regard the bench as an element of law enforcement, which of course it is not. But Barney was always an eager, quick-witted man. He has the power of growth, as all men have. Maybe he has exercised it since I knew him. He could be a good judge, if he gave himself the chance."

"You make him sound pretty rough," Benson said.

"No, no. I didn't mean that," Judge Turnbull said softly. "There is something in the calculated cruelty of a trial, Benson, that makes a judge cruel himself, unless he guards against it. And in guarding himself, he learns to look inward, to understand himself better. So he can grow, Benson. Beyond any man, a judge can grow in quality and meaning. It may well be that Barney has grown since his early days. Go gently with him, boy." The judge turned his face away from the sunlight.

"I will, sir. Do you think——"

Benson broke off. He leaned forward. Judge Turnbull's thin, narrow chest was lifting and falling with the slight, quick regularity of sleep. Benson slipped the cigar from the judge's fingers without disturbing him. He threw it and his own over the wall.

The fire is out, he thought dully. He stood there looking at the worn, melancholy face of the sleeping old man.

The judge seemed very old, lying back defenselessly with the side of his face in the harsh sunlight. His nostrils barely moved as he breathed. There was no longer much difference for him between sleeping and waking. A little blob of spittle formed in the corner of his dry lipless mouth. He looked nothing like the pictures of him that hung in every courtroom in the state. The great, strong, temperate man of the portrait is what people would think of when they remembered Amos Turnbull. As they damn well should. He was one of the men who had brought the law to a lawless land, not with the bravado of a gunslinger but with the love and courage of a decent man determined to make life possible and fruitful. There is a special place, Benson thought, for lawgivers.

He turned and walked away quickly through the ranks of patients sitting silently with their nurses, foundered in weakness, waiting to die in the sun. At least there was the sun, impartial in its warmth and brightness.

THE RINCON COUNTY COURTHOUSE looked drab and rather dirty in the hard morning light. There was a double row of people standing in front of the main entrance, where two deputies with their thumbs in their gunbelts kept them outside until the courtroom doors were opened. Arturo Campeón's was the first murder trial Rincon had seen in some five years, and the same people who had jammed the highway to Cobre Peak to see the spot where Roderick Duquesne had been killed were here now, jostling surreptitiously for a chance to witness the trial.

Benson leaned forward in the cab, told the driver to go around to the north quadrant. He sat back and took another paper from Mary who was perched tautly and hazardously on the edge of the seat, her thin face drawn with strain and excitement.

"Relax, Mary," Benson said. "You've done a fine job. This is just what I wanted. Now have you——"

"Oh, Mr. Kellogg, you don't know what it's been like!" she said. "I dream of that telephone sometimes and I could scream! I just didn't know what to tell people. I didn't even know where you were!"

"I was holed up, Mary," Benson said. He took out a folder from his thick briefcase and gave it to her. "I've made some notes I want you to type for me. Look up the references yourself. I don't want anyone to see this stuff."

"Oh, you can trust me, Mr. Kellogg," Mary said fervently.

"Why, I know that, Mary," Benson said in a gentle tone. "Now, what about the jury list?"

"I didn't get much information, Mr. Kellogg. It's a new panel. I checked the city directory and the county election board and one of the credit bureaus."

Benson took the stapled file. "I just wanted a clue, Mary. Thanks."

The cab pulled up outside the entrance to the county jail. Benson gave the driver a bill and got out. He closed the door and leaned in through the window. "Go get some fresh air, Mary, and try to relax. We're going to have a tough week."

"But, Mr. Kellogg, what about——"

"Later, Mary. I'll see you during the noon recess." Benson backed away and motioned for the driver to move on. He turned and went inside, pushed back the swinging gate beyond the booking desk and went down the narrow corridor toward the cell block. The deputy on duty unlocked the barred door.

"Newspaper boys are back with the sheriff, Mr. Kellogg," he said. His chin came up firmly like a man ready to have his picture taken. "They're looking for you. Want me to tell them ——"

"I'd be much obliged if you didn't tell them anything," Benson said quickly. "I don't have anything to say to them. How's my client?"

The deputy shrugged. "He was a snotty little punk a couple of days ago," he muttered. "But he's quieted down a lot since then. Ambulance brought him over an hour ago. Want me to bring him to the conference room?"

"The cell will do. I just want to see him for a minute."

The deputy led Benson down the iron hallway. He unlocked a cell door, stepped back to let Benson in and locked it again. "Holler when you're ready," he said. His boot heels were noisy as he retreated.

Turo Campeón was seated on the single steel bunk, staring down at the floor with a curiously composed expression. He brought his head up very slowly.

He looks like a young kid, Benson thought, and maybe looking like that will help him with the jury. The boy had been shaved that morning. His hair was closely trimmed and combed flat to his narrow head. He was wearing a new pair of dark slacks and a lightweight gray coat sweater that was fitted over his left arm, draped around his bulky cast, and held in place by a button at the waist. Mary had picked the clothes for the boy, and they seemed a good fit. The dressing on the side of his head was small and startlingly white against his hair.

"You're looking good, Turo," Benson said. "How do you like the new clothes?" He sat on the bunk beside the boy.

"They're okay," Turo said. "Kind of square-john, but they fit fine. Thanks, Mr. Kellogg. I didn't even think about what I was going to wear." His left hand lay palm up and re- laxed on the metal edge of the bunk. There was no tension in him that Benson could see.

"We'll get started in about an hour," Benson said. He put his briefcase down and took out his cigarettes. "I've got some instructions for you." He looked at the boy's quiet face. "Or should I start with a pep talk? Do you need one?"

Turo shook his head. He smiled thinly. "You can skip that," he said. "What do you want me to do?"

"Nothing very difficult. I just want you to know what to expect, how to handle yourself in the courtroom." He leaned back against the painted steel wall and brought up one foot, hooking his heel on the rim of the bunk.

"You'll be sitting at a table with me, to the judge's right. There'll be a deputy close by. The prosecutor's table will be on the other side, and there will probably be a table for reporters opposite the jury box. Get the picture?"

The boy nodded. He was looking down at the floor again.

"You will stand up when you're told to, which won't be often. The rest of the time you will sit at the table with me.

Don't slouch. Sit up straight and keep your chin up. Pay attention to everything. When there's a witness on the stand, look at him, but don't stare. Don't turn around or fidget. Don't frown at anyone, or smile at them. Sober, thoughtful interest is your line. The most important thing is to keep your mouth shut. I'll give you a pad and pencil so you can write me notes, but don't talk unless I tell you to. Remember there's a deputy right behind you and a flock of sharp-eared newspapermen. Got all that?"

"Yes. I don't write so good with my left hand, though."

"Okay, if you've got something to say, tap me on the arm and I'll lean over so you can whisper. Now, how are you feeling? You haven't been out of bed very long. Are you going to be able to sit in the courtroom for four or five hours at a stretch?"

"I guess so. I feel all right."

"If you get tired, or dizzy, tell me right away. We can always take a few minutes' recess. I'll arrange it with the judge. Should you have something with you, some medicine?"

"No, they didn't say anything about it."

"How do you stand with the hospital? Are you discharged?"

"Yes, they signed me out. They said somebody would be over here every morning to check up on me."

"All right. If you need anything more than that, for God's sake say so." He tossed his cigarette in the toilet bowl and leaned over to pull the lever. The boy was very still. He was too calm, Benson felt, too self-possessed in view of his situation. But as far as Benson was able to judge, it did not seem to be the excessive calm of emotional shock. The boy was holding himself very tightly. Benson got to his feet.

"That's about it, Turo. The deputy will bring you over to the courtroom in a little while. I'll be there to meet you."

The boy nodded.

Benson paused at the door. He turned back and put his hand lightly on the boy's shoulder. "Take it easy, Turo."

"Sure. I'm okay."

Benson turned away, dissatisfied and slightly confused. He

felt strangely helpless in the face of the boy's unexpected attitude. He called for the deputy and picked up his briefcase.

He walked quickly back toward the courtroom, going through the inner patio that was deserted now except for a few lackadaisical gardeners in jailhouse denims who were poking at the grass and flowerbeds. He went inside and down the corridor that was crowded with would-be spectators still barred by the closed doors. He worked his way slowly through the press of people and went into Judge Groat's chambers.

There was no one in the anteroom. The door to the judge's chambers stood open and Benson could hear voices from inside. He moved forward and tapped on the molding.

Judge Groat turned with a frown when Benson knocked.

"Well, Benson," he said sharply. "Willie found you, did he? Come in."

"I haven't seen, Willie, Judge," Benson said. "I just wanted to—— Good morning, Frank. Didn't see you there."

"Morning, Ben," Frank Sayer said heavily. He nodded from the deep chair beside the judge's desk. He leaned back and smiled at Benson—a sly, conspiratorial smile that was close to being a smirk. "I hear you had a little talk with H. L. Caine," he said softly. "He changed your mind for you, didn't he?"

Benson looked at him coldly. "Don't count on anything, Frank."

Sayer came forward in his chair. "What does that mean?"

"I wanted to see you, Benson," the judge said, overriding Frank Sayer with an unconscious and habitual arrogance. "I had to be sure that your client understands English adequately. I don't mean to have any complaints about it later. So, for the record, do you want me to appoint an interpreter?"

Benson considered it for a moment. "I don't think it's necessary, Judge. My client understands English well enough, but maybe from time to time, if it gets too thick for him, you'll allow me to take a minute to make sure he knows what is happening."

"Very well," the judge said briskly. He swung away from the mirror and took his large notebook from his desk. "Then I think we can——"

"Just a minute, please, Your Honor," Benson said. "There is another point about my client I wanted to bring up. He's just out of the hospital, you may remember. He's still a little weak and we may need an extra recess occasionally, so he can——"

"So he can work on the jury's sympathy," Frank Sayer said in a tight, nasty growl. "The hell with that."

"Do you want me to bring a doctor into the courtroom, Frank?" Benson said. "I can have one sitting beside the boy all the time. How do you think the jury will respond to that?"

"Let's have no bickering, gentlemen," Judge Groat said sharply. "I'll grant a recess whenever you ask me, Benson, but be discreet. I want no grandstanding. Anything else?"

"Exclusion of witnesses, Your Honor. I'd like you to invoke the rule."

"Frank?" the judge inquired.

Sayer shrugged. "All right with me. As long as it doesn't apply to investigators and medical witnesses."

"Which means it wouldn't apply to anyone," Benson said. "It would be best if none of the witnesses heard each other's testimony. It's in your discretion, Judge. I believe it would be helpful in this trial."

"Very well, very well," the judge said testily. "I'll invoke the rule. Make a room available for witnesses, Frank." He looked at Benson impatiently. "Anything else?"

"An item for Frank, since he's here," Benson said. "I've got a stack of subpoenas for all the prosecution witnesses." He smiled into Sayer's angry eyes. "But if Frank will assure me that he'll call them all, we could spare the sheriff some extra work."

"What are you talking about?" the judge asked.

"Frank isn't required to call a witness just because he endorsed the name on the information," Benson said. "At least one of those witnesses is out of town right now, Your Honor, sent away by the County Attorney. I want him in court. I'll subpoena if I have to."

"That's a lie," Sayer said hotly. "I didn't send anyone anywhere."

Benson spoke to Judge Groat in a level voice. "I've been away for a few days. I asked my secretary to check on all the prosecution witnesses. She discovered that Mr. Sayer's own chief investigator, Lieutenant Harry Jurgens, left town on Saturday night. His wife is not sure where he went, except that he left on official business. She doesn't know when he will be back."

"He is on official business," Sayer said angrily. "He's too damn busy to be hanging around a courtroom——" He stopped himself abruptly. He pushed up from his chair and stood close to Benson, chin out. "What could he testify to anyway?"

"Why did you put his name on the list in the first place?"

"Because he prepared a chart of the murder scene," Sayer said. "I've decided I don't need the chart, so why should I waste Jurgens' time?"

"But that's not all he can testify to, Frank," Benson said flatly, "and you know it. So do I. Jurgens made a very interesting phone call to Los Angeles and I want him to tell the jury about it. Now let's stop this horsing around. Either you get him here or I will. It doesn't matter to me how you want it handled."

"Damn it, Ben, what's got into you?"

"I just want the evidence produced in court, Frank. All the evidence."

Sayer's big mobile face flushed. He pulled in a quick, short breath and his shoulders bunched under his tight coat.

"I'll have no more of this," Judge Groat said in stern warning. "What is your answer, Frank? Will you give Benson the assurance he wants?"

"Let him do his own work," Sayer said in a thick growl. "I don't give a——"

"Very well, that's settled," the judge said. "You have your answer, Benson. Well, we aren't earning our pay in here."

He moved to the door to the courtroom and stood there stiffly, a thin and fierce symbol of authority.

"Do your fighting in court," he said with a tight, tilted smile. "Let's go, gentlemen."

THE COURTROOM was warm and stuffy after the judge's chambers. Benson followed Frank Sayer in from the rear entrance. Two assistants rose from the prosecution table to shake hands formally with Sayer. Benson went alone to his table and turned for a moment to look back at the crowded courtroom. The first rows of seats were filled with Judge Groat's half of the term's jury panel, fifty talesmen from which Arturo Campeón's jury was to be selected. The rest were spectators, representing the public—representing it rather poorly, Benson thought, unless you believed that Rincon's public was made up largely of avid-eyed, whispering women and weary old men who could find no other place to sit. The members of the petit jury were more assorted, the women younger and more alert, the men stiff and formal, somberly impressed with their responsibility. Benson nodded to them generally, turned and sat down. He put his briefcase on the bare, polished table.

Five men and one girl were seated behind the press table to his left. Two of the men rose and started toward him when he looked at them. A photographer backed away from Sayer's table, crammed a hot bulb in his pocket, twisted a new one in place and made a flashgun shot of Benson that caught him, he suspected, with his mouth open.

"What's the word, Ben?" one of the reporters asked. "Going to get him off?"

"Frank Sayer claims he'll get a verdict on the first ballot," the other said.

Benson smiled tightly. "To quote a favorite writer," he said, "Frank Sayer has crystal balls." He unstrapped his briefcase. "No comment, boys."

"Come on, Ben, give us a——"

"All rise," the bailiff shouted. He pounded his gavel vigorously, silencing the courtroom.

Benson got to his feet. The reporters hustled back to their places. There was a brief hush as Judge Groat came out of his chambers. He climbed three steps, pushed aside his high-backed chair and stood glaring out at the courtroom.

"The Superior Court for the County of Rincon is now in session," the bailiff intoned. "Honorable Bernard B. Groat presiding. Be seated."

The hissing whispers began again, as if someone had opened a steam valve. Many people cleared their throats noisily and scuffled their feet. Judge Groat waited impatiently, tapping a fingernail.

When the courtroom was quiet he lifted his head in a peremptory movement. "People against Arturo Campeón," he said.

Frank Sayer hitched himself a few inches from the seat of his chair. "Ready for the People, Your Honor."

Benson stood behind his table silently. The judge swung to look at him and Benson returned his gaze blandly.

The door to the staircase that led down to the underground detention room opened and Arturo Campeón was ushered into the courtroom. He walked in short, brisk strides. His left arm was gripped tightly by the starched deputy. The deputy came a few steps with him, let go and nudged the boy toward Benson's table. He went to his place near the railing.

Benson kicked back the center chair at his table and motioned for the boy to stand there. "Get your chin up," he said softly. Together they faced the bench. "Ready for the defense, Your Honor."

"Very well. Mr. Clerk," the judge said. He leaned back in his chair and opened the cover of his notebook.

The clerk bustled forward importantly, dug both hands deep into a flat open tub and tossed its contents lightly like a salad. He made a little flourish when he drew out a card at random. "John Eben Heller," he called. He tore the juror's card into three strips along the perforations. When the juror came through the gate, the clerk directed him to the first seat in the jury box.

The clerk handed a strip of card to Frank Sayer and brought another to Benson. He kept the third for his records and went back to his tub, scrabbling in it again and picking out a second card.

Benson checked each name against the list Mary had compiled for him. His information was scanty and gave little indication of a juror's quality, but at least Benson did not have to proceed blindly. He had some notion of each talesman's standing in the community, his occupation, voting record and financial position. Mr. John Eben Heller was fifty-three, worked as a cable splicer for the telephone company, voted Republican when he voted, which was not often, and had once had some trouble meeting his bills but was all squared away now. He was thick-bodied, slope-shouldered and looked a little unsure of himself. Take him or not? Benson wondered.

It was a question he would have to ask himself about each juror unless he was willing to accept the first twelve fished out of the tub.

Benson checked his file for each juror's name as it was called by the clerk. Each of the twelve card strips along the edge of his table had his notations scribbled on them for quick reference.

Five men and one woman sat in the front row of the box, six men behind them. Benson knew nothing about any of them that required a challenge. The last juror in the front row, Mr. James MacGruder, was a darkly scowling man who stared at Turo with a certain baleful intensity that made Benson uneasy. The others sat in stiff dignity and displayed no apparent animus.

When the box was filled, Judge Groat had the prospective jury sworn and then lectured them sternly and at length before putting the questions required by statute. None of the jurors asked to be excused on the basis of citizenship, illiteracy, deafness, religious scruples, ill health, criminal background or the urgent press of public duty. None admitted to any personal knowledge of, interest in or bias toward anyone involved in the trial. All professed to have no opinion as to the guilt or innocence of the accused Arturo Campeón.

While the judge was examining the jury, meticulously droning through the mandatory questions, Benson sat back, turned in his chair so he could inspect the double row in the box. In a few minutes he would have to decide whether to accept or reject these jurors. He had a searching list of questions which he planned to put to each of them, questions that went into religious and racial attitudes which might be a factor in the trial, questions that tested a juror's understanding of sexual aberration and were designed to elicit useful responses, particularly if a juror had any latent prejudice.

But surveying the faces in the jury box, Benson felt a sudden uncertainty, as if something were warning him that he might be close to making a mistake.

What, after all, did he require from this jury? He needed twelve moderately intelligent, fair-minded people who were capable of seeing Arturo Campeón as a young man in serious difficulty and not as a monster. He needed a jury that would not be overly responsive to Frank Sayer because of his eloquence or official position. He needed twelve people who could be moved to understand Arturo Campeón's motives and the actions that had stemmed from them.

Didn't he have that already? Four of the men who sat in the box were strongly marked with the muscles and calluses of physical labor in their youth, and it was reasonable to expect that they would be especially sensitive to the frenzy of revulsion that had led Turo to kill Roderick Duquesne. The solitary woman, Mrs. Anne-Marie Jordan, was an ex-stenographer, now a housewife and the mother of two girls. She would probably respond with a certain sense of horror when she heard of Duquesne's record.

The other prospective jurors were the sober business and professional people found on most panels, the blue-ribbon conservatives favored by every prosecutor. Seven out of twelve was probably the best proportion Benson could hope for. As juries went, he felt, this was not a bad one right now. He would greatly have preferred one or two Mexican-Americans among the twelve. There were three included in the fifty-man panel and Benson had twenty peremptory challenges he could exercise. The chances were fair that he could get one of the Mexican-Americans if he was willing to work for it. Against the possibility was the fact that every jury is always subtly flattered to be accepted without niggling questions. It would be a dangerous gamble, but mightn't it be worth taking if he——

"Very well, gentlemen," the judge said finally. "Examine for cause, if you please. You first, Mr. Sayer."

Frank Sayer was deep in a whispered huddle with his two aides, turning sheets in a fat folder. He had to be called again.

"The People have no questions for cause, Your Honor," he said with a flashing smile for the jury.

"Your turn, Mr. Kellogg."

Benson rose slowly. He came around the end of his table and walked toward the box. He stopped a few feet away where all the jurors could see him easily, and turned to the bench.

"Your Honor, I have one question to put to the jury. With the court's permission, I will ask it generally, of all jurors at the same time."

Judge Groat nodded.

Benson turned. He put his hands behind his back. "I am satisfied that all of you are prepared to serve well and honestly as jurors," he said. "But there is an element of the case you will hear that may present a problem for some of you. The defendant, Arturo Campeón, is a Mexican citizen. If any member of this jury feels he cannot, because of his personal feelings, render a fair verdict, I will excuse him. Just raise your hand, please, if the defendant's national origin prejudices his position in your eyes."

Frank Sayer growled softly from his table, muttering something that Benson could not hear, and laughing quietly with his assistants. Benson did not move. His eyes slowly traced along the row of jurors' faces, all of them attentive and alert. None raised his hand.

Benson smiled. He went down the length of the jury box, his hand sliding lightly along the wide mahogany railing. When he had reached the end, he turned.

If he did not intend to challenge either for cause or

peremptorily, he might as well make a gesture to indicate his complete confidence in the jury.

"The defense, Your Honor, is satisfied with this excellent jury. We will have no challenges."

Frank Sayer's chair scraped back. He rose quickly, red-faced. "Your Honor," he began in a loud, outraged voice.

"Never mind, Mr. Sayer," the judge said sharply. "The question was not put to you, Mr. Kellogg. You will be good enough to wait until the court inquires, if you please."

The heads of the jurors swung to look curiously at Benson. He bowed gravely. "My apologies, Your Honor. I merely wanted to express my sincere approval, but I will wait my proper turn." He went toward his table, hearing faint whispers from the spectators. The judge tapped his gavel as Benson passed behind Frank Sayer.

"Big grandstand play," the County Attorney muttered under his breath. "What do you think it'll get you?"

"A jury, Frank."

"If you have anything to say, Mr. Kellogg," the judge said with a subdued anger, "you will address the court properly."

"I'm sorry, Your Honor," Benson said. "I was answering a question for the County Attorney."

"Now, Your Honor," Sayer said belligerently. "We've had enough of this. I wish to protest the——"

"Not now, Mr. Sayer," the judge said. "Let's not start protesting this early in the game. I see that it is approaching twelve o'clock and I think we will take our noon recess. I shall expect to see both of you gentlemen return this afternoon in a better humor and a more courteous frame of mind." He turned his head slowly from Sayer to Benson. "I insist upon it," he said acidly. "Mr. Clerk."

"Hear ye, hear ye," the clerk called, "this honorable court stands in recess until one fifteen P.M."

WHEN BENSON came in his office door, Mary was just hanging up her phone. She snatched it up again swiftly.

"Here is Mr. Kellogg now," she said anxiously. "Oh dear." She looked at Benson with stricken eyes.

"Who was it?" Benson went by to his desk. He sat heavily and leaned forward to lift a napkin from a serving tray in the middle of his blotter. Two enormous sandwiches and a bottle of Mexican beer in a bowl of ice. He looked at them without interest.

"He wouldn't say. He had a kind of Mexicany voice. He said he had some information for you about the trial."

"He'll call again. They always do. I don't care about him, Mary. But if you get a call from someone named Harald Elsinore, I want you to find out where he is and let me know right away. He should have called before now."

"But what about this——"

"You don't win cases because of anonymous informants, Mary," Benson said tiredly.

"You win with cornball tricks, don't you, Counselor?" a bright, mocking voice said from the doorway. Burr Kellogg came sauntering in and dragged a chair up to Benson's desk. He inspected Benson's tray, picked up half a sandwich and sat back, swinging his big cordovan moccasins up on a corner of the desk.

"You'd better get a couple more of these, Mary," he said cheerfully. "Brother Benson has a guest for lunch."

He bit off a large semicircle, chewed quickly and swallowed. He looked at Benson with a wide smile that slowly grew into a looping grin. He put his head back and laughed with a whole-hearted infectious bellow that made Benson smile in response.

"What in hell is so funny?"

"You, Counselor. I almost popped a gusset when you pulled that corny stunt. That's what old Clarence Darrow used to do when he had a tough case. He'd take the first twelve men on the panel and when he accepted them, you'd swear he was decorating them for valor above and beyond. Of course, you didn't do so good with the speech, but then you didn't have much time. Frank recovered pretty fast."

"You were there?"

"For a while. I stopped to have a word with Frank on the way over here. God, he's hacked. You know, in all the years he's been prosecuting, nobody ever pulled that on him. It's such a musty old dodge that it's actually new. Congratulations, Counselor. You're a grand, dirty fighter."

"Go to hell," Benson said amiably. "I'm glad to hear Frank was upset."

"Upset?" Burr laughed. "The poor guy wants to knock three people off that jury. But you've fixed his wagon. He'll look like a jerk if he tries too hard now." Burr took another big bite and spoke with a full mouth. "You might say he was upset. If you like understatement."

Benson picked up the bottle of beer, flipped the cap, and pulled half of it down in one swig. He held the bottle out to Burr. "What are you doing in town?" he asked.

Burr made a casual grimace. "Just visiting. Curious about the trial. You know."

"Knock it off, Burr. There's a caucus in El Monte you wouldn't miss unless you had to. What's up?"

They stared at each other for a long moment. Then Burr turned his head toward Mary, who was still at her desk, not watching them but well within audible range.

"Would you see if you could get a couple more sandwiches, Mary?" Benson asked.

"Of course. Right away, Mr. Kellogg."

Burr leaned back and pushed the door shut behind her. He grinned at Benson. "You're right," he said easily. "Something is in the wind."

"Something political?"

"Don't say it like that, Ben. Politics isn't a dirty word. But yes, it is political, in a way. I don't have to go through it all again, do I?"

Benson's expression changed slightly. He started to say something, then stopped. He lit a cigarette, put it down and picked up a sandwich. "What are you talking about, Burr?" He bit into the sandwich.

"The same subject. H. L. Caine and the political future of our young and handsome hero, Burr Kellogg."

Benson swallowed quickly. "I thought I took him off your back. I told him——"

"I heard about it." Burr shrugged, unimpressed. "Caine wasn't convinced, I gather. Maybe you forgot to genuflect when you left the presence."

Benson stared at him, waiting.

"He wants insurance, I'm told," Burr added casually. "He's got a big deal cooking, maybe you know."

Benson shook his head.

"Yeah. King Caine has a large-type merger in the works. Most of the mineral rights in Venezuela or some place like that. He's putting together a new corporation that smells to me like an illegal cartel. Of course nobody has yet bothered to ask me what I think. Anyway, Caine is set to be kingpin, provided nothing upsets the program."

"And what is he afraid of?" Benson asked quietly.

"Hell, Ben, you know how these Latin Americans are about queers. If they knew about Caine's son, they'd start thinking things about the old man. They'd laugh him out of the country. Or smother him with pity. Either way, they'd stop taking him seriously. Caine doesn't like the prospect."

"Too bad," Benson said soberly. "What does he want?"

Burr put his feet down and sat forward. "How would you like me as associate counsel?" he asked abruptly.

"Is that the deal?"

Burr shrugged. "It's not a deal, Ben," he said patiently. "Nothing as dramatic as that. You make it sound like I'm poisoning the waterhole. We're just trying to keep Caine happy."

"I suppose you've already asked Judge Groat?"

"It's okay with him. And Frank is agreeable. What do you say, Ben?"

Benson put down the unfinished portion of his sandwich.

He scrubbed out his smoldering cigarette. "Will you answer a question first, Burr?" His voice was thin and tight but he was able to keep it level.

"Sure. What do you want to know?"

"If I took you on as associate counsel, I would still be running the show. What makes Caine so sure you could keep me from using his son's real name, if I decided to?"

"Hell, Ben, this is just a———"

Benson looked away. "I'm getting annoyed with your friend Caine, Burr. I told him to keep away from me. I'm beginning to wonder if it wouldn't be a good idea to tell the newspapers about Duquesne's father and get it out of the way once and for all."

Burr snorted. "They know all about it," he said casually. "Newspapers don't print stories like that about people like Caine. Of course, it would be different if you were to make it a matter of public record."

Benson nodded. "So all he needs to take care of is the trial record. And that's where you come in, is it? But even so, Caine wouldn't feel secure unless I was replaced as the boy's attorney. With me off the case entirely, he'd be okay."

Benson was speaking in a quiet, reflective tone. He turned back to look directly at his brother. "If I couldn't attend court, you would take over. We wouldn't have to get a continuance or a new trial if you were already on hand as associate counsel. Suppose I did accept you, Burr. What would be the next step? How did you plan on getting rid of me? Is Caine going to send someone to shoot me, or would he be satisfied with a broken leg?"

Burr shook his head slowly. He studied Benson with an incredulous half-frown. "You serious, Ben?"

"Does anything else make sense?" Benson demanded. "I won't drop the case as long as I'm physically capable of handling it. You know that. So does Caine."

"You ought to stop watching all those television shows," Burr said easily. "First thing you know you'll be———"

Benson slammed his hand down on the desk. "You damn

fool!" he said angrily. "You can't see it even now. You've hung a set of blinders on yourself. Are you really that hungry for a political job? Those bastards are using you to chop my neck. For Christ's sake, grow up, Burr!"

"Knock it off," Burr said roughly. "This is the big league, boy. You can't run things to suit yourself. Too many other people have a stake in this trial. You have to make some adjustments. Nobody's out to job your client, Ben, but you've got to give a little. Now let's get organized. We've got a lot of work ahead of us. Where do you want me to start?"

Benson sat back stiffly. He locked his hands together under the desk and squeezed hard, not speaking until he was completely in command of himself. "I can't figure out what it is you want, Burr," he said quietly. "I don't think you know, yourself. You say I'm being dramatic because you won't face the truth. You want to know what you should do first? I'll tell you. Go back to Nate Barstow and tell him exactly what I said. And while you're at it, tell him to get word to H. L. Caine for me. A clear warning, Burr, and my last. If I get one more message from Caine or any of his prat boys, I'm going to subpoena Caine and force him to identify his son in open court. Now go away, Burr. Report back to your boss. I don't want to look at you any more."

Burr came slowly to his feet. "That's a hell of a way to talk to me, Ben. You're going at this all wrong. I'll do what you want. I'll talk to Barstow and tell him what you said. But you're making trouble for yourself. I don't know if I'll be able to——"

"Go away, Burr," Benson said heavily. "Just please go away."

He saw Burr's big knotted hands draw back from the desk. Burr stood there silently for a moment, shifting indecisively. Then he turned on his heel. He opened the door and stopped. Benson did not look up. Burr went out and closed the door behind him, very slowly.

Benson sat unmoving, staring at his littered desk.

THE CLERK of the court had still not been able to find the right adjustment for one of the window shades, and when Benson rose with his client as Judge Groat entered, a thin, blinding band of sunlight danced off the top of the reporter's desk. Benson squinted and turned his head, waiting until the judge told the court to be seated. He felt dull and tired, almost listless, and the strongly directed light made it hard for him to concentrate.

"Mr. Clerk," the judge said testily, "please see what you can do about that blind. Now then, gentlemen, at the recess we had reached the point of peremptory challenges. We will go on from there, if you are ready? Mr. Sayer, will you challenge for the People?"

Frank Sayer came to his feet. "The People," he said reluctantly, "will excuse James J. MacGruder."

So the darkly scowling juror had disturbed Frank too, Benson thought. The chances were that Frank's decision was based on more important grounds than MacGruder's physical appearance. Frank had a file four inches thick and he knew everything worth knowing about every one of the fifty prospective jurors. Possession of that information was one of the powerful advantages that the current juridical process gave to the prosecution. Only an extremely wealthy defendant could compete.

The clerk sifted through his tub of cards again and fished out one. He called, "Harris A. Harris." He ripped the card into thirds as if he hated each piece.

Harris A. Harris was not a name Benson had to check. He had seen the name almost every day in large red letters on billboards and the muddy sides of trucks. Harris was a nurseryman and landscape architect and there were few areas of Rincon that had not been prodded by his green thumb. He was fifty-eight, Benson's records said, widowed, an aggressive Republican. His credit rating was excellent. Benson sat back as Judge Groat droned once more through the required pre-liminaries.

Frank Sayer beamed approvingly at the plum he had drawn from the clerk's grab bag. He cocked an eyebrow at Benson before he sat down. He snapped up one of the card strips and tossed it to an aide who riffled the file to find the right page. Together they studied the information, nodding wisely to each other.

"Examine for cause," Judge Groat said when he was finished with his warning interrogation. "Mr. Sayer?"

"No questions, Your Honor."

"Mr. Kellogg?"

"No questions, Your Honor."

"To peremptories, then," the judge said. "Mr. Sayer?"

Frank Sayer hesitated. He bent to scan the open page of his notepad. He rose very slowly and surveyed the jury with a confident smile.

"The People are well satisfied with this fine jury, Your Honor," he said.

"Mr. Kellogg?"

Benson came to his feet, deliberately slow. "The defense will excuse Harris A. Harris," he said.

Frank Sayer surged from his chair. "Your Honor," he shouted in a choked voice, "this is an outrage to the dignity of this court! I will not allow——"

The judge's gavel cut him off in midsentence. "This court is equipped, trained and able to manage its own affairs, Mr. Sayer," he said sharply. His thin, wattled face swung toward Benson. "Mr. Sayer feels you have changed your mind, Mr. Kellogg. Is that true? Do you wish to exercise your right to peremptory challenges?"

"Your Honor, I must protest any attempt to——"

"If you please, Mr. Sayer," the judge snapped. "The right of peremptory challenge cannot be denied to the defense counsel, although I must admit a more orderly procedure might have been followed."

"I apologize to the court," Benson said. He came around

the front of his table. "The County Attorney, however, is wrong in thinking that I have changed my mind. The court will recall that I was completely satisfied with the jury before the County Attorney challenged one of its members. It was he, Your Honor, who changed the situation, not I."

"I am aware of what has happened, Mr. Kellogg. I need no lectures from either side. You will step down, Mr. Harris. The clerk will select another name from the panel."

Judge Groat eased back in his chair. He eyed Benson narrowly from the shadow of his heavy brows. He was not frowning, but there was a speculative wrinkle across his forehead. He picked up the sheet that listed the statutory questions and prepared himself to examine still another replacement.

This time the clerk struck oil on Benson's claim. The talesman who came forward was Anthony John Ramirez, thirty-seven, a wholesale dealer in fruits and vegetables. His voting registration had lapsed, but four years ago he had been an undecided Democrat. His credit was shaky. He kept his eyes fixed somberly, unwaveringly, on Arturo Campeón as he responded to the judge's questions.

Ramirez would be the test, Benson realized. If Frank Sayer meant to keep his word, he would let the man stay. Benson did not expect it. He watched Frank bend for a whispered huddle with his two assistants.

Both prosecution and defense passed when asked to question for cause. Frank Sayer excused Mr. Ramirez on peremptory. No one was surprised, not even Mr. Ramirez.

That left two more Mexican-Americans on the panel of thirty-six that were still available. Benson still had nineteen challenges; Frank Sayer ten. On paper, the odds favored Benson, but it was now obvious that Sayer would save his challenges to use against the jurors Benson wanted.

"Mitchell J. Masterton," the clerk announced. He handed Benson the strip of torn card.

Mitchell Masterton was forty-six, an associate professor at Rincon State, a straight-ticket, never-fail Democrat. His credit was fair, within severe limits.

He looked good to Frank Sayer, and obviously he would make a fine, intelligent juror. Should he take him or try once more for a Mexican-American who might understand Arturo Campeón without explanation?

"The defense is satisfied with this jury, Your Honor," Benson said after a long hesitation.

Frank Sayer smiled with patronizing amusement. "I am pleased to join the defense attorney, for once," he said. "The People are also thoroughly satisfied."

"Swear the jury, Mr. Clerk," the judge said. He drew his notebook closer and opened its cover.

There was a rustling stir of preparation in the space below the bench. The court reporter snapped on his bull's-eye lamp and twiddled its beam onto his stenotype machine. He put an extra supply of paper in a box close at hand. The clerk intoned the solemn, ritual phrases with a firm, clear emphasis. ". . . well and truly try, and true deliverance make . . ." The jurors murmured their responses.

Benson sat back beside the boy, smiled at him, pleased to see him straight-backed and alert.

"Is it a good jury, Mr. Kellogg?"

"It'll do, Turo. No bastards on it, at any rate." As far as I can tell, he amended silently.

Frank Sayer turned with large, slow movements through the stapled pages of the statement he had prepared for his opening address. He had been over it a dozen times and by now most of its phrases came off his tongue with the ease of long practice. He changed a word with a scrawl of his pencil.

"Are you ready, Mr. Sayer?" the judge asked.

"Certainly, Your Honor." Frank Sayer put his statement down on the corner of his table where he could refer to it easily. He stood soberly facing the jury.

He was drawing out the suspense just a bit too much, Benson judged, but Frank was always inclined to be dramatic, he knew from transcripts of previous trials. Frank was too wise a bird, however, to expose his case by a lengthy preliminary statement. He put his intention to the jury in bald man-to-man terms. The People intended to show that Arturo Campeón had "brutally slain" a man named Roderick Duquesne in the course of a felonious attempt at robbery. It was a clear example of the statutory definition of first-degree murder. The defendant was young in years but old in crime. The prosecution, he said, would prove that Arturo Campeón had committed murder, as the People charged.

It was a brief, concisely worded statement of intent. Cleverly, Frank had made no reference to the death penalty in his opening. Sayer was going to demand capital punishment; that was obvious. But he did not direct the jury's attention to that fact. He wanted them first to concentrate on the evidence and not feel compelled to weigh it constantly, in bits and pieces, against the electric chair, for there was always a chance that a jury might, halfway through the trial, decide that the offense charged did not warrant the death penalty. Then they would stop listening to any evidence. But if Sayer could offer his evidence as a unit, in a calm atmosphere, he could afterward restate his position in higher, more emotional terms in his final summation. If he managed it adroitly, he could then ask for a first-degree conviction, and if his case had been well organized, he could expect that the jury would be in a receptive frame of mind.

When Sayer bowed and moved away, none of the jurors showed any response that Benson could notice. They had all turned toward Turo when Sayer first mentioned him, but only briefly, as if to make sure he was the one the prosecutor was talking about. They seemed a little surprised that he had finished so quickly. Their heads swung in unison toward the bench.

"Mr. Kellogg?"

Benson gave himself a moment to think before answering. He had intended to reserve his opening statement until after Frank Sayer had presented his case against the defendant. That was the routine of good procedure, for the jury was sure to forget what he said by the time he was able to put his own case. But now, thinking of Sayer's opening, he was not sure he had made the right decision.

Probably one day would be more than sufficient to offer the two or three witnesses that would constitute the case for the defense, which meant that both his opening and summation statements would come so close together that one would negate the other.

But most of all he was concerned about the effect Sayer had created in the collective mind of the jury. He had——

"Mr. Kellogg," the judge said impatiently, "do you wish to reserve your opening statement?"

Benson came to his feet. "No, Your Honor," he said quietly. "I think it might be best to have a word with the jury before we begin."

He moved across the wide bare space below the bench and stood with one hand on the railing of the witness stand. "Mrs. Jordan and gentlemen," he began, "the prosecutor in this trial, Mr. Sayer, has told you that he will prove the death of Roderick Duquesne was murder committed by the defendant, Arturo Campeón. Mr. Sayer said he will prove it. I say to you that he will not prove it. Roderick Duquesne did not die by murder.

"Mr. Sayer told you that Duquesne's death followed as a result of felonious assault by the defendant. There was indeed a felonious assault in this dark exercise, gentlemen of the jury, but it was not instigated by the defendant.

"We will learn, in the course of this trial, exactly what happened on Lookout Point in the early hours of April fourteenth. And we will learn why it happened. When all the evidence is before you, I am thoroughly convinced that you will discharge the defendant and allow him to continue his interrupted journey to his home.

"We are to try a difficult, complex case. It will be a trial for the defendant and for you, individually and as a jury, for you can never allow yourselves to forget that what you are deciding here is whether Arturo Campeón is to live or die. He is accused of first-degree murder, and if he is convicted, then he must die. The law of this state requires that punishment. Mr.

Sayer did not mention that when he addressed you. He would like to have you think that we are debating an impersonal and purely legal question and that after we have voted on it, we can go home and forget about it."

Benson looked gravely at each juror in turn, walking slowly down the length of the jury box.

"It will not be like that," he said soberly. "We are not watching television drama today. It is a young man's life you have in your hands. He is not an actor who can be brought to life again when the curtain goes down. If you determine that he should die, then he dies. And he stays dead. And none of you will go home and forget about it. You will live with it, for all of your lives."

He turned toward Turo, standing so that the jury saw him only in profile with the lines of troubled concern cut deeply in his lean, tired face.

"Arturo Campeón did not murder Roderick Duquesne. We will learn how Duquesne came to meet his death. The prosecution is about to present its case to you. I ask that you examine every statement, every piece of evidence, with a clear, questioning mind. You have sworn to do that. I ask nothing more."

Benson went back to his table, self-consciously aware of the stillness of the courtroom.

The judge tapped the metal end of his pencil against the base of his reading lamp. "Mr. Sayer, are you prepared with your first witness?"

"Yes, Your Honor, but it will take just a few minutes for him to get to the courtroom. I have sent for him. I thought, in view of the fact that——"

"Yes, yes," Judge Groat said impatiently. "I agree. We have gone forward fairly briskly this afternoon. Let's take fifteen minutes. Have your witness here when we return, Mr. Sayer."

The judge lifted a finger for his clerk. He got up, collected the skirts of his robe and went nimbly down the low steps to the door of his chambers.

TURO looked pale and tight around the mouth, Benson noted. "How are you making out?" he asked.

"Okay," the boy muttered. "It sure goes slow." He leaned toward Benson and whispered, "Uh, Mr. Kellogg, any chance I could—uh, go to the can?"

"Of course," Benson said quickly. "Good God, Turo, I told you to let me know if you wanted to take a break. There's no need to suffer. It's bad enough without that."

"You can say that again." The boy got up when Benson did.

All the reporters lunged from their table in a body, forming a clamoring ring around Turo and Benson, blocking away the deputy assigned to guard the defendant. Benson raised his voice to carry over their shouted questions. "It's no good asking him anything," he said bluntly. "I've told him not to talk. And you'll get no comment from me until the trial is over. Now, clear a lane for us, please. Deputy, can you——"

Roughly the guard shouldered a way between two reporters. He posted himself solidly in the doorway, excluding the newspapermen, as Benson took the boy's arm and went down the narrow iron staircase to the detention area below. He led Turo across the dark, low-ceilinged jail passage to a small conference room that would be reserved for them as long as the trial lasted. The deputy took up his station outside the glass door where he could watch, but not hear, what went on inside.

There was an open cubicle with a wash basin and a toilet bowl in the far corner beyond the scarred table and chairs that took up much of the space.

"Not very private," Benson said, "but I guess it's better than nothing. How about a Coke, Turo? The sheriff has a machine in the hall."

"Sure, that would be great."

Benson went to the door, rattling out change and giving

the deputy enough coins for three bottles. He stood in the open doorway, his back to the boy, while the deputy operated the machine. Benson brought two bottles back with him, gave one to the boy and emptied the other in two long thirsty gulps.

"Sit down, Turo," he said. He swallowed hard against the surge of compressed air in his throat. "Relax when you get a chance."

The boy sat carefully in the chair. He rested his thick cast on the arm to take the strain from the sling around his neck. He tasted the Coke and put the bottle down on the table. "You made a good speech, Mr. Kellogg," he said politely.

Benson stared at him. He sounded as if somebody had asked his opinion on an actor's performance, and he was trying to say something pleasant without committing himself. It was a strange reaction to sense in a defendant in a murder trial. Benson thought of questioning him about it, and then thought again. Hysterical, overwrought defendants were the rule, almost the invariable rule, he reminded himself. If you've got a calm and controlled one this time, for Christ's sake make the most of it and don't go sticking pins in him. After all, he can't do anything useful until the time comes for him to take the witness stand.

"Thanks," he said dryly. "Speeches don't mean much at this stage of the game. I just had to make sure the jury understood this was a murder trial and not an Elks convention."

"I guess that D.A. is pretty tricky, huh? I was trying to figure out what he was up to."

"He's out to convict you." Benson lit a cigarette. He looked up to see Turo studying him. He tapped his fist on the boy's knee. "Just stay loose in there, Turo. It's early innings yet. The prosecution gets to bat first, so it's going to be rough for a while. But we'll get our turn."

"How long is it going to take? Any idea, Mr. Kellogg?"

Benson shrugged. I really don't care for the boy's reaction, he told himself. You'd think he was trying to calm my nerves by asking me polite questions about my work.

"It's going to be a long time," he said brusquely. "It's going to go on and on until you'll feel like banging your head against the wall. Some people in your position do just that. It doesn't help but they do it anyway."

The boy's quick scowl was the old dark flare that Benson remembered. His eyes narrowed with the beginning of anger and there was nothing polite or hesitant about his voice. "I just wanted to know what's going on," he said tightly. "Don't worry about me. I'm not going to bang my head against any wall."

"The fact is, I haven't time to worry about you, boy," Benson said more easily. "That's your job. Here's the picture. We've got a jury and both sides have made their opening statements. Now it's up to the prosecution to make its case. They will put on a series of witnesses, and after Frank Sayer is finished with each one, I'll be allowed to cross-examine. Then when he's gone through his list of witnesses, I'll put on mine, and he will cross-examine them in turn. After that, I make a closing statement to the jury, Frank Sayer makes his, and the judge makes his. Everybody gets into the act. Then the jury goes out to its conference room and makes up its mind and comes back and tells us the verdict. That's how it goes. Anywhere from three days to a week. My guess is three or four days."

Turo nodded. "Yeah, I had an idea that was about it. Like in the movies."

"It's an old ritual, Turo. It doesn't change. Now let's get back upstairs, if you're feeling okay."

"Sure." The boy gulped his Coke and let Benson take the empty bottle.

"Wait here just a minute," Benson said. He went out to the hall and pushed the door shut behind him. He slid the empty bottles into the wall rack beside the Coke machine and turned to the watchful deputy. "What's your name?"

"John Monahan, Mr. Kellogg."

"Are you going to be on this detail all through the trial?"

"I reckon so. The sheriff said——"

"Fine." Benson took out his wallet. "I'd like you to do something for me, John. Get a few sandwiches and some candy bars each day and put them in the room here. Get some for yourself too. Oh yes, and ask the sheriff to send over a cot, will you? My client hasn't been out of the hospital very long. He needs to lie down once in a while."

"I don't know about the cot, Mr. Kellogg. I can handle the rest easy enough."

Benson gave him a ten-dollar bill. "Ask the sheriff, John. If he says no, tell me. I'd rather he did it as a matter of courtesy. If he won't, I'll get Judge Groat to issue an order."

"The sheriff won't like——"

Monahan broke off when a blue light flickered overhead. "Judge is coming back," he said.

Benson pulled the door open. "Let's go, Turo."

THE COURTROOM was quiet, drowsy with heat, when they came back. The patterns of shadow thrown by the slatted blinds were climbing diagonally up the wall behind the bench. Judge Groat leaned forward and cleared his throat. He glanced pointedly at Frank Sayer. The clerk got up languidly from his chair and picked up a thick, leather-bound Bible. He waited in front of the witness stand, facing the jury and staring moodily down at the floor between his shoes.

A stocky hard-bellied man in a light blue sports coat came around the end of the prosecutor's table and moved toward the clerk.

"Proceed, Mr. Sayer," the judge said.

"Yes, Your Honor. The People call, as their first witness, Deputy Sheriff Alvin Aldridge."

While the deputy was being sworn, Frank Sayer got up. He buttoned his tight-fitting coat, pulled it down smoothly and stroked his hand back over his thick pale hair. He had a small file card palmed in his left hand.

The deputy sat down comfortably in the elevated chair, crossing his knees and locking his fingers together. He was sedately confident, obviously accustomed to appearing in court.

In a brisk, businesslike manner, Sayer took him through the formal preliminaries. Alvin Aldridge was a veteran deputy of twenty-two years' service, a resident of Rincon County, and was principally assigned to investigation.

"Tell the court, please," Frank Sayer said, "where you were at three P.M. on Sunday, April fourteenth?"

"At the parking space called Lookout Point on Cobre Peak, six miles north of the city limits on Route 47."

"Why were you there?"

"I went to check a report that two boys had found a dead body on the rocks below the parking space."

Aldridge's face was expressionless. A dead body was all in the day's work for him. His deep, level voice did not emphasize the phrase.

Frank Sayer asked, "Did you find a body on Lookout Point?"

"Yes, sir."

"Were you the officer responsible for recovering the body?"

"I was, sir."

"Tell the court what happened."

Deputy Aldridge did not make his part sound particularly impressive, though any juror who had seen the rough and broken slope below Lookout Point could understand that for Aldridge to lower his bulky weight on a mountaineer's line was more of a hazard than should be required by routine duties. He had gone down alone, satisfied himself that the man was dead, tied another line under the dead man's arms and assisted in lifting him up to the paved area where the medical examiner was waiting.

"Did you find any identification on the body?"

"Yes, sir. There was a wallet with a driver's license and stuff like that."

"Were you in charge of the investigation made to determine the identity of the deceased?"

Frank Sayer stepped back and half turned as he put the question, not quite looking at Benson but obviously stiffening himself for an expected objection. This was the time, if Benson meant to challenge.

"Yes, sir," the deputy said evenly.

"Who was he? What was his name?"

Benson said nothing. He could see Frank Sayer's rigid shoulders relax gradually. The prosecutor turned back squarely to his witness.

"Roderick Duquesne, of Los Angeles."

"You traced his identity through the driver's license, among other things?"

"Yes, sir."

"Did the name Roderick Duquesne appear in a previous record of the Rincon County Sheriff's department?"

"Yes, sir. That was the name on the owner's registration certificate of a wrecked car we towed in Saturday night. Sunday morning, I mean. It was about four thirty in the morning."

"Who was driving the car when——"

"Objection," Benson said quietly. "This witness cannot offer the best evidence."

"Sustained," the judge said.

"That's all, Deputy. Thank you. Your witness, Mr. Kellogg." Sayer shrugged lightly at the jury as he went toward his seat.

"I won't keep you long, Deputy," Benson said. He came slowly toward the stand.

"You found something else in Roderick Duquesne's wallet, didn't you? Money, for example?"

"Yes, sir."

"Quite a lot of money, wasn't it? Several hundred dollars in cash?"

"That's right."

"And some five thousand dollars in traveler's checks?"

"Yes, sir."

"Deceased was also wearing or carrying an unusual amount of expensive gold jewelry, was he not? A cigarette case, a watch, a belt buckle, a ring, and so on?"

"Yes, sir."

"If I were to tell you that the total value of the jewelry Duquesne had on him was at least two thousand dollars, would you be inclined to dispute that estimate?"

"Well," Aldridge pursed his mouth. "It was valuable stuff, all right. I wouldn't argue if someone said it was worth what you said, but I don't actually know."

"Very well. So we have a total in cash, negotiable paper and jewelry of about seventy-five hundred dollars. And all this was still in deceased's possession when you found him. Is that right?"

"That's right, sir."

Benson made a note on the small pad he carried in his hand, breaking his examination for a moment to let the jury register the information.

"Now, Deputy," he went on. "To get back to your original testimony. What kind of a day was it Sunday afternoon?"

"Now, Your Honor," Frank Sayer said, rising. "How can a question like that be material to this trial?"

"Mr. Kellogg?"

"I can explain, Your Honor," Benson said. "However, the testimony will speak for itself, if I am allowed to continue."

"You are sure it is pertinent?"

"Absolutely, Your Honor."

"Proceed then, Mr. Kellogg. We will hold your objection in abeyance, Mr. Sayer, and give Mr. Kellogg a chance to make his point."

"It was a fine day," Aldridge said, holding his face soberly straight with a certain effort. "Clear sky. Awful hot for so early in the year."

"Visibility was very good, was it?"

"Yes, sir."

"Were you the only man who actually went down to the rocks where the body was found?"

"Yes, sir."

"Did your photographer make pictures of the body where it lay before you had it removed?"

"Yes, sir. He used a telescopic lens."

"Very well. Now, Deputy, when you were inspecting the body, did you notice what the ground around it looked like?"

Aldridge frowned. He leaned forward a little. "I don't believe I——"

"Let's approach it from another angle, Deputy. Earlier you testified that the body was found on a rock. There is also a certain amount of earth along that slope, caught in pockets of the rock, isn't there?"

"Yes, sir. A little bit."

"Enough earth so that there are some patches of grass and a few windflowers?"

"Yes, sir. And some shrubs."

"And the tracks of birds where they have been scratching at the ground. Did you notice any bird's nests?"

"I didn't happen to notice," Aldridge said patiently. "I was sort of busy."

"But you do remember seeing bird tracks?"

"Some. Yes, sir."

"Buzzard tracks, Deputy?"

"I object, Your Honor," Frank Sayer broke in. "How can this witness be expected to testify on that?"

"Why not?" Benson asked. "I can identify buzzard tracks. How do you know Deputy Aldridge can't?"

"I can't," the deputy said.

Judge Groat snorted. "You have your answer, Mr. Kellogg. Your objection is overruled, Mr. Sayer. Proceed, please."

"No more questions, Your Honor," Benson said. He eyed Sayer carefully as he went back. One of the prosecutor's aides was riffling a folder of photographs and whispering out of the corner of his mouth. Frank knew exactly what those last few questions implied and the expression on his face said he didn't like it at all.

"Dr. James Norwood," Sayer told the clerk, who repeated the name in a ringing voice.

Dr. Norwood was the county medical examiner, a pathologist at Rincon County Hospital and chairman of the local chapter of the A.M.A. When the doctor had been sworn, Benson offered to stipulate his qualifications as a medical expert and Sayer accepted with a show of gratitude. The doctor's testimony was brief. He had examined the body at Lookout Point, pronounced it well and truly dead and had later performed an autopsy. He described three knife wounds found in the lower abdomen. His dryly technical language took nothing away from the impact on the jury, Benson noted. Deceased, he said, might actually have been killed by the fall over the railing. He read a list of various contusions, abrasions and broken bones, especially multiple fractures of the skull, that made Mrs. Jordan gulp and look away from him. If he had not fallen, Duquesne might have lived a few minutes longer, the doctor guessed, but not more than five minutes at the most.

"Your witness," Frank Sayer said.

Benson rose slowly. He picked up the official autopsy report and a sheet on which he had scribbled notes.

"You first saw the body when it was raised from the rock slope below Lookout Point, did you not, Doctor?"

"That is right."

"You examined it merely to be sure it was dead. I mean, you didn't attempt an extensive examination on the spot?"

"No, not then."

"Were photographs made of the body at that time?"

"I believe so. I remember seeing flashbulbs going off, but I don't know whether——"

"Very well, Doctor. Now, when the body was brought to your examining room, was it in the same condition it had been at Lookout Point?"

"Yes, as far as anything important was concerned. We put the body in a carrier and then in the ambulance. It was taken directly to my laboratory."

"In your report, Doctor," Benson said, turning to the next-to-last page, "you have described three knife wounds, and several fractures of the skull which were the actual cause of death. You also listed a number of comparatively minor cuts and excisions, but your description of them was not detailed. Do you remember them clearly?"

"Yes, sir."

"What caused them?"

"Why, the fall. The body fell over that railing and scraped down a rough, broken slope before it landed on that rock."

Benson could see Mrs. Jordan wince. It would be wise to get off the subject as quickly as he could, but there were several points on which he needed the doctor's testimony.

"I don't wish to argue, Doctor," he said quietly. "But your report says nothing about the cause of five jagged tears in and around the knife wounds. It is true, is it not, that you found a certain amount of flesh and skin to be missing?"

"Yes, I assumed——"

"Please don't assume, Doctor," Benson said. "The missing portions were not found by your or by the sheriff's investigators?"

"Well, I don't believe anyone looked for them."

"So that we are left with the fact of their absence, but with no explanation. I ask you now, Doctor, if you are prepared to tell this court that all those cuts and excisions were caused by the fall and not by—other means."

"I wouldn't want to swear to it, but——"

"You are required to swear to it, Doctor," Benson insisted. "I now ask you, sir, if it is not true that a certain amount of the damage done to the body you examined was not in fact done by the tearing beaks of scavenger birds, and not the rocks?"

"Objection!" Frank Sayer snapped before the doctor had a chance to answer. "This witness is not qualified as an expert on scavenger birds."

"He is a medical expert, though," Benson said quickly. "I am asking for his medical opinion, Your Honor. He has already given his opinion on many of the wounds inflicted upon the deceased. I want to know his opinion of the others."

"Yes, the witness may answer." The judge made a brief note on his pad.

"The question, Doctor, was whether those cuts and excisions could have been caused by buzzards?"

"They might have," Dr. Norwood said. He raised his head to look over Benson's head toward Frank Sayer.

"Let me be sure that I understand you, Doctor," Benson went on. "It is your testimony that some of the damage done to the deceased was not caused by the knife wounds, nor by the fall, but by the action of buzzards after death. Is that right?"

"It might have been," the doctor said reluctantly.

"What is the likelihood, Doctor? What does your best judgment suggest to you? A strong likelihood?"

"Not strong, no. I wouldn't go that far."

"But a likelihood, all the same?"

"Yes, I suppose so."

That was as far as he could be taken down that road, Benson realized, and it was all that was needed. Benson shuffled the autopsy report behind his page of notes.

"Now, Doctor, I want to ask you about another part of your testimony. Will you please tell the court how the body was dressed?"

"Dressed?" Dr. Norwood straightened abruptly and scowled at Benson as if he suspected an outrageous flippancy.

"Yes, dressed," Benson repeated. "I assume he was clothed when you first saw him?"

"Of course, of course. It's all in my report, sir. Shoes and socks and underwear and trousers and a shirt. The brand names and laundry marks are listed in the sheriff's report. No coat. I understand the sheriff has the——"

"Just tell me what you saw yourself, Doctor. We'll get to the sheriff later if we have to. Did you undress the body?"

"Well, my assistant did it."

"But you were there?"

"Yes."

"You testified, Doctor, that the three knife wounds in the body were all in the lower abdomen, below the line of the umbilicus. Is that right?"

"Yes."

"In the area that would normally be covered by a man's trousers?"

"Yes."

"All of the wounds went from side to side, crossing what we might call the center line, I believe?"

"That is correct, sir," Dr. Norwood said impatiently. "It's all in the report."

"Were any of the knife strokes deflected by the zipper of deceased's trousers?"

"Not very much. One stroke, the second I described earlier, took a slight downward turn. The others were fairly straight."

"Now, to return to deceased's clothing, Doctor. Can you tell the court if the zipper of the trousers was cut by any of these knife strokes?"

"Yes, sir. If I may refresh my memory . . ." Dr. Norwood turned the pages of his report.

"Yes, take your time, Doctor."

"The left side of the zipper was cut once, Mr. Kellogg," the doctor said, tracing a finger down the page. "An inch and a half from the bottom where the zipper is joined."

"The left side," Benson said reflectively. He stepped away from the witness stand, retreating along the front of the jury box. "The left side," he repeated, looking at the jury. "You did say the left side, didn't you, Doctor?"

"Yes, sir."

Benson stopped at the end of the jury box, just beyond the last juror, Mitchell Masterton. "Will you please speak a little louder, Doctor? I don't think the jury can hear you."

"Yes, the left side only," the doctor said sharply.

"Thank you. I heard you very clearly then, Doctor. How in the world can you cut only one side of a zipper? Have you any explanation for that, Doctor?"

"I object," Frank Sayer said. He lunged up, leaning forward across his table. "It is not only argumentative, but immaterial and——"

"Sustained," Judge Groat said in a tired voice.

"Your Honor, this entire line of questioning is also immaterial and incompetent. It can add nothing to the evidence in Dr. Norwood's report."

"Mr. Kellogg?"

"I believe that my next question will show the relevance of this information, Your Honor. And witness is competent to answer, because I will ask for nothing but his personal observation."

"Put the question, Mr. Kellogg."

"Please tell the court, Doctor," Benson said, "whether the zipper was open or closed when you first saw the body."

"Objection!" Frank Sayer roared. "The question is clearly incompetent and irrelevant. This witness is here to testify to the cause of death."

"No, Mr. Sayer, I don't agree," the judge said bluntly. "Witness will answer."

"The zipper was open when I saw the body," Dr. Norwood said.

Benson remained in place, at the far end of the jury box, facing the witness stand. "Did I hear you correctly?" he asked. "The zipper was open?" The back of Frank Sayer's neck burned with a hot, angry flush.

"It was open," the doctor said again.

"And only one side of this open zipper had been cut. That is true, isn't it?"

"Yes."

"Underneath his open zipper, deceased was wearing a pair of shorts, wasn't he?"

"Yes."

"Were the shorts open also?"

"No," the doctor said. He seemed pleased to have a chance to say that.

Benson took a moment to consider his position. It is a cardinal rule of cross-examination never to ask a question unless you know what the answer will be. But Benson did not want to leave the jury with its present impression. Should he go ahead, or drop it where he was?

"The shorts were buttoned then, Doctor?"

"No."

Benson half smiled. "No buttons, Doctor? What was he wearing, the kind of shorts that are always open down the front?"

"Or always closed, depending on how you look at it," the doctor said.

"In this case, we will say they were open," Benson said. "Thank you. That's all."

"One moment, Dr. Norwood," Frank Sayer said hastily. He rose, waited for Benson to cross in front of him and then moved forward.

"You do not of your own knowledge know that the zipper of deceased's trousers was not torn open by the fall down the slope from Lookout Point. Do you, Doctor?"

"No, sir."

Sayer beamed at his witness. "Thank you. And you do not of your own knowledge know whether the cuts and excisions were caused by the fall or by scavengers. Do you, Doctor?"

"Well, I . . ."

"I mean, you didn't actually see any of these alleged buzzards the defense counsel has mentioned?"

"As a matter of fact, I——"

"What I am getting at, Doctor, is——"

Benson scraped his chair back noisily. "Let the witness answer," he snapped.

"You will address the court if you have something to say," the judge said testily.

"I'm sorry, Your Honor. But the prosecutor keeps trying to override his own witness. The jury has a right to hear his answers."

"Now, see here——"

Judge Groat's pencil tapped against his lamp gently, only once. It was warning enough. Both attorneys, red-faced and angry, turned silently to face the bench.

"The defense has a valid point, Mr. Sayer. Let the witness

answer. Now let us proceed without this constant bickering, gentlemen."

"Read the last question, please," Frank Sayer said to the reporter in a slow, thick voice.

The reporter reached over his stenotype machine, lifted folds of paper from the box and scanned them. He cleared his throat and looked up. Sayer nodded stiffly.

" 'I mean, you didn't actually see any of these alleged buzzards the defense counsel has mentioned?' "

"Answer the question, Doctor."

"I did see a few in the air, as I was driving up to Cobre Peak. I didn't see any on the ground," Dr. Norwood said.

Half a loaf for each of them, Benson thought. I wonder if Frank has sense enough to drop it there? He's already lost his point and he'll only make it worse if he goes on.

Sayer turned away. "Thank you, Doctor," he said over his shoulder. "That's all."

"Mr. Kellogg, have you any further questions for the witness?"

Benson looked up, startled. In the Rincon courts, a defense attorney has no definite right to recross-examination, although the prosecution is allowed redirect at any time. The decision rested entirely with the trial judge. Benson got up.

"I am grateful for your courtesy, Your Honor. I have no more questions for Dr. Norwood."

The doctor left the stand stiffly. Frank Sayer did not look at him as he went past.

"My next witness, Your Honor, will take some little time," the prosecutor said. "It is now past four thirty, and I thought Your Honor might prefer to——"

Judge Groat scooped up his watch. "Yes, we will adjourn for the day, gentlemen." He nodded to the clerk who was waiting with his gavel poised. It came down on the block in a brisk tattoo.

"This honorable court stands adjourned until tomorrow morning, Tuesday, April twenty-third, at ten A.M."

The jury scuffled along the enclosed box, stretching and muttering. Mrs. Jordan opened her handbag, took out a handkerchief and inspected her face in a pocket mirror. Mitchell Masterton folded a pad of paper he had been using for notes and stowed it in his pocket. John Eben Heller raised both his heavy arms and bent forward, his face pained.

Judge Groat stood behind the bench. He moved a few steps closer to the jury box and looked down. His lined face was stern and cold. He inspected the jury with his habitual glare.

"Gentlemen and Mrs. Jordan," he said in a thin, carrying tone, "I have observed some of you taking notes. If you feel notes will assist you in keeping the facts in mind, the court has no objection. However, you will deposit your notes in sealed envelopes with the clerk whenever you leave the courtroom. You may take them with you only to the jury conference room. Also, I wish to caution you once more about discussing this case among yourselves or with anyone else. If anyone attempts to discuss it in your presence, you will remove yourselves. If anyone persists in trying to discuss the case, you will notify me immediately. That is all. Good night."

Turo leaned to whisper to Benson. "We finished?"

"For today," Benson said. He gathered his papers together and slid them into his briefcase. "You've done all right, Turo. Get all the rest you can tonight. It will be a long day tomorrow."

BENSON stood on the courthouse steps watching the crowd drifting in batches down the cracked sidewalk. Through a gap in the slow procession he caught a brief glimpse of a high-shouldered man in a rusty black suit and an old black rancher's hat pulled low across his eyes. Benson went down the steps quickly. The man was out of sight before he reached the corner, lost somewhere in the stragglers moving toward the bus stop.

That couldn't have been the Dorado, he told himself. Just

some elderly cow person in his Sunday suit come to see the sights. The Dorado knew Benson didn't want him in the courtroom. And anyway, he remembered, Arturo's grandfather wasn't much of a hand with English and he couldn't very well bring an interpreter to court with him. Must have been someone else. But all the way back to his office, Benson found himself scanning faces along the streets, half expecting to spot the dark, wolfish face of the old man.

He went quickly through the crowded anteroom of B. Kellogg and Sampson and down the corridor with long strides. He pushed back the door of his office, took a step forward and stopped.

Jason Blumberg was sitting at Benson's desk, looking with flat, expressionless eyes at the door. His round elbows prodded the arms of Benson's chair. His hands were locked under his chin, thumbs tapping alternately at his fleshy chin.

He looks as if he's been waiting just like that for a long time, Benson thought. He nodded with a sour, impatient amusement and turned toward Mary's desk.

"I asked her to give us a minute alone, Benson," Blumberg said with a heavy sign. He cleared his throat softly.

Benson sat in the deep client's chair opposite Blumberg and put his briefcase on a corner of the desk.

"You've been avoiding me, young man. I don't like that," Blumberg said.

Benson nodded again. He took out his cigarettes and lit one. "I had to make some decisions," he said in a flat, slow voice. "I didn't want any more advice."

Blumberg's eyes half closed. His little button mouth twitched at the corners. "You are a singularly tactless man, Benson," he said coldly.

"I suppose so," Benson admitted. He directed a streamer of smoke against the polished side of his desk. "Right now, I'm a little tired. I've got a lot to do this evening, Mr. Blumberg. Could we get to the point, please?"

Blumberg's expression did not change. "In this firm, every partner handles his own work without interference. Without help or consultation unless he asks for it. That was the policy established by your father. I'm not sure it is the best policy for us any longer."

Benson nodded politely.

"I'm thinking of changing it," Blumberg said in a silky growl. "I'm thinking of making a lot of changes around here. Do you understand what I mean, Benson?"

"Not yet," Benson said indifferently. He could smell trouble in Blumberg's overly careful formality.

"Let me make myself clear, then," Blumberg said. "We won't waste time with accusations and explanations. What is past is past. I address myself to the future. Am I clear so far?"

"Of course."

"Good. I want you to know that I have just accepted a sizable retainer from Consolidated Copper. Sizable." Blumberg made a tasty shape with his mouth. "To earn that retainer and to make sure it is refreshed next year, we have to adjust ourselves to some necessary changes. We will need some new people. That means promotions for several junior partners. You understand?"

"I understand."

"Then, goddam it, straighten up!" Blumberg snapped. "Show some sense." He smiled earnestly, patiently. "I don't mean to shout at you, Benson," he added in a tone that was close to apology. "I get a little too emotional once in a while. You're busy and you've got a lot to worry about besides—" he made an aimless gesture with a pudgy hand—"this," he finished lamely.

Benson sat up and dropped his cigarette in the ashtray. "Have you ever talked to H. L. Caine?" he asked quietly.

"Only by phone."

"I think the man is insane," Benson said. "I have already agreed to do what he wants. He didn't have to scare me or bribe me. His sacred name doesn't mean a damn thing to the Campeón defense. Now what in hell do you think he's really after?"

Blumberg shook his head. He eyed Benson with a shrewd

half-scowl. "Maybe he's impressed with you, my boy. Maybe he wants you to handle all his business from now on."

"No," Benson said flatly. "Maybe he'd like to own me, just so he could have the fun of breaking me. He'd get a kick out of that, probably. Well, the hell with Caine. I haven't time to worry about him. Is that all, Mr. Blumberg?"

"That's all," Blumberg said with a note of subdued anger clear in his voice. "Think it over carefully, Benson. There's a lot at stake here. A big future or a big nothing. You follow me?"

"You're clear, Blumberg. Thanks for stopping by." Benson got up and walked past his desk to the windows. He stood looking out across the rooftops. He heard Blumberg close the door behind him.

He stayed there for a long moment, rubbing his chin thoughtfully and staring at his reflection with a rueful bewilderment. You are getting to be a loud, hard-nosed jerk, my friend, he told himself with a bitter distaste. Who in hell are you trying to impress? Caine is a vicious old monster, but he thinks he has reason to be worried and he won't get off your back until he hears the right words said in just the right way. So why not say them? You don't thumb your nose at people like Caine, not if you want to get anywhere. What would you stand to lose by being agreeable? Be a good boy and make Daddy proud of you. Speak softly and politely to your elders and betters and you'll be allowed to roll in clover. What's so hard about that? Benson grinned sourly at himself in the darkening glass.

He saw Mary open the door and come inside. He turned away from the window and sat behind his desk.

"Did Mr. Blumberg tell you?" Mary said in a strained voice.

"Tell me what?"

"About me? I wouldn't let him see your notes. My, he was angry! He said——"

"Don't worry about it, Mary," Benson said brusquely. "You were exactly right. Blumberg knows that. Will you get the notes, please?"

Mary hesitated, worrying her underlip between her teeth. Then, inwardly, she seemed to shrug. She turned away toward her desk and unlocked the center drawer with a key she wore on a chain around her neck.

"Any calls?" Benson asked. "Have we heard from Elsinore yet?"

"Not Elsinore," Mary said, her voice muffled. "You had two calls from El Monte. One about Elsinore from a Mr. Blue and the other——"

"Manny Blue?" Benson said. "What did he want?"

"He didn't say. He left a number. Shall I call him back?"

"I think you'd better," Benson said. He took the sealed envelope Mary gave him and unstrapped his briefcase to put it away.

Mary gave the number to the operator. She cupped her hand over the phone and looked over her shoulder. "The other one was the Mexicany voice again. He still won't talk to me. He says it's very important. About the trial. I gave him your home number, so I expect he'll——" She broke off to speak into the phone. She pushed a button switch to transfer the call to Benson's phone.

"Hi there, Counselor," Blue said in a loud, cheerful voice. "How's the trial going?"

"What do you want, Blue?"

"Just a few kind words, Counselor. I'm doing you a big favor."

Benson grunted. He propped the phone between ear and shoulder and used both hands to light a cigarette.

"The magic word is Elsinore. That make you happier?"

"What about him?" Benson asked sharply.

"You were pretty cute in L.A. I never figured you for a swifty. I guess you had a couple of chuckles, thinking how you outsmarted old Manny, didn't you?"

"You outsmarted yourself, Blue. Where is Elsinore now?"

"Right here, Counselor. Right in my pocket."

"He's been subpoenaed. I suppose you know that? Interfering with a witness under subpoena is a felony in this state, Blue."

"Now, don't go scaring me." Blue laughed easily. "You don't want little Harald hanging around town before you're ready to put him on the stand, do you?"

"What do you intend to do?" Benson asked shortly.

"Why, I intend to deliver your witness, Counselor. It takes a little time to get to Rincon, you know. We might have a breakdown in the desert and have to walk in. Maybe we won't get there in time. But me and Harald, we're on our way all the time. You know something, Counselor?" Blue added confidentially, "Mr. Caine has a lawyer who says we can't be touched if we can prove we've been on the way all the time. What do you think about that?"

"I think you'll get about five years to study some law books for yourself. Caine's lawyers are about as stupid as his detectives."

"My, my, ain't you the rough one, though," Blue said pleasantly. "We'll most likely be there when you want us, Counselor. You know what it depends on, don't you?"

"I know what you think it depends on, Blue," Benson said in a hard, tight voice. "I want to tell you something."

"Shoot, Counselor."

"I told Caine I had no interest in him. I told him I'd keep his name out of the trial as long as he kept his nose out of my business."

Blue whistled softly. "You said that? To Caine? I don't believe it."

"He's not God," Benson said angrily. "He's broken our agreement, so all bets are off. Tell him that, Blue. I'm under no restrictions. Court opens tomorrow at nine thirty in the morning. Unless you produce Harald Elsinore before then, I will make it my business to identify Roderick Duquesne by his right name. That is a flat promise, Blue."

"You could do that," Blue said easily. "But it wouldn't get Elsinore on the stand. You'll wind up getting your boy hung."

"I don't think so," Benson said, sensing the hesitancy in Blue. "If you aren't here by morning, I'm going to explain to Judge Groat just what you and Caine have been up to. I'm going to ask him for bench warrants for both of you. And after the court has seen you and heard your stories, I think the jury will suspect that you've been trying to frame my client. By the time I'm finished with you and Caine, the jury will want to hang you instead."

"Me! I haven't had a damn thing to do with——"

"Tell it in court. Tomorrow morning, Blue. Nine thirty, on the dot." Benson slammed the phone down. He took out his handkerchief and wiped the palms of his hands. He took in a quick, ragged breath. He looked at Mary.

"Did you hear that?" he asked.

She nodded, wide-eyed.

"Then forget it, please. I don't want Caine's name mentioned anywhere until I'm ready. All right?"

"Yes. Yes, of course, Mr. Kellogg. But won't that man, Blue——"

"Mr. Blue has been taken care of, Mary. He's in a rather vulnerable profession. He won't risk his entire future for any one client. He'll have my witness here by morning if he has to walk. If he should phone again, tell him to meet me in the courtroom. I won't talk to him anywhere else."

"Yes, sir."

Benson lifted his phone again, asked for an outside line, and dialed a familiar SIerra number.

"Miss Gilbert, please," he said when a girl's voice answered. "Benson Kellogg calling."

He covered the phone while he waited. "Mary, could you manage to come in early tomorrow? I have some——" He smiled and lifted one shoulder when he heard Joss's quick, excited voice on the line. She always sounded as if she'd just sprinted a brisk fifty yards out of sheer eagerness.

"Ben, I'm so glad you called. Where have you been all this time?"

"Hiding out," Benson said, trying to speak lightly. "Getting up my nerve."

"Oh, Ben! I am sorry. I was a pig, wasn't I? I don't know what gets into me sometimes. I should never have——"

"Home truths," Benson said thinly. "Hard to take, especially when they're true. Forget it, Joss. You didn't say anything that didn't need saying. Care to take a tired lawyer to dinner tonight?"

"Ben, I can't! Why didn't you ask me earlier? Sam Greenfield of Desert Modes just got in this afternoon. He's a little doll and I owe him a favor. I'm giving a cocktail party for him. Why don't you come, Ben? You know most of the people. We could chase everybody out by eight o'clock anyway, and go somewhere afterward. Will you?"

Benson made a sour face at the phone, but held his voice level and easy. "I guess not, Joss. Fact is, I'm in a lousy mood. I wouldn't be any good at a party. Anyway, I'd have to leave early. Got a stack of work to look at."

"Are you making excuses, Ben?"

Benson laughed. "No. Honest. Let's try again tomorrow?"

"Well . . ." Joss hesitated. Then in a softer, more personal tone, she said, "Is it all right, Ben? With us?"

"I want it to be, Joss," Benson said honestly.

"Then it is! Don't fret yourself, Ben. And stop working so hard all the time. How is the trial going?"

"About as you would expect."

"I don't know if that's good or bad. Should I ask?"

"No. There's nothing to talk about."

"That's not what the *Record* says. I haven't read it yet, but it looks like they gave you the whole front page. With a picture that makes you look a little bit dead. You will call tomorrow, Ben? Please?"

"Yes. Some time in the afternoon, probably. Good night, Joss. Have a good party."

"Yes, I will. Good night, Ben dear. I'm so very glad you called."

Benson put the phone down and rubbed a hand across his eyes. They felt sore when he touched them. He pulled the lids down gently and pressed in.

"You were saying," Mary prodded him timidly, "about tomorrow?"

"Oh yes. I want to stay current with my rebuttal notes. I'll write them up tonight. Could you come in early and type them for me? I'd like to have them when I go to court."

"Why, yes. I'd be happy to, Mr. Kellogg. What time? I could be here by six, if that's———"

"Not that early," Benson objected. "I didn't mean anything like that. Seven thirty or eight would be fine. I'll have an hour's work for you, probably. Can you make it by seven-thirty, do you think?"

"I'll be here, Mr. Kellogg. You can depend on it," Mary said fervently.

Benson took his briefcase from the desk and put his hat on the back of his head. "I'm going to bunk in at the Frontier tonight. You can reach me there for anything important. I'd rather you didn't, if you can manage to shortstop things for me."

THE EARLY-MORNING BREEZE struck cold from the snow-peaked Cobres and curled along the Rincon streets with the edge of chill that comes wonderfully to the desert just before the sun rises clear of the blind mountains. Benson left the hotel with a spring in his feet, rested after a good night's sleep, exhilarated as always by the cool, perfect brightness of the morning.

Only a soft pink light was burning in the reception room. Benson crossed and opened the door and moved down the dim corridor to his office.

Mary turned as he came in. She shut her eyes in a sigh of relief and held the phone away from her ear. She cupped her hand over the mouthpiece and expelled a soft explosion of air.

"It's that man Blue again," she said.

Benson nodded. "Put him on. Where is he calling from?"

"He's in town. At some motel." Mary tilted the phone toward her mouth. "One moment, Mr. Blue. Mr. Kellogg has just come in. He'll talk to you." She pushed a button to switch the call.

"Goddam, but you're a hard man to get to," Blue said angrily when Benson was on the line.

"I hope you're not trying to stall me, Blue," Benson said. "Where is Elsinore?"

"Stall? Who, me? Stall, hell," Blue said self-righteously. "Elsinore is right here. Pigsty Ten in the Pigsty Motel. Best in the glorious West, by actual test. He's sound asleep. And snoring."

"Then what's your trouble?" Benson asked. "Deliver him by nine thirty."

"I don't think you'll want me to," Blue said more quietly. "That's why I've been trying to get to you. Elsinore went hysterical on me last night. Threw an old-fashioned wing-ding. I had to give him something."

"What did you give him?" Benson demanded.

"You wouldn't want to know, Counselor. Just a little whatchacallit in an ampoule to make him sleep. Now, do you want him brought in this way, or do I let him sleep it off?"

"For how long?"

"Till noon maybe. He'll be up this afternoon sure."

"Let him sleep," Benson said after a moment. "But don't give him anything else, Blue. I want to talk to him, and for your sake, he'd better be coherent. Bring him to my office and wait till I get here. Do you understand that I'm not giving you any option, Blue? If you and Harald Elsinore are not in my office by the time I get back this afternoon, I'll apply for a bench warrant."

"You come through loud and clear, Counselor," Blue said cheerfully. "Caine gave me the word last night. I don't know what you did to him in L.A., but I've got your boy for you. Compliments of H. L. Caine. You want him now, you get him now. You want him later, you get him later. It's all one to me. Just don't forget that Caine is playing square with you.

He's expecting the same from you."

"The hell with Caine," Benson said. "Bring Elsinore here, Blue. I want him awake and able to speak for himself. Be here no later than four this afternoon." Benson hung up.

He pushed the phone away and took out his cigarettes. He lit one, tasted bitterness in his mouth and put it out after the first puff. He pushed up from his chair and went across to Mary, taking a thick, folded sheaf of papers from his pocket.

"This stuff should run to about fifteen pages, I'd say," he told her. "Triple-space them so I'll have room to make additions. Can you get through all that in time?"

"Oh, easily, Mr. Kellogg. It isn't even eight o'clock yet."

"Fine. I'm going out and get some breakfast and a shave. I'd like you to meet me in court at nine thirty. Bring the notes, if they're ready. One thing more." He fumbled through his pockets, ultimately locating what he wanted in a compartment of his wallet.

"These references," he said, giving Mary a slip of paper. "Cases I may want to cite if we get into an argument today. Wait till about nine o'clock and then phone Willie Rojas and see if he'll let us borrow the books from Judge Groat's library. If he can't, then get one of the office boys to carry our copies over to the courthouse and go with him to make sure they get there. Okay?"

Mary was interleafing carbons and onionskins. She nodded briskly.

Benson went down the hallway to the flickering tune of her electric typewriter.

EVERY SEAT in the courtroom was already filled when Benson walked past the main entrance where two amiably brusque deputies were waving latecomers aside. The local newspapers had been giving a lot of space to the trial. Any loyal subscriber who wanted to see the show for himself would have to show up before dawn to be sure of a seat. Benson opened the side door, nodded to the guard, and went in, crossing toward his table. He smiled at Mary and slid into the chair beside her. She sat behind a low barricade of law books with dangling strips of paper inserted to mark the sections he wanted to cite. At his place she had laid out a yellow notepad and several sharp pencils, the stapled notes she had typed that morning, a stack of small cards for messages and a thermos carafe with a matching plastic cup that looked like the set that usually lived on her office desk.

"Looks very efficient, Mary," he said in a low voice. "I never think to keep some water handy." He unstrapped his briefcase, took out three folders, squaring them with the far edge of the table. He picked up a pencil and began to read slowly and carefully through his notes.

He looked up when the deputy escorted Turo Campeón in from the detention room. The boy moved with a lithe, contained stride, easy in himself, and very quiet, much as he had been yesterday, Benson thought. There was about him an obscure sort of serenity that Benson could not understand. He nodded to the boy and went back to his work, leaving Mary to carry on a whispered, sympathetic conversation, which Turo tended to answer with single syllables or brief, expressive gestures of his left hand.

Frank Sayer entered noisily, flanked by two assistants ranging alongside like outriders. He made a formal, stilted point of shaking hands with Benson, keeping his big politician's head turned three quarters toward the photographers at the press table. After he had made his manners, Frank Sayer backed away and went into a sibilant, finger-stabbing conference with the clerk. Benson could tell by the sudden hush when Judge Groat came in from his chambers. He rose before the clerk could pound his gavel.

Judge Groat looked jaded and prickly, as if he'd had a bad night and meant someone to suffer for it. He glared down into the well of the court, counting noses. He greeted the court in a hoarse, rasping voice, told the reporter to note that defendant was present with counsel. He curtly instructed the

County Attorney to get on with it.

"Juan Elias Kleinschmidt," Frank Sayer called in a peremptory tone, as if he understood that the judge's testiness had to be answered by a show of brisk dispatch.

Benson watched the witness take the oath. Juan Elias Kleinschmidt, he thought. There was a name with the ring of the Old Territory to it. Kleinschmidt was a young, open-faced blond boy with the pink, hairless skin of a new baby. He was a civilian employee of the sheriff's office, ranking as a senior clerk. His primary function was to photograph whatever the sheriff told him to photograph. Most of the time that meant the sheriff himself. Kleinschmidt also photographed various kinds of evidence, including scenes of highway collisions and other crimes. He had taken several pictures of Roderick Duquesne's body, he said in answer to a question from Frank Sayer. He identified glossy prints the prosecutor handed him as ones he had shot and developed.

The fourteen photographs were stamped with an exhibit number and presented to Benson by one of Sayer's nameless aides.

"Now then, Mr. Kleinschmidt," Frank Sayer said, walking back toward the stand. "When you were——"

"One moment, please, Your Honor," Benson broke in. "I would appreciate an opportunity to inspect these photographs before we go any further."

Judge Groat bent a sidelong, suspicious gaze on Benson. With a barely perceptible movement he nodded.

Frank Sayer pulled in a long dramatic breath. He raised his eyes and shrugged for the jury with a wry, patient smile. He leaned against the railing of the witness stand, turned so that he could see Benson who had taken a long-handled reading glass from his briefcase and was leafing rapidly through Kleinschmidt's pictures.

Benson was looking for only one thing in each of the prints. Finally he separated the third one, put it on top, and shaped the pile together neatly. He put down his glass and came to his feet with slow deliberation, holding the pictures in one hand.

"The defense, Your Honor, objects to admission of any of these photographs," he said.

Frank Sayer sighed audibly. He lifted both hands helplessly to heaven. "Your Honor," he said in the voice of a man tried beyond endurance, "it is obvious that the defense is determined to——"

Judge Groat tapped his pencil against the base of his tall bronze lamp. "That will do, Mr. Sayer. Approach the bench, if you please, Mr. Kellogg. You too, Mr. Sayer."

Benson stopped to pick up his reading glass and a sheet of paper with a typed column of citations. He brought them with him and joined Frank Sayer at the corner of the bench farthest from the jury box. Shrill questioning murmurs from the spectators were graveled to silence by the clerk, who was leaning perilously back in his chair, straining to overhear.

"Well, Benson?" the judge said.

"The pictures Frank is offering are inflammatory and prejudicial, sir," Benson said in a low voice. "They are also inaccurate. They show deceased in a condition which even Frank does not contend was the fault of the defendant, or any other person."

"That's nonsense," Sayer said curtly. "Judge, I'm not going to stand here and——"

Judge Groat held up a thin trembling hand to stop Sayer in midsentence. "You will moderate your tone when you speak to me, Frank," he said sharply. "I will ask for your comments in a moment."

He brought his hand down and extended it toward Benson, fingers cupped. "Are those your citations, Benson? Let me just glance at them."

He scanned the sheet quickly, his dry, lipless mouth shaping the words as he read. Probably, Benson realized, there were not three judges in the state who could bring to mind the issues raised by those cases without checking the books. It was an impressive piece of professional competence.

The judge smiled thinly when he had finished. "Mr. Clerk," he said, "the jury will retire." He stared for a long, thoughtful moment at Benson. "I'll hear you, Mr. Kellogg," he said formally.

Frank Sayer whirled toward his table as the jury filed dutifully out to its waiting room. He snatched up a folder which one assistant had ready for him. He came back toward the bench in a stiff-legged angry stride.

It was too bad, Benson thought, watching him, that he had tipped his hand to Sayer yesterday. Surprised, the prosecutor would have been a lot easier to handle than he would be this morning with his rebuttal citations listed and his counter-arguments well in mind.

"To the first point, Mr. Kellogg," the judge said.

"I refer the court to *Janovich* v. *People,* thirty-two, one-seventy-five, and *Miranda* v. *People,* forty-two, three-fifty-eight, Your Honor," Benson said promptly. "The specific citations are on that sheet."

"In both cases cited, the trial court admitted photographs in spite of the defense contentions that they were gruesome and inflammatory," Frank Sayer put in quickly.

"Sir?" Judge Groat swung toward Benson.

"I cited those cases, Your Honor, to establish the fact that trial courts traditionally have wide latitude in admitting or excluding pictures that might be prejudicial."

"This court does not need instruction from counsel, Mr. Kellogg," the judge said stiffly. "I know what discretion I may exercise. Get to the point, if you please."

"These pictures, Your Honor," Benson said, putting the stack before the judge and weighting it with his reading glass, "these pictures show the body of Roderick Duquesne at various times on Sunday, April fourteenth. The body was found at three thirty P.M., so it is evident that no pictures could have been taken before that time. We have heard testimony that puts the time of death at approximately four thirty A.M. In the eleven hours intervening between death and discovery, the condition of the body was so altered by scavenger birds that any picture of it does not honestly represent——"

"That's specious reasoning, Your Honor," Frank Sayer snorted. "I don't concede that there was any alteration, but even if there had been, it would not affect this question. The ruling in *Young* v. *People,* thirty-eight, two-ninety-eight, has settled that."

"You're wrong," Benson said with a tight smile. "But allow me to return, Your Honor, to the matter of scavengers. We heard Deputy Aldridge tell the court yesterday that he had seen bird tracks near the body. We heard the medical examiner testify that he saw buzzards in the air. I now ask the court to inspect the pictures offered in evidence. The one I have placed on top has some interesting detail in the lower right-hand corner. You can make it out distinctly with that reading glass, Your Honor."

Benson stepped back and took a marked book from his table while Judge Groat was studying the photograph. The judge grunted. He handed the glass to Sayer and pointed to the corner of the shiny print. Benson opened his book and held it ready in one hand.

"Doesn't mean a thing," Sayer said brusquely. "Bird tracks. What of it? What does it prove?"

"Do the tracks remind you of anything, Mr. Prosecutor?" Benson asked quietly.

Sayer shrugged irritably. "Remind me of birds. So what?"

"Look again, and carefully this time. Notice the slightly webbed pattern of the feet outlined in the earth. Reminds you of a turkey track, doesn't it? There is an interesting kind of bird that is native to these parts, Mr. Prosecutor. You should know about them. They have been getting rather scarce lately, but you can still find plenty of them roosting around here. Tell the judge what they are called, Mr. Prosecutor."

"What?" Frank Sayer reared back defensively. His big chin came up. "How the devil would I know?"

"Turkey buzzards, Mr. Prosecutor," Benson said, driving it home. "What you see in that picture are the tracks of a turkey buzzard just six inches from the body of Roderick Duquesne. The turkey buzzard is a carrion-eating scavenger bird, Mr. Prosecutor. There is no mistaking those tracks. You may take my word for that. I'll bring experts to bear me out, if you wish."

"Your Honor," Sayer said quickly, "we're getting off the point. It doesn't make any difference if those tracks were made by turkey buzzards or swallow-tailed canaries. There's nothing in this picture that tells us when those tracks were made. They might be weeks old."

"They *might*," Benson repeated with a strong emphasis. "But a young man's life is at stake in this trial, Your Honor. I'm not satisfied with the prosecutor's casual dismissal of this evidence. He guesses that those tracks *might* have been made earlier. His guesses are not good enough, Your Honor. The burden of proof in this matter lies with the prosecution, and those tracks must be explained by something more solid than the prosecutor's guesses."

The judge tapped his pencil briskly before Frank Sayer could answer. "I've allowed a considerable leeway to counsel so far, Mr. Kellogg. I warn you that my patience has very definite limits. There will be no more personalities. To the point, if you please."

"Yes, Your Honor. I apologize. The critical fact is that those buzzard tracks exist, Your Honor. They cannot be brushed aside. They cannot, in fact, even be explained by the prosecution. The court heard the medical examiner testify that he found certain unexplained gouges and excisions on the body of Roderick Duquesne. An unknown amount of skin and tissue was missing when the body was discovered at three thirty P.M. The defense contends that with the evidence of the buzzard tracks in that photograph, with the evidence of the missing skin and tissue, we are justified in asking the court to exclude those photographs on the grounds that they do not show deceased's body in the same condition that the prosecution says it was left in by the defendant. Unless, of course," Benson turned to Sayer in polite inquiry, "the prosecution wishes to maintain that the defendant somehow transformed himself into a turkey buzzard?"

"I will ignore defense counsel's rudeness and flippancy," Frank Sayer said. "The situation is too serious for frivolous comment. I will merely remind the court that in *Young* v. *People,* which I have already cited, and in *Browning* v. *People,* fifty-three, one-seventy-four, photographs were held to have been properly admitted even though they did show a changed condition. The defense contention has no merit, Your Honor. The body of practice and precedent is against it. There is a special pertinence to the judgment rendered in *Young* v. *People,* which was also a trial for homicide."

"The prosecutor is in error, Your Honor," Benson said sharply. "Neither of the cases he cites are pertinent or material, in my view. In *Young* v. *People,* pictures were admitted which showed that deceased's head had been shaved by a doctor in order to treat wounds which later proved to be fatal. The condition was altered, it is true, but not in any way that worked to the detriment of defendant. The wounds were merely made more visible. They were not themselves altered. In the other case—*Browning* v. *People*—the court was upheld in a rape case when the trial judge admitted photographs of the prosecutrix' bruised and partially bandaged face. Any advantage accruing from the changed condition clearly benefited the defendant. In both cases, trial courts were upheld because the altered conditions shown by the photographs did not prejudice the defendant's position, and also because the altered conditions were fully and carefully explained to the jury. I submit, Your Honor, that in this case it is not possible to explain—or even identify—the altered conditions of Roderick Duquesne's body."

Benson reached up and laid his open book on the bench in front of the judge.

"A case which supports my contention, Your Honor," he went on, satisfied that he had the judge's complete attention, "is *Henderson* v. *Breesman,* seventy-seven, two-fifty-six, a civil case that involved liability for damage to plaintiff's car. The trial court was upheld when it excluded photographs that showed the car was not in the same condition as at the time of the alleged accident. The distinction here, it seems to me, is that it is not possible for the court to explain to the jury just where the alteration began—" Benson looked at Frank Sayer with a grim smile—"or where it ended."

The judge nodded, waiting.

"I believe that an extremely prejudicial situation would be created by introduction of those pictures, Your Honor. No man in this courtroom can honestly say that all the damage done to the body of Roderick Duquesne was effected by any human being or agency. I ask that they be excluded."

Judge Groat tapped the end of his pencil against his lower teeth, frowning at Benson. Without turning his head, he said, "Mr. Sayer?"

"Well," the prosecutor said slowly, "the defense has offered an imaginative and ingenious argument, I will say that." He brushed a hand back over his head, being careful not to muss his hair.

"No," the judge said bluntly, "you will not say that, Mr. Sayer. I did not invite your comment on Mr. Kellogg's argument. I asked if you wish to say anything further in support of your own position."

"Of course, I do, Your Honor," Sayer insisted, visibly annoyed. "I don't want to weary the court with repetitious argument, however. Defense counsel has been ingenious, but he has not been persuasive. The People, as I said earlier, have both precedent and sound procedure on their side. These photographs represent a major element in the People's case. I ask that the court admit them in evidence."

Judge Groat slid back in his deep chair. With the tip of his pencil he flipped open the cover of his leather notebook and turned two pages. He wrote several lines in an old man's shaky hand. He put his pencil down briefly and looked from Benson to Frank Sayer and back again.

"The objection is sustained. The photographs in question are excluded."

Both attorneys stood immobile before the bench.

"Mr. Clerk," the judge said briskly, "we will take fifteen minutes. You may then summon the jury." He rose, wrapped his gown around his legs and went quickly down the steps to the door of his chambers.

FRANK SAYER made a savage, incoherent sound in his throat. He swung away from the bench and went quickly back to his table.

"Oh, that was marvelous, Mr. Kellogg!" Mary said in a swift, excited gush. "I was holding my breath!"

"That's quite a judge we've got, Mary," Benson said quietly. "He's a lot sharper than I've been led to believe. I expected I'd have to spend all morning on this, but he was ahead of me all the way." He looked over Mary's head to Turo, smiling at the boy's quirked, admiring glance.

"You caught him coming right into the punch, didn't you?" Turo said. "Are the pictures important?"

"Not very, Turo. You go along with the deputy. I want to talk to Mary for a minute."

The boy got up readily and let Deputy Monahan lead him toward the staircase.

"I won't need you any more this morning, Mary. Probably not until late this afternoon. I'll want you on hand when we start fighting admission of the confession. You have my list of citations?"

"Yes, Mr. Kellogg. I've got everything ready."

"Good girl. Pack everything in a box or bag or something and make sure I have it this afternoon. The rest of the morning will be routine stuff, just a lot of sniping from ambush. You go along if you like. I imagine you've got a stack of work waiting for you in the office?"

"Well," Mary touched the back of her head with an exploring hand, twisting a dangling lock of hair. "I suppose I should— I hate to leave," she said with a rush, "but I'd better, I guess." She collected her handbag and file case and got to her feet. She took one step toward the door, turned and came back. "That's a very strange boy, Mr. Kellogg. The Campeón boy. Have you noticed?"

"Noticed what?" Benson frowned.

"I don't know how to say it. He's so—so detached. As if it was somebody else being tried and he was just here to watch. He—he isn't worried enough!"

"I've noticed, Mary," Benson said. "But I'm doing worrying enough for two, so the longer he stays out of it, the easier it will be. Let's not borrow trouble, Mary. Maybe he's just got a lot of self-control. It might not be natural, but it certainly is helpful just now."

"Well. If you say so, Mr. Kellogg." Mary gave him an uncertain smile and left by the side entrance, passing Turo as he returned with his guard. The jury shuffled in from their conference room and took seats in the box. They sat there blinking, each with a thoughtful scowl, obviously wondering what the devil had happened to Kleinschmidt and his photographs and wishing they could get away for a minute to buy a paper or ask someone what was going on.

Benson surveyed the jury impassively, inwardly delighted at the response he could sense in them. The pictures were not important, as he had told the boy. The jurors had earlier been told of the grievous wounds on Duquesne's body and Benson had seen their shocked faces. So he could not pretend that in excluding the pictures he had kept damaging evidence from them. But he had taken the first useful step in countering the prosecution's case—he had shown the jury that Frank Sayer was not entirely the dispassionate seeker after truth that he wanted the jury to think him. Although the jury did not know what had been decided about the photographs Sayer had offered, they would soon hear that the judge had excluded them. They would be less than human if they did not begin to ask themselves questions about the other elements of Sayer's case against Arturo Campeón. They would feel that the prosecution had probably been caught trying to sneak one over, and from now on they would be looking at Sayer with a more skeptical eye.

When Judge Groat signaled the County Attorney to resume his presentation of evidence, it was apparent to Benson that Frank also understood clearly what the setback had done to his prestige with the jury. He went carefully to work rebuilding his image.

He stood quiet and brooding in the broad band of sunlight that touched the floor in front of the jury box. He studied the jurors soberly, letting them see the unbowed figure of a man stalwart enough to withstand any anguish, any unfair treatment, if only he could present to them the simple, honest truth. He told the clerk to call Deputy Sheriff Houston Shriner. He waited patiently in front of the jury.

The deputy came forward from the hallway door. He shambled past the defense table, looking blindly forward. The knobs of his spine were visible under the fabric of his old, washed-soft shirt. He was thin and dried-out, with the emaciated quality that suggests chronic undernourishment. He raised a big-knuckled hand to take the oath. He climbed to the stand and settled himself on the edge of the chair.

He looks familiar, Benson thought. Then the man turned his head slightly and Benson remembered him. Shriner was the snarling, gun-slapping deputy who had tried to block him away from Lookout Point last Friday. He didn't look nearly so ferocious now, sitting there without his gun belt, running his hand along the railing and watching Frank Sayer with a flat, unwavering stare.

Turo's left hand reached across outside his bulky cast. A finger poked at Benson's elbow. Benson leaned over.

"That's the one," the boy whispered tightly, in a quick, animated tone that Benson had not heard from him since the trial started. "The deputy. He's the sonofabitch who kept hitting me when I was in the hospital."

"When they were trying to get a confession? That one?"

The boy nodded, keeping his eyes fixed hard and angrily

on the man in the witness box.

"Okay. Stop glaring at him. Sit back and leave him to me." Benson poured a glass of water and pushed it along to the boy. He slid his chair back and folded his arms, sitting so that he could see the witness and still keep an eye on Turo. This might be a very bad moment for the boy. Benson didn't dare give him a chance to explode. He could almost feel the tension in him. At the periphery of his vision he could see Frank Sayer approaching the witness.

The deputy had to say his name twice before it came out clearly. In an easy, businesslike manner, Sayer took him through the formal preliminaries, and by the time he was ready to put the important questions, Deputy Shriner had his nervousness under control and was answering firmly, at a normal volume. Shriner was a deputy of nine years' experience, a residence of Rincon County ("born in Conejo Canyon," he volunteered) and was principally assigned to traffic control. He had also been used as an investigator.

"That dirty sonofabitch," Turo muttered.

"Hold it," Benson said sharply. He put his hand on the boy's shoulder. "Leave it to me, boy. Just sit tight."

The judge tapped his pencil and turned in clear warning to glare at Benson.

"Your Honor," Frank Sayer said, "if the defense will allow me to——"

"Proceed, please, Mr. Sayer," Judge Groat said impatiently. "Let's have no colloquy."

"Of course, Your Honor." Sayer made a slow, stately bow and went back to his witness. "Tell the court, Deputy Shriner, where you were at approximately four thirty A.M. on the fourteenth of April."

"Parked on patrol two miles north of the city limits on Route Forty-seven," the deputy said in the measured singsong of a man parroting a rehearsed sentence.

"Why were you there?"

"Checking on speeders."

"And at the time in question, what happened?"

"This big fancy Rolls come bustin' down from the Cobres. My partner clocked it doin' about seventy-five, so we run out to flag him down."

"And did you intercept the car?"

Shriner shook his head. He hooked a finger in the collar of his shirt and ran it around. "Dint have to," he said in a satisfied tone. "That Rolls went plumb off the road and flipped."

"And what did you do then?" Sayer asked with an unusual patience.

"Went back and put out some flares and then went to see was the driver still alive."

"Go on, Deputy. Just tell it in your own words. Was the driver alive?"

"Sure he was. That's him settin' over there. He was bunged up pretty bad, but he was alive, all right."

In spite of Sayer's urging, Shriner would tell his story only in terse replies to specific questions. Sayer handled him gently, showing no sign of the irritation he felt. This was no time to distract the jury with brusque impatience. He led Shriner through his account with an understanding tolerance, but it took a long time.

Deputy Shriner had radioed for an ambulance, he said, after finding the driver of the wrecked Rolls Royce still alive. The only ambulance available was out on call, so Shriner and his partner took the driver to the hospital in their patrol car and stayed with him while he was checked in, stripped and carried to the emergency ward. Shriner identified the defendant, Arturo Campeón, as the driver after a long squinting inspection.

"Him, all right," he said flatly. For the first time, he smiled.

"What happened to the defendant's belongings?"

"I took charge of them," Shriner said. "Made up a list and put everythin' in a sack."

"I now show you a cigarette lighter," Frank Sayer said, picking it up from the reporter's table. "It is solid gold," he went on, savoring the phrase, "solid gold, and it is marked,

R. D. on the side. Can you tell the court whether you have seen this lighter before?"

"Took it off'n the Mex kid yonder," Shriner said.

"Objection," Benson snapped.

"Sustained," Judge Groat agreed quickly. "You will control your witness, Mr. Sayer. We will have no more of that."

"If you want to refer to the defendant, you will call him the defendant, or use his name. Is that clear, Deputy?" Sayer demanded with a cold savagery.

"Yes, sir. I dint mean——"

"I don't care what you meant. Answer the question and answer it properly. Where did you previously see this lighter which I have in my hand?"

Shriner gave a surly growl. He tipped his head toward the boy. "The—the defendant yonder had it in his pants pocket," he said in a mumbling tone.

"Speak more clearly, Deputy. The jury can't hear you. This solid gold lighter, marked R. D., was found by you in the defendant's pocket. Is that right?"

"Yes, sir."

"And did you search all his other pockets?"

"Yes, sir."

"Did you find any cigarettes?"

"No, sir. Not a——"

"Just answer the question. Did you find any cigars or pipe tobacco?"

"No, sir."

"You did not find anything to smoke, but you did find this solid gold lighter, marked R. D. in the defendant's possession?"

"Yes, sir."

"I now present this solid gold lighter marked R. D. for inspection by the defense." Sayer held it high and crossed the floor toward Benson, moving with a noticeable swagger.

"No objections," Benson said shortly. He did not touch the lighter.

"The exhibit may be accepted in evidence," the judge said.

"And now, Deputy," Frank Sayer said in a louder voice, "I wish to show you another exhibit and ask if you can identify it for the court?"

He held the jury's attention as he whirled dramatically to the table, tore open a sealed envelope and tipped a long dark switchblade knife out into his open palm. He carried it pinched between two fingers as he came along the front of the jury box.

Now it comes, Benson thought, watching the faces of the jurors. Every eye was on the knife which Sayer held balanced in his hand.

Benson gathered himself in his chair. He was going to make a damn fool of himself, but there was no hope for it.

Sayer approached the witness stand very deliberately. He brought the knife slowly down.

"Your Honor," Benson called.

The concentration was broken, not completely and not for long, but at least Frank Sayer would have to work to rebuild it.

Judge Groat turned, frowning.

"The light from that window, Your Honor," Benson said, pointing to the glaring band that lay across his table. "It is blinding me. May I ask the court——"

"Your Honor!" Frank Sayer roared. "These interruptions are ridiculous! Defense counsel has no right——"

Judge Groat rattled the tip of his pencil against the base of the bronze lamp. His hooded eyes closed briefly as if he prayed for patience. "The clerk will adjust the blinds," he said thinly. "Defense counsel will be good enough to make his requests at more opportune moments. The prosecution will proceed, Mr. Sayer."

Frank Sayer stood hunch-shouldered beside the bench, half turned from the jury box. His big body broke the shaft of light and made a shadow over Benson's table. Sayer was staring at Judge Groat with a curious, tight-lipped expression that was more speculative, Benson thought, than angry.

With a sudden flash of insight, Benson thought he understood what was in Frank's mind. At times this morning Judge

Groat had seemed to be wryly amused whenever Frank Sayer lost a point. The judge was not giving Benson any undue advantage, but he did appear to cut Frank off in midcomplaint with a certain uncharitable speed. What had caused that? Benson wondered. A falling-out of political allies? It might be. Who could have better, deeper reasons for dislike?

Sayer waited until the clerk had found a window pole to brace the slatted blind back against its frame. When the clerk had finished, the prosecutor turned toward his witness again.

He went through much the same procedure with the knife, though he did not now command the same hushed attention. When he snapped the blade open with shocking suddenness, he got his reward. In ragged unison, the jury gave a startled gasp.

Deputy Shriner identified the knife, said the blood stains visible on the blade had been there when he had found it in the defendant's pocket. Frank Sayer demonstrated the spring catch several times during his interrogation. Benson did not dare to object. He signaled Turo to sit up straight.

The knife was accepted in evidence and the bad moment was finally over. But it had been very bad, Benson knew, as he watched the stiff, troubled faces of the jury. From time to time they shot quick, almost furtive, glances at the boy and when they did, their expressions became masked and secretive, blankly sober.

Frank Sayer had been studying the jury too, and he further emphasized the impact of that wickedly curved fighting knife by leaving it, blade open, clearly in sight on a corner of the court reporter's desk. He asked the judge for a moment to study his notes.

In the stillness of the courtroom the prosecutor moved to his table and bent over an open notebook, his back to the jury. A shrill murmur rose for a moment among the spectators and died away by itself before the clerk could lift his gavel.

Benson sat straight and easy in his chair, making senseless notations on a pad, inwardly fuming. Frank Sayer was getting every ounce of advantage out of that knife and there was not a damn thing Benson could do about it. Any action now would merely add to Sayer's advantage. And, he suspected, Judge Groat would probably kick him out of court if he interrupted again without good reason.

Finally Frank Sayer straightened. He picked up a small card and came back toward Shriner.

"Now, on the following day, Deputy, or the late afternoon of the same day, I should say, did you——"

Judge Groat tapped his lamp with his pencil.

"Mr. Sayer, since you seem to have concluded one section of this witness' testimony, perhaps this might be a good time for us to break for lunch." He nodded to the clerk and rose eagerly with the sound of the gavel.

"NOT SO GOOD, huh?" Turo asked under his breath. His eyes followed Shriner as the lanky deputy climbed down from the stand and crossed toward the prosecutor.

"It wasn't good," Benson muttered. He was watching the jury half fearfully, and as he had anticipated, several of them looked back at Turo as they were filing from the jury box. That was a bad sign at any time.

"They looked kinda scared when he popped that knife, didn't they?" Turo said.

Benson turned to him angrily. He opened his mouth, then closed it again, clamping his teeth hard together. The boy sounded grotesquely casual, as if he were watching a play in which some mildly interesting things had been happening. What in hell was wrong with him?

"Benson?" a voice called. "Benson, may I come inside?"

He swung his chair around. "Joss, what are you doing here? Come in, of course." He got up and opened the low gate in the railing for her. "Just a minute," he said. He motioned to Turo. "Go along with the deputy and get your lunch. Lie down for a while afterward. It's going to be a long day."

He loaded his briefcase quickly and left it on the clerk's desk. He came back and took Joss Gilbert's arm in a warm, close grasp.

"My God, you look good," he said softly. "New hat?"

"New everything," she smiled. "Drumming up trade. Anybody who is anybody is attending court these days."

"You were here? What for? I thought——"

"Well, if you're going charging at windmills, I want to see how it all comes out," she said with a mocking glance that had in it the faint, saving hint of malice. "You're doing better than I expected."

"Win a little, lose a little," Benson said. He led her down the long aisle toward the door. "We made some yardage with the photographs, but that knife was a kick in the teeth."

"Yes, it was, wasn't it? I was watching the jury."

"So was I."

"Are they likely to——"

"Not here," Benson said in a quick, warning tone. He made a gesture at the crowd slowly moving out of the courtroom. "Can you have lunch with me?"

"I was hoping you might ask me," Joss said. "That's really why I wore my fancy new clothes. I didn't know if you could take time out for lunch in the middle of a trial."

"I've got an hour," Benson said. "And I've done all my homework. Last-minute cramming isn't much use unless you're looking for something specific. Frank is still at bat. All I can do is throw him my fast curve and hope he'll pop up."

Joss paused at the top of the courthouse steps, shielding her eyes from the dazzle of sun in the streets. "But it isn't actually much like a ball game, is it?" She studied Benson, candidly concerned. "I saw Frank when he was waving that knife. He was like an animal. It's the first time I ever realized that a trial is actually a kind of warfare."

Benson nodded soberly. "It's supposed to be a search for truth, with the judge acting as referee. It works out to be trial by combat. A battle of wits. It's our system and it's probably the best system any people ever developed. But it still isn't very good."

Joss touched his hand lightly. She was seeing him now with a heightened awareness, as if they were strangers newly met. It was his quality of self-containment, she felt, that would keep him always partially a stranger to everyone. The long planes of his facial muscles seemed unresponsive to nervous stimuli, holding, even in animation, a grave, reflective stillness. It was the face of a man who could seldom allow himself the solace of flinching, and to Joss that was a disturbing incapacity. She gripped his hand tightly.

"You are worried, aren't you?" she said, half surprised. "I've never known you to be so worried before. What is it, Ben?"

Benson smiled with a slow reluctance. He led her down the steps and across to the shaded side of the street. "You're getting pretty sensitive to my moods, Joss."

"I always have been, Ben. That doesn't mean I like being that way. I prefer men to be responsive to me. Tell me, Ben."

He shook his head. "Nothing to tell. A case of buck fever, probably. Nothing tangible, anyway. Sure, I'm a little jittery, I guess. I'm responsible for that boy's defense. If I goof, I can't just shake his hand and apologize."

"But when you mentioned the jury, I got the impression you had something more concrete in mind."

"Maybe I do," Benson admitted slowly. "A jury is twelve different people, but after a while it develops a single, collective personality. I can't get the feel of this jury. There is sometimes a certain advantage to the defense in having the prosecution open a trial because the extra time gives the defense a better chance to sense the mood of the jury. But with this one—I just don't know."

"What are you looking for?"

"It's hard to explain, Joss. Whenever you try a case you always know that every juror will be asking himself two questions about the defendant. Is he guilty? Do I want to see him punished? The two questions are not always answered the same way. In this case, I'm beginning to suspect the jury is edging toward a decision on the second question without even considering the first. Do you see what I mean?"

"Tell me."

"When Frank flashed that knife, something happened to everyone on that jury. I think that, right this minute, they'd like to see the boy punished. For something. I think they are building up a sense of general antagonism toward him. They just don't like him."

"No, they don't. Do you like him, Ben?"

Benson stopped suddenly, looking at her. He did not answer.

A CREW of county maintenance men was just leaving the courtroom as Benson entered by the side door. He stood aside to let them pass in line, each gripping a section of a long ladder. Benson looked at the last window, noticed the new, startlingly white blind, and grinned. The judge was giving him no further excuse for interruption.

The afternoon atmosphere of the courtroom was sluggish, almost somnolent, as it always was. The coolers were running full blast, the overhead fans rumbling drowsily, and now the direct sunlight had moved away from the windows. Yet the long, high-ceilinged room was overly warm and stuffy. The jurors would be falling asleep if the trial began to drag.

Judge Groat arrived with an air of bustling efficiency, as if he alone could be trusted to keep the trial moving along with no dawdling nonsense. He brought the court to order, recalled Deputy Shriner himself, reminded him that he was still under oath and gestured for Frank Sayer to pick up the questioning again. He leaned forward, pencil in hand.

Frank Sayer was on his feet, ready. "I was asking you, Deputy Shriner," he said, "about the events of late Sunday afternoon, April fourteenth. You were on duty at that time, were you not?"

Shriner nodded. He cleared his throat noisily and tried again. After a couple of words his voice steadied. "Yes, sir, I was," he said thinly.

"What was your assignment at that time?"

"Answering the phone. Squeal phone, they call it. For when people call in to complain about sumthin or other."

"You had been on patrol duty most of the night and you were still on duty late that afternoon? Why was that?"

"Well, it was Sunday," Shriner said with a little shrug. "Married men like to git home Sundays. Me, I got no family. I fill in for a couple hours after I have me a nap."

Frank Sayer smiled at him approvingly. "Fine," he said warmly. "Fine. Now, Deputy, tell the court what happened that afternoon, in reference to the defendant, Arturo Campeón."

"Well, along about four thirty, Al Aldridge called in on the radio."

"That was Deputy Alvin Aldridge?"

"Yes, sir. Deputy Aldridge. He was out at Lookout Point. Had a dead body there. Aldridge said the dead man was somebody called Roderick Duquesne. Well, sir, it just so happened that I was down to the county garage about noon when the tow car dragged in that wrecked Rolls, so I——"

"One moment, Deputy," Sayer broke in hastily. "This Rolls-Royce you refer to was the same car which you saw the defendant crash on Route Forty-seven earlier that morning?"

"The very same one," the deputy agreed. "I never in my life seen a car like it. Well, when I was on my way back to the office, the tow-car man said could I carry his report in with me. Which I done. Report had the name of the owner on it."

"The name of the man that owned the Rolls-Royce?"

"Yes, sir. You're right. There was a registration card on the steering post, like there has to be in California. Man's name was Roderick Duquesne."

"I see. So when Deputy Aldridge told you the name of the

dead man he found on Lookout Point, what did you do?"

"Naturally, I told him we picked up the fellow that killed——"

"Your Honor!" Benson came to his feet in truculent objection.

Judge Groat smacked his hand down angrily. He nodded to Benson. "One moment, Mr. Kellogg." He turned to the court reporter. "You will strike that answer. The jury is instructed to disregard it."

Frank Sayer brought his clenched fists up on his hips. He inclined forward, glaring incredulously at his witness.

"Very well, Mr. Kellogg," the judge said.

Benson rose. His voice was thin with strain. "The witness on the stand, Your Honor, is no ordinary witness. He is an experienced deputy who has been trained in the behavior expected of witnesses. He cannot be considered an ordinary witness who may have stepped over the bounds through ignorance. Nothing excuses what he has done. His answer was prejudicial in the extreme. It is my opinion that it was meant to be."

"You need not labor the point, Mr. Kellogg," Judge Groat said. "Are you making an objection, or a motion?"

Benson hesitated. It was tempting, especially as he saw the frozen intensity of Sayer's expression, but Benson put the temptation aside. The deputy's statement alone was not adequate grounds for a mistrial. If Benson moved for a ruling, it would surely be denied. He would, of course, have a chance to debate it and his argument might do something to counteract the effect of Shriner's testimony. But not enough, he decided.

"I am making an objection, Your Honor," he said finally. "Mr. Sayer should not——"

"Objection sustained," the judge said impatiently. "You may leave Mr. Sayer to me." His lowered head swung toward the County Attorney and his heavy eyebrows pulled together. "Mr. Sayer," he said in a biting tone, "I am shocked and surprised that an attorney of your experience and merit should permit this display. I shall have more to say to you later. I now warn you that if your witness once more violates the rules

« 374 »

of this court, I shall hold you equally responsible with him. As for you, Mr. Witness, watch your step. Another violation will send you to jail for contempt. This court finds your behavior inexcusable and will so inform your superiors. You will proceed, Mr. Sayer, if you please."

"Yes, Your Honor," Frank Sayer said in a subdued voice. "May I tender my sincere apologies to the court? I would like to associate myself completely with the opinion Your Honor has expressed of this witness' behavior. Now then, Deputy, think before you speak again. What did you tell Deputy Aldridge when he called you on Sunday afternoon?"

Deputy Shriner could not speak. The savage disapproval of the judge and of both attorneys had struck at him with the shock of a flash flood. He swept a trembling hand across his sweaty forehead. He licked his dry lips. He tried to swallow, and even across the room Benson could hear the brittle click in his throat.

"You told Deputy Aldridge that the registered owner of the wrecked Rolls-Royce was Roderick Duquesne. Is that correct, Deputy?"

Shriner nodded. His mouth opened as if he had spoken, but there was no sound.

Frank Sayer motioned to the clerk. He stepped back and let the clerk approach the witness stand with the thermos of water he always kept on hand for stricken witnesses. Shriner gulped from the paper cup. He gave it back to the clerk with an awkward movement, letting it drop before the clerk could catch it. The cup clattered hollowly on the floor. The clerk kicked it aside and went back to his place.

"Is that correct, Deputy?" Sayer asked again.

Shriner nodded once. "Yes, sir," he said hoarsely.

"Try to speak louder, Deputy. Now, what action did you take as a result of your conversation with Deputy Aldridge?"

"Went—went to the County——" Shriner coughed. He wiped his mouth with the edge of his hand. "Went to meet him at the County Hospital," he said more clearly.

"You went to meet Deputy Aldridge at Rincon County Hospital. Why? In response to his request?"

"Yes, sir," Shriner said.

"Why did he want you with him?"

"Because it was me that picked up the—the defendant in the first place. I knowed about the car and—and all."

"Yes, I see. Did you then go to the County Hospital and did you there meet Deputy Aldridge in the prison ward of the hospital?"

"Yes, sir."

"And what did you do there?"

Shriner looked at Benson from the corner of his eye. He pursed his dry lips, then said, "Talked to the defendant."

"Did the defendant make any statement in your presence?"

Judge Groat turned even before Benson had come to his feet. His expression put the question.

"Yes, Your Honor," Benson said promptly. "The defense certainly does object to any reference to any alleged statement."

Judge Groat closed one eye. He lined up the tip of his pencil with Benson's head, like a gunner handling an aiming stake. "On what grounds?" he asked.

"May we approach the bench, Your Honor?"

Judge Groat pushed his chair back slightly. "Come up, Mr. Kellogg," he said in a resigned tone. "Mr. Sayer?"

The attorneys met at the side-bar, maintaining a space between them of several discreet inches. Deputy Shriner watched them suspiciously, his scrawny neck twisted hard around.

"Well, Benson," the judge said, "let's have it."

"No statement has ever been made voluntarily by the defendant, Your Honor," Benson said flatly. "The defense requests a hearing to that point, without the jury."

Frank Sayer snorted heavily. "Oh, Christ," he muttered.

"Objections, Frank?" the judge asked.

"It's a damn waste of time," Sayer growled.

"The two authorities are Wigmore and McCormick," Benson said equably. "They agree that the trial judge should always exclude the jury and hear evidence on both sides. I can cite three local and recent cases to support their opinion."

"It won't be necessary," Judge Groat said with a trace of a smile. "Frank isn't objecting; he's just complaining. How long will it take? Any estimate, Frank?"

"Shouldn't take long," Sayer said, shrugging. "I will have four witnesses. Three, I mean," he amended hastily. "They are ready and waiting."

"You came prepared, I see," the judge said dryly.

"I saw this coming," Sayer agreed.

"I know why you saw it coming, Frank," Benson said tightly. "Because I told you it was coming. Remember? And there's another reason too. Would you like me to tell the judge?"

"All right, all right," Judge Groat said quickly. "Let's get to work, gentlemen. We'll take a break and give the jury a chance to withdraw delicately." He grinned suddenly, fiercely, and lifted a finger for the clerk. "The jury will retire until summoned," he announced. "We will take ten minutes, Mr. Clerk."

"TAKE A BREAK, Turo. Go stretch for a while," Benson said. "This is the big one coming up."

"Okay." Turo stood and flicked a thumb over his shoulder for the deputy.

Benson reached down for the flat carton in which Mary had packed his reference material. He stacked a double row of books along the edge of the table and laid three manila folders beside them. He shoved the box under the table.

And where, he asked himself, is our wandering Mary? It's going to be a hell of a chore to chase references and argue at the same time. He shifted irritably, looked up and made himself smile reassuringly at Mary's flustered, apologetic dash across from the doorway.

"Oh, Mr. Kellogg," she said breathlessly. "I'm so sorry! I got caught at——"

"Plenty of time, Mary." Benson poured a glass of water for her. "Sit back and catch your breath. I'm going out for a smoke. Back in a minute."

Benson put up his hand to wave the reporters back as he went out. They were forever trying. They figured they just might catch him in a talkative mood some time. But not today. He slipped along the crowded corridor to the first door and then out into the open courtyard. He lit a cigarette while he was walking down the narrow tiled path toward the central fountain. There was a low granite lip around the small pool. Benson propped a foot on it and leaned forward, blowing smoke rings into the rainbow spray.

It was a fine day. There was an immaculate sky and the sun was like new brass. It wasn't as warm as it had been the past few days. It was a day for riding easily through the springtime desert, for swimming in a mountain stream, for walking down the Rincon streets and watching the pretty girls.

A day, he reminded himself, to be getting the hell back to work. He took his cigarette stub to a sand jar near the door and went inside again, arriving in his place just as the judge was climbing up to his high platform.

"Mr. Sayer, are you ready?"

"Yes, Your Honor. I now call Deputy Sheriff Alvin Aldridge."

"One moment, if the court please," Benson said quickly. "There is already a witness on the stand, one that the defense has not yet had a chance to cross-examine."

The judge blinked. "Mr. Sayer?"

"This is an examination separate and distinct from the trial, Your Honor. Deputy Shriner will return to the stand after the court has ruled on the question of admissibility."

"The defense will insist upon a positive assurance that Deputy Shriner will be called as a witness during this examination," Benson said. "He is available now. He introduced this question himself, and I want a crack at him."

Judge Groat stood his pencil on end and wobbled it for a moment. "No, Mr. Kellogg," he said. "The People may present their evidence in whatever manner the County Attorney thinks best. Deputy Shriner, I believe, has already been subpoenaed as a defense witness?"

"Yes, Your Honor, but he is——"

"No, Mr. Kellogg," the judge said again. "Deputy Shriner is available to you in this hearing. You may call him yourself if the People do not. Proceed, Mr. Sayer."

Deputy Aldridge, having been sworn previously, took the stand, settled himself with his usual deliberation, and folded his arms. He would be an entirely different proposition from Shriner, his posture said. He was the sheriff's prize court man, the one who collected evidence, helped to prepare and present it, and could be trusted never to blow a case by losing his temper or by letting anyone confuse him about anything.

Frank Sayer established the background with a few brief questions. Deputy Alvin Aldridge had identified Duquesne's body on Lookout Point. He had then called the sheriff's office and been told by Shriner about the wrecked Rolls in the county garage and about the injured prisoner in the County Hospital. He had instructed Shriner to collect his partner and meet him at the hospital. His calm and skeptical expression suggested that he was sorry he'd ever thought of it, but nothing in his words or voice was directly critical of Shriner.

Aldridge and the others had met with the intern on duty, a Dr. Morris Elman, to determine whether the prisoner could safely be questioned. The doctor went with them to the ward where the prisoner was interrogated.

The session took only half an hour, due to defendant's weakened condition. Arturo Campeón was coherent and in command of himself, Aldridge maintained firmly. He freely confessed to killing Roderick Duquesne and to stealing a gold cigarette lighter. No threats or force were used. Campeón admitted he had been forced to kill because Duquesne had resisted while Campeón was trying to rob him at knifepoint.

Aldridge identified the confession Frank Sayer showed him. The defendant, Aldridge said, had signed it in the presence of himself and the doctor and the two other deputies, all of whose signatures appeared in the lower margin. The defendant had signed with a left-handed *X* because his right arm and collarbone had been broken and were bound in a cast. Aldridge then, in a slow and portentous monotone, read the brief confession.

"You may cross-examine," Sayer said to Benson. He handed him the confession and went back to his table.

"This is an unusually short and informal document, is it not, Deputy?" Benson asked. "Not the sort of detailed confession the sheriff's office normally offers in a trial?"

"It is short," Aldridge admitted warily.

"Come now, Deputy. I asked if it was not informal and unusual. Didn't you understand the question?"

"I understood, sir," Aldridge said. "It is not the routine form of confession. May I explain?"

"I was about to insist," Benson said wryly. "Explain, please."

"I went to the hospital unprepared, sir," Aldridge said. "Deputy Shriner told me about the prisoner in the hospital and about the wrecked car. Naturally, I tied it all together in my mind and I thought I'd better get right over there. I came straight from Lookout Point. I had a notebook, but none of the people with me could work a typewriter or take shorthand, so I wrote out a very brief statement myself. The defendant signed it."

"In the presence of the people whose names appear on the confession?"

"Yes, sir."

"Were all those people present at all times during the entire interrogation?"

Aldridge thrust out his lower lip and drew it in slowly. "I —am not sure, Mr. Kellogg. There was some moving around. We weren't there very long."

"Will you please answer the question I asked you, Deputy? Were the people who witnessed this document—Deputy Houston Shriner, Deputy Juan Montero, Dr. Morris Elman, and yourself—present during the entire period of the interrogation?"

"I don't remember, sir. I'm sorry. Dr. Elman was called away for a while, I recall. I think Deputy Shriner was present most of the time. Deputy Montero went out once."

"What about you? Were you present for the entire time?"

"No, sir. I stepped out for a minute."

"What for?"

"To answer a call of nature, sir," Aldridge said primly.

Benson waited for the inevitable titter to subside. He looked closely at Aldridge. "Do you know, Deputy, I am getting a very peculiar impression from your testimony. Apparently no one of your witnesses can tell us about the interrogation. Am I right in saying that?"

"Not exactly, sir. But their signatures indicate that they were present when the defendant signed the confession, that's all."

Benson rubbed the edge of his chin with his thumb. "So we are offered four witnesses to a confession but not one of them is qualified to tell the court what went on in that ward while Arturo Campeón was being questioned. Is that right?"

"No, sir," Aldridge said patiently. "One of us can tell you about every minute. But all four of us can't. What I mean is——"

"Never mind, Deputy. The court is aware of what you mean. I ask you now if this peculiar situation was deliberately contrived by you?"

"Deliberately?" Aldridge stared, blankly innocent. "There's nothing unusual about it, Mr. Kellogg. Routine procedure, you might call it."

"No, that's not what I'd call it, Deputy. I'd say it was something close to criminal conspiracy."

"Your Honor!" Frank Sayer shouted. "Counsel has no right to abuse this witness."

"Objection sustained," Judge Groat said wearily. "You know better than that, Mr. Kellogg. Let's have no more of it."

"I'm sorry, Your Honor. Now, Deputy, let's explore this peculiar and unusual situation a step further. If I told you that two minutes after you began questioning Arturo Campeón he had been beaten by one of the men present, what would you say?"

"I would say that was a lie, sir," Aldridge said promptly.

"Why do you say that? Were you there?"

"Yes, sir."

"That's what I've been trying to find out, Deputy. Were you also present during all of the preceding two minutes?"

"Yes, sir."

"We have managed to isolate two minutes. Now we have a witness to that time. We are going to cover the entire half hour in two-minute sections, Deputy. As I call them out I want to know if you were present, and for how long. When we have your movements charted, we will consider the other players in this game of musical chairs. Now, let's hear about the second two-minute period, Deputy. Were you present—or absent?"

It went on for more than an hour. Aldridge could not be shaken. He was often vague, sometimes deliberately so, Benson thought, but not to a degree that wasn't consistent with the normal confusion of any witness. He insisted that at least two of the four witnesses had been present during each two-minute period that Benson called out with his sharp, demanding "Present—or absent?"

Aldridge was not to be shaken, but by the time he had left the stand, his testimony had taken on a characteristic flavor he had not intended. He had flatly denied that any threats or coercion had been applied when he was present. His answers had been straightforward, seemingly candid, but somehow they dangerously skirted the border of downright evasion. Benson glanced at the closed, thoughtful face of Judge Groat before he dismissed the deputy. Aldridge's adroit testimony had left Benson with no lever to use; he could do nothing more with the man. But there would be other witnesses, and it was not likely that they would all have Aldridge's training or impervious composure.

Dr. Morris Elman came and went quickly. He had accompanied the three deputies to the prison ward, ascertained that the defendant was in condition to answer questions, and had then withdrawn. He had returned about fifteen minutes later, checked the patient again, and gone away again. He had been summoned when the confession was ready. He had seen the defendant make his mark and had then signed as a subscribing witness to that act. When the deputies left the ward, the defendant had been resting comfortably. The doctor smiled when he said that.

Benson made the doctor explain in detail the injuries the boy had sustained—four ribs, right collarbone, right arm, all broken; multiple lacerations and contusions, including a long and jagged scalp wound. He had been given sedatives when he had been brought in, but the doctor insisted their effect had worn off before he had been questioned.

Benson stared at him for a long moment. "I hope to God, Doctor," he said very quietly, "that you are someday heartlessly abandoned when you are in need of help, as you abandoned the boy you were supposed to protect. Now get off that stand, Doctor." He made a snarl of the last word.

Dr. Elman went away with a dazed expression. What had he done? What was everybody so hot about?

Judge Groat gestured for Benson. He leaned forward and spoke softly, and very decisively. "Easy, Benson," he said. "Stop making speeches to the witnesses, or I'll have to stop you."

"Yes, sir. Man to man, Judge, what do you——"

"No, Benson. In this court I'm not a man. I'm a judge and I'm telling you what to do. You go do it."

"Yes, sir."

Deputy Houston Shriner shuffled to the stand and took his seat with a pained slowness, as if he knew what was in store for him.

Frank Sayer had only a few questions to put to him. Shriner had been in and out of the ward during the interrogation, he said. There had been no force or threats of force used in his presence. He had heard the prisoner admit his guilt and had later witnessed him making his mark. Frank Sayer nodded to Benson.

« *383* »

"Who actually wrote this document, Deputy?" Benson asked, holding up the confession.

"Why, uh, Deputy Aldridge wrote it out," Shriner said.

"But you were holding a metal automatic pencil all the time you were present, were you not?"

"I—uh, maybe I was."

"Answer the question, Shriner," Benson said. "Remember you are under oath. Speak up. Were you holding a pencil?"

"I had a pencil," Shriner said slowly. His thin face was drawn and gray and ugly.

"What for?"

"What?"

"I said, 'What for?' Why did you have a pencil?"

"Why, I don't know. I just did. All deputies got to carry a pencil."

"What were you doing with the pencil?"

Shriner shook his head. "Nothing."

Benson stepped back. He went to his table and took the glass of water Mary handed him and drank it down. He turned, bracing both hands on the edge of the table and leaning back. He spoke to Shriner from there.

"Let's get the picture straight, Shriner," he said. "The defendant was lying in a hospital bed, cranked up high. He was almost sitting upright. You were standing at his right side near the head of the bed. Deputy Aldridge was sitting in a chair beside the bed, on the left side. Deputy Montero was standing at the foot of the bed, and Dr. Elman whipped in and out without stopping anywhere for long. Have I got it right?"

Shriner nodded cautiously. "That's how it was sometimes."

"Well, those are the times I'm talking about," Benson said. He came slowly forward toward the stand. "You are standing at the head of the bed. You have a pencil in your hand. Right?"

"Yes, I guess so."

"What portion of the defendant's anatomy was closest to you, Shriner?"

"Huh, why, I don't—" Shriner pulled his chin in tightly— "don't believe I particularly noticed," he muttered.

"You were standing at the head of the bed, on the right side, and you didn't notice," Benson said incredulously. "Do you expect anyone to believe that? Look at the defendant, Shriner. He's sitting over there behind me. Look at him."

Shriner turned an alarmed stare toward Turo.

"What do you see on his right shoulder?"

Shriner swallowed. "Cast," he said in a strained voice.

"A cast," Benson said. "Good for you. It's exactly the same cast he was wearing Sunday afternoon. But you don't remember. You were standing inches away from his right shoulder, according to your own testimony, all the time you were in the ward, but you can't recall that he was wearing a heavy white cast over his right shoulder and arm. Of course you had a pencil in your hand, didn't you? I suppose you were busy with the pencil?"

"What? I don't——"

"Never mind, Deputy, we'll come back to it. Now that you have been reminded that the defendant was wearing a cast over his right shoulder, I would like you to tell the court if you knew at that time what the cast was protecting." He saw Shriner blink with his habitual defensive bafflement, and went on. "Did you know what was under the cast, Deputy? Did anyone tell you? Did you bother to ask?"

"I object, Your Honor," Frank Sayer said, breaking in before Shriner could reply. "Witness has no competence in medical matters. This entire line of questioning is incompetent and immaterial."

"The prosecutor is mistaken again, Your Honor," Benson said with an edge of anger. "My question asks for human, not medical judgment. I want to know if this witness knew then that under the defendant's cast there was a broken collarbone and a broken arm, both of them exceedingly painful injuries. It seems to me a simple and relevant question, Your Honor. May I have his answer?"

"The witness will answer," Judge Groat said. He kept his narrowed eyes on Frank Sayer for a thoughtful moment.

"Well, Deputy?" Benson demanded.

"I—I knowed he was bunged up some," Shriner said hesitantly. "I dint rightly know how bad."

"You didn't care, either, did you?" Benson said in a deceptively mild voice. "You just stood there at his shoulder hitting him over the cast with that pencil. He passed out two or three times from the pain, but that didn't bother you, either, did it?"

"I object!" Sayer shouted.

"To what?" Benson turned to him belligerently. "Don't you have guts enough to let him answer?"

"I protest, Your Honor," Sayer said, reddening. "Counsel is bullying this witness and insulting——"

"I am trying to cross-examine a witness in a murder trial, Your Honor," Benson said with a fierce calm. "The court will recall that defense counsel was earlier reprimanded for interrupting. I now ask the court to reprimand the prosecutor for unwarranted and nonsensical objections that are merely designed to get his witness off the hook."

Judge Groat put his pencil down carefully. He blocked it against his notebook. He picked up his gavel, studied it for a while and then cracked it down smartly on its block. He waited with a baleful intensity for complete silence.

"I will say this only once," he announced softly. "I have permitted great latitude in this trial, recognizing that vital issues are at stake and tempers are often sorely tested. The court's patience has been exhausted. The next unrestrained outburst will result in citation for contempt. I consider both sides equally at fault. Your objection is overruled, Mr. Sayer. You will proceed, Mr. Kellogg. With caution."

The delay had given Shriner time to find a wavering determination. He denied that he had ever touched the defendant with his pencil or anything else. His voice cut out on him occasionally, as if his was a ghostly denial scored on an old Ediphone cylinder, but his answer, when it was audible, never changed. No threats or force had ever been used in his presence. It was past four-thirty when Benson gave up and dismissed him.

Shriner's usefulness to the sheriff's department was destroyed, but his fearful, self-protective testimony had not been broken.

Shriner came down from the stand hunch-shouldered, with an air of animal shyness. His bleached eyes watched Benson warily as he edged past and went toward the door, his feet flapping under weak ankles.

Benson sat in his chair and took another drink of water. Frank Sayer got to his feet, full of confidence. Shriner had been his weakest link, but even under Benson's savaging, his testimony had stood up.

Benson wished he had a cigarette. He wished he could think of something to wipe that fat smirk off Frank's fat face.

"Your Honor," Sayer said blandly, standing comfortably before the bench, hands locked behind his back. "The People have established the *prima facie* case required for admission of this confession. We will call no other witnesses."

Benson rose, startled. "What about Montero? I want him on the stand."

Frank Sayer smiled gently, pityingly. "Deputy Montero is on detached duty, Your Honor. The defense may call him, of course, if he has been served with a subpoena." He eyed Benson and his smile widened with malicious amusement. "Montero's name was not endorsed on the information," he added.

Which means, Benson thought with a sick awareness, that I booted one. I didn't subpoena Montero. It never occurred to me that Frank wouldn't call him. I didn't check and it's too late to do anything about it now. I don't know where the man is and it's a cinch Frank won't help me find him. I couldn't possibly get him here in time.

Benson forced a tight smile in acknowledgment. He wasn't going to let Frank know he had slipped one in under his guard. He sat again as if to consult his notes. He was looking at Turo out of the corner of his eye, trying to decide about him.

He had no substantive evidence to offer except for the boy's testimony. And how much weight would Judge Groat give to that when there were three prosecution witnesses to contradict it? Putting Turo on the stand would be a move of desperation, but what choice did he have?

He could limit the boy's testimony to the question of the confession, and Frank would not be allowed to cross-examine on any other aspect of the case. But he would be giving Frank a useful advantage, for the prosecutor had not yet had a chance to test the boy's intelligence and stamina under pressure. Giving Frank a practice session was not good sense. But, again, what was the alternative? If he let the issue go by default, the confession would be read to the jury, and then Turo would be cooked.

"Well, Mr. Kellogg, it rests with you," the judge reminded him. "The People have no further evidence. Does the defense wish to present a witness?"

"Your Honor," Benson said soberly, "the absence of the witness Montero is surprising and disturbing to the defense."

"It is your responsibility to subpoena defense witnesses, Mr. Kellogg."

"I realize that, Your Honor. I was not suggesting that Montero's absence is due to anything but a regrettable oversight. With time it could be rectified. It is now past four thirty, Your Honor, and I would like to request an adjournment at this time. Every effort will be made between now and tomorrow morning to locate Montero."

"It can't be done, Your Honor," Frank Sayer said positively. "Deputy Montero has been detailed to attend the highway patrol school at El Monte. He is due to report there tomorrow morning. Until then he is on leave and the sheriff's office does not know where to find him."

"The defense would like to try, Your Honor," Benson said urgently. "I recognize the request is unusual. However, the law in capital cases is tender of the defendant, and this could be extremely important to the defense. The only effect of an early adjournment would be the loss of half an hour of the court's time. It would not, in any event, be possible to conclude this examination today."

"Do you intend to call witnesses even if you do not succeed in locating Deputy Montero?" the judge asked.

"Yes, Your Honor."

Frank Sayer grinned suddenly. His eyes glinted as he looked at the defendant.

"The People have no objection, Your Honor," he said blandly. "I was merely pointing out that Mr. Kellogg may find it impossible to locate Montero and get him here by tomorrow morning. If the court feels the defense should be allowed to try, the People are agreeable."

"The People's wishes are not pertinent, Mr. Sayer," Judge Groat said in a tired voice. He wrote a line in his notebook and closed the cover. "Very well, Mr. Kellogg. The court will grant your request. I shall expect to see you here tomorrow morning prepared to conclude in a very short time. Is that clear?"

"Yes, Your Honor. I'm grateful."

A noisy bustle filled the court after the clerk gaveled for adjournment. Benson rummaged for a blank subpoena and sat to fill it out. He slid it across to Mary.

"Whip down to the sheriff's office with this, Mary. I'll see you at the office later."

"Yes, sir." Mary bent quickly to the floor to get her bag. She crammed a flat straw hat on the back of her head. "Do you want me to tell the sheriff anything special, Mr. Kellogg? About Montero, I mean?"

Benson shook his head wearily. "Don't bother, Mary. The subpoena is just a matter of form. The sheriff isn't going to find Montero. I doubt if he even tries."

"But then why——" Mary choked off her protest and blushed at her temerity.

"I just wanted to break off here," Benson explained. "Maybe I'll get a brilliant idea overnight. Maybe Frank Sayer will drop dead. Go along now, Mary. I'll be in later." He leaned past her to look at Turo. "Okay, boy?"

Turo nodded dully. He made a sketchy circle with his thumb and forefinger.

BENSON came down the corridor in a rush, his arms cramped and aching from the load of books and papers he was carrying. He went inside his office and let everything drop onto Mary's desk. Then he saw the two people waiting in the customers' chairs against the wall.

"You're late, Counselor," Blue said in an exaggeratedly buoyant tone. "Me and Harald were getting itchy, weren't we, pretty boy?"

Harald Elsinore glanced up at Benson. His eyes were inflamed, dark-rimmed. He pulled in a quick gasping breath and nodded jerkily.

"How are you feeling, Harald?" Benson asked quietly. "Are you all right?" He dragged a chair across and sat in front of Elsinore.

"Yes, thank you," Elsinore said in a reedy voice. "I've been—upset, but I'm all right now."

"He's been mourning his queen," Blue said with a harsh, barking laugh. "Real tender feelings, that's Harald." He wedged a cigarette in the corner of his wide mouth and squinted at Benson through the smoke.

Benson turned to look at him, frowning. The calm cheerfulness that had seemed to be Blue's basic quality had subtly altered and Benson wondered if that was because of Elsinore. A man like Blue might respond peculiarly to someone like Elsinore, he suspected, becoming aggressive and overly assertive, as if his masculinity were somehow threatened by Elsinore's mere existence. He turned back to Elsinore.

"I'm glad to hear you're all right, Harald," he said easily. "I've made a reservation for you at—" he hesitated, then went on smoothly—"at a local hotel. You can say good-bye to Mr. Blue."

"Not so fast, Counselor," Blue said abruptly. "Not so damn fast. Manny just ain't ready to say good-bye yet. There's maybe a couple things we want to talk about first."

"No," Benson said. "There's nothing to talk about. Goodbye, Blue."

Blue thumbed a folded envelope from his breast pocket and tapped it on the arm of his chair. "Message from the boss," he said with a small, cynical smile. He leaned over, took the cigarette from his mouth and ground it out in an ashtray. He straightened, breathing out a thick, pale streamer, still smiling. He scaled the envelope into Benson's lap. "Read it, Counselor. Then we'll talk."

Benson's face went pale and hard. He picked up the heavy envelope in fingers that were awkwardly slow. He held it up in both hands, looking over its edge at Blue. He tore it with a clumsy carefulness, as if he had to get it in two exact halves. He put the pieces together and tore it again. He got to his feet, took one step and flicked the scraps into Blue's chair.

Blue leaned back with a quizzical half-smile, cheerful and tolerantly indifferent. "I was supposed to get an answer," he said mildly.

Benson's voice was low and furious, tight with a depth of anger that was almost out of control. "You've got your answer," he said thickly. "You bring me one more message from Caine and I'll make you eat it."

"What the hell are you so mad about?" Blue asked. "It's just business, Counselor."

"My business, Blue. Not yours. And not Caine's. You are in my town now, Blue. You don't mean anything here. I could have you thrown into jail for what you've done, and if you give me one more smart word, I'll damn well do it."

"You serious?"

"If you're not out of my office in two seconds, I'll show you just how serious I am," Benson said.

Blue spread his legs and stretched them out. He brushed the scraps from his jacket and brought his heavy arms up over his head in a pose of complete relaxation. He grinned at Benson.

"Jesus, Counselor, you are a real old-fashioned desert tough when you get hot, ain't you? Tell you what I'm——"

Benson moved while he was talking. With one hand he

bunched up a wad of cloth on Blue's shoulder and jerked him from the chair in a staggering circle. He stepped back precisely, turning on his heel. He tucked his chin down as Blue swung a fist. When Blue was near the open door, he shoved and released his grip.

Blue reeled, off balance, into the hallway. His legs crossed and he tripped heavily to the floor. He rolled with the motion and came up swiftly in a lithe motion like a cat. His thick, sloped shoulders bunched under his coat. His face was dark and sullen, stupid with fury.

Office doors opened along the corridor and heads were thrust out, turned toward Blue as he moved in quick, padding steps toward Benson.

"What do you think you're doing?" someone shouted.

"Come on, Blue," Benson said softly. He braced himself in the doorway. "You've been spoiling for this since I first met you. Come and get it."

Blue stiffened. He lowered his arms slowly. He brushed one hand aimlessly down the front of his coat. His eyes came up and caught Benson's. "Another time, Counselor," he said in a choked voice. "Another place. Not on your own home ground. We'll settle this, don't think we won't." He took a long, endless breath and made his broad, tanned face stretch back in a strained and empty smile. "A pleasure, Counselor. I'll deliver your message."

Benson shrugged away the excited questions of the people in the corridor. He went back into his office and closed the door. He sat stiffly in the chair at his desk, looking at the floor. He braced his elbows on the desk, holding his face in hands that were still trembling with tension. He sat for a long moment, raging in his mind. When he was again his own man, he put his hands down and looked at Elsinore.

"Childish exhibition, wasn't it?" he said with a faint, self-mocking smile. "I don't think Blue and I are ever going to be friends."

"He is a vile man," Elsinore said shakily. "Detestable. You have no idea what he did to me when——"

Benson made a curt gesture. "We have a lot to talk about, Harald. Let's not waste time on Manny Blue. Do you have your bag with you? We'll walk over to your hotel. I want to tell you about the trial. You'll have to be ready to testify tomorrow or the day after. Let's go, Harald."

THE MOON was visibile very early that night, before the sky was solidly dark. The watery light it washed over the windows made them mirrors that held a vague and wavering image of the room. Beside Benson in the bed Jocelyn Gilbert lay breathing softly and regularly, her arm curled up behind her head, a wide band of pale hair spread across the pillow where it drifted hazily toward Benson.

He was thinking that he could remember with clear, sharp pleasure every moment they had spent together, especially the moments at night when he was briefly and completely master, then completely defeated in the roaring, pounding climax of the highest moment. She was eager, sweet, insistent. She was close to being perfect, he suspected. At least, she was for him.

"Happy?" she asked in a secret whisper.

"I thought you were sleeping."

"I was, for a minute. But I could tell you weren't. What are you thinking about, Ben?"

Benson shook his head. "I wasn't thinking. I was just lying here like a snake on a warm rock, being happy I was alive."

"You're tired, aren't you?" Her hand touched his lightly.

"No, I'm all right. A little depressed, I guess. Frank Sayer is making a chump out of me. That's enough to make anyone depressed."

"There's more to it than that."

"Yes, there is, but let's not talk about it, Joss."

"Tell me, please."

"I dump too much of it on you."

"No!" She rose up on her elbow, looking down at him. "No, you don't, Ben," she said earnestly. "That's just the trouble. You never tell me enough. I never know——" She smoothed back the heavy fall of long hair. "I'm sorry, Ben," she went on in a small, knowingly contrite voice. "I hate to prod you constantly. I just feel so lost sometimes. As if you didn't need me, or want me around."

"No, it's never that, Joss," Benson said slowly. "I'm not used to talking about—things like this. I'm learning. Give me time. A lot has been happening to me lately. I haven't had time to sort it out. Don't get impatient, Joss."

"I'm not, Ben. I just want to know we're together, actually, really together."

"There's not much doubt about that, is there?" Benson said with a soft laugh.

"You know what I mean, Ben."

"Of course I know. I want the same thing, Joss. I'm getting fed up with this hit-and-run stuff. It's been great, but now it's time we shifted gears."

"What are you saying, Ben?"

"I want you to marry me."

She lay back quietly, her profiled face shadowed and secret in the darkness. Moonlight touched the high curve of her hip and made it glow.

"Just me, Joss," Benson went on gently. "I want you to marry me. Not La Cañada and its people, not a law practice, or a certain way of living. I want you to marry me and live with me. I'm beginning to understand what you were getting at a while ago. I was drifting in a sort of half-life, I think. Half-lawyer, half-rancher. I wasn't anything all the way. I didn't care much about anything especially. I do now, Joss. I care about you. I love you. I think we'd be happy together."

"Oh, Ben!"

"Don't cry, Joss. I don't want——"

"Ben, you idiot, I'm not crying." She held her arms up to him. "Come here, Ben."

He moved warmly beside her and kissed her with a slow, gentle insistence.

"Can you stay, Ben? Please?"

"I should get back to the ranch tonight. I haven't been out there for the best part of a week. I need some fresh clothes."

"And you need to know that everything is running just right."

"I'm responsible for the ranch, Joss. You know that. I can't brush it aside. But I haven't thought about La Cañada for days. It isn't really any competition for——"

She silenced him with her hand across his lips. "I know, Ben. I do understand. I don't know why I have to be so bitchy about it. When are you going to marry me?"

Benson pushed up. He swung his bare feet to the cold tiles of the floor and sat there looking at her. "Soon, please," he said quietly. "When would you like, Joss?"

"Right now is what I'd like. But we'll wait till the trial is over and things are normal again. I don't want to marry a man with one eye on his law books." She rolled toward him and her hand touched him wantonly. "Do you have to go right now, Ben? Are you in a hurry?"

"Hurry?" he said, leaning down. "Who's in a hurry?"

She came to him with a surge of emotion that surprised him. He kissed her hair, cupping his trembling hands behind her head and holding her close.

BENSON drove fast through the night, whistling over the shrill sound of the desert wind. It was chill now and very clear, with a lowering moon that made the sterile earth shine like phosphorescent waves at sea. Beyond Kellogg Junction, where the road lifted toward the Gritones, the wind turned cold, and carried a taste of bitter dust.

The loom of the mountains made a lee, cutting off the wind. It was quiet again and Benson could hear himself whistling a brisk and bouncing and slightly flat version of a tune he could not identify. He repeated the most familiar phrase again, and then grinned suddenly. "I'm getting married in the morning," he sang in a loud, bellowing voice. "Ding-dong, the bells are gonna chime." He couldn't remember any more words, except the final line which he repeated several times, roaring at the sky. "Get me to the church, get me to the church, get me to the church on ti-i-i-ime!"

He slowed to turn at the base of the mountains, then eased forward on the accelerator again, and sat up straight, watching his strong headlights strike and bounce from the harsh ridges.

Below, on the floor of the mountain valley, he could see the long sharp plumes of a car's lights just entering the narrow road, heading toward him. Benson slowed gradually and stopped. He rammed the gearshift into reverse, cocked his arm on the seat and backed up to the flat space where there was room for two cars to pass. He edged carefully to one side, dimmed his lights and turned off the ignition. He lit a cigarette and slumped down lazily, hat over his eyes, listening to the echoes of the car struggling up the slope in second. One of the pick-up trucks, he guessed. Hell of a time for anyone to be heading for town. He brought his arm up, skinned back his cuff and puffed rapidly on his cigarette to get enough light to see the dial. Past one thirty. Awful damn late for a working ranch hand to be up. The oncoming lights struck the side of the pass high up, swept around and lowered suddenly as the truck nosed into the pass. Benson tapped his horn lightly, twice.

The truck swerved toward him, skidding. It slid to a stop, inches from Benson's fender.

"Patrón!" a deep, growling bear's voice shouted. "This is good luck! Where the hell you been?" Clemente turned off the motor and came back to Benson's car. He slid in beside him.

"At the ranch, all is well. Regular, al menos. I am going to Kellogg Junction, patrón."

"You old tomcat," Benson grinned. "Well, on your way, Shameless. I'm going to bed."

"No, patrón," Clemente said soberly. "I do not go for pleasure. Nacio who sweeps at the Wild West Saloon—you remember Nacio, patrón? With the very large hands and hair like a woodpecker?"

"What about him?"

"He telephoned me tonight. At the Wild West is a situation of much gravity. He wanted someone from La Cañada to know. In your absence, patrón, I agreed to come. I have told no one."

"About what?" Benson said impatiently. "What's going on at the Wild West that we care about?"

"It is the blonde young wife of the brother of the patrón," Clemente said heavily. "Drunk. Very drunk, Nacio says, and making of herself an exhibition for the bellacos of the saloon."

Benson sat up quickly. He snapped his cigarette out onto the graveled roadway and with the same motion, switched on the ignition. He cramped the wheel hard over and shot the car back in a tight arc. It took him two tries to get it turned toward Kellogg Junction. He slammed it into high and roared over the pass and down the long slope.

"We can help nothing if we die in the car, patrón," Clemente complained. He held his hat with one hand.

"What else did Nacio tell you?"

"That is all, patrón. That the Señora Kellogg was there alone, very drunk. Nacio was afraid there might be trouble."

"There will be," Benson said positively.

He went over the graveled rises at a dangerous pace, almost leaving the road. He took the curves in long, powered skids that sprayed crushed rock far out into the desert. He came into Kellogg Junction too fast and had to swing out onto the highway for fifty yards before he could slow enough to turn back toward the darkened village.

He swung right at the second corner and rolled quietly down the street. Two of the old movie-built saloons were lighted dimly. The ramshackle one at the far end would be the Last Chance, Benson remembered. He turned his car around, facing the highway, and parked in front of the first. It was too dark to read the sign, but he knew the place. He nudged Clemente and crawled out after him.

The Wild West Saloon was a wide, false-fronted frame

building, its faded paint cobwebbed by the sun. Benson detoured around a broken place in the boardwalk. He stopped in the band of light that seeped through the grubby sand-scratched window of the Wild West. He touched Clemente's arm.

"Stay beside the door," he said in a low voice. "Don't take a hand unless I call for you."

"Patrón." Clemente lifted a pocket of his horsehide coat and pressed it up so that the leather outlined the shape of a long-barreled pistol.

"We won't need anything like that," Benson said sharply. "Leave it in your pocket. Come on."

He pushed back the splintery swing doors and went inside. The air was thick and reeked of smoke and spilled beer. It had been ten years since he had last been here, but nothing had changed. Nothing would ever change until the movie people came back.

The Wild West had been built as the set where the dancing heroine did her stuff on the little kerosene-lighted stage at the rear and where the hero won all the villain's money at the faro table and finished up by fighting him up and down the narrow flight of stairs that led to a railed landing that had doors leading nowhere. The long mahogany-veneered bar was a good piece of work, not much improved by use. The old Lily Langtry poster was almost too worn and dark to read now, but the fat, titian-haired nude over the bar was bright and rosy as ever, still holding up that glossy spray of cherries and giving the boys a smoldering eye. The place was false and cheap and obscurely nasty. As it always had been.

Four half-asleep men perched on bar stools with their big hats pulled over their eyes and the one-inch heels of their oil-cloth boots hooked on the rungs. A dozen tables ran in staggered series down the side wall, only two of them in use. The jukebox beside the door belched when a coin dropped. A trio of mariachis backed by a giddy-ap guitar lurched into a falsetto attack on "Noche de Ronda." Benson went toward it, hooked a toe under the power line leading to the jukebox and yanked the plug. The sudden silence was something you could feel.

Benson heard his shoes making the only sound. The man behind the bar looked up with a quick aggressive scowl and moved around the far end, wiping his hands on his dirty apron, making muscles dance in his big hairy arms.

"Turn that juke on, buster," he said in a practiced snarl. "I'll break your——" He stopped when Benson came into the focused light from a bare overhead bulb. "Kellogg? What are you——"

Benson made a quick, tight gesture, waving him away. He threaded through the maze of tables and chairs. Three tired young whores looked up as he passed their table. Only their eyes moved. Their faces were dull and blank.

Even in the dim light of the saloon, Paula's streaky blond hair was a vibrant note. She was facing away from Benson. There was a man on each side of her, each with an arm up over the back of her chair. Paula was wearing a low-necked Mexican blouse with elastic smocking to hold it up. The hands of both men were sliding it gradually down. The whores nudged each other and sat up to watch.

The bartender cut through the tables and caught Benson's arm before he reached Paula. "What do you think you're doing?" he growled. "We don't want no trouble here, Kellogg."

"You've already got it," Benson said bluntly. "Do you know who that lady is?"

"Lady? What lady? Her, you mean?" He flicked a thumb toward Paula. "You mean that——"

"Don't say it," Benson said in sharp warning.

"Now wait a minute. Just wait a goddam minute. She come in by herself. Dint nobody drag her. Starts buying drinks and——" His heavy eyebrows knotted together slowly. "Say, who is she, anyway?"

"Trouble," Benson said. He pulled his arm away and put a hand flat on the bartender's chest. "Get in my way and I'll bring a dozen hands down here and pull this joint over your ears. Move!" He prodded with a stiff finger.

"Listen, Kellogg. For Christ's sake, we don't want no bad trouble here. I got enough to sweat about. Now, be reasonable, goddam it." He glanced nervously at Clemente, dark and glowering beside the door. He shifted back under Benson's pressure, indecisive. Benson moved toward the table.

The man on Paula's left had his soft white hand on her bare shoulder, stroking gently. The other hand, wide and broken-nailed and dirty, was hooked slightly under the edge of Paula's blouse, drawing it down. Benson reached out angrily, snatched both hands away in a swift, savage grip. He let the soft one go, but pulled the other up and around, bending it back against the wrist, bringing its owner from his chair with a muffled shriek of pain.

The man was thin and dark, with the long sideburns and narrow mustache of a movie badman. He was dressed for the part in black jeans and boots, a black shirt with grimy white piping and a black hat cocked back over his stringy black hair. His mouth was open and he was shouting something that Benson did not listen to. He put one hand flat against the man's nose and heaved with all the weight of his body behind his arm. The man went spinning back, taking two chairs with him, and sprawled on the floor.

Benson turned away in time to see the other man push back from the table and lunge toward him. He had chosen the wrong one first, he realized then. It was Soft-Hands who was the real badman. He had himself rigged out as a sin-palace gambler, with a boiled shirt and string tie. He had a thin-lipped mouth made for sneering. And he had a thin and wicked switchblade knife open in his soft white hand.

"Don't, Ace!" the bartender shouted. "Don't touch him, Ace, for Christ's sake. That's Ben Kellogg!"

"Ain't that nice?" Ace whispered. "Ben Kellogg. Imagine that." He padded around behind Paula, moving carefully now that Benson was watching. His thin mouth lifted at the corners in an unconscious smile of enjoyment. He slid toward Benson, holding his knife low. He profiled, stabbing the air in tight, flickering motions like a snake testing the atmosphere with his tongue.

Paula lifted her head dazedly. She brushed back her hair

in a bewildered gesture. A blond tendril fell drunkenly over her forehead in a shaggy question mark. Her eyes swept, out of focus, around the room. "Ben?" she said in a child's querulous voice. "Did you say——"

"Don't move, Paula," Benson said, urgently quiet. He reached back with one hand, eyes always on the shifting blade. His hand brushed the back of a chair. He grabbed it and swung it up and around, jabbing its legs at the knife. Soft-Hands retreated warily.

Benson crouched a little behind the barricade of his chair. He felt like saying, "Come on, Ace, old friend. Come and get it," as he had to Manny Blue. He felt loose and almost happy now, with all the long day's tension washed out of him and only a hot, high-keyed eagerness in his muscles.

Soft-Hands swept up his open hand, chopping at the chair. He took a quick, sliding step.

Clemente fired a shot from his position beside the door, and the world froze in place.

The first to recover was the bartender. He snatched up an empty beer bottle from the table, swung it up and cracked it against the back of Soft-Hands' skull. The man stiffened against the impact. His neck twisted. He cocked his head, staring blindly at Benson with eyes rolled up into his head, still smiling. He folded in slow motion, as if a movie director were coaching him—knees first, then left hand on floor, roll to left hip, then left shoulder, let knife drop very reluctantly. Then collapse. Soft-Hands collapsed with a grunt. He hit the floor with the side of his head.

"He'd of killed you," the bartender said with shrill certainty. "That Ace is a wild man sometimes. You're damn lucky, Kellogg, and you better know it. Now, git that babe outa here. I give you a break. You give me a break. I don't want no bad trouble here." He pointed a thick finger at the first man who was climbing awkwardly to his feet. "You stand right there, Blackie. By Christ, I'm stoppin' this right now. Git her outa here, Kellogg."

Benson put his chair down and leaned on the table beside

Paula, breathing heavily. He drew Paula's blouse up into position. He bent down, cupping his hands under her elbows and bringing her up to her feet. She wobbled against him, her head lolling back on a limp neck. Her eyes were glassy, pinkly moist. Her lipstick was smeared across her face.

"Ben?" She slumped in his arms and giggled. "Broth' Ben. What're you doing here?" She patted his cheek playfully. "Have lil drink, Ben. Meet friends. Ver-ry 'tractive boys. Movie stars . . ."

"Let's go for a ride first, Paula," Benson said.

"Inna mint. Have lil drink firs', meet friends. Nice boys. Somebody t'talk to."

She giggled again, helplessly, as Benson scooped her up with a hand under her knees. Benson carried her down the long room toward the door. Clemente hooked back the swinging doors and held them. He stayed where he was as they went through, holding his pistol down against the side of his leg, watching the long room.

Benson moved, stiff-legged and clumsy, toward his car. He hoisted Paula and put her over the door into the front seat. She lurched back, arms spread dramatically wide, hair over the back of the seat. "What a bewful night, Ben. Bewful. But's lonesome. Always lonesome out here . . ."

Benson grunted. He rummaged in the deep pocket of her skirt where he could see a bulge. The bulge was a wallet, empty now, and a key holder. Benson put the wallet back as Paula groaned and bent forward suddenly, gagging.

He yanked her arm, turning her toward the door and lifting her so that her head hung over. He moved back too slowly to escape all of the vomit, but he missed the worst of it. A pale sickly pool gathered in the dust beside the car. Paula retched in long, hawking gushes, smearing the side of the car. Benson used his handkerchief to mop his trousers and shoes, then threw the handkerchief away. He went around the front of the car, paying no attention to Paula's strangling gasps, and reached in to tap his horn button twice.

Across the street, angled beside a tall mesquite, he could

see the low, snub-nosed outline of a sports car. Paula's, he thought. He waited for Clemente to come backing out of the saloon, gun in hand.

"Put that damn thing away," he said. "You shoot somebody and we'll really be in a mess."

"Just blanks," Clemente said with a darting smile. "Sounded real, no?"

"Put it away," Benson said. "Come over here." He led Clemente across the street and made sure he understood how to work the controls of Paula's car. When Clemente drove off cautiously in low gear, Benson went back to Paula.

She was still curled over the edge of the door, but she seemed to be better now. She was breathing in quick shallow gulps, trying to hold her hair away from her face. Benson got in, unlocked the glove compartment and took out a box of tissues. He dropped it in Paula's lap. He rummaged in the compartment for the half-pint of brandy he always carried. He broke the seal with his thumb and took a long drink. Paula sat up weakly when he started the motor.

"Sick," she muttered. "So sick, Ben."

"Me too," Benson said, almost to himself.

HE STOPPED BRIEFLY at the cattleguard entrance to Burr's house until Clemente caught up, then waved and drove forward over the clanking iron pipes and up the dark avenue of Lombardies. He cut the motor and drifted up close to the side entrance. He got out and walked back to Clemente.

"Just leave the keys in the car. I'll see the señora inside. Wait for me."

"Patrón, the señora. Is she—"

"Just the stomach. She'll be all right," Benson said. He went around behind his car toward Paula who was resting with her arm over the door, her head nestled in the crook of her elbow.

"Let's go, Paula," he said briskly. "Bedtime."

"Don't be—cheery, Ben," she muttered against her arm.

"I don't feel cheery," he said honestly. "Get out of my car and let me go home to bed."

Paula pushed herself up wearily, eyes closed. "Ben, I——" She shook her head. "So sick. Sorry, Ben. So 'shamed. I—I don't know what to do."

"Go to bed," Benson said heavily. He opened the door, holding her erect with one hand. "Come on."

Paula turned away from him. "Rest a mint," she said indistinctly. "Jus' a mint."

Benson shrugged. He lowered her head to the seat and went back for her keys. At the screen door of the terrace entrance he lit a match, thumbing the keys apart.

"You don't need a key," a thick, blurred voice said from the terrace. "Door's open. Who is it?"

"Burr?"

"Yeah. Hi, Ben."

"Damn you," Benson exploded. "Get your ass out here and haul your wife out of my car."

"Paula? You got Paula with you?"

Benson could hear movement behind the screen. A dull yellow buglight came on and Burr's bulky silhouette filled the doorway.

"What's Paula doing with you?"

"You tell me," Benson said in a voice that shook with anger. "She's your wife. Don't you——"

"We had a fight," Burr muttered, thick-tongued and slow. He pulled the door open and came outside. "I was stoned when I got home and Paula got mad. She went storming off somewhere. She's a——"

"The hell with what she is," Benson said sharply. "Just get her out of my car."

"Okay." Burr brushed past him. He opened the driver's door and knelt on the seat, bending over. He raised up again, glaring at Benson. "She's passed out," he said. "Smells like a distillery. What have you——"

"Not me," Benson said sharply. "I found her like that.

Let her tell you about it, if she wants to. You need some help or can you manage her by yourself?"

Burr stared at him tightly for a moment, then nodded curtly. "I can manage." He slid Paula toward him and lifted her easily. She buried her nose in the pocket of his shoulder and murmured something.

"Can you wait a minute, Ben?" he asked. "I'll just be a minute."

"No, I want to get home. I'm beat."

"Just for a minute, Ben. It's important. I've got something to tell you. I was going to hunt you up anyway. I just didn't have the heart for it when I got home. Okay, Ben? Will you wait?"

"All right, all right. Shake it up. Clemente is waiting out here, too, so don't waste any time."

"Won't be a minute."

Benson held the door for him, closed it on the latch and went back to his car. He picked up the flask of brandy and signaled for Clemente. They sat together in the car, sharing the bottle and waiting for Burr.

He was gone longer than a minute but not much longer. Benson left the brandy with Clemente, got out and climbed the low steps to the screened terrace.

"What's on your mind?" he said in a brusque, unsympathetic tone.

"Ben, what happened to her? She's a mess." Burr showed him a damp washcloth he had wiped across Paula's face. The smears of lipstick and crusted vomit and dirt were a sickening mixture.

"I don't think anything happened to her," Benson said stiffly. "You'll have to ask her."

Burr stared at him soberly. He sat down in a wicker chair. He looked as bad as Paula, Benson thought. He'd probably been asleep in the chair when they drove up. His inflamed eyes were not tracking well. He continually licked his cracked lips. His voice came as a thin, brittle croak. "What are you so mad about?" he asked.

"I'm not mad," Benson said. "What's on your mind?"

Burr looked up at him, dull-eyed and somber. "I guess we're not friends any more," he said slowly.

Even now, Benson thought angrily, he's playing the charm racket. He's made it work for him all his life. Everything had come to him almost without effort and it probably wasn't his fault that he had gotten into the habit of assuming that everything and everyone would always fall in with his pattern. Maybe it wasn't his fault, but that didn't make it any less irritating.

"What's on your mind?" he said again.

Burr sighed. He rubbed the heel of his hand across his eyes. "This isn't easy for me, Ben. I feel like a prize jerk." He turned his head away. "I got back from Monte this afternoon. Had a session with Nate Barstow. He set me right on a few things."

"Such as what?"

Burr waggled his head. "About what you'd expect. I was wearing a set of blinders, I guess. Ben, honest to God, I thought they were on the level. No——" Burr checked himself abruptly. "No, I guess I knew what they were. I was trying pretty hard to kid myself. I would have played along with them probably, but Nate Barstow made it so goddam obvious that he had been setting me up as a patsy. He was kind of mad because I didn't learn my lines fast enough."

Benson sat down beside him. There was something in Burr's voice and manner that troubled him deeply. "What happened?"

Burr made a disgusted sound in his throat. He drained the last watery inch in the bottom of a glass and set it down noisily. "They suckered me. Or maybe I should say they let me sucker myself, and, boy, I was eager to do it, too. That's a laugh, huh? A smart, tricky guy like me getting sandbagged by a pack of cowboy politicians. Old Nate straightened me out fast. And for keeps."

"You aren't making much sense, Burr. What happened?"

"I went barging in on old Nate. You wanted me to deliver a message. I delivered it all right."

"What about it?"

Burr shrugged. "Even now I don't know if old Nate really meant to put the muscle boys on your trail, but he sure as hell did mean for me to be running the Campeón trial before it was over. He couldn't believe I was stupid enough to think anything else. It was like being hit in the face with a bucket of cold water. It chilled me, I can tell you. I pulled up short with my big stupid mouth open and just stood there."

"It was pretty obvious, Burr."

"Not to me," Burr said hotly. "By God, it wasn't obvious to me. Maybe I was a jerk, maybe I was willing to close my eyes to a lot of crappy shenanigans, but I wouldn't go along with a thing like that. Why, all the way up to Monte I was trying to figure out a way to explain you to Barstow without making you sound like a self-righteous damn fool. There's another laugh for you, if you're in the mood for laughs."

"I'm not."

"I guess not. Well, that's it, Ben. I stepped into something over my head. I was wrong as hell. I know that. I'd like to apologize."

"The hell with it. We don't need apologies, Burr. What happened between you and Barstow? Are you still his fair-haired boy?"

Burr shifted his shoulders restlessly. "I don't know. I doubt it. After what I told him, I don't believe old Nate is ever going to want to see me again. I blew one right off the ceiling."

"He's probably heard worse," Benson said calmly. "A politician must be used to it. He isn't going to junk a promising candidate that easily."

"That's what they keep calling me," Burr said heavily. "A promising young man. I've been a promising young man since I got out of the navy. That's too long a time, Ben. It doesn't go with a thick waistline and thinning hair. I don't kid myself any more. I don't believe the promise is going to be redeemed. I'm that honest with myself."

"You're that sorry for yourself," Benson said bluntly. He dropped his hands smartly down on the arms of the chair as if to rise. "That all you wanted to say?"

"It doesn't mean anything to you, does it?"

"Not much. I knew you'd see what was going on, sooner or later."

Burr looked at him morosely. "You think I'm a horse's ass, don't you? You and Paula. She's got the notion I married her just to get a wife who'd make a good hostess for a rising young politician. That's why she ran out on me tonight."

"Is that why you married her?"

Burr shook his head positively. "No. I knew she'd fit, all right. Hell, she'd fit anywhere. But that's not why I asked her to marry me."

"Then tell her. And make her believe it. I think she got pretty far away from you tonight. You'd better convince her quick, before she goes all the way."

"What do you mean? Did she say anything about——"

"She didn't say a word. She was in no condition to talk when I found her."

"Ben?" Burr got up stiffly. "Ben, could you talk to her and try to——"

"No! Goddam it, no! I won't carry your marriage on my back, Burr. If it means anything to you, get to work on it yourself. You convinced her once. Do it again. And this time make it stick. But don't ask me to take a hand. I won't do it."

"I shouldn't have asked you, Ben," Burr said in a contrite mumble. "I'm a little shook, I guess. Everything just went to hell all at once. I'll be okay. Thanks, anyway."

Benson put his hand on the heavy muscle of Burr's shoulder. "Sure, you'll be okay. Get some sleep."

"Ben, I didn't mean——"

"I know you didn't. Don't worry about it."

"Thanks, Ben." Burr held the screen door for him. He tried to smile but something went wrong with his face. Benson could see the deep, unbelieving bewilderment that had Burr caught as a man is caught in a nightmare. Burr had seen a part of himself that he did not recognize, a stranger long denied, even now not accepted or understood. He was not frightened, or not very much, but he was watching himself with a wary kind of mistrust. The quick and sure and headily confident days were not possible for him any more. He was bewildered by a new view of himself.

"Will you shake hands, Ben?" he asked as Benson went past.

"For Christ's sake," Benson snarled, "don't make such a big thing of it. Sure, you've been a jerk. Barstow made you see it and now you've lost some of your confidence. Well, damn it, that's part of the business of growing up. It's not going to kill you." He locked his long fingers around Burr's hand. "You don't have to worry about a thing. You're a good man, Burr, in any company. You've proved that often enough. Maybe you weren't as good as you thought you were, but you sure as hell aren't as lousy now as you think you are. You belong somewhere in between, where most of us have to live. You'll throw this off pretty quickly. You'll be up again, roaring at the moon. And when you are, I hope you'll remember how you felt tonight."

"I'm not likely to forget," Burr said. "Good night, Ben. Thanks."

"Good night," Benson said.

He went down the steps and got in under the wheel. Clemente lay back, more than half asleep, the empty brandy flask held in his big hands.

Benson backed and turned and drove down the long avenue. In his mirror he could see the lonely shadow of his brother on the dimly lit terrace. He saw him sit down heavily and cover his face with his hands as a man does when he tries to control an intolerable pain.

BENSON stopped his car outside Clemente's house and shook the foreman awake. He waited until he saw him unlock the door and turn to wave. Then he drove away up the winding road to the ranch house.

His strong lights swept along the retaining wall of the terrace, glinted on the glass of the living-room wall, and straightened as the car completed the turn and climbed. The beams lifted slowly, striking brilliance from the windshield of a car parked beside the steps, facing down the drive. A black car, Benson noted as he came closer. In the desert, where a dense pale dust settles on everything, black cars are not common. Usually they are official cars, or the semi-official kind like hearses and rented limousines. This one did not have an official license number. Benson rolled up and stopped beside it.

He could see the heads and shoulders of two men slumped down in the front seat. They sat up. Each opened his door and stepped out into the driveway, visible now in the reflection of Benson's lights.

That was Guillermo Rojas nearest him, Benson realized. And the man on the far side was a taller, heavier and hairier version of Willie, with a strong familial resemblance.

"Willie?" he called. "Did you want to see me?" He opened the door and got out.

"Ben! Boy, am I glad to see you! Me and Johnnie were about to give up on you. We been waiting since about midnight."

"What's it about, Willie?" Benson shivered suddenly in the chill air from the mountain. "God, it's cold out here. Let's get in out of the wind."

He led the way up to the front door, unlocked it and ushered them inside. He flipped on the lights and gestured for them to sit.

"I guess you could use a drink, couldn't you? I know I could. Brandy be all right?"

"A little brandy would be very fine, Ben," Willie Rojas said politely. "You have a very beautiful place here. I'm only sorry we came by darkness. It must be beautiful in the sunlight."

Benson poured brandy in three glasses and distributed them. "This is the good time of year for La Cañada," he said. "Come out some day soon for a visit, Willie." He dropped into a deep chair and lifted his glass in a brief salute. "Y pesetas," he said. "What's up, Willie?"

"It is Johnnie," Willie said, indicating with a motion of his head the silent young man beside him on the couch. "Let me make you acquainted with my nephew, Deputy Sheriff Juan Alonzo Montero." He grinned at Benson's expression. "Surprised, eh?"

"Surprised is not the word," Benson said weakly. "How did you find him?"

"I didn't have to find him, he found me," Willie said.

"I have been trying for three days to telephone you, Mr. Kellogg," Montero said in a deep, soft voice.

Benson tossed off his drink and shook his head. "So you're the anonymous caller, are you? I wish I'd known. Why didn't you explain to my secretary?"

"Now, that's just why we come out here in the dark of night, Ben," Willie said earnestly, hitching himself forward. "You've got to understand what we're up against. Young Johnnie and me. You know what my job is. You know what Johnnie's job is. We can't either of us afford to stick our neck out. I told Johnnie we could count on you. We can, can't we?"

"Whatever you say, Willie," Benson said soberly. "Let me talk to the deputy for a minute and then we'll decide how to handle it. Is that all right?"

Willie nodded, beaming. "See, Johnnie? I told you it would be strictly okay."

"Do you know why I've been trying to locate you, Deputy?" Benson asked.

"Call him Johnnie," Willie insisted. "We're all friends here. Right, Ben?"

"Sure we are," Benson agreed. "Johnnie?"

"I read it in the papers," the big young deputy said. "Anyhow, I knew all the time, but Aldridge said to keep shut. I told him I wasn't going to lie for him or that old prick, Shriner, so he had me sent off to highway-patrol school. He didn't want me around where you could ask me questions."

"We'll come back to that part in a minute," Benson said

tightly. "I want to know more about Aldridge's part in this. But first, tell me about the confession. Were you present in the prison ward while Aldridge was interrogating my client?"

"Most of the time, yes, sir. Aldridge sent me out for a while. Told me to take a walk. The kid was ready to sign when I came back."

"Tell him about the pencil, Johnnie," Willie said excitedly.

"Let him tell it his own way, Willie," Benson said quietly. "What about it, Johnnie?"

"I saw Shriner crack the kid over the shoulder a couple licks when I was coming back. He was unconscious. Aldridge gave him some water and brought him around and the kid put his *X* on the paper and that was that.

"You actually saw Shriner hit the boy?"

"Yes, sir."

"And you know that Aldridge saw it, too?"

"Sure, he was right there next to him."

"Did Aldridge and Shriner know then that you had seen Shriner hit the boy?"

"No. The doctor came in right behind me and I figured I better not say anything while he was there. I talked to Aldridge on the way back. I was a little sore, maybe." The deputy lifted his deep-set eyes to Benson's. "He was a Mexican boy. Shriner didn't like Mexicans. I kind of got my belly full of Shriner."

"Yes." Benson rubbed his tired eyes. "Is this the truth, Johnnie? You aren't lying just to get a Mexican boy off the hook?"

"Now, look here, I don't——"

"That's what the County Attorney is going to say," Benson went on calmly. "You'll have to answer him."

"I'll answer him, all right," Montero said angrily. "I'll ram it down his throat."

Benson grinned at him. Montero looked as if he'd do just that. "What did Aldridge say when you told him you had seen Shriner hit the boy?"

Montero made a quick gesture as if to throw something away. "Tried to talk me out of it. When that didn't work, he told me to keep my mouth shut. Said the kid would have a lawyer protecting him from now on and he wouldn't get another chance to try for a confession, so this one would have to stand. He said he'd boot me off the force if I didn't go along with him."

"Could he do it?"

"Get me canned? Sure. Aldridge runs the department. I thought everybody knew that."

"I didn't know it. What about the sheriff?"

Montero laughed scornfully. "That's a good one. What about the sheriff? He's got the Sheriff's Posse that meets on Saturdays and rides out into the desert. And he's got the Junior Posse that meets on Sundays and rides out into the desert. And during the week he's got the Chamber of Commerce and the Rotary and the Kiwanis and the——"

"So he lets Aldridge run the department?"

"Right."

"I see. Then it was Aldridge himself who had you sent away? I mean, could he do that himself without even consulting the sheriff?"

"Sure. I heard him give the order. Sheriff wasn't anywhere around."

Benson leaned back in his chair and closed his eyes. Montero had given him a powerful weapon. But how should he use it, to get the most benefit for his client? He was too tired to think clearly. He'd decide in the morning. He looked up suddenly at Montero. "What's going to happen to you if you testify?"

"That's why I brought him to you, Ben," Willie broke in quickly. "If Johnnie was to go to the judge by himself, pow!" Willie pounded a thick fist on the couch. "Aldridge would chop his neck. But I figured you would know a way to get Johnnie's testimony into the record without it costing him his job. Deputy sheriff is a good job, Ben. Johnnie wants to keep it."

"He will," Benson said firmly. "I'll make that a flat promise, Johnnie. I think I can even promise you that you won't have to worry about Aldridge or Shriner. Somehow I don't think they'll be on the payroll much longer."

Willie nudged his nephew. "What did I tell you, huh? You listen to your Uncle Willie, boy, and you won't go wrong."

"Now, what about you, Willie?" Benson asked. "Do you want to keep out of it? There's no reason for you to appear, unless you want to."

"No, sir," Willie said, shaking his head. "I don't want to appear in anything. It would put me in bad with Judge Groat. Might even make the judge look bad, his clerk taking a hand in a case he's trying. No, I have to stay out of it, Ben."

"Okay, Willie. That's easy. We'll just leave it that Johnnie came alone to see me. There's no need for your name to come into it. Is that okay?"

"That's fine, Ben. Just the way I wanted it. I knew you'd handle it. I tell you, it's a good feeling to deal with a gentleman. With a guy like Frank Sayer, you never know where you stand. With you, no sweat. Well," Willie dusted his hands together in a satisfied gesture, "all set, are we? What do you want us to do, Ben?"

Benson yawned slowly. He glanced at his watch. "It's past three o'clock. I think we'd all better get some sleep. Why don't you go on home, Willie? Johnnie can bunk here and drive in with me in the morning. And you can be flabbergasted when we show up in the judge's chambers tomorrow morning. I'll count on you to get the judge there by eight o'clock. Can you do that?"

"Count on me, Ben." Willie smacked his meaty hand on his nephew's knee. "Well, Johnnie, all set? You know what you're supposed to do?"

Montero nodded. His heavy brooding young face lightened with a trace of a smile. He drew in a quick, relieved breath.

"Everything's rosy now, huh?" Willie said delightedly. "This boy was really worried, Ben. You should have seen him. He knew he had to do something, but it looked like he was going to cut his own throat, no matter what he did."

"No, nothing's going to happen to Johnnie," Benson said. He struggled up from the soft chair. "Willie, I don't have words to thank you for what you've done."

"Might get your boy off, huh?"

"It gives him a little better chance, at least. He's still up to his neck in trouble, but it isn't over his head yet." With a hand on Willie's shoulder, he urged him lightly toward the door. "Sorry you had to lose a night's sleep, Willie."

"It was worth it," Willie said fiercely. "By God, it was worth it. Eh, Johnnie?"

"Sure was," the deputy agreed.

"Good night, Willie. Thanks again. See you in the morning. Eight o'clock. Right?"

"Right. You just wait and see how surprised I'm going to be when you and Johnnie come walking into my office. Good night, fellows. You do what Ben tells you, Johnnie." He flipped a buoyant salute and went bouncing down the steps toward his car. Benson slid the door closed and came back. He filled Johnnie's glass and his own.

"I guess you'll be glad to see a bed, Johnnie," he said in a weary voice. "Bring your drink. There's a guest room next to mine you can use. Toothbrush and shaving gear in the bathroom. Pajamas in the dresser."

He took the young deputy down the hallway, showed him the room, made sure he had everything he needed and said good night.

He went into his own room, shedding clothes at every step. He washed sketchily, yawning, surprised at the runnels of dirt that sluiced from his hands. He stumbled toward his bed and dropped on it heavily. He set his alarm for six o'clock and rolled over with a groan. The overhead light was still burning, but he was too far asleep to reach up and turn it off.

"BUT WHY did you bring this young man to me?" Judge Groat demanded in a testy, tired voice. He cleared his throat noisily and used his handkerchief to pick something off his tongue.

Benson took a moment to organize what he wanted to say.

It had been an active, crowded morning so far. Up at six, breakfast conference with Montero to draw up his deposition, a fast drive into town for this meeting in the judge's chambers.

Frank Sayer sat across from him, his feet propped on the edge of the low table. After hearing what Montero had to say, his healthily pink face had gone blotchy with strain. He was caught in a still apprehension.

Montero stood rigidly in front of the table, big hands locked behind his back, his broad dark face impassive. He had spoken in a clear, unemotional tone, had said exactly what needed to be said, and had answered every question Frank or the judge could ask. He had taken a lot of pounding from Frank, but the sober truth of his evidence had not been brought seriously into question.

"Well, Benson?" the judge said impatiently.

"I could have waited until court convened, Your Honor," Benson said evenly. "I could have let you and Frank hear Deputy Montero's testimony at the same time it went on the record. I thought this was a better way. Provided we can reach a sensible agreement here this morning."

"Explain yourself, please," the judge said.

"Yes, sir. I'd welcome the opportunity. I wonder if it mightn't be best to ask Deputy Montero to wait in Willie's office for a few minutes?"

The judge nodded. "Thank you, Deputy," he said coldly. "Do you mind? You might ask Willie to get us all some coffee, if you would."

Montero stiffened and saluted. He pivoted precisely, strode to the door and went out quietly.

"All right, Benson."

"We've got a serious problem, Judge. It's obvious that Aldridge and Shriner perjured themselves yesterday, but——"

"No, it's not obvious," Frank Sayer said heatedly. "It's one witness against two. Against three, if you count Dr. Elman."

"We won't count any of them," Benson said. "And never mind the crap, Frank. This issue is going to be decided by

Judge Groat, not the jury. So we don't need any speeches. The simple fact is that everybody in this room is absolutely convinced that Deputy Montero was telling the unvarnished truth."

"No, by God——"

"Just a moment, Frank," the judge broke in. "Let Benson finish, please."

"Thank you, sir." Benson said. "If I were to put Montero on the stand, you would be forced to take official notice of the situation. That would probably mean perjury indictments against Shriner and Aldridge. There wouldn't be any alternative, if Montero's testimony is before the court. I'd hate to see that, sir. We obviously don't have a very good sheriff's office in this county, but I can't believe it deserves that kind of publicity."

Judge Groat nodded impatiently as if he had already moved far ahead of Benson's argument. "What do you suggest?"

Benson stroked his chin. This was the crux of the problem. He had thought of moving for a mistrial, but there was little to be gained by that. He would just have to go back to court another time. But now, if he went on with the trial, he could logically expect a certain friendliness from Judge Groat, for there are few things a judge dislikes more than declaring a mistrial. It was worth trying, he thought.

"None of this questionable evidence has yet been presented to the jury, Your Honor. If Frank is prepared to withdraw the confession, we can let the matter drop right here. Provided——"

Frank Sayer gave a smothered snort. "Ridiculous, Your Honor! I won't consider——"

"I asked you to let him finish," Judge Groat said in a fiercely quiet voice. "If you will be so kind?"

"But, Judge, I can't sit here and——" Sayer silenced himself at a glare from the judge.

"What is your proviso, Benson?"

"About what you would expect, Judge," Benson went on. "Shriner and Aldridge have to be kicked out. It can be done quietly, but it has to be done. And Deputy Montero has to be given some firm assurance that no attempt at reprisal, official or unofficial, will be tolerated. I was hoping you might issue a warning to the sheriff, sir."

"I would be willing to do that in any case, Benson," the judge said. "Be sure to remind me. Very well, Frank. What were you about to say?"

"One thing more, sir," Benson put in hastily.

"Yes?"

"If we can't reach an agreement, if we go on with this and I put Montero on the stand to testify, then I will be compelled to ask the court to investigate the part played in this matter by the County Attorney. It is not beyond possibility that someone in his office may have known that the confession was illegally forced from the defendant."

Frank Sayer hadn't even considered that aspect, Benson could see. The county prosecutor had been so busy thinking of a way to get his witnesses out of trouble that he hadn't thought about being in a bind himself. Sayer's face flushed with angry blood. His voice was thinned with strain as he spoke to the judge.

"Your Honor, I swear—" he swallowed painfully and went on more slowly, fighting for calmness—"I have never in my life knowingly presented perjured evidence in any court, Judge. I think my record speaks for me on that. Shriner and Aldridge both assured me that they had employed no coercion in taking that confession from the defendant. I have no reason to doubt them. I have no valid reason."

"I warned you last week, Frank," Benson said sharply. "Did you investigate then?"

"Why should I?" Sayer snapped. "Every jackleg defense counsel always screams about confessions. I've never had a confession disallowed in my whole career. Many of those confessions were obtained by Deputy Aldridge. Why should I doubt him now?"

"Because he's a liar," Benson said flatly. "Because——" He broke off when Willie tapped on the door and came backing into the room carrying a tray of filled coffee mugs from the corner restaurant.

"This one is yours, Judge," Willie said expansively. "Two sugars, no cream. The others are raw." He passed the cups around and stood back, beaming at Benson.

"Thank you, Willie," the judge said. "We'll be a little longer." He nodded in dismissal.

"You were saying, Benson?" the judge inquired.

Benson began to continue, then stopped himself. He had given the judge his evidence and his arguments. There was no profit in boring him with repetition.

"I've finished, Your Honor," he said. "It's in your hands."

"Your Honor," Frank Sayer said in a quick, penetrating voice, "I would like a chance to——"

"In a moment, Frank," the judge said, not looking up from his coffee. He blew on it meditatively. "I want to think about this quietly for a while. I'll excuse you now, Benson. I want to have a talk with Frank before we convene."

"Yes, sir," Benson said. He put his untouched mug on the table and moved toward the door.

"I should probably thank you, Benson," Judge Groat sighed. "Maybe I will, later on. I'm in no mood for it now. Ask Deputy Montero to wait, will you please?"

"Yes, sir," Benson went out and swung the door shut behind him. He could hear Frank Sayer's voice rising strongly as the door closed.

"Did he give it to you, Counselor?" Burr grinned at him from the far side of Willie's desk where he was lounging in one of the hard chairs, hunched down comfortably and looking as well rested and vigorous as if he'd spent the night in bed. Even his eyes were clear, Benson noted with some envy.

"He didn't say," Benson muttered. "What are you doing here, Burr?"

Burr put his feet down on the floor and sat up. "Willie said I could wait here. I wanted to talk to you, Ben."

Willie gestured surreptitiously to Montero and got up from his chair. "Johnnie and me are going to catch a smoke. Give us a call if the judge wants us, will you, Ben?"

"Sure," Benson said absently. He watched them go out.

"Did you arrange that too?" he asked Burr.

"I guess so. I told Willie I wanted to see you alone for a minute if he could fix it for me."

"What for?"

"I have to eat some worms. It's easier in private."

"Don't play games with me, Burr. I haven't got time for that. What do you want?"

Burr stiffened. His broad muscular face firmed into hard planes under tension. "I meant it, Ben. I'm not playing games. I came to apply for a job."

"What is this? Damn it, Burr, I don't——"

"Can you find room for an associate counsel, Ben? Or an errand boy? I'm available."

"And what about Nate Barstow?"

"I didn't ask him," Burr said tightly. "I didn't even tell him. I'd like to set things straight, Ben. You ain't exactly making it easy, boy."

"Does it have to be easy?" Benson demanded.

Burr flushed. He shook his head. "It has to be the way you say, Ben. I had some time to think last night, after you left. It's not much fun being me right now. I've been acting like a kid in a candy store, snatching up everything in sight. I guess I've got a moral bellyache."

"You don't have to make a gesture, Burr."

Burr's chin came up quickly. "I'd like a chance to square myself."

"You'd wreck your chances with Barstow."

"So?" Burr eyed him clearly.

Benson turned away. "You're a damn fool," he muttered.

"I know, Counselor," Burr agreed cheerfully. "How about a job?" He looked at Benson, and a slow wide grin came blossoming.

AS SOON as court convened, Benson introduced his new associate counsel. When he and Burr were seated, Judge Groat leaned pointedly forward, turned toward Frank Sayer. In a subdued voice the County Attorney asked the court's permission to withdraw the alleged confession. The motion was granted without discussion, but only the court reporter heard the judge's ruling. The rest of the court was bathed in a surging wave of whispered comments, excited speculations. Two of the men at the press table edged out and clattered toward the door.

"How did you manage that?" Turo asked under his breath.

"He whipsawed him, boy. A tricky lawyer, this," Burr said casually, tapping the boy's shoulder.

"Don't start cheering yet, damn it," Benson snapped. "We've got a long way to go."

"Mr. Clerk," the judge said when the court was quiet enough for him, "you may summon the jury."

The twelve talesmen filed in from their conference room, blinking in the brighter light. They were frowning with resentment and curiosity, visibly annoyed at having been shut away a second time while opposing attorneys argued a tricky point before the judge.

"Gentlemen, Mrs. Jordan," the judge said when the jury had finally seated themselves. "We will resume the taking of testimony where it was broken off yesterday. Mr. Sayer?"

Frank Sayer came to his feet. He was too old and experienced a hand to be thrown off his stride by an adverse ruling, but there was something suspiciously unsure and rather tentative in his manner at the moment. It was not natural to him. Benson noted that the juror in the end seat, the one nearest the prosecution table, was frowning speculatively at the County Attorney. What was that juror's name? he wondered. Number Six. Of course. That was Mitchell Masterton, the instructor from Rincon State. A man perceptive to moods, apparently. That might be useful later on.

"May we approach the bench, Your Honor?" Frank Sayer asked.

"Come forward."

"I had Shriner on the stand when we broke," Sayer said

in a hoarse whisper when they were huddled at the far end of the bench. "I'll have to recall him, just to dismiss him, but I don't want Ben asking him any questions about the confession. Or about anything else."

"Benson?" the judge said.

"I won't touch on the confession, Judge," Benson said. "I do have a couple of questions for Shriner. I'll have to get answers from him or Montero. Which, Frank?"

"Hell, take them from Shriner. Just stay off the confession."

"All right, gentlemen. Let's get moving. We've wasted far too much time already."

Deputy Houston Shriner was recalled to the stand, reminded that he was under oath, and immediately referred to the defense counsel for cross-examination.

"A few questions about the wrecked Rolls, Deputy," Benson began. "You said that you inspected the interior of the car after you pulled the defendant out. Am I right?"

Shriner, frightened now and jittery about his job and his future, was an even less satisfactory witness than he had been previously. He could hardly force his voice into the range of audibility. He managed a thin "Yes" after some visible effort.

"Inside the car you found deceased's baggage and some items which were not listed on the sheriff's inventory. True, Deputy?"

"I reckon," Shriner croaked.

"Did you also find several wads of Kleenex that had been soaked with blood?"

"Yes, sir."

"How many wads?"

Shriner shook his head. "Don't know," he said, eager now to give an acceptable answer, but unsure about what was expected of him. "Five or six, maybe."

"When you hauled the defendant from the wreckage, he was severely wounded, was he not? Among other injuries, he had a deep scalp wound, did he not?"

"I reckon he did. He was some bloody."

"But the scalp wound was not bleeding when you saw him, was it?" Benson demanded. "The flow of blood had already been stopped by applying the Kleenex, had it not, Deputy?"

Before Shriner could answer, Frank Sayer rose in strident objection. "Calls for a conclusion of the witness, Your Honor. Clearly inadmissible."

"Sustained."

"Let's approach it from another direction, Deputy," Benson said. "Did you observe that the scalp wound on the defendant's head had already stopped bleeding when you found him in the wrecked car?"

Shriner cast a perplexed glance at the prosecutor. He seemed to shrink inside his faded shirt. "Don't know," he said indistinctly. "I was kinda busy. Dint rightly take notice was he bleedin' or not."

"Tell the jury, Deputy, what became of those wads of bloodied Kleenex."

Shriner shook his head. "I don't—I reckon . . ." Shriner gave it up and shrugged helplessly. "I reckon they all got lost. Just bloody wads of paper. Nobody thought to keep 'em."

"Just bloody wads of paper that had the defendant's blood on them." Benson said, emphasizing the point. "Were you responsible for disposing of them, Deputy?"

"Dint nobody dispose of 'em," Shriner said with dogged insistence. "I reckon they just blew away when we was towing that car into town. Windows was all smashed and like that. They jest blew away."

"They just blew away," Benson repeated with a slow, heavy disgust. He turned to face the jury. "And if I hadn't asked you about them, you would have forgotten all about them, wouldn't you, Deputy?"

"Huh?"

"You do remember that you saw those bloody wads?"

"Yes, sir."

"Did the defendant have time or opportunity to use those

« 423 »

wads of Kleenex after the crash?"

"Why, no. He was knocked plumb out."

"So the blood on those wads of absorbent tissue came from an injury that must have been sustained at some time prior to the crash. Isn't that so, Deputy?"

"Objection," Frank Sayer said.

"I withdraw the question, Your Honor," Benson said. "I don't think the jury needs the answer. I have no further questions for this witness."

Burr leaned toward him as he sat down. "You put it across, all right," he said softly. "The jury got the point. Just sock it home in your summation and you've got it made."

"You're awful damn optimistic," Benson growled.

"Maybe," Burr whispered. "I've been watching Frank. He's about ready to climb the wall. He was counting on that confession."

But not having the confession did not seriously cramp the prosecutor's confident style, as far as Benson could tell. Frank Sayer scribbled a couple of notes and sent one of his anonymous aides out with them. He called the first of a series of minor, corroborative witnesses to clean up the loose ends.

A flabby, expensively dressed man from California was presented as an "exclusive" jeweler who owned a large and expensive shop in Beverly Hills. He identified the cigarette lighter in question as one that he had himself sold to Roderick Duquesne two years before. The initials engraved on it were in a discursive medieval script that, the jeweler claimed, he alone used. Benson asked no questions. Ownership of the lighter was not in dispute.

Frank Sayer asked for a moment before calling his next witness. One of the B. Kellogg and Sampson office boys, a tall, skinny youth who had been waiting just inside the door, took advantage of the lull to slip through the railing. He handed a sealed envelope to Benson.

"She said to wait for an answer, Mr. Kellogg," he whispered.

Benson ripped the envelope. "Dear Mr. Kellogg," he read. "I saw Harald Elsinore this morning, as you said I should. He was in a highly nervous state. He did not even want to get out of bed and I'm afraid I had to bully him a little bit. I gave him some aspirin and made him eat some tea and toast. He is much better now, though still very nervous. I think it would be best for me to stay with him until you want him in court. I am just a little afraid that he might run away if I don't."

"Oh, Christ," Benson groaned. He read the final line. "I have never met such a very GENTLE boy. Yours sincerely, Mary (Mrs. George M.) Shipton." She had underlined "gentle" three times.

"Tell her to stay with him, Tommy," he said to the boy. "Then you'd better come back here and wait. I'll want Elsinore this afternoon, probably. You'll have to go and get him. Tell Mary to make sure he gets something for lunch, but to keep him in his room until I send for him. Got all that, Tommy?"

"I got it, Mr. Kellogg. Back in five minutes."

"No hurry. Just wait at the side door so I'll know where to find you."

Benson slid the note across to Burr, and gave his attention to the witness Frank Sayer was questioning. The insignificant little bald man was the sheriff's property clerk. He described Roderick Duquesne's baggage and made a professional guess as to its value. It was, he said, expensive, and had been made to fit the deceased. He knew this because he had compared the measurements of the clothes with those of the deceased.

"Just one question," Benson said when the witness was referred to him. "You mentioned the clothes that you compared with deceased's measurements. We know that Duquesne was a large and muscular man, so can you——"

"We know nothing of the sort, Your Honor," Frank Sayer objected. "That is an assumption of a fact not in evidence."

"Quite right," Judge Groat said. "Sustained. Ask your questions in the proper form, if you please, Mr. Kellogg."

"I'm sorry, Your Honor," Benson said. "Will you tell the court," he asked the witness, "what general size deceased was? Tall or short?"

"Quite tall, sir."

"How much taller than the defendant?"

"Four or five inches, I would say."

"That would make Duquesne six feet, possibly a bit more?"

"Yes, sir."

"And how heavy was he?"

The witness pursed his lips for a moment, then hazarded, "One hundred and eighty pounds, thereabouts. Definitely a heavyweight."

"What was his collar size?"

"Sixteen inches."

"Sleeve length?"

"Thirty-five-and-a-half inches."

"His chest?"

"Forty-two inches, sir."

"Waistband?"

"Thirty-one inches."

"Thirty-one?" Benson echoed as if he could not believe it. "You did say thirty-one inches?"

"Yes, sir. That's what his trousers measured."

"Thirty-one inches." Benson swept his coat open with both hands and hooked his thumbs under his belt. He drew them slowly forward as if measuring his own waistband. "Duquesne was over six feet tall, a heavyweight. He had a thirty-one-inch waist and a forty-two-inch chest. Well, maybe we can't be sure that the deceased was a large and muscular man, but it does sound as if he must have been."

"Your Honor!"

"Yes," the judge said sharply. "We will have no more of that, Mr. Kellogg. You will save your speeches until the proper time."

"Certainly, Your Honor. I have no more questions."

Burr winked at him as he sat down.

Sayer's assistant slipped through the gate and squatted beside the prosecutor's chair. He whispered something urgently, making an audible hissing. He laid a page of his notebook close to Sayer's hand.

"Your Honor!" Sayer lunged to his feet. His big mobile face was smooth with renewed confidence. "At this time the People request the court's permission to call a witness whose name is not endorsed on the information. Her name was not known to the People until a few minutes ago."

Judge Groat frowned with a trace of suspicion. He tapped his pencil absently against his lower lip. "Mr. Kellogg?"

What the hell has Frank got hold of now? Benson wondered. He glanced at Burr, who shrugged in response. That's all there was to do, Benson realized, just shrug it off. He had no valid basis for objection if the County Attorney honestly maintained that the witness was unknown to him until this minute. He rose reluctantly.

"The name of this surprise witness, Your Honor?" he asked.

"Miss Alice McCoy," Sayer announced cheerfully. "Miss McCoy is a nurse-in-training at Rincon County Hospital, Your Honor. Until this morning the People were not aware that she possessed information of value to this court."

"Do you object, Mr. Kellogg?"

"No, Your Honor," Benson said, knowing it would be useless to protest. "I have no objection to this witness. I think it might be possible to object to the prosecutor's inadequate preparation, but I will not object formally."

He sat down. "Nothing else you could have done," Burr assured him quietly.

Miss Alice McCoy was very young, visibly nervous, but not awed. She was wearing her best as a gesture to the court, a blue-and-white-figured suit with a small flowered hat to match. She carried a pair of starched, never-worn white gloves in one moist hand.

"You are Miss Alice McCoy, a nurse-in-training at Rincon County Hospital?" Sayer asked.

"Yes—yes, sir."

"Now, don't be nervous, Miss McCoy. Just take your time. Please tell the court if you were on duty at approximately three P.M. on the fifteenth of this month? That was Monday afternoon," he added as he saw the girl hesitate.

"Yes, sir, I was."

"Did you, at about that time, have a conversation with the defendant, Arturo Campeón?"

"Not—not exactly a conversation," the girl said cautiously.

"But you did talk to him, however briefly, and he replied?" Sayer insisted.

"Yes, sir."

"Tell the court, please, what was said at that time. First, Miss McCoy, tell us where the conversation took place."

"In—in the prison ward," she said. "He was in bed. He had a little temperature and I gave him an alcohol rub."

"You knew who he was, did you not, and of what offense he stood charged?"

"Oh, yes. He had just come back from justice court, he said. He was real mad at his lawyer, and the police. And—and he said . . ."

"Yes, Miss McCoy," Sayer urged. "Go on, please."

The girl gulped a quick breath and rushed into it. "He said he had killed that—that bastard, and he wasn't trying to deny it. He just wanted everybody to shut up and not talk about it any more."

"Are you absolutely sure he told you he had killed Roderick Duquesne?"

"That's exactly what he said," the girl answered positively. Her little button chin tensed and came up sharply at the mere suggestion that she might not be telling the truth.

Benson stared at her, feeling sick. All that work, all those lucky breaks, that had kept the confession from the jury had just gone down the drain.

"Your witness, Mr. Kellogg," Frank Sayer said with a blandly malicious smile.

Benson did not move. Goddam that boy, he thought

savagely. How many times did I tell him to keep his mouth shut?

Benson got up like an old man and walked across to the witness stand. What could he ask her that would take some of the sting out of her testimony? He couldn't think of a thing. Alice McCoy was very obviously what she seemed to be, a young and eager and honest girl who had told the truth as she knew it.

"How old are you, Miss McCoy?" he asked quietly.

"Nine—nineteen, sir," she said timidly, almost as if it was a shameful fact.

"How long have you been training as a nurse?"

"Just five months, sir."

"So when you tell the court that the defendant had a slight temperature, you do not offer that as a medical fact, but merely as your personal opinion?"

"What?"

"He might have been running a fever, might he not?" Benson went on. "You didn't take his temperature, did you?"

"No, sir."

"So when the defendant returned from justice court on Monday which was only one day after he had been seriously injured in a car wreck, he was running a temperature that might have been a fever. Isn't that true?"

"I—I don't know what——"

"Very well, Miss McCoy," Benson said gently. "I think the facts are clear. You had a conversation with the defendant who was feverish and so uncomfortable that you gave him an alcohol rub to ease the discomfort. That is the time at which he allegedly told you that he had killed Roderick Duquesne. Can you explain to the court why he picked on you for this sudden admission? Why, Miss McCoy? Were you good friends?"

"No, of course not. I didn't even——"

"You didn't even like taking care of him, did you, Miss McCoy?" Benson demanded. "You didn't try to hide your disapproval, did you? You didn't do anything especially nice for him, no extra little attentions that hadn't been ordered. I want to know why this incredible statement was made to you. Have you any explanation to offer the court?"

The girl shook her head. "No. I don't know."

"Was it because you had badgered him half out of his mind, Miss McCoy? By your own admission you were alone in the ward with him. By your own admission you disliked him and made sure he knew it."

"No, I didn't——"

"By your own admission," Benson went on ruthlessly, "the defendant made this statement merely to cut off any more discussion about it. Those are your words, Miss McCoy. We know the defendant was in pain. We know he was feverish. We know he wanted to be left alone. He would have said anything just to get you to shut up. Isn't that true, Miss McCoy?"

The girl's shoulders pulled together protectively. She shook her head.

Benson moved closer, his hands on his hips, inclined forward. "Answer me, Miss McCoy," he demanded.

The girl slid back in her seat, wide-eyed, shocked to silence.

"Didn't you badger him into it, Miss McCoy? Didn't he make this so-called statement to you merely because he was in pain and wanted only to be left alone? Wasn't he willing to say anything if only you would stop pestering him?"

"Oh, no!" She covered her mouth with a quick, awkward gesture of both hands. The loose ends of her gloves swung up and hit her small hat, tilting it. "Oh-h-h."

Benson stepped away, shaking his head. "Just how many people did you tell about this alleged confession, Miss McCoy?"

The girl prodded at her hat. "Nobody," she said in a rising tone. "I didn't tell anybody."

"Then will you explain just how the County Attorney came to call you as a witness? How did he know you had anything to say?"

"Well, I might have . . ." the girl hesitated. She flushed splotchily and her small pretty face knotted with a flicker of anger. "I just happened to tell my boy friend," she said with a resentful little flounce. "And maybe I mentioned it to my supervisor. I think I probably did."

"I think you probably did, too," Benson agreed. "And I'll bet it got better each time you told it."

Frank Sayer scraped his chair back noisily. "Your Honor, counsel has no right to——"

"I withdraw the question, Your Honor," Benson said wearily. "I am finished with Mr. Sayer's surprise." He made a curt motion of his hand and turned away.

"What do you think?" he asked Burr.

"She got to them," Burr said in an undertone. "You could see it sink in. You didn't hurt her much. They still believed her."

Benson nodded. He looked once, bitterly, at Turo and bent to study his notes. The confession itself was not particularly damaging, as long as it was not coupled with the suggestion that the boy had killed while trying to rob Duquesne. The fact of the killing itself was not to be disputed. Benson planned to have the boy admit it when he testified. But he had also been counting on the dramatic effect of the boy's free and frank admission. Now, after hearing Miss McCoy, the jury might be inclined to suspect the boy had been forced into it.

Frank Sayer and his two assistants held a quick, muttered conference at their table. Judge Groat restrained himself for quite a while before tapping impatiently on the base of his lamp. "Well, Mr. Sayer?"

Frank Sayer rose and pulled down his coat smoothly. "Your Honor," he said, "the People rest."

Judge Groat glanced up at the big clock over the entrance. It was not quite eleven thirty. "You have already made your opening statement, Mr. Kellogg. Are you ready now with your first witness, or would you rather begin after our noon recess?"

"My first witness is here, Your Honor," Benson said. "His testimony will take only a few minutes."

"Call him, then, if you please, Mr. Kellogg."

A slouching, scrawny young man with a prominent Adam's apple and a cocksure, offhand bounciness came loping in, took the oath, and identified himself as Dr. Charles Gordon Hill.

"Where were you, Doctor, at about five A.M. on the fourteenth of April?" Benson moved slowly toward the witness stand.

"On duty in the emergency ward at Rincon County Hospital."

"At about that time, were you called upon to treat the defendant, Arturo Campeón?"

"I was." Dr. Hill put his head on one side and studied the boy. "Yes, sir," he said decisively.

"Please tell the court what injuries you treated. In laymen's language, please, so that we can follow."

"Scalp wound," the doctor began in a nervous staccato. "Broken right arm. Broken right collarbone. Four broken ribs. Scratches and abrasions."

"It is the last item that I wish you would explain in more detail, Doctor," Benson said. "Where did you find those abrasions and so forth?"

"Both elbows, both shoulders, both buttocks."

"Again, Doctor, I refer you to the last item. What was the extent of the scratches and abrasions in the area of the buttocks?"

"Not severe. None of the scratches required anything more than a light dressing."

"How was the defendant clothed when you first saw him?"

Dr. Hill shrugged. "I don't believe I noticed. I had more important things to think about."

"Of course," Benson said in a conciliatory tone. "I appreciate that, Doctor. I merely want to know if there was anything unusual about his clothing. Was there any item missing?"

"Well, his shirt was torn pretty badly."

"Was he, Doctor," Benson asked pointedly, "wearing a pair of trousers?"

"Why, yes."

"What was the state of those trousers? Were they whole, or were they torn?"

"They looked all right to me," Dr. Hill said. "A little dirty, but they weren't ripped or anything like that."

"You did not notice the scratches and abrasions on the defendant's buttocks until after you had removed his trousers, did you, Doctor?"

"Well, I couldn't very well have . . ." Dr. Hill made a quick vague gesture.

"Please finish what you were saying, Doctor."

"Just that the buttock injuries were hidden by the defendant's trouser's, that's all. I didn't see them until he was undressed."

"Thank you, Doctor. That will be all."

Frank Sayer glanced up as Benson turned away. He was rubbing his chin. His long lower lip was caught lightly between his teeth. He blinked and sat up straight. "I have no questions for this witness, Your Honor," he said.

"Very well. We will now recess until one thirty this afternoon." Judge Groat signaled the clerk and got up with a spry alacrity that suggested he was in urgent need of a respite.

Benson pulled at Burr's arm, keeping him in his seat. "I want you to have lunch here with Turo. Can you?"

"I can," Burr said with a scowl. "I sure as hell don't want to."

"I'm not pleased about the way he's behaving," Benson said earnestly. "He's got a damn strange attitude. I can't figure him out. See if you can get him to talk about it."

"Okay, if you say so." Burr turned and went out quickly, trailing the boy and his guard. Benson sighed and sat back in his chair, looking absently at the stacks of books and papers on his table. He stripped off some pages and put them in his pocket. The courtroom was almost deserted as he went out.

BENSON detoured several blocks into the old Spanish quarter and ate his lunch in a nearly empty restaurant near the old rail freight yards. He gulped down his meal and was outside again in less than half an hour. He walked very slowly through the noontime crowds, enjoying the flare of the desert light, the weight of the sun on his back, the slow movement of brittle-dry air that stung his nostrils. He turned in reluctantly at his office building and rode up in an overloaded elevator.

He opened his office door and went inside. He was almost at his desk before he saw the tall slender man who unfolded himself like a jackknife from the couch. He stood, gaunt and high, outlined against the brilliant windows. Benson blinked. For a moment he did not recognize him. Then he smiled and held out his hand.

"Fitz," he said pleasantly. "I haven't seen you in town for a year. I didn't know you in your city clothes."

"You're a bit of a stranger yourself, my boy," Fitz said. "Haven't been eating or sleeping much, I hear. Margareta is worried about you. So am I."

"I've had to concentrate on the trial, Fitz. No time for the ranch right now. How are things with you?"

Fitz tilted a thin hand from side to side. "So-so," he said casually. "I'm just off for Alaska. Stopped in to say good-bye —and God bless. Had a most enjoyable stay."

Benson grunted. He went around and sat behind his desk. "Sudden decision, isn't it, Fitz?"

Fitz stroked a finger slowly along his bristly mustache. "Not sudden enough, I'm afraid," he murmured. "Stayed on rather longer than I'd intended. Been feeling a little uneasy about it, as a matter of fact." He looked up at Benson very soberly.

"What's on your mind, Fitz?"

"Nothing there's any need to talk about. Never much value in rehashing things, to my way of thinking. Fact is, I was a trifle pissed the last time we spoke. May have said a word or two I didn't entirely mean. I thought I'd grown out of that sort of thing, but I dare say none of us get much wiser with age. I just stopped off to make sure there were no hard feelings. Wouldn't like to go off, having you think . . ." His light, very distinct voice dwindled inconclusively to silence. He made a slow, uncertain gesture with one hand.

"What you said was very useful to me, Fitz. I didn't take any offense, if that's what you mean."

But that wasn't quite what he meant, Benson knew. There didn't seem to be much point in approaching any closer to the real issue. Fitz was embarrassed, he could see. It was not, Benson thought, a situation that would be improved by discussion.

It was not pleasant, seeing Fitz like this. Benson was used to his moving and talking with the exuberant spontaneity of a young boy, not sitting in watchful stillness like an aging and cautious man who guards his treacherous tongue as a man must when he knows he is not among friends. This attitude did not suit Fitz at all. His habit was to play the good and gallant and reckless soldier whose quality was to make grown men recall for just a moment, the wild sense of adventure that had informed them as boys.

"I've been reading about the trial the past few days," Fitz said with a forced brightness. "Sounds rather like a shilling thriller in spots. The newspapers don't seem to think you have much chance of winning. The law is against you, I gather?"

"Let's say that it is not for us. We'll have to let the jury decide." Benson took out a cigarette and tossed the pack across to Fitz. "I'll be sorry to see you go, Fitz. You're leaving just before the big rodeo parade. Why don't you stick around awhile longer?"

"No," Fitz made a curt waggle of his head. "Plans all made. I've a long way to go and I'm told it isn't wise to count on decent weather in Alaska much after summer."

"I'd like to see that part of the world myself," Benson said uncomfortably. "Never been up there. What are your plans, Fitz? Going to head back before the first snow, I suppose?"

"Well, I'll clear out of Alaska before then, at any rate. I've been looking into the shipping schedules to Hawaii from there. Thought I might put the old Deusenberg on board and sail off to the islands. Make a nice change."

"Sounds great," Benson muttered. He made himself smile at Fitz. He didn't want to analyze his feelings. He knew that much of the regard and affection he felt for Fitz would never diminish. But it would be foolish to pretend that nothing had changed between them. "I'm sorry you're going, Fitz," he said honestly.

Fitz shook his narrow, handsome head. "It's time I was moving along," he said easily. "I'm taking away some very pleasant memories."

"I'm glad of that," Benson said clumsily. "Fitz, I wish——"

"Shouldn't be surprised if I wished much the same thing," Fitz broke in briskly. Benson's inarticulate hesitancy seemed to give him a new confidence. He leaned back slightly and caught a lifted knee between his hands. "Going to marry that girl?"

"Next week, probably," Benson said. "Fitz——"

"Too bad I can't come to the wedding. Mightn't be in the best of taste, in any event. I'll send you a present, though. What would you like? Sealskin parka? Nice grass hula skirt?"

"With the girl still inside," Benson said with a stiff attempt at a smile.

Fitz rose, quick and angular. He put out his cigarette. "Thanks very much, my boy," he said quietly.

It was a brief handshake. They looked at each other silently, full of words they could not say. Benson knew that in saying good-bye to Fitz he was closing the door on a meaningful part of his past. No one else could bridge the gap between the present and those nearly forgotten days in England when he had been married so very briefly to Liza FitzAllen. After Fitz left, the memory of Liza would grow dimmer with time, until it would merge gradually with a vague and jumbled memory of the terror and excitement of the war years.

Fitz straightened himself to a soldierly squareness.

"Keep in touch, Fitz."

"I will, my boy," Fitz said, lying amiably. "Best of luck." His thin hand rose and fell in a short, choppy salute. He swung the door shut behind him with a decisive click.

Benson gave Fitz a few minutes to get clear of the building. He sat very still, suddenly tired, watching his cigarette smoldering to ashes in front of him, purposely thinking of nothing at all. He could not allow himself to remember. In less than half an hour he was due in court, and he did not dare handicap himself with memory.

He went out quickly, speaking to no one. He moved along the busy streets, squinting in the harsh sunlight, forcing his mind to consideration of the case he was to present in court. He pulled away irritably when a hand hooked his elbow from behind. He took another step before looking around.

"Sorry, Burr," he said dully. "Didn't realize that was you."

"Wake up, Ben, you're sleepwalking." Burr looked at him sharply. "You okay?"

"Sure. Just—thinking. Did you see the boy?"

Burr shrugged. He fell into step beside Benson. "I saw him. We had some jailhouse coffee and some jailhouse baloney. And the kid gave me a candy bar for dessert. I saw his grandfather, too. And that, let me tell you, is a spooky old boy."

"The Dorado?"

"Was he one of those?" Burr whistled softly. "I can believe it. And I'll bet Pancho Villa was a little bit uneasy, too, whenever the old boy was around."

"What was he doing there?"

"Damned if I know," Burr muttered. "He just came in with the jailer, asked the kid if he was all right, asked if he wanted anything. The kid answered and the old boy turned around and stamped off. Didn't say a word to me, didn't even look at me."

"I wish to hell he wouldn't hang around," Benson said. "But I guess Turo needs some moral support. What did you think about him?"

"Hard to say. I'd bet ten to one he's not a fairy. That's one of the things you were worried about, wasn't it?"

"One of them," Benson admitted. "But right now I'm more concerned about his strange attitude."

"You've got reason to worry, I'd say," Burr agreed. "I can't figure him out. He needs a good kick in the ass. For a minute I was thinking maybe he was on some kind of dope. He just sits there and answers politely but it's all pretense. He doesn't really listen. I don't think he gives a damn." Burr stepped around two women waiting at a bus stop and bowed his apologies.

"I never saw anything quite like it before, Ben," he went on. "The average guy on trial for his life, even a grown man with good steady nerves, will be jittery and tight. His belly is in a knot and he'll probably vomit if you touch him suddenly. But this kid . . ." Burr shook his head. "I just don't know what to say."

Benson nodded heavily. "I know what you mean. But he can't be taking dope; there's no way he could get it."

"He reminds me of an old experienced con, just going through the motions," Burr said. "As if he knows the fix is in and all he has to do is sit there and tough it out."

"Fixed," Benson repeated. "I never thought of that. Do you suppose the Dorado might have told him——"

"No, I meant just the opposite," Burr broke in. "That the kid thought the trial was fixed against him, so there was no chance at all for him to win."

"What?"

"I think the kid expects to be convicted. That's why he's so calm. He's resigned to it, like an old Indian waiting to die."

"That's nonsense, Burr," Benson said angrily. "He can't ——" He stopped suddenly, remembering something. "What did he say to you?" he demanded.

"Nothing useful, Ben. Maybe I just pulled something out of the air. Forget it." He eyed Benson curiously. "But you just got a hot flash, didn't you? What's on your mind?"

Benson shook his head. "I was thinking of something Clemente told me about the old man," he said slowly. "I'd forgotten until this minute."

"What was it?"

"Some superstitious business about the Dorado killing Turo unless I convinced him the boy was innocent."

"Innocent of what? We know damn well he's guilty. At least he did scrag Duquesne. There's no getting around that."

"You know what he's thinking of," Benson said soberly. "He doesn't care about Duquesne; he's worried about Turo. The Dorado is a Mexican. If he thought his grandson was actually a practicing homosexual, he just might . . ."

"Yeah," Burr said. "Maybe so. I'd better have a talk with that old boy and see if——"

"No!" Benson said quickly. "Let him alone, Burr. You'd never talk him out of anything. Anyway, we could be completely wrong about him."

"But damn it, Ben, you have to do something. You can't let the kid take the stand if that's his attitude. He'd hang himself."

"We don't have any choice," Benson reminded him. "Turo is the only witness who can tell the jury what actually happened on Lookout Point. The only one. Without his testimony, there's no chance of winning."

"And damn little with him," Burr muttered.

"Let it go over till morning," Benson said. "I'll try to jack him up before he takes the stand. He's got guts. I think I can put some stiffener in his spine."

They turned at Courthouse Square and crossed the street. Benson moved stiffly, with a growing fear that was like ice in his mind.

THE CLERK'S GAVEL brought Benson out of his introspective concentration. He stood up beside Burr, seeing Turo rise with them. The boy was calm and self-contained. He seemed to be paying strict attention, but as Burr had seen, it was little more than polite pretense.

There was something tragic and deeply disturbing, Benson thought, about a defendant who is at ease in a courtroom where he is on trial for his life. It is unnatural to a degree that makes for revulsion. Benson hoped fervently that none of the jurors sensed the strangeness of Arturo Campeón. But Number Six, Mitchell Masterton, was just the perceptive sort of man who might sniff it out.

"Well, Mr. Kellogg?" Judge Groat said. He rose and twitched at his gown, and sat again.

"The defense calls Detective Lieutenant Harry Jurgens," Benson told the clerk. Before he went toward the witness stand, he bent to whisper in Burr's ear. "Tommy should be waiting at the side door. Tell him to hotfoot it over to the Frontier Hotel and tell Mary to bring Elsinore to the witness room right away."

"Will do," Burr said readily. He slid from his seat.

"You are Detective Lieutenant Harry Jurgens," Benson asked the witness, "currently assigned as chief investigator in the office of the County Attorney?"

Jurgens was an alert, wiry man with pale red hair and the kind of skin that turns thick and red in the sun. He had a responsive Jewish face, lean and flexible.

"Were you one of the county officers who assisted the County Attorney in preparing the prosecution's case against the defendant, Arturo Campeón?"

"I was."

"One moment, if you please, Your Honor," Frank Sayer called. "The People ask for a show of proof on this witness. I want to know how his testimony can be relevant to any matter at issue in this trial."

"Very well. Come forward. You too, Mr. Kellogg."

Benson went back to his table. Burr slid a sheaf of stapled papers toward him, and winked. "Give it a slow build-up."

"I know," Benson said grimly.

"I will make three separate offers of proof in respect to this witness, Your Honor," Benson said.

"Three! What kind of foolishness is this?" Sayer demanded.

"This witness' testimony is relevant and material for three distinct reasons, Your Honor," Benson insisted. "I'm not going to lump those reasons together and run the risk of an adverse ruling because the court disagrees with me on one or two of them."

"Very wise," Judge Groat said thinly. "Proceed, please."

"I intend to show that the deceased was widely known as a man of turbulent and violent disposition. Evidence of the character of deceased is always relevant, Your Honor, when defense contends that there is a strong presumption that because of his reputation, deceased was more likely to have been the aggressor than a defendant of peaceful reputation."

"No, sir," Sayer stated flatly. "It won't wash. Such evidence would be admissible only after defense has made a *prima facie* showing of self-defense. It's a dubious point anyway. The law makes no distinction between the murder of a bad man and the murder of a good man. It is the murder we are concerned with here, not deceased's reputation."

Judge Groat waggled his pencil in front of his eyes for a thoughtful moment. "I am inclined to agree with Frank on that," he said in a dubious tone. "What is your second offer, Benson?"

"Lieutenant Jurgens' evidence is part of the *res gestae,* Your Honor," Benson went on. "Ordinarily, I realize, such testimony would not be admissible, but here we are concerned with the situation discussed by both Wigmore and McCormick, both of whom agree that evidence of other criminal acts may be admitted if such evidence directly establishes some essential element. The decision balances on the probative force of the evidence offered."

"And what would be the force, Benson?" the judge asked.

"In the first place, we will complete the story of the crime for which defendant is on trial. Only the defense is able, and willing, to do that, and the jury has the right to the whole story.

The other reason touches upon my third offer of proof." Benson paused, waiting until the judge signaled for him to go on.

"And this, I suspect," the judge murmured, "is the nub?"

"It may well be, Your Honor," Benson said. He turned a page of his notes. "The defense will show, through testimony by Lieutenant Jurgens and another witness, that deceased had a strong propensity for sexual aberration. In *People* v. *McDaniel,* eighty, three-eighty-one, the ruling is directly to the point. May I read an excerpt, Your Honor?"

"If it is brief."

" 'There is still another relevancy to the evidence herein adduced,' " Benson read in a low, clear voice. " 'Certain crimes today are recognized as stemming from a specific propensity for sexual aberration. The fact that in the past one has given way to unnatural proclivities has a direct bearing on the ultimate issue whether in the case being tried he is guilty of a particular unnatural act of passion. . . . This propensity tended to establish the offense for which the defendant herein was being tried, much as the symptoms of a known disease suffered in the past tend to establish the presence of the same today.' " He folded his papers together and held them behind his back.

"The ruling cited, Your Honor, refers to admission of evidence against a defendant. If such evidence can be admitted to convict, it seems mandatory that such evidence should be admitted when a defendant wishes to offer it in his own behalf. A later ruling in the same case goes even farther in extending the rule to include unnatural acts of the same type, committed with persons other than those named in the charge."

"But these acts are not charged in the information, Your Honor," Frank Sayer said with some heat. "We don't care whether an unnatural relationship existed between defendant and deceased. We are concerned only with murder."

"We intend to show that deceased's death was the direct result of defendant's instinctive and violent revulsion against homosexual attack by the deceased. I ask for a ruling, Your Honor."

"I maintain my objection, Your Honor," the prosecutor

said forcefully. "The defense is touching on dangerous ground in asking for admission of evidence that is largely hearsay and totally irrelevant to any offense charged by the People."

Judge Groat scribbled in his notebook, head down, intent. After a moment he looked up and said, "No, I am going to overrule you, Frank. You may have an exception. Let's proceed, Benson."

Benson let out a pent-up breath in a silent gasp. He went back to his place on legs that almost shook with relief. Burr took the folded papers from his hand. Benson was surprised to see that he had wadded them tightly in his fist.

"Go get him, Ben. He's all yours." Burr said admiringly. "Don't forget you can declare him a hostile witness if he tries to evade any of your questions. Sic 'im, boy!"

Benson grinned briefly. He picked up a sheet with the transcribed notes of his interview with Captain Valentine.

"Now, Lieutenant Jurgens," he said, "the court has ruled that you may tell us about your investigation. I am interested principally in one aspect of it. I ask you now whether in the course of that investigation you uncovered evidence showing that deceased, Roderick Duquesne, was a person of turbulent and violent disposition?"

Jurgens eyed him with a full, bold stare that was close to challenge. He nodded slowly. "Yes, sir," he said in a flat, authoritative tone.

"Did you also find evidence showing that deceased, Roderick Duquesne, was widely known for his strong propensity toward sexual aberration?"

Benson slowly retreated along the jury box as Jurgens said, "Yes, sir."

This was the first reference to homosexuality the jury had yet heard, and Benson wanted to be sure they understood the significance of Jurgens' testimony.

"What form did Duquesne's sexual aberration take, Lieutenant?"

"He was known to be a homosexual," Jurgens said.

"Will you repeat that, please, Lieutenant?" Benson asked.

"I don't believe the jury could hear you."

"I said he was a homosexual," Jurgens said again at exactly the same volume. He studied Benson with a half-hidden derision.

"A homosexual, Lieutenant?" Benson said. "What sort?"

Jurgens frowned suspiciously. "I don't understand the question, Counselor. He was a homosexual, a sodomist."

"You say that Roderick Duquesne was widely known to be a sodomist. I asked you what variety of sodomist, Lieutenant. Active, or passive?"

Jurgens shook his head. "I don't know what those terms mean," he said irritably.

"The terms explain themselves, Lieutenant," Benson said, standing now at the far end of the jury box. "But let me see if I can help you out. An active sodomist is that masculine participant in one of the five acts of sodomy who plays the part of the male. The passive is that masculine participant in such an act who plays the role of the female. I ask you again, Lieutenant, which sort was Duquesne?"

Jurgens flushed hotly. He ran a finger along his high-bridged nose and shrugged. "I don't know. I didn't know there were two kinds."

"Let me try to help you again. You received certain information concerning Duquesne's reputation from various sources, among them the chief of the confidential squad of the Los Angeles Police, a Captain C. G. Valentine. Is that correct?"

"Yes."

"And Captain Valentine read to you a long list of offenses which Duquesne was known to have committed. Is that true also, Lieutenant?"

"Yes."

"All of those acts contained a common element of violence, didn't they?"

"Yes."

"And many of those acts———"

"Your Honor!" Frank Sayer rose beside Benson, brushing

past as he moved around his table. "Your Honor, I must ob-ject to the constant references counsel is making to specific acts which are not relevant or admissible in establishing the reputation or character of deceased."

"In this case, Your Honor," Benson said, staying where he was and talking to the back of Sayer's head, "there is a pertinent exception to the rule the County Attorney has cited. In considering Roderick Duquesne's character, we are establishing a distinctive plan or device which followed a remarkably similar, if not identical, pattern through most of deceased's adult life. To establish that pattern, it is necessary and permissible to refer to specific instances and relate them to the common, unvarying pattern of deceased's behavior."

"Objection overruled," the judge said.

Frank Sayer shot an infuriated glance at Benson as he resumed his seat. He scraped together a miscellany of loose papers and bent over them.

Benson went on patiently and methodically, asking Jurgens if Captain Valentine had told him of the separate entries on the report which Benson had seen in Los Angeles. Jurgens replied stolidly, unemotionally, volunteering nothing, but admitting that Captain Valentine had indeed told him of all the charges and suspicions listed against Duquesne. By the time Benson was finished, the jury was staring with a certain numb astonishment at the witness, slightly horrified and wondering what new piece of revolting information he would offer next. Mrs. Jordan, the lone woman juror, was white and drawn about the mouth. She could not look at the witness.

"Are you now in a position, Lieutenant," Benson asked, "to tell the court whether the active person who committed this active series of unnatural criminal acts, was an active or a passive homosexual?"

"I guess he was active, all right," Jurgens said in a surly undertone. "I don't think anyone told me that, though."

"I hardly think anyone had to tell you," Benson said. "How many times was Roderick Duquesne questioned by the Los Angeles police on charges of homosexual assault?"

"Four or five times, as I recall."

"Four or five times the deceased was suspected of forcing boys or young men to unnatural sex acts," Benson said, talking to the jury. "That is your testimony, Lieutenant?"

"Yes, sir."

"Thank you, Lieutenant. Your witness, Mr. Sayer."

"I have no questions for Lieutenant Jurgens," Frank Sayer said without rising from his chair.

Benson glanced inquiringly toward the defense table. Burr nodded quickly.

"The defense will call——" Benson began.

Judge Groat's light pencil tapping silenced him before he could announce Elsinore's name.

"We will take fifteen minutes first," the judge said. "Mr. Clerk?"

NONE OF THE SPECTATORS left the courtroom during the intermission, and only two of the jurors took advantage of their chance to stretch their legs. Everyone seemed to sense that Lieutenant Jurgens had merely been the first of a series of witnesses who would be testifying on the real background of the crime charged against Arturo Campeón. Nobody wanted to run the risk of missing any of the scandalous bits.

"Call Harald Elsinore," Benson told the clerk when court had reconvened.

Elsinore had been waiting near the door and he came in promptly. Judge Groat glanced at him casually, then stared. He followed the willowy young man's progression with a tight, questioning glare.

Benson was watching the jury closely. As he had expected, it was Masterton who first turned to study Turo after his first brief glimpse of Elsinore. His sharp intensity indicated that he had immediately noted the remarkable resemblance between Elsinore and the defendant and was trying to see if there was special meaning to it. Then Mrs. Jordan caught it.

She pinched the fleshy tip of her chin as she turned from one to the other.

That close and unexpected resemblance, Benson thought, was at least half of Elsinore's value to the defense. His physical appearance alone would be strong corroboration of his testimony.

Elsinore was very pale and tense. He was dressed as for a funeral in an almost-black suit of summer silk that shimmered with an inner gleam. He wore a black necktie with a tiny white figure. He held up a trembling right hand, affirmed his oath in a reedy voice, and took the stand. He looked once at Benson, then down at the narrow railing in front of him. He did not move as Benson approached.

"Your name is Harald Elsinore?"

"Yes."

"Why are you here, Harald?"

"What?" Elsinore glanced up through lowered lashes. "Why, I was——"

"I issued a subpoena, did I not, that required your attendance at this trial? You did not come here of your own free will, did you?"

"No," Elsinore said thinly.

"I subpoenaed you so that you could tell the court about the background and reputation of Roderick Duquesne. You have special and personal knowledge of Duquesne as a result of an intimate relationship that lasted for some five years. Is that correct?"

Elsinore nodded. "Yes."

"During the period of that intimate relationship, you learned much of his past history. Through your own observation and what you were told, you came to understand what motivated him. Is that a fair statement?"

"I—I suppose it is."

"Well, let's just see if it is," Benson said patiently. "I want you to tell the court, briefly and in your own words, what you know of Duquesne's background, what his family life was like, the sort of boy he was, the sort of man he finally became.

Just go ahead, Harald."

Elsinore drew in a shaky breath and lifted his shoulders. He spoke in a toneless, erratic voice that had great carrying force.

The jury listened intently. There were none of the usual restless sounds from the spectators. Judge Groat sat without moving, chewing lightly at the tip of his pencil, his tired, lined old face growing more and more bleak and still as Elsinore continued.

Elsinore dismissed Duquesne's parents with a few curt sentences. ("Well-to-do," he called them.) He told the jury how Duquesne's mother had killed herself, leaving her body to be found by her fourteen-year-old son. Mrs. Jordan made a short, choked sound. The rest of the jury sat hunched and concentrated.

Benson stood well back from the witness stand. He did not need to prompt Elsinore or ask any questions.

Elsinore's voice broke when he told of the venereal disease Duquesne had contracted during his school days and the revulsion toward females that Duquesne justified as a result.

"He often said," Elsinore went on, "that the very same horrible thing had happened to Oscar Wilde when he was at Oxford. That was the reason for—for Roddy's change of attitude."

Again it was Masterton who caught the allusion first and completely. He seemed to stiffen in his chair.

"Later," Elsinore went on, "Roddy liked to give his friends engraved cigarette cases to commemorate great occasions because he had read that Oscar Wilde used to do that, too."

He spoke briefly of Duquesne's professional skill and his gradually increasing discontent. Elsinore's account then began to falter as he groped for details that did not come readily to mind. Benson moved toward the stand.

"During the time you knew him, did Duquesne have any intimate relations whatever with women?"

Elsinore told the jury at some length of Duquesne's fradulent marriage which had been intended from the first as a cynical camouflage. He made the serious mistake of sneering at the young actress who had entered into the deception with Duquesne. Benson got him off the subject quickly.

"Now, Harald, I want you to tell the jury how and where and when you met Duquesne, what your first experience with him was, and how your relationship developed."

This was the part that would ruin Elsinore in the estimation of the jury, Benson realized. It couldn't be helped, though, and it was better to bring it out now than wait for Frank Sayer to expose it on cross-examination.

Benson could almost feel the waves of savage disapproval in the courtroom as Elsinore stumbled through a transparently expurgated version of his days with Duquesne. It took four insistent, demanding questions from Benson before Elsinore would admit that he had been attacked by Duquesne and forced to submit to homosexual rape the very first time they had been alone together. And that, in effect, was all that Benson wanted from him.

Harald Elsinore had told the jury that Duquesne had at least once before committed homosexual attack on a young man. Everything else he had said was merely corroborative of that one stark fact. Duquesne's character and reputation were now clearly apparent to the jury.

But the same could be said of Elsinore's. Benson took another hour with him, putting quietly and patiently a series of questions aimed at demonstrating Elsinore's passive nature, his incapacity for decision, his feeble sense of reality. It did little good, he suspected, but at least the jury was no longer thinking of Elsinore as a slobbering monster.

"Your witness," Benson said finally. On the way back to his table, he noticed that Turo Campeón was not merely pretending an interest now. The boy was watching Harald Elsinore with a tightly fascinated, unbelieving stare.

Burr leaned toward him and muttered, "I'd hate to be in that little punk's shoes. Frank is going to butcher him."

"I know," Benson said.

It was a few minutes before Elsinore understood what was happening to him. Sayer began in a mildly skeptical tone that progressively hardened to open contempt. Elsinore shrank into himself protectively as the cross-examination went on. Within five minutes he was on the verge of tears. His voice went shrill.

There was no protection Benson could offer Elsinore. Sayer ripped him apart time after time, snapping out questions with a fierce disgust that visibly shook the witness.

Elsinore was forced to recollect every unsavory episode of his homosexual experience from its beginning ("I was thirteen," he finally admitted) to his presently unattached status, which, Sayer insinuated, was not as unattached as Elsinore pretended.

Elsinore had stupidly tried to claim that Duquesne's attack on him had been his first homosexual experience. Sayer had demolished that self-serving pretense with almost no effort. The history that followed was a sordid, stomach-turning account.

Out of his excessive eagerness, the prosecutor made one mistake. He tried to suggest that Elsinore's experience with Duquesne had not been the long and intimate association that Elsinore said it had been. He lost the jury on that one, Benson felt, especially when Elsinore, to bolster his claim, recited what he said was Duquesne's favorite justification for his way of life: "I am one, my liege, whom the vile blows and buffets of the world have so incensed, that I am reckless what I do to spite the world."

And Elsinore said it with a readiness and confidence he had seldom shown on the stand. That was the last moment of firmness or credibility that Elsinore was allowed.

Frank Sayer moved in for the kill, pushing him with ruthless severity to a frenzied and incoherent defense of homosexuality. The jury listened incredulously as Elsinore spoke wildly of Shakespeare and Socrates, quoted from Burton's *Terminal Essay* and the apologies of Donald Cory. He was in midstride with a garbled version of Kinsey when Sayer cut him off.

"No, no, that's enough," he growled. He wiped his mouth

with a flipped-open handkerchief as he walked back toward his table. He was shaking his head at the jurors as he went by.

"Have you finished with this witness, Mr. Sayer?" the judge inquired.

"My God, yes, Your Honor," Sayer said heavily. "I've finished with that—" he swept a hand through the air in a slashing gesture—"that creature."

Elsinore came down awkwardly from the stand, almost stumbling. What had been the total effect? Benson wondered. It was always difficult to gauge the impact of any testimony, and in Elsinore's case it was doubly confusing. He left the stand discredited and broken, in the eyes of the jury a corrupt, unrepentant pervert. Sayer had sharply emphasized the fact of Elsinore's jealous anger when he learned of Duquesne's constant promiscuity, fixing firmly in the jury's awareness Elsinore's classic motive for wanting to destroy Duquesne's reputation. What would the jury choose to believe?

For nearly three hours Elsinore had held them fascinated with dread and horror at the picture of the homosexual world he had drawn for them. They would believe without question that he had been part of that world for most of his life. And even though they despised him, they would be inclined to believe him when he identified Duquesne as an active homosexual. But would they believe that Duquesne had been a homosexual rapist?

"Bad," Burr said quietly. "That punk better change his name again and head for the hills. Frank slaughtered him."

Benson nodded. It had been bad. Elsinore had been the best available witness but, he suspected, not good enough. He could not pretend he was surprised by what had happened.

Judge Groat tapped his pencil tiredly against his lamp. "That's all for today," he said. "Nine thirty tomorrow, Mr. Clerk."

Benson intercepted Turo before the boy could leave. "Tomorrow's your big day. I'll be in to see you about seven thirty and we'll take a couple of hours to go over your testimony. Okay?"

"Sure." Turo was looking over Benson's head toward the spectators who were filing from the courtroom.

"Are you feeling all right?"

"Sure." Turo turned away and led his guard toward the staircase.

Benson watched him out of sight, frowning.

"One thing Elsinore did," Burr said easily, stretching far back in his chair. "He certainly convinced me that Duquesne was overdue for killing."

THE LIGHTS in the houses of La Cañada were coming on one by one as Benson stood watching from the big window of the living room. He was holding a telephone to his ear with two fingers, listening with a numbed sort of patience.

"No, Mary," he said after a moment. "You were right to call me. Did you give Elsinore any money?"

He listened for a moment longer, spoke briefly, and hung up. He went slowly back through the long room to the corridor and along it a few steps to the dining room. Jocelyn Gilbert glanced up, holding her coffee cup poised.

"It was just Mary," Benson said. "God, I'm beat." He pulled his necktie down and opened his collar. He shoved his half-filled plate aside and poured more wine into his glass.

He looked out through the high windows at the looming mountain, purple-dark now and ominous with shadow. Joss reached over to touch his hand. She was wearing a heavily embroidered blouse and matador pants in a dull silk that was the palest shade of pink Benson had ever seen. Nothing could have been more becoming.

"I suppose you heard about Harald Elsinore?" he said.

"I read about him." Her voice was tight, rather flat. "The papers were full of him." She shuddered and sat back. "What a horrible little monster."

"Amen," Benson said. "Definitely not an admirable type, as Fitz would say. Mary just told me he's ducked out."

"Who? Fitz or Elsinore?"

"Well, both, as a matter of fact," Benson said. "Fitz took off for Alaska this afternoon. Didn't I tell you? Anyway, Mary was calling about Elsinore. I promised him a little money for coming here to testify. He left without collecting. I don't know where he went."

"Do you care?"

"No. I'm not even curious about him, but he's probably in a bad state. Frank Sayer took the hide off him in long thin strips. Basically, that was my fault; I brought him here. I promised to help him get settled somewhere when the trial was over."

Joss put her hands up hard against the sides of her very pale face. "Ben, can't you see? He doesn't want to have anything to do with you now. I read the papers. He went out of that courtroom in tears. I used to think pansies all loved to publicize themselves, but Elsinore must be different. I wouldn't be at all surprised if he blames you for everything that happened."

"I suppose so." Benson sighed tiredly. He took the cup of coffee Joss handed to him.

"Does his testimony mean that———"

"Let's not talk about the trial tonight, Joss," he said quickly. He took a sip of the coffee, scalded his mouth, and cursed softly. "I'd like to put it aside for a while. Let's go in and play some music and forget the whole damn thing. What say?"

"I'm on," Joss agreed. She rose and came around the table, putting her arms on his shoulders and bending to kiss him warmly. "Poor dear Ben. You look so tired. Come in and stretch out. I'll put on some early Dorsey and we can neck for a while. Then I'm going home. What you need is a good night's sleep. By yourself."

Benson snorted. He got up and followed her into the living room. He sprawled on one of the long couches and shut his eyes, letting the slow, powerful surge of the music work into his brain with a soothing insistence.

Joss sat on the floor beside him. She rested her head on

the cushion beside his chest and listened contentedly, making small quiet sounds in her throat.

Benson was almost asleep when he heard a struggling motor slow at the foot of his driveway. It roared once, then throttled down for the climb to the ranch house. A moment later a second car followed. Benson groaned and opened his eyes. The approaching headlights made strange patterns in the darkened room.

"Stay where you are," Joss said. She got up, snapped on some shaded lights and went to the door.

"The first one is Paula's little bug," she said. "I can't see the other one. I wonder . . ." She slid back the door and went out onto the terrace.

Benson pushed himself upright, put his legs down and got unsteadily to his feet. He slid his necktie up into position. Joss came back. She pushed the door farther open for the two people behind her.

"Paula," Benson said politely, smothering a yawn. He looked beyond her to the slow-moving little man balancing himself on a cane in the doorway. "Tim Cook. What brings you two here?"

"We didn't come together," Paula said flatly. "He just followed me up the road."

"Lucky break for me," Tim said easily. "That's a real tough grade to drive at night. How are you, Ben? I'm not disturbing anything, am I?"

"Just a quiet evening," Benson said ambiguously. "Sit down, Tim. Can I get you a drink? What would you like, Paula?"

"I—I don't want to stay, Ben," Paula said diffidently. "Could you—could you walk me to the car? I just wanted to——" She broke off and brushed her hair back with a distracted gesture. "You don't mind, Joss? I won't keep him long."

"Of course not," Joss said a little too quickly. "Let me get you a drink, Mr. Cook." She directed Tim toward the small bar, keeping her back turned as Benson went out on the terrace with Paula.

"I'm sorry, Ben. She doesn't like me, does she?"

"I never asked her," Benson said bluntly. "She never told me. What do you care?"

"I don't, I suppose," Paula admitted. "I'm just feeling so rotten and insecure that I bust out crying if anyone bats an eye at me. I'm a mess, Ben."

"Hangover," Benson said with no sympathy in his voice. "Did you run out on Burr again?"

"No. Oh, no. I left a note for him. In case he looks for me, which isn't likely. He's working and I didn't want to break in on him. We—we aren't getting on very well just now."

"Don't tell me things like that, Paula. Keep it for yourselves, if you really want to work it out. If you drag in a third party, everything will go plumb to hell."

"I know. I do know, Ben. I didn't come to dump my problems in your lap. I just—wanted to say thank you, Ben. For last night. I'm very grateful. I don't remember everything, but—enough."

"It's all right, Paula," Benson said gently. "All in the family anyway. You aren't the first of us to go into a flat spin. Forget it. How is Burr?"

"He's quiet. So very quiet, Ben, and—polite. I hardly know him." She looked up at Benson suddenly, her eyes clear and bitter. "You don't know how it's been with us since Burr bought this notion of being Attorney General." She drew in a shallow quick breath. "He was like a greedy child, like a greedy, lost child. But—but maybe you do know. He was the same greedy child when he took all the money your father left and fixed it so you almost lost the ranch. He's not a——"

"Paula!" Benson said harshly. "Paula, stop it! You don't want to say these things."

She did stop, abruptly. She shuddered and turned her head away. "He's changed, Ben. Burr isn't like that now. It's as if something scared him. He's very quiet now, and—watchful. He said he was working on something for you."

"Yes, we're drawing up submissions for charges. Don't worry about him, Paula. He's got some things to work out in his mind. From what I've seen, this isn't an easy time for him."

"I'm glad he's working with you, Ben. I'm glad he has you to turn to."

Benson looked at her in the darkness. He led her down the stairs and opened the door of her car. "I'm glad too, Paula. He's a great help," he said. "Go home now, Paula. You can't solve anything here."

"I know," she murmured. "I wasn't trying to. . . ." She slid in behind the wheel with a lithe motion. "I'm not going to lean on you for support, Brother Ben. I just lost sight of what I really wanted. Just for a little while. I'm over it now. I love your brother, Ben. I love him and I'm going to keep him and make him happy, if I have to break his neck. I've got a lot to offer—pride and affection and a certain talent for enjoyment. I can even make a good living, if it comes to that. I don't want you to think——"

Benson stopped her with a hand on her shoulder. "Hush, Paula. Don't tell me. Tell Burr," he said softly. "Any sane man would thank God if you loved him. Give Burr a chance. I think that—for a lot of reasons—he's taking this as badly as you are. He's a very complex and troubled fellow right now. I'm damned if I understand him, and I've tried. But I like him, Paula. I think he'll do. If you are willing to help him once in a while."

"I mean to, Ben," she said firmly. "Thank you. Thank you very much. Now go away, please. I want to sit here by myself for a minute. I might even cry. And then I'll go home. Please, Ben? Just leave me alone now."

"Sure." Benson leaned to kiss her lightly. "Good luck. To both of you." He went back up the stairs without looking back. He closed the sliding door behind him.

Joss measured him with a speculative, sidelong glance as he came inside. He shook his head slightly.

"I guess I picked a bad time to come calling," Tim said. He got off the bar stool and hobbled across the floor. "I didn't have any choice, to tell the truth. I'm on an errand, Ben."

He was speaking in a flat, impersonal tone, the sort of

voice that suggests the speaker is not offering his own words or ideas and does not want to be held accountable for them.

"If it has anything to do with Barstow, forget it, Tim," Benson said. "Let me make you a fresh drink." He took Tim's glass and went past him to the bar.

"I don't want a fresh drink," Tim said stiffly. "I want to speak my piece. You won't like it, I guess, but I have to do it." He stood, stabbing the tip of his cane at the rough hearthstones. "Caucus is about over," he said quickly. "They'll be announcing the names of the candidates in the morning."

"Why tell me? Burr is the one who——"

"Burr's name won't be on the list."

Benson sat up straight. He put his feet down. "You'd better explain that," he said, grimly quiet.

"Damn it," Tim snapped, "I explained it a long time ago. Burr's got a rap on him. One of the big moneybags says he won't do. That's all the caucus has to hear. So Burr is out and ——"

"Does he know?"

"Not from me. It'll be announced in the morning papers."

"Who chopped him? Barstow?"

"Now, you don't have to ask me a question like that," Tim said in a bored voice. "You know damn well who chopped him. Your old friend H. L. Caine."

"Caine! Why would Caine——"

"Because your little brother couldn't deliver the goods," Tim said roughly. "He was given one assignment and he blew it. In that league you don't get a second chance."

"He was supposed to deliver me," Benson said heavily. "That's what you mean, isn't it? Did you actually think he could? Are you people insane enough to think that anybody— anybody—can be delivered?"

"It can be done," Tim said. "It has been done. Burr couldn't do it, though, so Burr is out." He shifted back to put his shoulders against the high fireplace. "And don't bother blasting me. I know what you're thinking. Maybe I'm thinking the same thing. But nobody ever asked me what I think. I'm just running an errand."

"What errand?" Benson demanded. "Why come here and tell me that——"

"I think it's just a trifle too obvious, Ben," Joss said gently. "This—gentleman is trying to recruit another B. Kellogg."

Tim looked at her for a long silent moment, meeting her level candid gaze with a certain reluctant admiration. "You're sharp," he said. "Or maybe I'm getting clumsy."

"Now I know you people are insane," Benson said tightly. "You cut the belly out of my brother and then you expect me to——" He made a quick angry gesture. "Why? Can you tell me that? Why in God's name come to me?"

"Because you delivered," Tim said emphatically. "That's all there is to it, Ben. You said you were going to do certain things, and you did them. You made a deal with Caine, and you kept it. That's what counts in this business. Maybe you haven't been reading the papers lately, but you're getting a lot of pretty valuable publicity. You could parlay it into something good, if you wanted to."

"Something like Attorney General?"

"That's what I was supposed to tell you."

Benson put his glass down, awkwardly abrupt, his hands hard with nervous cramp. He went toward the long glass wall. He stared out blindly at the dark shadows of the high mountain valley.

"Joss?" he asked quietly.

She smiled up at him brightly. "It is tempting, isn't it? Such fun to be the Attorney General. All that madly gay social whirl in El Monte. It would be awful to turn it down, wouldn't it?"

And then she added, with a gentle coarseness that Benson remembered with delight all his life, "Tell the nice man where he can shove it, Ben."

Benson almost choked. He gulped from his glass quickly, swallowing several times before he was able to talk.

Tim Cook hobbled clumsily across the room, retrieved his

hat and turned when he was near the door. "You don't have to tell me."

"There is one thing I'd better tell you, Tim," Benson said coldly.

"Say it."

"I could make you take him."

"Burr?" Tim looked at him sharply.

"There is still one more day to go in the Campeón trial," Benson went on. "I still have to make my final plea to the jury. Until now the dead man has been referred to as Roderick Duquesne. I could call him Robert Caine, if I wanted to. It's not over yet, Tim. Don't you think Caine might bring a little pressure to bear on Nate Barstow, if he was afraid I might name his son?"

"He might," Tim admitted warily. "Are you going to do it?"

"Do you think that Caine's pressure might be so effective that Barstow would want Burr as his candidate after all?"

"Might."

"You know."

"I know."

"That's all I wanted to tell you, Tim. I'm not going to do it. Not because of Caine, or his son. To my mind, Burr made a big mistake when he tied up with Barstow. I'm glad to see him out of it. For a while, at least."

"What does that mean? For a while?"

Benson smiled, and for the first time, it was a wide and genuine smile. "You've thrown away a fine, talented candidate, Tim. Burr has every qualification for political office in this state. He wants to try his hand and I'm going to help him next time."

Tim wiped the back of his hand along his chin. "Next time?"

"He doesn't need Barstow or his broken-down machine. We can raise plenty of campaign money ourselves and build a better organization. There'll be a next time, Tim. You can take that as a promise. And Burr will be running all-out against Barstow's candidate. And he'll win."

Tim studied him, pinch-faced and sober. His tight expression eased gradually. He laughed, a sudden, explosive bark that seemed to catch him by surprise. "Jesus!" he muttered. "Maybe you'll be needing an errand boy when you're ready to move, Ben. I'll be wanting to make a change by then, I imagine. Let me know in plenty of time." He eyed Joss briefly and turned away, shaking his head judiciously. "See you around." He pushed the door open with the rubber tip of his cane and made his way carefully out across the uneven flagstones of the terrace.

Benson sat heavily on the couch and looked at Joss with a submerged and baffled laughter in his eyes.

"Yes, he is a darling and comical little man," Joss said in a sardonic tone. "But we haven't time to discuss him now. Get my coat, dear Ben, and let's be moving."

"Moving? Where?"

Joss rose briskly and held both hands to draw him up. "You really don't want Burr to get the news from the morning paper."

"I'm thick tonight," Benson said apologetically. He came up with Joss's pull and held her close in his arms. "You are real sharp, lady, just as Tim said. And pretty damn wonderful, too. I was proud of you. Did you see Tim's face?"

"Did you see yours?" Joss chuckled throatily. "You are pretty wonderful yourself, Counselor. Now get my coat and let's go have a nice family row with the Burr Kelloggs."

BENSON skidded his chair away from his desk and rubbed his eyes very gently. The morning light in his office was coming strongly in the windows behind him. He reached back to tilt the slats of the blind, then got up and turned off the office lights.

Burr was lying flat on the couch, a big arm up over his face. Benson tapped his foot as he came back to his desk.

"I'm not asleep," Burr said lazily, "just slightly dead. You are a bear for work, boy. Let's see how you've fiddled that draft." He stretched out a hand for the papers Benson slid toward him.

"It's about the way we wrote it the first time. I've been trying to simplify the language. I don't want Judge Groat stumbling over it."

"I don't think it makes much difference how you say it, Ben. I just can't see the old boy accepting it for charge. He might, but don't count on it. You'll make a lot more yardage with the first two submissions, I'd say."

"The two on intent?"

"That's where you'll be shooting directly at the heart of Frank's case," Burr said positively. He sat up, yawning. "To prove first-degree murder, Frank has to prove malice and premeditation. He's got that stolen cigarette lighter which suggests the kid was out to rob Duquesne. That means the killing was felony murder, and that's first-degree. But you've got another explanation for the lighter, and the jury might believe you. The other touchy area is the little flicker of time after the kid kicked himself free from Duquesne and fell out of the car. Frank is going to try to stretch out that time, Ben. He'll be trying to prove that it was long enough so that the kid could have escaped if he'd wanted to. You'll have to nail that one, Ben."

"I intend to," Benson said.

"Make it strong, Counselor. The kid hangs if the jury believes he had a moment to think about what was happening. Premeditation can occur in the time you take to snap your fingers. Make sure the jury knows that Duquesne was right on top of the kid all the way. And keep harping on those pants."

"Pants? Oh, the boy's——"

"Sure. Make sure the jury has a picture of the kid with his britches at half-mast. How the hell could he have run away, even if he'd had time, which he didn't. Get it? Gives you two shots at the same target. Then when old Groat tells the jury they can eliminate premeditation, if they believe what the kid has told them—why, you're home free, and the kid gets off.

Or he gets clipped for manslaughter, at the worst."

"That's an awfully negative approach, Burr," Benson said dubiously. "I don't like it very much."

"I don't exactly love it myself," Burr agreed. "But I think it's your best pitch. All negative evidence ain't bad, you know. Think of the cheers that go up to heaven when the Wassermann is negative. Or the rabbit test. Don't get greedy, boy. Take what's there to be taken."

"I'm not refusing anything, Burr," Benson said. He swung a big foot up on the desk and leaned back. "I'm going to emphasize premeditation. But I'm not going to stop there. Even I know enough of juries to be leery of a purely negative plea."

"You've got the positive approach all lined up. We've been working on it half the night, and I still say it won't hold water, Ben. You're asking the judge to instruct the jury that this kid had a legal right to defend himself from homosexual attack. You even ask him to call it rape. But homosexual attack is not rape. It isn't even a felony in our statutes. Legally, the kid overdefended himself. He committed a criminal act."

"Maybe not. The statute isn't that definite, Burr. You're reasoning from negative evidence again. I remember that Judge Turnbull told me it was a point worth arguing."

"But Groat won't let you argue it. He'll just look at your submission privately, and then accept or reject it."

"Before that, I'll have a chance to explain it to the jury. That's permissible, and by God, I'm going to put it to them no matter what Groat thinks."

"And no matter what I think," Burr grinned suddenly. "You're getting real ferocious lately, boy." He got up from the couch, stretching. "It's coming up for eight o'clock. Let's get some breakfast."

"Hell, is it that late? I've got to get over to the jail." Benson scooped his papers together, took them over to Mary's desk and scribbled a hasty memo for her.

"Want me to come along?"

"I can probably handle him better by myself, Burr. I don't want anyone distracting him."

"You're not getting jittery, are you, Counselor?" Burr squinted at him shrewdly through half-closed eyes.

Benson forced a tired smile. "A little, maybe. I'd probably be scared to death if I had time for it."

THERE WAS still one thin spear of morning sunlight that escaped the newly fitted blind. It fell slantingly across the courtroom from behind the jury box. Arturo Campeón walked through it on his way to the witness stand. He was supporting his bulky cast with his left hand. He took his hand away, touched the clerk's Bible with his fingertips and repeated the oath in a calm, unemotional voice.

He got up on the elevated stand and sat, half turned so he could rest the weight of the cast on the arm of the chair. He looked toward Benson who had not yet left his place at the defense table. Briefly he glanced out into the courtroom, then back again to Benson.

The courtroom was very still as Benson got up. He came forward deliberately, his mouth nervously dry, dots of sweat starting along his forehead.

He had not been nervous earlier that morning, but now, after two hours with Turo in his cell, he was not only nervous, he was downright alarmed. Nothing he could say had seemed to get through to the boy.

At least, Benson told himself, there was no danger of Turo's overdramatizing his story on the stand. The real danger lay in the opposite direction—that he might testify in such flat, matter-of-fact terms that the jury would be alienated by his unnatural composure.

The Dorado's thin, high-shouldered figure had just been leaving the jail corridor as Benson arrived. But the boy had not mentioned him, and Benson, after giving him a few opportunities, had not dared to raise the subject himself. If the Dorado had appointed himself a judge with the power of life and death over his grandson, the damage had already been done. And,

Benson thought, one more judge wouldn't greatly alter his problem. He still had to convince the jury. He would worry about the Dorado later.

"State your name," he told the boy.

"Arturo Dos Santos Campeón."

"When and where did you first meet the deceased, Roderick Duquesne?"

"Late Saturday morning," Turo said. "I was thumbing a ride south out of L.A. He gave me a lift."

"This is the morning of Saturday, April thirteenth?"

"Yes."

"Had you ever seen, or even heard of Roderick Duquesne before that time?"

"No."

"Where were you going?"

"I was headed home. To Mexico."

"Specifically where?"

"The city of Chihuahua, in the state of Chihuahua."

"Did Duquesne offer you a ride all the way home?"

"No. He said he was going to take the coast road down to Manzanillo, but he'd give me a lift as far as Rincon."

"Did you and Duquesne make any stops before the time he turned off at Lookout Point?"

"A couple times. For gas. We got something to eat at a drive-in."

"Tell the jury what happened at the drive-in," Benson said. He moved a step back and rested one foot on the edge of the stand. He kept his eyes on the jury as Turo told them about Duquesne's fumbling with his lighter at the drive-in restaurant, how he had forgotten it in the minor confusion of paying the bill and had not thought of it again. The boy admitted he had stolen it.

"You had the lighter in your possession before you and Duquesne arrived at Lookout Point?"

"Yes."

"Why did you steal it?"

"I was broke," he muttered. "I thought maybe Duquesne

wouldn't even notice it was gone. He was using the dash lighter all the time."

"After you and he left the drive-in, did you stop anywhere else?"

"Not till Lookout Point."

"You drove straight through? What time did you get to Lookout Point?"

"I don't know. It was still pretty dark. I was asleep. Duquesne did all the driving."

"What woke you up?"

"Duquesne. He——" Turo hesitated. He drew in a quick breath. He was looking over Benson's head, at the spectators in the back of the courtroom.

"Tell the jury in your own words, Turo," Benson said quietly. "You were asleep in Duquesne's car. He parked at Lookout Point and then woke you up. How?"

"He was kissing me, slobbering over me," the boy said in a flat, mechanical voice. He closed his eyes for a brief moment, then looked down at Benson.

There was a quick stir in the jury box. Mrs. Jordan slid her chair back, as if instinctively she wanted to get up and leave before the boy said anything more.

Turo went on soberly, speaking in a low, clear tone. He was as baldly factual as Benson had feared he would be. Even when he was speaking of his nightmarish fight with Duquesne, he made it sound like something he had witnessed from a distance.

The jury listened to him with close, troubled attention. Most of them were frowning. When Turo finished telling the jury how he had taken Duquesne's car and later wrecked it on the way to town, Benson shifted quickly forward.

"Why did you kill him?" he demanded in a voice as harsh as Frank Sayer might have used.

"I told you," the boy said, scowling. "He was trying to——"

"But you had a knife. Duquesne was unarmed. Why didn't you run away?"

"I never got a chance to run. He was on top of me all the time," the boy said. "My pants were down around my knees. I couldn't move. Duquesne was right on top of me."

"You want the jury to believe that you used your knife merely to make Duquesne get away from you?"

Turo stared darkly at Benson, eyes narrowed. "Yes," he said, his voice tightening suddenly and uncontrollably. "That's just how it was."

That was the attitude he wanted to see in the boy, Benson thought with an edge of relief. Now Turo was beginning to sound credible. The note of grotesque detachment was no longer in his voice.

He led Turo again through his story step by step, goading him to a determined, positive response on each point. This was more like it, he was thinking. Gradually, something of the blind, terrified panic of that savage moment on Lookout Point was being re-created in the courtroom, and Turo himself could feel it again as it had been then. His voice became the tight, trembling voice of a young man fighting for control, and for his belief in a sane world. The jury, Benson believed, was beginning to understand.

"After Duquesne fell over the railing, what did you do?" he asked.

"I didn't know he was gone for a minute," Turo said. "I pulled up my pants and tried to stop the bleeding on my head. There was blood all over. I was bleeding like a bull."

"How did you stop the bleeding?"

"Duquesne had a box of Kleenex in the car. I used that. Didn't do much good, but I could see a little better. I—I was afraid I was going to bleed to death."

"And then you drove away from there in Duquesne's car? What were you planning to do?"

"I don't know. I was panicky. I wanted help. I was bleeding like a bull. I guess I passed out while I was driving."

"And the next thing you knew, you were in the prison ward at Rincon County Hospital. Is that right?"

"Yes."

Benson shifted so that he was facing the jury. "Turo, tell the court truthfully, did you at any time intend to kill Roderick Duquesne?"

"Christ, I just wanted to get him off me," the boy said shrilly. "How many times do I have to tell you?"

"Just once, Turo," Benson said quietly. He waited until the boy's angry eyes came up to meet his, and he smiled confidently. Turo was fighting for his life now, with all the hot, controlled intensity possible to him. He was ready for Frank Sayer now, Benson thought. "No more questions," he said.

FRANK SAYER moved in, head lowered. He silently pounded a fist against his open palm as he studied the boy. His tone at the beginning was quiet, thoughtful, restrained.

"Did you tell the jury the truth about what happened on Lookout Point, Turo?"

"Yes," Turo said tightly.

"All of it?"

"Yes."

"Can you give the court any reason why Roderick Duquesne should pick on you for his—attentions?"

"I don't know," Turo said warily.

"Did you encourage him?"

"No! I told you——"

"I heard what you said. We'll leave it there for the moment. So you didn't entice Duquesne. It just happened. If it did happen."

"Yes."

"Now let's talk about the lighter you stole from Roderick Duquesne. When did you decide to rob him?"

Turo took his time, Benson was pleased to see. "I didn't," he said after a moment.

"You didn't?" Sayer bugged his eyes to show the jury how surprised he was to hear that. "Didn't you just admit that you stole his lighter?"

"I didn't mean . . ."

Slowly, Turo, Benson said in his mind. Go very slowly now, boy.

"It's hard to tell just what you mean. One minute you say you didn't rob him and the next minute you say you did. Now, which do you want the jury to believe?"

"I didn't say that."

"No? What did you say?"

"I stole the lighter. It was there on the car seat. I didn't steal anything else."

"But you tried to, didn't you?" Sayer bored in, pressing Turo hard. "You saw all the money Duquesne was carrying, and the minute he stopped to rest, you snapped out your switchblade and threatened to carve him up if he didn't hand it over. But he didn't hand over, did he? He was a little more than you bargained for. He fought, and you killed him. Now, tell the truth, boy. That's the way it happened, wasn't it?"

"No," Turo said calmly.

"You knifed him and he fell over that railing and you were too yellow to go down and get the money you'd killed him for. So you just stole his car and everything in it and took off. Where were you going when you ran away?"

"Objection, Your Honor," Benson said mildly. "Even I can't figure out what question the prosecutor is asking. He's making speeches at the witness."

"Yes, it was a little complex," the judge agreed. "Be more specific, Mr. Sayer."

"Yes, Your Honor." Sayer turned back to the witness stand. "Flight, Turo, that's what we're discussing. When you stole Duquesne's car and ran away, where were you headed?"

"That's no improvement, Your Honor," Benson insisted. "The prosecutor cannot claim the defendant was fleeing, when defendant has already testified that he left to get medical assistance. The prosecutor is making an improper insinuation to the jury, under the guise of asking a question."

"No," the judge said firmly. "I don't agree, Mr. Kellogg. The County Attorney may categorize the acts of defendant as he sees fit. He is not required to accept defendant's interpretation. I see no impropriety in the question. Proceed, Mr. Sayer."

"Well, Turo?" Sayer demanded impatiently.

"I was going to find a doctor," the boy said stubbornly, taking his cue from Benson.

"To find a doctor. You had just stolen an expensive car. You knew Duquesne's expensive clothes and baggage were still in it. But you were going to drive it into town and give yourself up. Is that what you expect the court to believe?"

"I was bleeding," Turo said. "I wanted a doctor."

"You were bleeding," Sayer said reflectively. "You were bleeding from a scalp wound that you didn't get until you wrecked Duquesne's car."

Turo sat back stiffly in his chair. His narrow face went cold and empty. He lifted his hand to touch the small pad of bandage on the side of his head. He seemed then to sense for the first time the menace of Frank Sayer. Benson could see his eyes half close, as if he were withdrawing into himself.

"I must remind the prosecutor, Your Honor," Benson said, coming to his feet, "that he has not asked a question."

Sayer nodded tightly. He rephrased his statement, making it a question. In effect, Benson realized, Frank Sayer was now testifying himself, putting his version of the case before the jury in a long, linked series of questions. The boy's constant and determined denials might not be as persuasive with the jury as the counterarguments that Sayer slyly buried inside his questions. It was clever work, the sort of thing only a clever and experienced prosecutor could get away with. Benson fidgeted. He could hear Burr mumbling irritably beside him.

But Frank Sayer, for all his cleverness, was taking too much time.

On his notepad Benson ticked off the points one by one as the prosecutor challenged the boy's story at every turn. Through his questions, Sayer bluntly insinuated that Turo had invited Duquesne's homosexual advances, that there had been neither attack nor resistance, that there had been no fight until Turo had tried to rob Duquesne, that the boy's scalp wound had

« 469 »

been caused in the wreck and not by fighting Duquesne, that Turo had stolen the lighter just before he had killed Duquesne, that he had then stolen Duquesne's Rolls and tried to escape to Mexico. Sayer missed nothing, he conceded nothing. He prodded at every possible weakness, worried away like a terrier at every statement not supported by solid evidence. His hard, driving voice beat upon the defendant like a tangible force, goading Turo again and again to angry, resentful outbursts.

But Turo was coming out of it fairly well, Benson judged. Benson glanced quickly at Burr, saw him nod in agreement. The boy was doing all right. Sayer was devious, merciless, taunting, trying his damnedest to break the boy, to open a small crack into which he could work a crowbar and pry apart the entire fabric of the defense. The boy gave him no chance for that. Turo was trembling now, and frightened, his voice strained and thin with vehemence, but he was firm in his denials. And, Benson believed, he was credible. The jury was not turning against him.

This was the essence of the trial, Benson knew. The jury was now being forced to decide between Sayer's interpretation of the facts and Turo's. The sort of slanted argument Sayer was making should have been reserved for his final summation, but Sayer, stretching the bounds of proper cross-examination, was giving himself an extra session to make his case. He was also beginning to lose the jury's attention. Mrs. Jordan dabbled her handkerchief distractedly at the corners of her mouth. Mitchell Masterton folded up the wad of paper he was using for notes and put it in his pocket. He stroked the side of his pencil along his chin, his eyes fixed on a point above Turo's head. In the chair closest to the witness stand, John Eben Heller was sitting glassy-eyed and sweating in the narrow strip of sunlight from the window behind him.

Frank Sayer ran his eyes along the faces of the jurors briefly. He went back to his table and sipped from a glass of water. He muttered something to an assistant, then came back toward the stand.

"We heard you tell the court about your criminal exploits in Los Angeles," he said. "I'd like to hear a little more about that. How many felonies have you committed so far?"

"I don't——"

"Objection," Benson said quickly. "The question is completely improper, Your Honor."

"It is certainly proper as an assault on the credibility of this witness, Your Honor," Sayer said hotly. "The defense opened this door itself. I want to go through and see what's on the other side."

"The question is proper only if the prosecution is prepared here and now to offer proof that the defendant has ever been convicted of a felony. A mere denial by the defendant, Your Honor, cannot wipe out of the jury's mind the prejudice created by the question itself. I challenge the prosecutor to present such proof to the court. I know that he cannot, Your Honor, because no such proof exists. I ask that the question be stricken from the record."

"Mr. Sayer?" the judge asked, "can you offer proof?"

"Not to this specific matter, Your Honor," Sayer admitted, "but we know that——"

"The question will be stricken," Judge Groat said, leaning down to address the court reporter. "Proceed, Mr. Sayer."

"Well, we know you're a thief," Sayer said angrily, turning back to the boy. "You've admitted that yourself. You stole Roderick Duquesne's Rolls-Royce. You stole his gold cigarette lighter. You were convicted once for stealing from an employer who trusted you, and arrested on several other occasions. That's true, isn't it?"

"Yes."

"Now I want you to tell the jury just how you made a living in Los Angeles after you were fired for stealing. Isn't it true that you offered yourself as a male prostitute to homosexuals?"

"No! I never did anything like that!"

"You did openly associate with various young men known to the police as perverts, did you not?"

"I—I knew some. I never——"

"And when Duquesne saw you, he recognized the signs right away, didn't he? You enticed him, meaning to rob him if you got the chance. He didn't have to force you, did he? You offered yourself to him. Isn't that true?"

"No! It's not true! Damn you, I never in my life——" Turo half rose from his chair, choking and red-faced. Tears of rage stood bright in his eyes. After a moment of strained tension, he sat again, very slowly and stiffly.

Frank Sayer posed before the stand, hands cocked on his hips, shaking his head, saddened and disgusted. He stepped back.

"The jury doesn't need to know anything more about you," he said in an ugly tone. "That's all. I have finished with this witness, Your Honor."

Judge Groat looked inquiringly toward Benson.

"Yes, Your Honor," Benson said promptly. "I will ask one question, on redirect."

He got to his feet, staying behind the table. "Turo," he said easily. He waited for the boy's head to come up and around. "The prosecutor has insinuated that you are a homosexual and that you invited Duquesne's perverted advances. I want you to tell the court if you have ever at any time had any experience of any homosexual act?"

"No." The boy swallowed tightly. He turned his eyes toward the back of the courtroom. "I swear to God, I never have," he said.

"Thank you, Turo. To quote Mr. Sayer, I don't think the jury needs to know anything more. I am finished, Your Honor."

"Mr. Sayer?"

"No, Your Honor."

"You may step down," the judge said to the boy. Turo looked up at him dazedly and nodded. He braced his cast with his left hand and got down from the stand.

"Have you any other witnesses, Mr. Kellogg?"

"No, Your Honor. The defense rests."

"Very well. You may submit your requests for charges at

this time. We will take our noon recess now, Mr. Clerk. Court will reconvene at one fifteen."

B E N S O N sat opposite Burr at a table in a remote corner of the Stockmen's Club dining room, staring absently at his plate, fingering half a sandwich.

"Want to talk about it?" Burr asked.

"Not now."

"What were you doing, rehearsing your speech to the jury?"

Benson shrugged. "I suppose I was." He bit into his sandwich and chewed slowly.

"I told you Frank could be rough."

"You told me."

"He put the kid over the jumps. That's his job. But young Señor Campeón came through pretty well. No defendant ever comes out of it clean, you know that. A good prosecutor can make anyone look bad, if he tries hard enough. You should see what Frank has done with some of the bums I've defended."

Benson didn't answer. He put down his sandwich and finished his coffee.

"But I got some of them off," Burr went on casually. "Most of them, as a matter of fact. You never know what a jury is going to do."

"That's a thought to hang on to," Benson grunted.

"Look, boy," Burr said earnestly. "You knew this was going to happen. The kid tells a plausible story, but it's just his unsupported word, for the most part. Frank Sayer would be a damn fool if he didn't try to poke it to pieces, and Frank, I can tell you, is not a damn fool when it comes to trying a case in court."

Benson glanced up sharply. "He missed something today," he said in a strange voice.

"What?"

"He let up too soon. Something was happening to the boy

there at the end. Didn't you notice?"

"Not especially. What do you mean?"

"I don't know how to put it," Benson said uncertainly. "I sensed something. Can't say just what it was. Frank had the boy crying. That was a bad moment. Why did Frank let up on him?"

"Yes," Burr said thoughtfully. "I see. But it wasn't all that obvious, Ben. The kid was beginning to tighten up, but he's got the guts of a burglar. I guess Frank didn't see much chance of getting anything more out of him. The kid may have been crying, but he sure as hell wasn't giving Frank any aid and comfort. Anyway, by that time Frank had to close up shop. He was stretching his cross out too long as it was. The jury was beginning to fidget."

"Maybe so," Benson said, unconvinced. "Well, this is no time to hash it over. Let's go, Burr. I want a last look at my notes before court convenes."

Burr laughed at him. "It never does any good, Counselor. Forget it. Let's take a walk. You've got a good argument all set. You've been over it a million times in your mind already."

"At least that often," Benson agreed with a faint smile. "Think it'll do?"

"It'll do," Burr said firmly. "I like it. You come close to selling me. If I was on that jury, I just might give it to you." Burr signed the check and got up. Benson went to collect their hats from the attendant. He waited at the entrance while Burr stopped to pick up a copy of the *Rincon Record* from the stack on the porter's desk.

"They've got another picture of you, Counselor. One of Frank. One of the boy. Want to see?"

"No."

"These guys are having a hell of a time trying to report Elsinore's testimony. Little too gamey for a family paper, I suppose."

"Or any other kind," Benson said.

He held the door for Burr, who moved through lightly, still reading. He slipped the second section out as he stepped to the sidewalk. "What was the name of that private detective Caine sent down with Elsinore? The guy who wanted to bust your head?"

"Manny Blue."

"Poor Manny Blue." Burr tilted the paper so Benson could see the brief story he was marking with his finger.

" 'L.A. Investigator Crashes on El Monte Freeway,' " Benson read aloud. "Broke his neck, I hope?"

" 'In critical condition,' the story says. Couldn't have happened to a nicer guy, eh?"

"Not one of my favorite characters," Benson said. "Come on, Burr. We've only got a few minutes."

"Softly, softly, catchee monkey," Burr said genially. "They can't start without you, Counselor. You're the star."

IN THE HIGH drowsy-warm courtroom, Judge Groat mounted to the bench. He opened his leather notebook, tested the point of his pencil against his thumb and glanced at Benson.

"Can you give the court some estimate of the time you will require for summation, Mr. Kellogg?"

"I will be brief, Your Honor," Benson said promptly. "May it please the court," he said, advancing toward the high railing of the jury box. "Mrs. Jordan, gentlemen. We have spent a long and difficult time together. In the course of this trial we have been forced to consider things that sicken and dismay all decent people. And now that we have finished, you twelve citizens, representing the people of Rincon County, will be required to decide whether Arturo Campeón is to live or die."

The courtroom was hushed as Benson turned with one hand on the railing and looked over his shoulder at Turo, who sat, pale and hunched, watching Benson with a close, curiously furtive intensity. Beside him, Burr nodded grave encouragement.

"We have heard a lot of evidence in the past few days," Benson went on, facing the jury again. "Much of it has been confusing. The prosecuting attorney has seen to that. He is an experienced and very successful prosecutor, who likes to win all his cases. He often seems more interested in winning than in establishing the truth. Today we have all listened with some astonishment to his reshaping of simple, provable facts into a totally false picture. Let us review together some of those facts—some of that evidence."

Benson paused to glance at the page from his notebook that he held cupped in his hand. He scored his thumbnail under the first, one-word reminder: *Fight*.

"We all remember how vigorously Mr. Sayer tried to deny that the defendant had fought with Roderick Duquesne on Lookout Point. The prosecutor, through insinuations, attempted to show that there had, in fact, been no fight, merely a murderous, unprovoked assault by the defendant. All of the defendant's many injuries, Mr. Sayer contended, were caused by the car wreck, not in the fight with Duquesne.

"We know that is not true. Simple logic proves that Mr. Sayer has again distorted the truth. I will remind you of the testimony given by Deputy Sheriff Houston Shriner, a witness called by the prosecution. Deputy Shriner told us of finding— and later conveniently losing—five or six blood-soaked wads of Kleenex in Duquesne's car immediately after the wreck. Those wads were used by the defendant in his attempt to stem the flow of blood from a deep scalp wound inflicted by Duquesne. There is no other possible explanation for them. The scalp wound was inflicted before the wreck, or there could have been no blood-soaked Kleenex found at that time. Mr. Sayer cannot deny their existence. He cannot deny their meaning."

Benson moved a few restless steps along the railing. He stood looking at the jurors for a silent moment.

"Much of the evidence in this trial has been sordid. I share your feeling of distaste. But neither you nor I can ignore that evidence. I must refer now to the criminal and perverted assault made upon the defendant by Roderick Duquesne, because that assault was the reason for the fight and for Duquesne's death. I ask you to recall the evidence given here by

Dr. Hill, the intern at Rincon County Hospital who first treated the defendant. In addition to more serious injuries, the defendant also had a number of scratches and abrasions on his buttocks—injuries made when, as the defendant told us, he managed to kick himself away from Duquesne. In the scuffle, he unlatched the door with his elbow and fell heavily to the ground outside. It was then that he suffered those injuries which Dr. Hill told us about. His bare flesh was torn and scratched when he fell because, as he told us, his trousers had been pulled down to his knees by the pervert who was trying to rape him.

"I will not dwell on this point any longer. It is clear to any sensible mind that the abrasions on Arturo Campeón's bare flesh were the result of a savage and relentless attack made by Roderick Duquesne. The critical item of proof is furnished by the defendant's trousers, which Dr. Hill found had not been torn or damaged in any way. Obviously those trousers could not have been in their normal position when Arturo Campeón suffered cuts and scratches on his bare flesh. Again, I must emphasize that there is no other explanation possible. Mr. Sayer's insinuations are exposed by evidence which he cannot refute."

Benson slid his thumb down to the second line of his notes: *Knife.*

"We have seen," he went on more confidently, "that the prosecutor's attempt to deny a fight took place has been proven foolish by the evidence which you yourselves heard in this court. There was a fight, as the defendant told us, and in the course of the fight, Roderick Duquesne was killed. The defendant killed him with a knife which he managed, after a considerable struggle, to take out of his pocket.

"Mr. Sayer, you will remember, made much of that knife. He went stalking around the courtroom, waving it overhead, hoping to convince you that the mere ownership of that knife was reason enough for you to convict the defendant. Now that, members of the jury, is ridiculous.

"In this part of the world almost every man carries a

knife in his pocket. I have one which I've carried since the day my father gave it to me on my sixth birthday. And I'd be willing to make a small bet that half you gentlemen on this jury have knives in your pockets too."

In the first seat John Eben Heller snorted. He wiped a hand soberly across his big red face.

"To a man in this part of the country," Benson said, "a knife is primarily a tool. And a spring-bladed knife is an unusually useful tool. Mr. Sayer pretended great shock at the opening mechanism of this knife. Mr. Sayer was born and raised in this county and he knows that when a man is earmarking range cattle, he can't afford two hands to open his knife. It's about all he can do to get one free. No, it won't do. Mr. Sayer's expression of shock just doesn't ring true."

Benson moved a step along the front of the box. "When your natural defenses have been beaten down by a powerful opponent," he said quietly, "you will snatch up anything that comes to hand as a protection. It might be a carpenter's hammer, a butcher's cleaver, a plumber's wrench, or a Western man's knife. All of them tools, members of the jury. First and foremost, tools. But all capable of being used as weapons in a moment of peril.

"I am not attempting to tell you that it is all right for a young man to use a knife to kill if he happens to have one in his pocket. I merely say to you that the fact that Arturo Campeón had a knife in his pocket does not make him either more or less guilty of the offense with which he has been charged. Mr. Sayer has tried to make something more of it. Mr. Sayer has not succeeded."

Robbery. Benson looked quickly at the note.

"A large part of the prosecutor's skill has been devoted to an attempt to convince you that the only dispute between Roderick Duquesne and the defendant arose because the defendant tried to rob this very wealthy and corrupt man.

"I ask you to consider this point with extreme care. If you believe that was the reason for the defendant's actions, if you believe he wanted only to rob Duquesne and was not trying to defend himself against Duquesne's homosexual assault, you will have found the defendant guilty of murder. Robbery with a deadly weapon is a felony, and any death resulting from a felonious act must be considered to be murder. The fact is, members of the jury, that there was no robbery, and no attempt at robbery.

"You heard a prosecution witness testify that Roderick Duquesne retained in his possession a total of seventy-five hundred dollars in cash and valuables. The prosecutor has tried to claim that the defendant killed Duquesne and was then too frightened to climb down and take from the body the money for which he had killed. Mr. Sayer wants you to see Arturo Campeón as a vicious, inhuman killer, not frightened for a moment of a man who outweighed him by almost fifty pounds and who was both taller and stronger. But, somehow, he was too scared to climb down a rocky slope and collect the money. Mr. Sayer cannot have it both ways. If the defendant was one of those people, he cannot have been the other. The truth is that Arturo Campeón is neither one of those mythical creatures that Mr. Sayer invented.

"The defendant admitted that he stole Roderick Duquesne's lighter when Duquesne carelessly mislaid it at a drive-in restaurant. He still had that lighter in his possession when he was found in the wrecked car. Mr. Sayer wants you to accept that lighter as proof of an intent to commit another and more serious crime.

"This is the nub of the problem you must decide. You have been given two versions of the same fact. You must determine whether Arturo Campeón or Frank Sayer has offered the correct version. Of the two, only Arturo Campeón was present and is in a position to tell us exactly what happened. Frank Sayer has a vivid and skillful imagination, but that is not enough to set against the testimony of the defendant. And keep always in mind: it is up to the prosecution to prove its case. Mr. Sayer cannot present a wild and baseless speculation and expect you to base your verdict upon it.

"I repeat, your decision turns on this point. The defendant has openly admitted that he killed Roderick Duquesne. If you choose to accept Mr. Sayer's version of his intent, if you believe Arturo Campeón killed in an attempt to rob, then you have convicted him of murder."

Benson moved back from the jury box.

"I am confident," he said, "that you will not accept the prosecutor's unproven, imaginary explanation."

He put both hands in his pockets, lifting and squaring his shoulders under his light coat.

"And now," he went on, "we must consider what really did happen on Lookout Point, and why Roderick Duquesne was killed.

"To normal and mature people, a homosexual is no part of life. If they think about such a person at all, it is with contempt or pity or anger, often a combination of all those responses. To us, these people are revolting because they pervert the most meaningful relationship in human experience. We are disheartened. Our common reaction is to ignore such people. None of us likes to talk about them.

"So I must apologize to you. I have to talk about them. I will be as brief as I can be in justice to my client.

"I saw your faces yesterday when Harald Elsinore was on the witness stand. I think I felt what you were feeling. I cannot apologize for bringing him here, however, for it was necessary for me to produce a witness qualified to tell you what sort of person Roderick Duquesne actually was. Only someone like Harald Elsinore could have known."

Benson paused. Mrs. Jordan was biting her lips. Her eyes shifted distractedly away from Benson. John Eben Heller pursed his mouth as if he wanted to spit. Benson hurried through a résumé of Elsinore's testimony.

"It is possible to feel pity," he said. "Duquesne could have made of himself a useful and admirable citizen, a good and trustworthy friend. He did not. He was stronger than most men, and a good deal richer. He used those assets to beat young boys into submitting to his perverted appetite and to buy them off afterward. He died, finally, because he found one boy who resisted successfully. And now, I must speak of the defendant and tell you the sort of person he is.

"I have called him a boy during this trial. That is not accurate, of course. Arturo Campeón is twenty-one, and that is a man's age. The law is very definite on that point. Arturo Campeón, for all his youthful appearance, is legally a man, and that is why he stands before you charged with murder.

"If he were still under age, I do not believe Mr. Sayer would have charged him with murder. The laws of this state are not easy to understand on this question. Judge Groat will explain the law bearing on this trial when Mr. Sayer and I have finished, but I would like to say something about it before then."

Benson stood with an elbow propped on the railing of the witness stand. This was it. This was the crux of his plea to the jury. He drew in a slow breath.

"Our statutes," he began soberly, "list the most serious crimes, the felonies. Rape, for example, is on that list, as you would expect. But the legislature did not see fit to add the category of homosexual rape. Girls may be raped. But boys cannot be, according to our legislature. If a boy is under twenty-one, then the statutes referring to child molestation apply, and any pervert attacking a young boy commits a felony. If Arturo Campeón were under twenty-one, or if he were a girl, he would not now be in this court charged with murder. But he is twenty-one, and very much a man. And he is charged with murder.

"Arturo Campeón defended himself against a proven pervert, a corrupt and savage homosexual attacker with a long, incredibly long, record of homosexual rape. But the law in our state does not list homosexual rape as a felony. The law, therefore, implies that Roderick Duquesne's attack was not the sort of crime which a young man may resist with any amount of force necessary. You may find this unbelievable, as I do, but it is so.

"I cannot tell you to disregard the law. Judge Groat will explain the law to you and you must accept his version, not mine. You are not allowed to say to yourselves, 'The law is wrong here; we know better and we're going to do what we think is right.'

"You cannot ignore what the legislature has said about the law. You cannot ignore what your hearts and minds say about justice. The legislature has given us the law. But no law and no legislature can force a jury of free citizens to send a young man to his death when the conscience of the jury tells it to set him free."

And that, Benson told himself silently, is about as far as I dare push that one. I'm surprised old Groat didn't cut me off long ago.

"The law," he went on carefully, "says that Arturo Campeón would have been justified in defending himself if he had feared for his life. Arturo Campeón has not claimed that he was frightened to the point of panic and terror. He gave his evidence in this court as honestly as any witness could, and he told you that he does not remember being afraid. He woke up, dazed with sleep, to find a powerful and determined homosexual tearing his clothes off. His reaction was fury, and that, I believe, would be the reaction of all normal men. Even then, he fought only to get away. He managed, bleeding from a severe scalp wound, to get out of Duquesne's car, but Duquesne would not let him escape. He pursued the defendant, sure that his big muscles and fat wallet would succeed again as they had so often before. And so he was killed. No, members of the jury, Arturo Campeón does not say that he was afraid for his life. But he did fear for something which to him is as important, possibly more important, than his life."

Benson came slowly forward to a position in the center of the jury-box railing. He took his hands out of his pockets and locked them behind him, surprised to feel them damp with sweat.

"Nowadays," he said, "in a complex and sophisticated world, if a man dares to speak of honor as a motivating force, the best he can expect is laughter. We have all become a little fearful of letting anyone know that we treasure our honor as we do our lives. When our ancestors pledged their 'lives and sacred honor,' they were pledging what they believed were the two equally vital elements of human existence. The world has changed since then. But not all men have changed with it. To Arturo Campeón, the honor of his person and spirit is just as worthy of defense as his life."

Benson brought up his right hand and swept it across his damp forehead.

"Roderick Duquesne," he said in a lowered, deliberate voice, "was a corrupt pervert. Judged even by homosexual standards, he was despicable. He was the sort they call a 'scalp hunter,' a pervert who delights in overpowering hetero-sexual victims. He lived, as all homosexuals must live, in a criminal world. It is not for us to condemn or justify that world. We are concerned here only with the character of one such person, Roderick Duquesne. Mr. Sayer will tell you that Duquesne's vile character is no reason why he should have been killed. Mr. Sayer will be right, for the law protects the worthless with the best. Duquesne's character does not justify his death, but members of the jury, it most certainly does explain it!

"We heard Harald Elsinore tell us much of Roderick Duquesne and his life. Elsinore quoted a line from Shakespeare that he said was Duquesne's constant justification. I think it tells us something important about Duquesne's character, for that self-excusing quotation, full of whining bluster, was taken from the mouth of one of the most depraved characters Shakespeare ever created, a man known to us only as The Second Murderer. It is such a man with whom Duquesne identified himself.

"You saw the tragic figure of Harald Elsinore, and you heard what he suffered from Duquesne, from the first rape through the final abandonment. You have heard what Duquesne did to others like Elsinore. And what he tried to do to the defendant. Duquesne was one of those damned souls, 'done with Hope and Honor, lost to Love and Truth.' And in charity, we might add, as Kipling did about those other men who were 'damned from here to eternity,' that Roderick Duquesne also 'knew the worst too young.' We have heard from Elsinore how Duquesne was made vulnerable by his mother, much as Achilles; there was never much chance for him.

"But there is a chance for Arturo Campeón. It rests with you. The prosecutor has tried to plant in your minds the suspicion that Arturo Campeón was himself a pervert who enticed Roderick Duquesne. That was a shameful thing for Mr. Sayer to have done, and I think he already regrets it. But whether or not Mr. Sayer has the grace of repentance is not important. The facts are clear. Only in the dark movements of Frank Sayer's mind does this suspicion exist. He has, of course, offered no evidence. There is no evidence to offer. We know that Arturo Campeón defended himself with every ounce of his strength and determination against a known pervert with a long record of homosexual rape. To say that this was a fight over a robbery is preposterous, for how could Arturo Campeón have suffered those scratches on his bare buttocks, unless the fight progressed exactly as he has told us it did? If he had welcomed Duquesne's advances, there would, obviously, have been no fight. Mr. Sayer is again trying to have it both ways and in trying, shows us that he is wrong about both.

"No, members of the jury, we are not in any doubt about what happened on Lookout Point. We see them in sharp outline, the brutal pervert and the young man who fought him off. We have seen the motives that governed them. And I think we have seen into their hearts.

"Arturo Campeón fought to save himself from homosexual rape. It is up to you to say whether he was right. Should he have given in, surrendered his integrity and honor and self-respect? For keep clearly in mind, members of the jury, Duquesne permitted no other alternative. Either Arturo Campeón surrendered, or he fought. He chose to fight. It is impossible for me not to admire his resolution.

"I have finished now, members of the jury. Mr. Sayer will make his final summation, the judge will charge you, and you will then retire to your conference room and there you will decide if, in defending himself, Arturo Campeón offended the peace and dignity of this state. I believe he supported it, elevated it. I ask you to find him not guilty."

Benson bowed stiffly to the jury, thanked them, and went back to his chair, walking through a heavy silence on legs that tended to flutter under his weight. He sat down and wiped a hand across his forehead. He looked at the film of moisture on his finger and let out a long, sighing breath.

Burr poured a fresh glass of water and pushed it along the table. He winked cheerfully at Benson.

Judge Groat made his chair squeak as he rocked back. He tapped his pencil on the lamp. "We will take ten minutes before we hear Mr. Sayer," he said to the jury. "Mr. Clerk?"

BENSON lifted his hand slightly off the top of the table and watched it tremble. "Look at that," he said under his breath.

"It's always that way," Burr said with a grin. "Sometimes it's all you can do to get back to your seat. You did all right, Ben. That female juror, Number Three, was nodding in time with you like she was listening to the preacher laying down the gospel judgment. And old Frank was making notes like a fool. You've made him rewrite his whole speech, I'll bet. You're quite a cornball spellbinder, Brother Benson."

"Yeah," Turo said. "You sounded good, Mr. Kellogg." His voice came huskily, uncertain. "I just wanted you to know . . ."

"I'm glad you approve, Turo," Benson said quickly. "Want to go downstairs? You'd better hop."

"I guess I will." The boy got up reluctantly. He leaned on the table for an instant. "Thanks, Mr. Kellogg." He went out, cocking his thumb for Deputy Monahan.

"Feel okay, Ben?" Burr shifted to the chair next to Benson.

"I'm all right," Benson muttered. "But, by God, that stuff takes it out of you. I feel as tired as if I'd been climbing Cobre Peak with a horse on my back. Is it always like that?"

"It is with me," Burr said. "Watch when Frank finishes. He'll come dragging back on his hands and knees." He looked up directly at Benson and smiled. "I liked it, Ben," he said sincerely. "If it was up to me, I'd give it to you."

"Let's not start cheering yet," Benson said. "What I'm really worried about is the judge's charge. The jury won't let the boy off if he tells them there is no legal justification for the killing."

"Groat probably won't go that far," Burr said comfortingly. "His charges are never what you could call harsh. Even if he does, you struck a blow for freedom in your argument, boy. You just got it in under the wire, too. Old Groat was reaching for his gavel when you changed the subject."

"I wondered why he didn't cut me off."

"You were too fast for him. It was borderline stuff, anyway. Groat usually gives you a lot of leeway in summations."

The jury came filing back eagerly without waiting for the clerk to call them. They shuffled along the narrow aisle to their places. The deputy brought Turo up from the detention room, arriving just as Judge Groat popped through the door from his chambers and climbed to the bench. He nodded briskly to the clerk. Frank Sayer rose at his table, shooting his cuffs, pulling down the tail of his coat.

"Very well, Mr. Sayer," the judge said.

Sayer strode along the front of the jury box with a slow steadiness, as if he kept rhythm with a funeral march. He was not there, his manner said, to exhort the jury to vindictive revenge, but to consider with them, decent citizens all, what disposition they should properly make of the prisoner before them. His expression was dramatically somber.

When he spoke, he held his voice to an even tone, as though supported by such inner conviction that he did not need to emphasize it.

"A man lies dead," he began solemnly. "He died at the hand of the young man who is seated opposite you. Arturo Campeón has admitted he killed Roderick Duquesne. In the course of his lengthy testimony he admitted many other things which are worth remembering, and before you retire to decide upon your verdict, I would like to speak to you about some of those other admissions the defendant has made."

He brushed his hand over his head, fingering the closely cropped hair in the back, looking up at the ceiling, his mouth pinched up thoughtfully.

"First," he said emphatically.

Burr leaned over to prod Benson. He jerked his thumb toward the side door. There, peeking under the restraining arm of a deputy, Benson could see the strained, harassed face of his secretary. She gestured to him urgently from the hallway.

"Mind the store," he said quietly as he passed behind Burr's chair. He nodded apologetically at the bench and went softly toward the side door. The deputy stepped aside to let him out.

"What is it, Mary?"

"Something terrible, Mr. Kellogg," she almost wailed. "I just don't know how to tell you."

Two courthouse employees turned in the hall to stare, hearing the choked intensity of her voice. Benson took her arm gently, eased her along the corridor and out into the brightness of the central courtyard. He led her toward a low stone bench. He sat beside her and took out his cigarettes.

"Now, take it very easy, Mary," he said calmly. "Just sit back and tell me what's wrong."

Mary lowered her head a little and stared at her hands that gripped her bag like bird claws.

"The—the police phoned me at the office a little while ago. Because—" she took a moment for a quick, steadying breath— "because he had one of your cards in his pocket. Nothing else, they said. Just your card and—and the note written on it."

"You're not being very clear, Mary," Benson said gently. "Who had my card? What note?"

"Elsinore. Harald Elsinore."

Benson stiffened. The stone bench was suddenly cold against his back. "What about him?"

"The police said he—he killed himself," Mary told him.

"In the washroom on the bus station. He took something, some kind of pill, and he tied a necktie around a pipe and then around his——"

Benson put his hands over hers and held them firmly. "That's enough, Mary. Be quiet now."

He sat there stiffly, looking at the central fountain with a chill, unchanging stare. That poor bastard, he thought numbly. I should have expected something like this when he disappeared yesterday. I saw him go out of the courtroom like a dead man. I should have known then.

"They—the police—" Mary coughed away an obstruction in her throat and went on more quietly—"they wanted to know if you were going to claim the——"

"The body?" Benson said. "Yes. I guess it's up to us to bury him. He didn't have any family, at least not any family that would want to claim him."

It's about the least you can do for him, he told himself. You should have seen this coming. You didn't even think about him after he left the courtroom. You saw what Frank Sayer did to him on the witness stand. All Elsinore's puny little self-protective devices were blown to hell after that. He was naked to himself for the first time in his life. Of course he killed himself. What did you expect? "Didn't you say he left a note. What was in it?"

"Nothing, really," Mary murmured into her handkerchief. "Just a line. He said, 'It's better this way. Far, far better.' That's all. It—it made me cry."

"Yes," Benson said. That sad, silly little jerk, he thought. Sidney Carton Elsinore. It is a far, far better thing I do than I have ever done.

But who in hell did he think he was sacrificing himself for? Who was the Lucy Manette in this piece? Benson groaned inwardly with sudden knowledge. Arturo Campeón, of course. The boy who resembled him so closely. Of course Elsinore would respond to that resemblance and see in it something more than reason justified. He was an overwrought, unbalanced hysteric, and it was to be expected that he would make some kind of highly emotional transference when he saw the boy.

And so Elsinore had probably had a brief moment when he saw himself a hero, testifying to save an innocent boy who was, in Elsinore's view, not Arturo Campeón, but Harald Elsinore, younger and with a life before him. And then Frank Sayer had stuck a pin in his balloon. So Elsinore had killed himself.

"I'll be going back to the office now, Mr. Kellogg," Mary said. She gathered her feet carefully under her. "I thought you should know about this as soon as possible."

"Yes. Will you call the police when you get back? Tell them to let me know when they want to release the body."

"I will, Mr. Kellogg. Right away. I—I'm very sorry, Mr. Kellogg. He was such a *gentle* boy. Will it make any difference to the trial?" She tipped her head toward the courtroom.

"I don't think so, Mary. I don't see how it could." Benson dropped his cigarette in the tall sand jar beside the bench and got to his feet.

He walked with her along the narrow interior colonnade, turned in at the first door and went along to the courtroom.

FRANK SAYER was still talking to the jury when Benson came in and moved quietly back to his seat. Burr looked up inquiringly. Benson shook his head.

Judge Groat sat with his forehead cupped in his hand, making desultory notes. He glanced at Benson, frowning, then turned away.

Frank Sayer spoke with earnest force, pounding hard at the jury with the power and flexibility of his orator's voice. He moved hardly at all, made no nervous gestures or distracting grimaces. Occasionally he shifted a few steps along the front of the jury box, his eyes steadily on the faces of the jurors, sensing their responses with the sure instinct compounded of native ability and long practice.

"The defense has made much," he said smoothly, "of a supposed homosexual element which it has injected into this trial by foul, disgusting testimony from foul, disgusting people. I say to you, members of the jury, that the entire question is a side issue. It makes no difference whether there was a homosexual relationship, willing or otherwise, between deceased and defendant. No plea of self-defense has been offered by the defense in this case, and no such plea could legally be made. Arturo Campeón's motives are not an issue. He killed Roderick Duquesne; he has admitted it. No explanation he has offered is legal justification for that killing. Therefore, the People demand that you find him guilty of murder in the first degree.

"Finally," Frank Sayer tilted his head back and let his voice deepen in peroration. "I will remind you that the evidence shows no reason for leniency or compassion. The defendant, Arturo Campeón, who sits there so coldly before you, is not a remorseful young man, ashamed and sorrowful for what he has done. There is no repentance in him. He is proud of it; he would do it again. And, members of the jury, if he goes free from this courtroom, he probably will do it again. For he will have gotten away with murder. Why shouldn't he kill again, if he knows there will be no penalty demanded of him? Who can say which of us may be his next victim? The defendant has committed murder. Cold-blooded murder! It is your duty to the people of this state to accept your responsibility squarely and in accordance with the laws of this state."

He brought his hands together slowly at the waist, clenched them hard, and bowed. "Thank you."

Benson leaned to one side. "How did it go?" he asked Burr.

"Short and nasty," Burr muttered.

"Sure was," Turo said. "The bastard."

Judge Groat tapped with his pencil. "Members of the jury," he began, "it now falls to me to explain the law to you. What I am about to say is the final authority. In our legal system it is for the jury to determine facts, for the judge to determine the law. Listen then," he said with slow, heavy emphasis, "to the law."

Benson leaned back inattentively as the judge explained in simple terms the distinction between first-degree and second-degree murder, interpreted the meaning of "reasonable doubt," defined "presumption of innocence." In every capital case, the trial judge uses much the same words, taking them from thousands of previous charges that he has read or delivered. There is a tendency for the judge to drone, for it is old and tedious stuff to him. But Judge Groat was meticulous and careful, understandable beyond any possibility of confusion. Benson did not listen closely. He was waiting for the judge to get to the meat of his charge.

Judge Groat spread open his notebook, passing on to more specific points. He reviewed the testimony of each witness with succinct clarity, commenting on the debatable aspects which, he warned the jurors, were for them to decide.

Then he came to the testimony of the defendant and Benson sat up alertly. The judge underlined several words, made a brief correction, and went on.

"The act itself is not in dispute. Defendant has admitted killing Roderick Duquesne. He has denied killing willfully or with malice aforethought. The question of intent is, therefore, in dispute, and is for the jury to determine."

Judge Groat separated a sheet from his notebook and held it tilted to the light. He read in a solemn, measured voice the two paragraphs which Benson and Burr had labored over the night before. The matter of the cigarette lighter, he told the jury, was seriously important. If the jury accepted the People's contention that the lighter had been stolen when defendant and deceased were together at Lookout Point, and was merely the first item of loot in what was meant to be a felonious robbery, then the jury found the defendant guilty of felony-murder. Any death resulting from a felonious act was, by definition of law, murder. However, if the jury believed the defendant's account of stealing the lighter surreptitiously at an earlier time and another place, then the lighter itself should have no bearing on their verdict. So much for the lighter.

Burr winked and blew out an exaggerated breath as Judge Groat turned to the second page of the charge. Again, evidence bearing upon the question of intent was in dispute. Did the defendant, having momentarily freed himself from deceased's attack, have an opportunity to escape? The length of time involved made no difference. If the defendant was free, for however short a time, and had willfully returned to fight with deceased, then the jury would be right in assuming that Duquesne's death had been premeditated. On the other hand, if the jury believed that defendant had been given no respite from the attack, that deceased had followed him immediately from the car and forcibly prevented him from escaping, then it could not be said that Roderick Duquesne met his death by a premeditated and malicious act by the defendant. To this point, the evidence of the injuries to defendant's buttocks, the judge added dryly, and the state of his trousers gave a certain credence to defendant's account.

Both of them, Benson thought gratefully. Judge Groat read both of them just the way we gave them to him. Everything we asked for, and a bit more. For the judge was not finished with the question of intent.

"In listening to heated arguments by opposing counsel during this trial, the jury may have gained the impression that the manner in which deceased met his death should somehow be an element in assisting you to reach a verdict. This is not so. The manner of death is of no meaning to you except as it assists you in determining the intent of the defendant. I will remind you that it is the act which you are considering here, not the means by which that act was accomplished.

"In a trial for first-degree murder, the most important question for the jury to answer is, what was the intent which motivated the act? Death of a human being is not, of itself, always punishable, or even reprehensible. We know that in time of war it may be honorable and admired, as in the case of a soldier. It may be accidental and forgivable, as in the case of a doctor whose patient dies on the operating table. It may be accidental and punishable, as in the case of a man who kills another involuntarily in an automobile crash. It may be criminal and fall within one of the three categories I have explained to you—that is to say, manslaughter, second-degree murder, or first-degree murder. These many and important distinctions turn upon the question of intent. It is for the jury to determine intent, according to the evidence they have heard."

Benson sighed quietly. There was little comfort or loss in any of that. Groat had just tossed it in the jury's lap. Still, he could have been tougher.

The judge turned a page. He paused for a sip of water before going on, and something in the way he glanced sharply around the courtroom warned Benson that he was coming now to the really critical point.

"The defendant has suggested to you, in justification, that he killed Roderick Duquesne in order to protect himself from an assault by deceased which was committed with the intent to force defendant to an unnatural sex act. The laws of this state do not define sodomy as a felony, and therefore, make no provision for personal defense against it, however natural and instinctive it may seem to many people. Defense counsel has suggested that Roderick Duquesne's assault might be equated with rape, and he invited you to compare defendant's position with that of a young girl who had killed in order to protect herself from sexual assault. I say to you that this contention is without merit. You will dismiss it from your minds."

"Jesus!" Burr groaned. Benson shook his head slowly.

The judge closed the cover of his notebook with a small, decisive smack. In the silence he put his hands down flat on it and leaned forward. Benson listened to him, almost dazed with shock.

"The possible verdicts you may reach are these," the judge said sharply. "If you find that Roderick Duquesne met his death as the result of a felonious act on the part of the defendant, then you must find him guilty of murder. If you find deceased met his death due to any wrongful act by the defendant and that his death was due to malice and premeditation, then you will find him guilty of murder. If you find that Roderick Duquesne met his death as the result of a wrongful act by the defendant, but that death was not due to malice or premeditation, then you will render a verdict of manslaughter. If you are convinced beyond a reasonable doubt that none of these definitions explains the way in which Roderick Duquesne met his death, then you will bring in a verdict of not guilty.

"You will reach your verdict without any considerations of bias or prejudice for or against defendant or deceased. You will not allow yourselves to be influenced by feelings of sympathy, or disgust. You will consult your own consciences, and each other. The jury will now retire."

He tapped his pencil briskly and pushed his chair back from the bench. The clerk swung his gavel vigorously. He announced that the court was adjourned until the jury had found a verdict. It was four o'clock.

THE NEWSPAPERMEN sprinted from their seats as if the clerk's gavel had been a starting gun. They gathered first around the defense table.

"Come on, Ben, be a sport. We let you alone, didn't we? The trial's over. Give us a statement. Say something, damn it! We've got to file!"

"Beat it," Burr growled ominously. He beckoned Deputy Monahan forward. "Take the kid downstairs, John." He brushed the reporters back with a quick gesture. "Go on, beat it. What the hell is there to say until the jury comes in? Go ask Frank. He's always willing to say something foolish."

"The judge ruined you with that charge, didn't he?" one reporter said challengingly.

"Beat it." Burr waved him away. "Better catch Frank before he ducks you."

The reporters left in a clamoring rush. Burr jerked his

head at Turo. "Don't worry, kid. Go take a break. Have John get you something to eat. It'll be awhile yet. Jurors always have to talk it up before they vote."

"You're sure it's all right to——"

"Yeah, sure," Burr said easily. "Take off. John will get you back in plenty of time."

When the boy had gone, Burr sat again in his chair, turning it to face Benson. He waited a moment, then reached out and punched Benson's arm lightly.

"I need a cigarette, Counselor. Join me in the garden?"

Benson followed him absently out of the courtroom. He stood by while Burr told an attendant they would be out in the courtyard, then let Burr push him down the corridor and out into the still bright, warm enclosure. They sat on one of the low stone benches near the fountain.

Burr pushed a lighted cigarette between Benson's fingers and sat back easily, one foot propped up on the bench. He blew out a long plume of smoke.

"Old Groat is getting rougher every day," he said cheerfully. "I never heard him give a charge as strong as that before. Downright tyrannical."

Benson grunted. Absent-mindedly, he put out his cigarette.

"Relax, Ben. You did all you could."

"I loused it up," Benson said in a dull, depressed voice. He drew in a ragged breath and looked around him. "I had a brave, smart idea," he said quietly. "I was going to prove that a boy has a legal right to defend himself against homosexual rape. Harald Elsinore is dead because I tried to prove something that can't be proven in our state. Elsinore is dead, and in a little while, Turo——"

"What's that about Elsinore?" Burr demanded.

"He killed himself," Benson said heavily. "In a public toilet at the bus station. He took poison and then hanged himself, just to make sure."

"Jesus!" Burr breathed. "It's a damn good thing he waited until after he'd testified."

"Good for whom?" Benson asked. "If he hadn't come here

to testify, he would not have been destroyed. You saw what Frank did to him. Elsinore would still be——"

"Oh, the hell with Elsinore," Burr said brusquely. "He was a natural-born casualty if one ever lived, a cinch for the high dive sooner or later. And don't think his testimony wasn't useful. It established the background, boy, and you needed that. Now the jury knows——"

"It knows the judge told them not to——"

Burr snorted. "You weren't watching them, boy. I was. You seem to have the nutty idea that the jury is going to follow Groat's charge just because that's how things are supposed to be done."

"But he said——"

"Yeah, yeah. Juries aren't supposed to find on questions of law. I know what the books say. I'm trying to tell you how it really works. Juries *do* find on questions of law when they take the notion. They have the power, and they damn well know it. If movies and television have done anything, they've shown people that a jury can be a buffer between law and the person. Every once in a while a jury decides to write some law of its own."

Benson looked at him, frowning. "Do you really think there's a chance they might——"

"That's what I've been trying to pound into your thick head, boy. You opened up a big dirty bagful of worry for the people on that jury. They don't want to hang a kid for killing scum like Duquesne. You gave them an excuse for letting him go when you told them to think of him in the same way they would think of a girl who killed a rapist. By God, that stung them, Ben. Groat told them they couldn't draw that comparison, but he didn't make it stick. We've got a chance, Ben."

"You are without a doubt the most stupidly optimistic sonofa——"

"Don't say anything you'll be sorry for in the morning." Burr grinned. He handed Benson another cigarette and held a light for him. "Sit back and relax. You've beat yourself into the ground on this case. No wonder you've got the sick horrors."

He put his foot down and turned to face Benson. "If you want to know something, Counselor, I've felt like cheering, the way you put your head down and went bulling into this case. You've done enough work for ten trials. I wouldn't have done it, I can tell you that, not for this kid. I never thought he had the ghost of a chance."

Benson turned away quickly. "Let it go, Burr," he said in a strained undertone.

They sat quietly, listening to the random sounds of people passing on the narrow walks, the slow and aimless chatter of three prisoners in jailhouse denims who were squatting together in a far corner, transplanting half-grown flowers in the circular beds. The afternoon was very warm and still. The air, after the courtroom mustiness, was brilliantly fresh. It carried the thin dusty fragrance of desert scents.

The brief desert spring was nearly over now. The pink and yellow and blue ephemeral flowers were almost gone. They never lasted long. Not what you could call dependable types, Fitz used to complain. He wasn't much of a dependable type either. Ephemeral Fitz. Lots of color, lots of surprises. Not much staying power. Good-bye, Fitz.

Beside him Burr drew in a long audible breath. "Breeding weather," he said lazily. "Smell it, Ben?"

Benson nodded. He was grateful for Burr's cheerful and easy manner but he could not respond to it.

"What happens next, Ben?"

Benson looked up.

"After the trial, I mean," Burr said. "We're about finished. What next? Going to marry Joss?"

"Next week, probably."

"Then what?"

Benson shrugged. "I haven't thought that far. Take a trip somewhere, I guess, if that's what Joss wants. Maybe just hole up at the ranch for a while."

Burr snorted lightly. "The hottest lawyer in the state, and he wants to hole up. You know what you are, boy?" He laid a finger along his nose. "You're a crypto-cowboy. A horseback rider. A fornicating equestrian."

"Amen," Benson said mildly. He grinned in spite of himself. "What the hell are you getting at?"

"Am I getting at something?"

Benson looked at him sharply. "Yes," he said flatly. "What's up?"

"Old Ben," Burr laughed. "I try a subtle wind-up and he yells for me to throw the ball. Okay. I quit Blumberg. Told the old boy farewell."

Benson rubbed his chin thoughtfully. "Why? Because they swiped your nomination?"

"No," Burr said quickly. Then, "Well, maybe that was part of it. Jake should have gone to bat for me. But he never backs a loser. I wrote him a sharp little note last night. Guess how long it took him to answer it?"

"Tell me."

"Hell, I don't know," Burr said easily. "Maybe he sat up with it all night, but I doubt it. One of the office boys brought the answer early this morning. 'Sorry you feel that way, but if that's the way you feel, maybe you'd better resign, resignation accepted.' Jake's inimitable style."

"Good," Benson said. "You should have done it long ago. You don't need Blumberg any more than you need Barstow. You've been bringing in more than your share of the business for years. Go your own road, Burr."

"I . . . uh . . ." Burr cocked an eyebrow. "I was hoping you might come along with me. We'd make a pretty good team, Ben. What do you say?"

"Maybe," Benson said slowly. "Very appealing, as a matter of fact, but this is a hell of a time to talk about it."

"Best time in the world. Win or lose, you want to stay busy, Ben." Burr slapped his hand hard on Benson's knee. "Give me a firm answer, boy. What'll we call the new shop? B. Kellogg and—what?"

"None of that crap," Benson said sharply. He made a brusque, slashing movement with one hand. "We've had enough of that B. Kellogg business in this family. If you've got a brain in your head, you'll——" He swallowed heavily and forced himself to speak more calmly. "Remember Dad, Burr. Dad was a pretty fair lawyer, successful enough, but he was a miserably unhappy man most of his life. A lot of it he brought on himself, and the biggest foolishness was to call himself B. Kellogg, Jr. He never did get out from under the long shadow. That's not for me, Burr. I'll join you in a new office and welcome the chance. I don't want to stay with Blumberg any longer. But I won't join if you're setting up to be another B. Kellogg. No more pipe dreams for me."

"What did I say to bring all that on?" Burr muttered.

Benson didn't answer. He had already said too much.

"Ben, are you sore?"

"Hell no, Burr. I'm flattered. I'd be glad to go in with you. Kellogg and Kellogg. Right?"

"Isn't that what I said?" Burr demanded. He stared blandly at Benson, his tongue poking a lump in his cheek.

"I heard you say it," Benson agreed.

Burr put his head back and roared that big loud cheerful bellowing laugh. "Old Ben," he said, almost choking. "By God, we'll show 'em, won't we? We'll get every——"

Benson turned as a uniformed attendant whistled from the colonnade behind them.

"What is it, Charlie?" Burr called. "The jury?"

"Right," the uniformed man shouted. "They've got a verdict, Mr. Kellogg! You better git in here."

THE COURTROOM was unnaturally quiet. Benson and Burr took their seats at the defense table, leaving the chair between them for Turo. The court attendants were in place, waiting. Frank Sayer sat with his legs out straight, slumped at his table, his heavy face lined and tired. He lifted his head in a quick, confident movement when he noticed Benson looking at him.

Deputy Monahan brought Turo through the door, holding

him lightly by the left elbow. He let go and moved, almost tip-toeing, to his chair near the railing. Turo nodded to Benson and slid into his chair. Judge Groat surveyed the courtroom with a somber glare. He pointed the end of his pencil at the clerk.

"Summon the jury, Mr. Clerk."

They came in quickly. It had taken them little time to find a verdict, but considerable strain, Benson judged. Mrs. Jordan's eyes were strangely bright, as if she had been crying, and her face was very carefully powdered to hide the fact. Mitchell Masterton entered with his head down and stumbled clumsily along to his seat. John Eben Heller, the Number One juror, remained standing. He was obviously the foreman. His round red face was tight with the pressure of the occasion and the public prominence of his position.

The blinds had been opened now in the late hours of the afternoon and the light came strongly from behind the jury box, glazing the faces of the jurors and making them vague with haze.

"Arturo Campeón," the clerk said briskly, "please rise and face the jury."

Benson nudged the boy and got to his feet with him. Burr rose, closing in. Benson could feel Turo trembling. And he could feel a hot, strangling constriction in the pit of his stomach.

"Members of the jury," the clerk said, turning, "have you agreed upon a verdict?"

John Eben Heller nodded nervously. He coughed once and licked his lips. "We have, sir," he said firmly.

"How say you?" the clerk intoned. "Do you find the defendant, Arturo Campeón, guilty or not guilty?"

"We, the jury, find him," Heller looked for the first time at Turo, "not guilty."

The courtroom erupted with noise. John Eben Heller seated himself heavily and mopped his streaming scarlet face.

Turo stood stiffly, white-faced and silent, beside Benson. His eyes turned to watch Frank Sayer come across to the defense table with his big hand outstretched, his broad face creased in a smile for the photographers who were snapping flashguns in salvos. Benson shook hands.

"You really showed me something, Ben," Sayer said, his heavy voice riding over the surge of noise. "I still don't know how you pulled it off."

Benson nodded. The hell with it. He was too tired to respond. He thanked Sayer and sat again in the chair beside Turo.

The clerk's gavel was pounding constantly, cracking in futile protest. Gradually its incessant dull thudding worked its usual magic. The courtroom grew quiet again.

Judge Groat stared down morosely at the cover of his notebook, waiting until the silence was complete enough to suit him. Then he looked at the jury.

"At this stage it is customary for the trial judge to thank members of the jury for attentive and conscientious service. It would not, however, be fitting for the court to thank a jury which has reached a verdict not warranted by the laws of this state. The court appreciates the emotional considerations that prompted your verdict. You may believe you have applied a higher law in finding your verdict. In the days to come, each of you must decide that for himself. You are dismissed, members of the jury."

The judge pulled the edges of his robe closer together in front and looked down at Turo.

"The sheriff will release the prisoner from custody," he said. "We will adjourn until tomorrow morning at nine thirty, Mr. Clerk." He got up and turned toward the door to his chambers.

"Is that it, Mr. Kellogg?" Turo asked thinly. He held his cast with his free hand and stood up.

Benson nodded. He smiled at the boy and slowly the smile broadened as he realized it was all over. And successfully over.

Almost. Turo's eyes lifted beyond Benson, his face very still as he watched the narrow, black-coated figure of his grandfather come through the gate and into the well of the courtroom.

Benson rose quickly. The Dorado's eyes, as always, were shadowed in his dark, emaciated face. He stood with his long chin aimed directly up at Benson. His hands were in the pockets of his coat.

In that quiet moment the courtroom seemed to be absolutely silent. As he waited Benson could hear in his mind the deep growling voice of Clemente, warning him again. "He is a killer, patrón. He will kill the boy. No matter what happens in court, he will kill the boy unless——"

Benson shifted warily between the Dorado and his grandson. "Señor Darango," he said. "Did you want to see me?" Then he remembered the old man had little English and he said the same thing again in Spanish.

"To see," the Dorado said. He looked at the boy. In turning, the late sunlight touched his flat yellowish eyes. He nodded to Benson. "To see and to say my thanks for that which you have done."

And what have I done for you? Benson wondered, watching the Dorado carefully. Did I get the boy off just so you could kill him yourself?

"I have seen and I know," the Dorado said. "You fought for my grandson as you said you would fight. All that happened here was not clear to me, but enough." The dark ivory of his face was tight with strain, the lipless mouth drawn back hard against his teeth. "We did not agree what you were to be paid. I have come to pay you now."

"There is no need," Benson said stiffly. "The county will pay me."

The Dorado glared up arrogantly. "No gringo pays for me, or for my family." He took his left hand out of his pocket and dropped a heavy oblong package on the table beside Benson.

Burr got to his feet and came around to look at it. The package was covered with rawhide that had been sewn on when it was wet. In drying, the hide had shrunk tightly, outlining a double row of coins and welding them into a solid brick. Burr flicked a fingernail along the coins. There were twenty-five in each row, fifty coins in all. The rawhide was old, almost black with time. It smelled sweet and was hard as stone.

"Big ones," Burr muttered. "Five-peso coins, I guess."

The Dorado stepped back and bent over the court reporter's desk for a moment. He came back with Turo's switchblade knife in his hand. He gestured for Burr to hold the package firmly. He stuck the point of the knife in the rawhide and snapped his wrist. He sliced off one of the last coins as if he were taking off the end of a sausage. He closed the knife with a sharp click.

"My God!" Burr said softly. "It's gold!" He picked up the coin from the table, holding it on his palm. "One of the old fifty-peso gold johnnies."

"Las cincuentas del oro," the Dorado agreed.

"Twenty-five hundred pesos in gold," Burr said under his breath. "I wonder what that's worth in spending money?"

"That stuff has to be illegal," Benson said. "It was all called in."

"Sure. I guess he had it buried in a sand dune ever since his days with Pancho Villa. But don't worry about it. I'll figure a way to cash it in. There's a small fortune here, boy."

Benson turned back to the arrogant old man. "It is too much money, señor," he said stiffly. "I cannot accept so much for——"

The Dorado silenced him with a peremptory gesture. "When will Arturo be freed?" he demanded.

Benson looked around the courtroom. Most of the spectators had left. Frank Sayer was just going through the door to the judge's chambers. He waved to Benson. Deputy Monahan stood waiting for Turo, lounging patiently with his back to the bench.

"Burr," Benson said, "take Turo over to Monahan for a minute. I want to talk to Señor Darango privately."

"Right." Burr dropped the Dorado's block of coins in his pocket and took Turo's good arm lightly, nudging him away.

Benson propped himself against the edge of the table and folded his arms. Now his eyes were on a level with the Dorado's and he looked into them silently, gravely.

The Dorado held himself stiffly. Turo's knife was almost

hidden in his clenched fist. "I asked you, señor, when will Arturo be freed?"

"I heard," Benson said. "And I understood. Let me ask a question. If Turo is free to go with you, where will you take him?"

"Home, of course. To Chihuahua. Why do you ask?"

"Will he arrive?"

"Arrive?"

"Will he be alive when you get there?" Benson demanded.

"Aah!" The Dorado let out a thin breath. His bleak bony face relaxed for the first time. "That. It is that."

"Yes," Benson said soberly. "I require an answer, señor."

The Dorado brought his right hand from his pocket. With slow formality he placed it flat over his heart. "The boy is my life, señor. My honor. My future."

"Do me the favor to answer clearly," Benson insisted. "The jury has said the boy is innocent. What do you say? Innocent—or guilty?"

The Dorado's hand wadded the cloth of his coat. "I say that he is innocent, señor. I say this now. This I swear."

"On your honor."

"On my honor."

Benson took a quick breath. "Then Turo is free to leave any time, señor. Will you come with me, please."

He walked with the Dorado across the bare floor toward the bench where Turo was waiting. Benson called to the deputy and indicated the Dorado. "This is Turo's grandfather, John. Take him and the boy along with you and see they get out all right, will you?"

Deputy Monahan made a sketchy salute. "I'll take care of it, Mr. Kellogg." He tapped Turo's shoulder and said, grinning, "Come along now, Mr. Arturo Campeón. You better get yourself out of my jail or I'll have to start charging you rent."

"You mean that's all?" the boy asked. "I can go? Right now?"

"Any time, Turo," Benson said.

The boy looked up somberly into the remote yellow eyes

of his grandfather. He nodded silently, as if a message had passed between them. He held out his left hand to Benson.

"I don't have the words to thank you, Mr. Kellogg," he said awkwardly. His eyes did not turn from the Dorado.

"It's all right, Turo," Benson said uneasily. He did not like the silent tension between the old man and the boy. Maybe it would be best if he waited until——

The Dorado's left arm came up in a stiff, broken motion. He held the switchblade knife by one end, poking it clumsily at the boy's shirt pocket. When his fingers fumbled, Turo helped him.

The Dorado nodded. He tapped his knuckles against the boy's chest. "For such a reason, use it quickly again. Not ever for a lesser reason." His voice thinned with strain until it was barely audible. "You have done us honor." He gripped Turo's thin shoulders suddenly and pulled him into a close, hurting embrace, the abrazo of complete acceptance. Benson could hear the breath whistle from the boy's throat.

The Dorado drew his grandson around and led him quickly away, following the deputy toward the door.

Burr grunted softly and shook his head. "I don't know why," he said, "but that old boy makes me look around for a place to hide."

"Yes," Benson said.

"Do you think the kid will be okay with him?"

"Yes."

"Are you sure, Ben?"

"I'm sure. The boy is practically home right now. He'll make it, Burr."

They stayed where they were, unmoving. The Dorado and his grandson went out the door. Neither of them looked back.

Bart Spicer

Born in Virginia in 1918, Bart Spicer spent his early childhood
in various parts of the British Empire. He enlisted in the
Army during World War II and rose to the rank of captain in
the South Pacific. Mr. Spicer began writing as a journalist.
Before the war he wrote for the Scripps-Howard Syndicate and
was a radio news writer as well. After the war he worked for
three years in public relations for Universal Military
Training and a year for the World Affairs Council. Mr.
Spicer's first book, a mystery, was published in 1949. Entitled
The Dark Light, it won Dodd, Mead's $1,000 prize. Of the
dozen he has written, the most recent is *Look Behind You,*
published in 1960 under the pseudonym of Jay Barbette. Of his
four historical novels, the most recent is *The Day Before
Thunder,* also published in 1960. Mr. Spicer has traveled
widely and lived in England, India, Africa, France, Spain,
Mexico and many parts of the United States including
the Southwest. His wife, Betty Coe Spicer, collaborates with him
on the Jay Barbette mysteries.